The
BiniSphere

The BiniSphere

By Joseph W. Foster

PsyConOps
Publishing

Joseph W. Foster

For information contact the publisher at:
info@psyconopspublishing.com

Library of Congress Cataloging – in – publication data
Foster, Joseph W.
ISBN-10: 1-7320712-3-3
ISBN-13: 978-17320712-3-0
Published by: PsyConOps Publishing
Copyright © 2020 J. W. Foster
All rights reserved.

Cover design by Andrew P. Rushakoff,
andrew@artoftherush.com

Acknowledgments

The plot for this story was developed several years ago while my wife, Elaine, and I were driving along the mountainous roads of Nebrodi National Park in northern Sicily. The story grew, twisted and folded as I explored the history, customs, and traditions of the Sicilian culture. Throughout all of this, Elaine encouraged me to keep writing, editing and revising. We make a good team; my creativity and her tenacity made this all possible. Thank you darling.

I'd also like to acknowledge my beta readers, Rick Huber, Steve Kumin, Tim Randle, Rich Edmondson, and Steve Foster, for their many hours of review and feedback, and my copy editor, Lisa Baci. With their commitment and insights, we made a good story even better.

Prolog

March 1938

Ettore stood on the aft deck of the *M/S Regina* and checked the luminescent dial on his watch. It was 10:55 p.m. Looking up, he saw the dim outline of a new moon and a night sky glowing of the Milky Way. His sunken eyes followed the ocean of stars down to the smooth surface of the Mediterranean Sea. The starlight reflected off the water's surface and merged with a glowing stream of phosphorescent plankton left behind by the ship's wake. Before the ship's departure, he'd sent a telegram to Antonio Carrelli, the director of the Naples Physics Institute.

```
Dear Carrelli,
I've made a decision that has become
unavoidable. There isn't a bit of selfishness in
it, but I realize what trouble my sudden dis-
appearance will cause you and the students. For
this as well, I beg your forgiveness, but
especially for betraying the trust, the sincere
friendship, and the sympathy you gave me over
the past months. I ask you to remind me to all
those I learned to know and appreciate in
your Institute, especially Sciuti: I will keep a
fond memory of them all, at least until 11 pm
tonight, possibly later.
    Respectfully yours, Ettore Majorana
```

Committed to this new path, Ettore had withdrawn all his money from the Banca di Palermo and booked passage for Naples.

The trail of plankton recorded the ship's path as it steamed northeast, away from the northern coast of Sicily. Ettore rechecked his watch. It was 10:59. He lifted his canvas bag from the deck and climbed over the iron rail. When the watch's second hand reached the top of the dial, he took a deep breath and jumped. It was 10 meters to the water's surface. Ettore's thin, wiry body hit hard, but the pain of the impact paled in comparison to the shock of the cold Mediterranean Sea. He plunged deep underwater, where the powerful wake from the ship's twin screws tumbled him, twisting and turning. Clutching tightly to his buoyant bag, he eventually rose. Breaking the surface thirty seconds later, he turned and watched the ship steam away. Ettore knew he wouldn't survive long in the frigid water. It was Saturday, 26 March 1938, and the end of the only life Ettore had ever known.

Salvatore eyed the massive ship as it swept through the dark waters. He wasn't happy. It was too far away.

"Harder! Row harder!" he yelled.

The three oarsmen, already out of breath, rowed faster. At precisely 11 p.m., Salvatore sighted an imaginary line. It ran from the bow of their skiff, through the stern light of the *M/S Regina*, and off to a familiar star in the constellation Argo Navis.

He yelled again, "I am on the bearing. Faster, we are out of time!"

He pulled the tiller to the left and pointed the small craft straight for Argo Navis. They were moving north at 4 knots. It was going to be close, too close.

Salvatore had assured Ettore it was simple vector analysis. That had convinced him. Ettore had little experience with the world outside of his laboratory and secluded office in the Physics Institute at the Sapienza - Università di Roma. Explaining the plan using vectors, rates, and precise timing transformed a colossal feat of daring into a logical progression of events. Even Ettore, one of the most preeminent physicists on the planet, appreciated the beauty of it. But, as with any experimental procedure, there must be an analysis of variables, an appreciation of the significance of small errors when compounded, meant the difference between right conclusions and wrong ones. And sometimes, such as now, the difference between life and death. Ettore knew the stakes were high, but he had little choice; his disappearance had to look like a suicide. If they found him, the world would soon learn of his discovery.

Salvatore planned to intersect the ship's path at 11 p.m. His only concern was the risk of collision. That would ruin not only Ettore's plans but Salvatore and his crew's plans for a long and glorious life. But with his strong oarsmen, the risk was slight. They could maneuver away from the ship's path.

"The damned wind," Salvatore muttered. "Whoever heard of the winds dying in March?"

He'd calculated the average speed of their journey, assuming the prevailing southwesterly winds in March. They would propel their sailing skiff north on a broad reach with plenty of leeway built into their arrival time. In case the wind died, an infrequent occurrence in March, he also estimated their speed given four sturdy men with oars. His plans fell apart at the last minute. Salvatore and the others were pushing hard to launch their skiff down the rocky shores of Mongerbino. Marco, the strongest of his oarsmen, was guiding the massive bow of the boat into the breaking waves when a rock under his foot slipped away. He fell into the shallow water. No one had noticed until his screams in the dark brought them to a stop. It was too late. Marco's forearm had snapped as soon as it came between the plunging keel of the boat and the rocky bottom.

Handicapped by the lack of wind and a missing oarsman, Salvatore's 30-minute margin of error had disappeared.

It was now 11:25. Salvatore scanned the surface of the water looking for signs of the ship's phosphorescent path. He saw only reflected stars.

One of his oarsmen spoke. "Sal, the glow does not last this long. We are too late."

"Everyone, stop!" Salvatore yelled.

The crew shipped their oars and sat in silence, scanning.

"Ettore!" he yelled. "Ettore!"

They listened as the skiff glided through the water.

"Ettore!"

Only the gentle splash of waves against the gunnels broke the silence.

"Keep paddling!" he yelled.

The three sweat-drenched crewmen rowed further north for another minute and stopped again.

"Ettore!" he yelled. "Ettore!"

This time Sal heard a sound. He turned toward it but saw nothing.

"Over there, quick!"

Off to the east, he saw a dim silhouette.

The boat surged forward as the crew pulled with urgency. Salvatore pushed the tiller to port until they were lined up on the shadow.

They closed the remaining meters and found a canvas bag floating in the water. Then, they saw Ettore's head. The crew hauled him over the rail and into the boat.

"Are you alright?" asked an oarsman.

Ettore mouthed words but was unable to speak.

"He is hypothermic, get him out of those clothes," ordered Salvatore.

His crew pulled the wet clothing from Ettore's body, while Sal unwrapped a bundle of woolen blankets. Buried in the center was a scaldaletto, a brass bed-warming pan. It was filled with simmering coals. Once exposed to the open air, the embers glowed with renewed energy. Salvatore spread the warm blankets on the deck.

Ettore, stripped naked, was placed on the blankets and wrapped up tightly. Only then, enveloped in the lifesaving heat, did he manage a weak smile.

"W-w-w-what-t-t t-t-took so lo-o-o-ong?"

Salvatore placed the scaldaletto on the deck next to Ettore's head and draped a blanket over it, creating a small shroud of warmth.

"The fishing is amazing this time of night," Sal said. "We must have lost track of time."

Ettore smiled at his friend and closed his eyes. His body was wracked with shivering, but he knew he'd survive.

Ettore was sitting at a small wooden desk in a bedroom of Sal's home when he heard a tentative knock at the door. Without turning away from his work, he asked, "Who is it?"

The door hinges creaked.

"Signore, I have brought you some dinner. Please, take a small break from your work."

"I am not hungry! Go away!"

The young woman, dressed in a dark woolen skirt and white billowy cotton blouse, mustered her courage and entered the small bedroom. She walked over and dropped the tray onto his desk, splashing red wine onto his papers. Ettore jumped from his chair; his six-foot frame towering over the tiny woman.

Isabella, Sal's daughter, was 15 years old. She had flowing, dark brown hair that curled just below her smooth shoulders. Her olive skin was flawless, still moist from working in the kitchen. Growing up in a home of science, she understood the mercurial moods of a superior mind. This time, she chose to fight instead of flee. She cut Ettore off before he uttered a word.

"Signore! My father has told me little of who you are or where you came from, but you will not misbehave in our home. You have not eaten for days and I have made you a nice meal. You will sit down and enjoy it, or I will spoon feed it to you."

Ettore surveyed her with interest. Since his arrival a week ago, he had paid little mind to signorina Isabella Germanni. She had stayed mostly in the background. Beyond their initial introductions, they had not shared more than a few words. She was right; he had not been polite, and why should he? His work was all that mattered. He looked down at the steaming plate of spaghetti aglio e olio and the freshly baked bread, and his mood lifted.

"I apologize, signorina. Thank you very much. I am sometimes too involved with my work."

"I understand. My papa behaves the same when he is on the trail of discovery. It forces me to treat him as a child. It is for his own good."

Ettore looked directly at Isabella. She had her father's green eyes sparkling with a wisdom he would not have expected in such a young woman. For the first time since he had been rescued, Ettore smiled.

"Your father is a fortunate man in many ways." He reached for the plate, twirled the long strings of pasta around his fork and stuffed the food into his mouth. After swallowing and taking a sip of wine, he said, "You have permission to adjust my behavior whenever you feel it appropriate."

Encouraged, Isabella walked back to the door.

"Very well, please enjoy your meal." Before stepping over the threshold, she turned again to face him. With a hopeful smile, she added, "If you bring your plate down when you are finished, I will serve you a fresh cannoli and espresso."

"Now you have my attention," Ettore replied before turning back to his papers.

Ettore and Salvatore had climbed halfway up the mountainside. It was a warm, breezy day, the sun shined brightly. They had been climbing over the rocks for almost an hour. Reaching a sizeable windswept tree, Salvatore sat in the shade.

"Sal, you almost succeeded in killing me last week. Are you trying again?"

"What are you complaining about? It all worked as planned. Aside from Marco's broken arm, no one is the worse off."

Ettore sat next to him and looked down at Canneto di Caronia and the turquois blue Mediterranean.

"Maybe, but your error analysis left a lot to be desired. I can only pray that it does not portend the quality of your research."

"Bini, you know as well as I, there are no guarantees… with our research or with our lives. Randomness happens. We deal with it."

"Well, I am still feeling the random results of my alleged suicide. Do you think anyone has noticed I am missing yet?"

"Of course," Sal said. "Your disappearance is going to be one hell of a mystery."

Ettore "Bini" Majorana was 31 years old. He had a Moorish appearance, with straight black hair and intense dark eyes that penetrated the few people he allowed into his small circle. Bini was a shy, introverted man. A mathematical genius, he lacked the social skills required to maintain all but the most drought-tolerant relationships. Sal was one of the few.

Ettore's thoughts drifted back to the world around him.

"Why did you bring me up here? Surely not for a philosophical discussion about my life and death."

"Come." Sal replied, "Let me show you."

Sal stood and skirted sideways along the boulders. Ettore followed.

"It is not much farther," Sal said.

Five minutes later, Sal stopped at an outcropping of rocks the size of small houses and waited expectantly for Bini.

When he caught up with Sal, Ettore paused to catch his breath and asked, "Now what?"

Sal smiled and waited.

The mountain wind shifted slightly, and Ettore felt a cool, moist breeze blow across his face. It had a musky scent of earth and ocean and mildew. He looked at his friend.

Sal pointed at a large crevice between the rocks. "Welcome to our new research facility."

Sal removed two large flashlights from the green canvas backpack he was carrying and handed one to Ettore.

"Follow me."

Ettore and Salvatore climbed down into a vast network of volcanic tubes; caves formed by ancient lava flows.

"As the lava flows toward the sea, the outer walls cool and solidify," said Sal. "The molten inner core continues to flow inside these insulated tubes until the volcano subsides. The remaining lava flows out, and voila, a huge underground labyrinth. These tunnels run for miles."

"How are we going to afford all of this?"

"The Don is our friend, and just as importantly, our benefactor. We are already putting your ideas to the test."

"But why would the Mafia want to help us?"

"Let us say it is in their best interest. They know what you and the Via Panisperna Boys have been doing, and they do not like the idea of the Nazis having nuclear weapons."

Ettore belonged to an exclusive group of brilliant young scientists led by the Italian physicist, Enrico Fermi, the "architect of the nuclear age." The nickname of the group came from the address of the Physics Institute, at the Sapienza - Università di Roma. Via Panisperna, a street in the center of the city, got its name from a nearby monastery,

San Lorenzo in Panisperna. It was 1934 when their group had made the famous discovery of slow neutrons which later made possible the nuclear reactor, and then the construction of the first atomic bomb. But only Ettore knew the truth of what they had discovered.

"It will be very expensive," said Ettore.

"Yes, and I have gone to the deepest pockets in Sicily and Rome." Sal slowed his pace, searching for some shred of approval.

Ettore stopped walking and grabbed Sal by the arm. "You did not tell them, did you?"

"I did not offer details. I just told them, if your theories are correct, we can stop both the fascist and the communists."

"But, Sal, it will take decades to build. The technology does not exist."

Ettore's expression grew tight and worried.

"That is why I went to the famiglia. Governments are too shortsighted, too political. They would never be able to commit to such a long-term effort. Or keep it a secret."

"And the family can?"

"Yes. They believe in you, Ettore. You are one of us, and the family knows it is the only way to stop them. Fascism will destroy the Mafia. Communism will destroy the Mafia. They can only thrive in a free society. And you know what happens when someone in the famiglia breaks a secret."

"I do not like it," Ettore said. "Where is that money going to come from? Extortion of the poor, corruption of the rich?"

Sal smiled. "Ettore, the family has its tentacles in every aspect of our society, and not just here in Sicily, in all of Italy. The heads of the families have come together, and in a rare event, they have all agreed. A tax will be levied on every bribe, on every transaction."

"That is insane. The Mafia has no central command, no leader. They are like an octopus without a head. Who is going to organize it? Enforce it?"

"They know what is in their best interest and, as I said, they believe in your work. Bini, the next thing I tell you is the most important. It must stay with you to your dying day."

"I am not sure I want to know."

"There is a central power, a head to your octopus. Our friends have convinced the leaders of the most powerful and secretive society in the world that your work will save them as well."

"Our friends? Who?"

"Joliot-Curie, Fermi, Oppenheimer and Carrelli."

"They all know?"

"They have read your papers, Bini. They do not know you are alive and well, but they can see what is coming. Because of them, we will have unlimited funding to continue your work."

"But why? And how would they have contact with the mafia?"

"They have had no direct contact. The final convincing was from you, in a letter you had written to your friend."

Sal removed a folded piece of paper from his pocket and opened it. "This telegram came yesterday. News of your disappearance has spread throughout the world."

Ettore took the telegraphed news article and read.

The Northern Gazette, Alberta, Canada.
A young scientist who probed deeply into the secrets of Nature has vanished after declaring that science has gone far enough. Now he is being sought in all the monasteries in Italy. He is Ettore Majorana, world-famous atom-splitter, praised by Lord Rutherford. Shortly before he disappeared, he wrote to a friend: "There is a point where science must stop. I want to return in time to God."

"Sal, why would this convince the famiglia to provide unlimited funds?"

"The Cosa Nostra is already convinced. But they are not the only organization that requires a free world for their survival."

❖

December 1938

Sal led Antonio through the labyrinth of tunnels as the sound of construction echoed off the volcanic walls. They soon walked through a large opening and stepped onto a natural stone balcony. Nine months had passed since Sal had first shown the caverns to Ettore. During that time, their team had achieved the colossal feat of moving their entire above-ground research facility.

Standing at a rough, wrought-iron railing, Ettore watched the activity 30 feet below him.

"Ettore," Sal said. "This is Antonio. He is responsible for arranging much of the funding for our work."

Antonio, in his mid-fifties, was impeccably dressed in a 3-piece black suit and wingtip shoes. He wore gold-rimmed glasses and a small Catholic crucifix was pinned to his lapel. He nodded to Ettore and offered his hand.

"It is a pleasure, Dr. Majorana. I have long admired your work."

Ettore avoided the man's gaze but nodded.

"Thank you," he mumbled.

The three of them looked down into the massive cavern. A concrete cube sat at the center of the room, dominating the space. An array of pipes, cables, and supporting superstructures surrounded the enormous block of concrete. Evenly spaced on one face of the cube was an array of three-inch diameter holes. The high-pitched sound of a boring machine filled the cavern. Cooling water sprayed out of a borehole, covering the floor with a slurry of concrete mud.

Sal explained, "This small reactor is for only one purpose, Antonio… to prove that Ettore's calculations are correct."

"How long before you are finished?" Antonio asked. He had the look of a man who was not in the habit of waiting.

"Several more months," Sal replied.

"Months? That means more funding." Antonio removed a perfectly folded handkerchief from his breast pocket and wiped his brow. Staring down at the cube again, he said, "Well, in truth, it is hard to believe it is going to happen at all."

"Yes. Thanks to your generous funding. And do not worry. We too feel the pressure. It has been four years since Fermi unknowingly split the atom during his uranium experiments. Someone other than Ettore is going to discover this oversight. When Fermi realizes what they have done, the world is going to change. Power over this knowledge will mean power over this world."

Antonio looked at Ettore.

"Your partner does not appear as confident as you."

"Do not mind, Bini," Sal replied. "He is always worried. It is his nature."

"He is going to run," muttered Ettore.

"Who?" asked Antonio.

"Fermi, he has to."

Antonio looked to Sal for an explanation.

"The fascists," explained Sal. "They are going after the Jews. It will not be long before these poor souls are purged from Italy."

"But certainly not Fermi. He is a treasure…"

"They will take him!" Ettore interrupted. "The Nazis. His wife is Jewish. When they realize… when Fermi realizes what he has done, there will be no going back. They will have the power to annihilate the earth."

"Are you sure this will be enough to stop them?" Antonio asked, waving his arm toward the reactor.

"Si`," replied Sal. "As I said, if Ettore's calculations are correct…"

"No," Ettore said. "It will not be enough. We can only pray that the Americans will figure it out in time."

"I do not understand," said Antonio.

"Our work is going to take decades," Ettore said. "We understand the physics, but the technology does not exist. We must develop new materials, new techniques. It is the only way we can stop this madness. In the meantime, we must watch and wait."

"There must be something else we can do?" asked Antonio.

Sal looked at Bini and waited. Bini nodded before turning his attention back towards the construction below them.

"Before his disappearance, Ettore sent some of his research to the Americans," Sal said. "It will give them enough of a head start."

"But can they be trusted with this knowledge?" Antonio asked.

"We have no choice, and we have not shared everything," Sal replied. "There are still some secrets only we possess. We have faith that the recipient will do all he can to protect us."

"Who can you possibly trust with that knowledge?"

"We are not at liberty to share that information, but rest assured, he is a pacifist and can be trusted to help maintain a balance of powers."

"Very well," replied Antonio looking increasingly skeptical. "If you say it will take decades before your machine is operational, what will you be testing in a few months?"

"What you see in front of you is a scale model," Sal said. "We will test this at a range of a kilometer. We have placed a radioactive plate up on the surface."

"But you said you cannot control the reaction."

"Si`. We do not control it. We allow it to become unstable, to reach critical mass. Since it is such a small reaction, we can contain it.

"How do you aim it?" Antonio asked. "You cannot see through the mountain."

"The aiming of the neutrino beam is a whole other problem," said Sal. "The final machine will be 100 times this size and must rotate freely in both azimuth and elevation. We must also develop a sensing technology to precisely aim the beam at our nuclear targets. For now, for this experiment, we have surveyed the location of our test panel so it will be in line with the beam, and still, that is not sufficiently accurate. We will slowly move the target back and forth, waiting for it to heat up."

"You will have someone near the target? Is that not dangerous?"

"No, the neutrinos pass right through us. We have coated the surface of the target with paraffin. As soon as our man on the surface sees the wax melt, he will call down to us on the telephone."

"How will we ever be able to find a target on the other side of the earth?"

"That is what Ettore has been working on. We know the basic building blocks required to build a sensor, but as I said, the technology does not exist."

"So, you have built a gun, but you cannot aim it?"

"We told you from the beginning," said Sal. "It will take a long time to complete. You must be patient. Ettore has already completed the plans for steering the reactor."

Antonio shook his head. "Do you realize the amount of money we are spending here?"

"I understand, but you must remember," Sal said. "We are trying to save mankind."

"But you may already be too late."

"Well then all your money does not matter, does it, Monsignor Costa?"

Ettore turned and stared at the well-dressed man with fresh eyes.

"Costa? Bishop Antonio Costa? The treasurer of the Vatican?"

November 1977

Ettore was asleep in the worn, leather recliner. Papers were scattered on his lap. More were stacked on the side table, along with a handful of #2 pencils and a sharpener. A few of the papers had sailed across the room, settling by the hearth of the basalt fireplace. The scribbled equations, notes, and diagrams no longer made sense to anyone but Ettore.

Holding the baby gently in her arms, Isabella walked across the living room and knelt next to him.

"Bini... Bini, wake up. Meet your new granddaughter."

Ettore opened his eyes. He smiled at his wife of 33 years, glanced at the baby, and fell back to sleep.

Isabella kissed him on his cheek and walked back upstairs to return the newborn.

Ettore, now 71 years old, had surrendered the fight. Ever since Sal's death, a few years earlier, he no longer had the desire or physical capability to continue his research in the caverns below. Sal had always been the patriarch of the family, the leader, the commander. His passing had been a shock. Every one grieved but eventually recovered... except for Ettore. Over the years, Sal had become Ettore's best friend, his research partner, and even his father-in-law. Now it was over.

With Ettore's decline, Isabella had become the head of the family. She had a natural ability to bring people together. All of Ettore's research had been passed on to their two children. Their daughter had inherited Ettore's genius, their son inherited Isabella's love for family and community, her compassion and spirituality.

Over the decades, the research facility had grown by an order of magnitude. The funding continued to pour in as tensions between the world's nuclear superpowers spiraled out of control. Ettore and Sal's dreams of a nuclear-free world had yet to be achieved and yet they always made progress. It wasn't necessarily a race against time, it was a race against technology. Their mission was to stay at the forefront. As world knowledge of nuclear physics grew and expanded, as new materials, tools and techniques were developed, their team of scientists grew with it. The Vatican's financial support and the famiglia's worldwide network of criminals allowed the closely held results of other nation's research to pour in. But the newfound knowledge never poured out, thanks to the Cosa Nostra's life or death grip on absolute security. All their efforts were focused on a single goal: to generate the most powerful beam of energy known to mankind.

Isabella was standing at the kitchen counter, preparing dinner, when her son walked in. He hugged her.

"I have put father to bed. He asked for you."

She turned quickly to face him. "He spoke?" she asked.

"Si`!"

"He has not said a word in days."

"You have been up all night helping with the birth of my niece. Go rest with him while I prepare dinner."

Isabella nodded and wiped her hands on a dish towel.

"I will just take a quick nap. Wake me when dinner is ready."

Ettore no longer had the strength to negotiate the staircase, so they had moved his bedroom into his old office on the first floor. Light was streaming in through the open window as the curtains danced with the cool November breeze. Isabella walked in and sat on the edge of the bed. Ettore's breathing was shallow, his normally flushed face white. His papery-thin skin revealed greenish-blue veins above his temples. She placed her warm hand on his head and stared at the only man who had ever rivaled the strength of her father. Ettore opened his eyes. Their gazes met and a flood of emotions passed between them. Fear, regret, and love. Ettore shrugged his shoulders, cocked his head to the side, and raised an eyebrow. He smiled, reached for her hand and fell back to sleep. Isabella lay next to him and put her head on his shoulder. Ten minutes later, her warm tears fell onto his motionless chest.

A Week Ago

Johnson slipped on his headset and activated the mike. "Okay, folks, today will be our final test. We'll reposition our line-of-sight from nadir to zenith at 1800 hours Zulu. Guidance, set the swath to sweep across sol at 1835 Zulu. Any questions?"

The room was silent.

Dave Johnson stood at his console mounted on a raised platform and surveyed the room. It was roughly 30 feet by 30 feet and filled with nine triple-monitor computer stations. Each station had a black placard with white letters: *Propulsion, Guidance, Sensor Payload, Power, Data Processing, Image Analysis, Computer Systems, Comms,* and *Quality Assurance*. Sitting at each station was a member of his team, everyone an expert in their field. They'd practiced each step of their mission. All knew what needed to be done.

"No?" Johnson asked. "Good. Everyone check in on the board, and we'll get this day started."

Johnson looked down at his computer monitor and watched as each station checked in, rectangular boxes on the screen switching from yellow to green. Johnson waited until all stations were a go. After a full minute had passed, Sensor Payload remained yellow. Johnson craned his neck up and to the side to get a clear look at the station. The chair was empty.

"Where the hell is Sergeant Connors?" Johnson yelled.

In his earlier years, Lt Col Dave Johnson had been an F-16 fighter pilot and flight test engineer. After being injured in an ejection seat failure, he'd been reassigned to the National Reconnaissance Office's KH-11 Operations Center. As the Lead Engineer, Johnson was responsible for the last of the KH-11 reconnaissance satellites. Designated USA-245, NRO's most sophisticated spy satellite had been launched into orbit two weeks earlier. Johnson and his KH-11 system operators worked in the Area 58 control room, a large, windowless, two-story concrete building at Fort Belvoir, Virginia. They'd been conducting an extensive battery of health checks, calibrations, and data collections to ensure that the USA-245 was fully functional and ready for operational use.

The KH-11's classified electro-optic payload consisted of three sensors: a high-resolution multi-spectral visible camera, a long-wave infrared imaging camera, and the first-of-its-kind Phase Inverted Tracker or PIT sensor. During daylight hours, the payload's visible camera provides enough detail to tell the difference between a soldier in uniform and a civilian in jeans. The infrared camera was lower resolution but capable of detecting temperature differences measured in the tens of milli-Kelvin or .02 degrees F, day or night. It could distinguish between a breathing and non-breathing body lying on the battlefield, even detect footsteps crossing cold terrain based solely on the thermal signatures left behind by a person's shoes. The third sensor, the PIT, was an altogether different animal. It didn't image people, or buildings or missiles or ships or tanks; it had only one use, to precisely track a unique signature.

The KH-11 operators had one more test to run, and they always saved this test for last. Failure could destroy their cameras. The highly sensitive visible and infrared cameras had an inherent flaw: they could be damaged by excessive incoming energy, such as the sun passing through their field-of-view. But the sun wasn't the problem. The sensors were carefully controlled and were always pointed down at the earth's surface. The problem was from a newly emerging threat. Because of recent advances in high energy lasers and optics, unfriendly nations had the capability to destroy the sophisticated sensors in a matter of seconds. These ground-based directed energy, or DE, systems were simple and very powerful. Using large steerable mirrors and powerful chemical lasers, a pulse of high energy radiation could be directed towards any satellite orbiting the earth. Because of this threat, the new KH-11 optics were equipped with high-speed, mechanical shutters that automatically activated at the first sign of a DE attack. The shutters were essentially a set of sophisticated Venetian blinds placed across the front aperture of the shared optics. The edges and back-sides were coated with light-absorbing carbon black that would eliminate any stray reflections that affect the quality of the imagery. When activated, the shutters could snap shut within milliseconds, the polished titanium front surfaces reflecting any incoming hostile energy off into space.

The time had come to point the multimillion-dollar cameras at an intense heat source, a source large enough to fill the entire field-of-view of the cameras, a source capable of destroying the cameras if the thermal shutters failed to operate quickly. The approved test plan was to point the cameras directly at the sun, but a few of the scientists disagreed with that approach. Redirecting the telescope away from the earth required added expense in energy and prevented the controllers from measuring the accuracy of their algorithms to geolocate the offending energy source. Lastly, the energy of the sun was so intense that the heat could damage the cameras, even if the shutters worked correctly.

Johnson was stepping down from his platform when Connors burst through the control room doors.

"What the hell, Connors!"

"Sorry sir, I was in the break room watching CNN."

"Are you kidding me?" Johnson said. "Are you asking to get fired?"

"No, sir. You don't understand. It's Mount Etna in Sicily. It just erupted."

"Thanks for the update," Johnson said. "Now get your ass back to work."

"But I have an idea that can save fuel and lower the risk of damage to the sensors."

"We've already reviewed and accepted the test plan. This mission is a go. Everybody's waiting on you. Get back to your…"

"But sir," Connors interrupted. "I did some quick calculations. This is perfect."

"What's perfect?"

"The spectral flux density of the molten lava is a closer match to the threat. The eruption is huge. It will fill the field-of-view. It's a better and safer test."

"Everyone stand down," Johnson shouted. He trained a hard stare on his excited technician. "Connors, you had better be right. Get on the phone with Dr. Jacobs right now. If he agrees, we'll make the change."

Connors picked up the phone and dialed their chief scientist while one of his men pulled CNN up on a huge flat screen monitor mounted to the wall.

The newscaster was still reporting.

"…Mount Etna, Europe's most active volcano, has erupted again, causing nearby airports and airspace to close. Mount Etna hasn't had an eruption of this magnitude since 1999."

An hour later, Lt Col Johnson received a phone call. He talked for several minutes before hanging up.

"Connors! Good work. Jacobs agrees. Guidance, get the new coordinates set in. Jacobs says the plume is being swept southeast. Bring the swath in from the northwest to avoid any obscuration."

The small group of NCOs and scientists returned to their consoles and prepared for the final test.

The KH-11 satellite raced across the sky at 18,000 mph, at an altitude of 200 miles. The onboard sensor package operated in several different modes. It could be pointed straight down and push-broom its way across the surface of the earth, or it could be locked onto a specific earth coordinate, providing longer dwell times to capture dynamic scenes. It could also be locked onto a moving object and track it across the ground or sky. For this test, the satellite was realigned so that the sensors would push-broom across the Tyrrhenian Sea, north to south, at an azimuth and elevation angle that allowed the sensor field-of-view to intersect Mount Etna. After all the parameters had been set, the KH-11 operators nervously watched the flat screen monitors as high resolution imagery of whitecaps and the occasional fishing boat, passed by. The northern coast of Sicily appeared at the bottom edge of the overhead displays and worked its way up towards the center.

The NCO stationed at the Guidance terminal announced, "Two minutes, twenty-five seconds to intersect Mount Etna."

"You had better be right, Connors," said Johnson, as he nervously tapped his pen on the computer console.

The coast of Sicily slid further up. Just before the shoreline reached the center of the screen, Johnson's pen fell to the floor. The screens had all gone dark.

Mike Sheehan stared out his office window on the top floor of the LX2 building at the Liberty Crossing Intelligence Campus in McLean, Virginia. The LX1 building, across from him, housed the National Counter-Terrorism Center and the National Counter-Proliferation Center, or NCPC. Prominent on his desk sat a picture of two young men, both dressed in military uniform, one a Marine corpsman, the other, a Naval officer. He looked down at the picture and then back at NCPC and shook his head. Sheehan hated the Iranians. He'd lost his younger brother over 30 years ago, during the Iran hostage crisis, and couldn't stand the idea that Iran was now close to having a nuclear weapon. How was this possible? But he already knew. The left-wing passivists. Those never ending talks and never ending sanctions meant nothing to those rag-heads. The only thing that got their attention was brute force. And now that the Russians were helping them... he was sick of America being shit on. The Russians and the Iranians needed to be put in their place for good.

Over the last 30 years, Mike Sheehan had successfully fought his way up through the Mississippi political machine. He'd started his career in the Navy, as an engineer, working on nuclear submarines. After his brother's death, he resigned his commission and left the military to pursue a career in politics. It was his dad's idea. An aging congressman from Mississippi, he'd said, "You want to do something about your brother's death? Get in the game. You won't get justice takin' orders from a bunch of paper pushers in DC."

Sheehan was now in his 60s. His chin tuck and Botox treatments had lost their effect as his skin continued to sag with age and the abuse of his vices. He'd stopped dyeing his hair a year ago, when his wife finally convinced him he was being vain and looked more authoritative with the grey. Even at five feet, five inches, he had a commanding presence, using his loud, baritone voice to his advantage.

Sheehan also had an uncanny sense of knowing which way the wind was blowing. No matter how foul the stench, he'd take the path of least resistance. He was extremely ambitious and had latched onto the coattails of then presidential candidate, James Blake. Sheehan had been promised a position in the new Cabinet if he delivered Mississippi during the Republican presidential primaries.

He accepted the mantle like a dog with a bone. If it brought results, either from his misbegotten efforts or the efforts of others, it justified the means. Within the Administration and out, there was a debate whether he'd actually delivered, or whether the win had been the inevitable result of Mississippians' ability to ignore corruption at all levels of government, voting for a candidate who knew nothing about the needs of rural southern folks, while promising them everything. Either way, it worked. Within weeks of Blake being sworn into the presidency, Sheehan was appointed deputy director of national intelligence. He wasn't exactly happy with the junior Cabinet appointment, but he knew he wouldn't be there for long. The job was important and high profile. He was responsible for coordinating intelligence operations focused on the counter-proliferation of nuclear material.

Sheehan's phone buzzed and his secretary's voice announced over the intercom, "Deputy Director, I have Mr. Howell on the phone for you."

Sheehan picked up the phone and pressed "Line 1."

"Howell," he said. "It's about time."

"We just verified it sir. It was a hostile emission that destroyed the PIT camera."

"But you said the shutters should have snapped closed. Did they fail?"

"That's the problem sir. They didn't fail. The PIT camera was destroyed milliseconds after the shutters had activated."

"I don't understand," Sheehan said.

"The shutters were closed. It was no laser. The only radiation capable of taking out the PIT sensor is the same radiation that the camera is designed to detect: Majorana neutrinos."

"Holy shit! "

"Yes, sir. Someone has figured out how to produce a high intensity neutrino beam and they've figured out how to

23

aim it. And that's not all. The beam has apparently degraded the satellite's nuclear power plant."

"What?"

"We were able to duplicate the phenomena. We ran some experiments. At high enough intensities, the Majorana neutrinos interact with radioactive material."

"Any kind of nuclear material?"

"Yes, sir."

Max Howell stood almost six feet tall. He was originally from Scotland but looked and dressed as if he were a native cowboy. He had a slender build and a bushy red mustache. His daily attire was Wrangler jeans, a western shirt, and cowboy boots. He was also the station chief of the Nevada National Security Site. He and his team supported Sheehan and the NCPC in Washington, DC. Located in a remote, highly secure site in southern Nevada, the NNSS conducted experiments in support of the nation's nuclear deterrent. They were considered the nation's experts in detecting and locating dirty bombs, loose nukes, and other radiological sources. Howell had worked for NNSS for over 29 years. He was a nuclear physicist, and even though he was considered management, he still liked getting his hands dirty.

"How did we miss this?" Sheehan asked.

"It's reasonably straight forward," Howell said. "We've had neutrino beam technology for some time now, just not at these power levels. In fact, every two seconds, the Fermilab particle accelerator, just outside of Chicago, fires a beam carrying a trillion neutrinos at particle detectors in northern Minnesota, more than 450 miles away. We do it a little differently here, with a nuclear reactor. We orient the thorium-fluoride nanotubes using super-conducting magnets then radiate them with an intense stream of neutrinos from one of our reactors. The nanotubes convert the normal neutrinos into Majorana neutrinos, and they're all heading in the same direction. It's essentially a sub-atomic laser. We call it a 'phaser'."

Sheehan said, "If someone built a device like this, a phaser, will it produce sufficient energy to take out a warhead?"

"That's the million-dollar question. As you know, we've built a prototype right outside our reactor. The process is very unstable. We've conducted small-scale experiments successfully, but the reaction goes critical when we increase the size and power. It's the avalanche effect. When we reach a certain level of power, we get too much stray radiation. We have no way of controlling it."

"If you could control the reaction, what do you need to build a larger device?"

"Well, sir, we'd need about 60 or 70 kilograms of the nanotubes and time to…"

"We have 100 kilograms spread around the world at different sites," Sheehan said. "Is that enough?"

"Yes, that's plenty, but you do realize this is just experimental. You'd never be able to deploy it."

"Why not?" asked Sheehan.

"There's no way to point the beam. We'd have to rotate the entire nuclear reactor to aim it, which is quite impossible."

"Can't you use mirrors or lenses or something?" he asked.

"No, sir. There's no such thing as mirrors for neutrinos. We can collimate and fine-tune the beam using the magnets to position the nanotubes, but that's the extent of it. It shoots in one direction only."

"Then let's build a new reactor, one you can steer!" Sheehan said. "How long will that take?"

"Given unlimited resources, not long at all. We can have it all up and running in two to three years."

"Two years!"

"Yes, sir," Howell replied. "Building a nuclear reactor from scratch, one that we can move, that we can point in any direction with extremely high accuracy, will take a lot of work. Two years is optimistic."

"Max?" Sheehan asked. "Why can't we use one of our subs?"

Max had intimate knowledge of the nuclear power plants used on modern submarines, having been involved with the design of many of the sub-systems. He thought for a minute and said, "We'd have to use one of our Ohio-class ballistic missile subs. They're the only ones with a reactor large enough to power the phaser. But again, we'd never be able to get the accuracy we need. Can you imagine trying to point an 18,000-ton submarine with enough accuracy to hit a target thousands of miles away?"

"Then we just get closer, damn it! All I'm hearing from you is whiney bullshit. How long before you can have something operational?"

"If we recall all the stockpiled nanotubes from the PIT program and if we have immediate access to one of our Ohio-class subs and unlimited support, we could dismantle and reassemble our prototype inside the sub in less than a month."

"I want it up and operating in two weeks, and money is no object."

"But Deputy Director, I don't think you realize how dangerous this is. We can't control the reaction. You wouldn't want a sub's nuclear missiles within a thousand miles of this."

"Howell, someone in Sicily has already solved that problem. I'm sending a team over there to track these people down. We're going to move so fast they won't know what hit them."

The DDNI shook his head. "How can an island whose only claims to fame are the Mafia and square pizza have gotten their hands on something this powerful?"

Chapter 1

Present Day

It was 4:15 on a cold October morning. Perry's alarm had sounded 15 minutes earlier. He woke disgusted with himself. He felt old, his head throbbed, his back ached. He hadn't slept for more than a few hours. Perry slipped sweatpants and a sweatshirt onto his 6 foot, 2 inch, 180 pound frame, and looked in the mirror. He had dark circles under his blue-gray eyes and hadn't shaved in five days. His usually close-cropped, light-brown hair hung over his ears. Perry decided he'd let it grow out. Aside from the lack of sleep and a stiff back, he was in reasonably good shape but not due to any commitment to a healthy lifestyle. He could only thank his parents rugged maritime genetic stock for his hardiness. They'd been hard-drinking, hard-smoking, hard-fighting people that lived well into their eighties.

Perry walked barefoot across the wooden planked floor and down the narrow staircase. Reaching the kitchen, he turned on the espresso machine and added water. He poured enough coffee beans into the grinder for a single cup and inhaled the nutty, smoky, caffeinated aroma. A few minutes later, he carried his cappuccino outside. Sitting on his porch chair, he looked out over the dark waters of Linekin Bay.

Perry's home in Ocean Point, Maine, could be charitably described as a classic down-easter summer cottage. His ex-wife, Julie, said it was a hovel that should have been burned to the ground decades ago. The mustard-colored, cedar-shake cottage had a high-pitched roof with two gabled windows and a long porch that ran the entire length of one side. It had three small rooms on the ground floor and three even smaller rooms in what looked more like an attic than a second floor. The small kitchen accommodated a porcelain-coated, green and white, cast iron stove that he'd converted from kerosene to propane. The black sink was also cast iron. It was called a "dry sink" because it had to be wiped dry after each use to prevent rusting. The refrigerator was an expensive, retro-looking, cream-colored appliance with curved edges and chrome hardware. The cottage had belonged to Perry's father. After his death, it became Perry's and it was his most valued possession. After his divorce, Perry had packed his bags and moved to Ocean Point, leaving Boston and Julie in his rearview mirror.

"I deserve this," he muttered to himself. "What should I expect? Doing nothing but sitting in front of my computer for two months."

The night before, he'd been reaching into the top of his closet when electric jolts of pain shot through his lower back. Marta, his housekeeper, had just finished making dinner for the night and helped finish the packing, which, in his case, wasn't all that much, while Perry popped a healthy dose of Tramadol and lay on the couch.

"You should take better care of yourself," Marta said.

"I'm fine. I just twisted the wrong way and pulled a muscle. Thanks for helping, I don't know what I'd do without you."

"I think you'd be doing this packing yourself," she said. "You're just making excuses. The surgery was over a year ago. The doctors said it was a complete success, but you had to stay active and exercise to keep your back muscles strong. You've been ignoring their advice."

"Yeah, maybe." Perry reached out, took Marta's hand and stared at her. "But, I'm serious," he said. "I don't know what I'd do if you left me, too."

Marta smiled. "Try not to be mad at Miss Julie. She left because she had to. Now it's time you start taking care of yourself."

"So, you are leaving me, too?" Perry smiled back.

Marta was his therapy. She helped fill the void when Julie walked out. She was 63 years old. She'd immigrated from Pakistan with her family when she was a teenager. Perry had originally hired her as a caretaker for his dad. Now, she was taking care of him. After working her day job, she'd come over three times a week to cook meals and clean the house. Perry led a simple life and could easily take care of those things himself, but he just couldn't bring himself to let her go.

In the bright light of a new day, Perry finished his coffee, opened the porch door, and walked back inside. He went to the couch where Marta had left his backpack. All it contained was a change of clothes, his shaving bag, and a large laptop computer. He gingerly lifted it to his shoulders and walked around the living room. The pain wasn't bad.

"Thank God," he said to himself. "The meds are working."

Perry Franklin was 46 years old and had supposedly been retired from the CIA because of his "disability," but he suspected there was something else. As far as he was concerned, he'd fully recovered from his injuries, and his tracking technologies were critical to national security. His missions required a certain finesse, the kind of expertise only he'd been capable of delivering. Perry was no spook, no special operator with years of training and field deployments. He just had a natural talent, a knack for seeing and understanding details in his environment that others missed. The gift of eidetic spatial recall gave him a level of situational awareness that was impossible to pass on to operatives in the field. No one came close to outperforming him. His lack of field training and killer instincts allowed him to blend into hostile environments without looking like GI Joe in a kufi. Nobody suspected him. He had a deer in the headlights quality to him that was disarming. And up until last year, he'd had a perfect record. He was good at what he did and never understood why they canned him.

Perry dropped the backpack by the front door and went back upstairs to get showered and dressed.

Perry had received Stan's email two days earlier.

Hey Franklin,
How's the new life treating you? Have you thrown that noose over the beam in the attic yet?
So, we're having some technical problems and I think your skill set might be helpful. Would you be interested in coming back to do some on-call work for us?
Stan

Lieutenant Colonial Stan Sheppard had run the United States Army Special Operations Command, or USASOC's, 7th Group Special Reconnaissance Branch before being reassigned to the Office of Technical Service at the CIA's Directorate of Science and Technology. When he and his wife moved one more time, from Eglin AFB, Florida to Northern Virginia, he promised her, it was their last. Stan had quickly taken Perry under his wing as soon as the PIT technology began development. In the blink of an eye, Perry's career changed from that of a scientist at the NCPC, to a "technical field consultant" for the CIA, responsible for transitioning his tracking technologies from the laboratory into the field, from experimentation to operation. That was five years ago. Over that time, they'd become close friends. Stan was ten years older and several inches shorter than Perry. He had a hard, rough exterior and a gravely, commanding voice with a southern Alabama accent. His demeanor kept everyone at arm's length, except for Perry.

The hardened warrior and the geeky scientist made for an odd team, akin to Steve Wozniak partnering with Rambo, but it worked.

Perry had read Stan's email and understood the words clearly enough. Stan's use of the word 'technical' meant national technical means, or NTMs, which translated into overhead spy satellites. His use of 'skill set' and 'on-call' meant that he wanted Perry to go back into the field to finesse another target. Perry replied:

> *What? First, you guys fire me, now you need something from me? SNAFU and FU!*
> *Forget it! I'm done.*
> *Now can you tell me how to tie this damn knot?*
> *Franklin*

The morning after replying to Stan's email, Perry was drinking his second cup of coffee while reading magazine articles about backpacking around the world. He was halfway through a blog about hiking 500 miles on the Camino de Santiago when he felt a familiar chill on the back of his neck. Something wasn't right. He sprung to his feet and had already reached the door when he heard footsteps on the front porch. Two men dressed in cargo pants, short-sleeve shirts, and hiking boots were approaching. Perry recognized the clothing. It was 5.11 tactical gear. It looked like anything you might find at L.L. Bean in Freeport, but it wasn't. The clothing was over-the-top rugged and included strategically placed hidden pockets to conceal a variety of accessories for the modern professional. The cargo pants had slots for knee pads, gun magazines, and knives. They even included a canvas strap on the back to allow a buddy to drag your carcass out of the line-of-fire with one hand while returning fire with the other. The casual observer wouldn't have noticed the subtle differences, but Perry had a closet full of the same stuff. He swung the door open.

"Too bad the 5.11 folks don't produce a better variety of clothing," said Perry. "It's not exactly covert when a coupla' tough-looking operatives like you stand next to each other."

"Good morning, Franklin. Sorry for the intrusion, but we need to talk face-to-face."

"Thomas, I already told Stan to go to hell. I'm not interested. You and Samuels can keep the bullshit and head straight back home."

Both Thomas and Samuels stood about 5' 10" and weighed in at around 180 pounds. Thomas had bright blue eyes while Samuel's were hazel green. That was about the only difference between them. They both had an outdoorsy, mid-western, baseball, hot dogs, and apple pie look. Their smooth facial features were clean-shaven. They wore their brown hair at medium length and had no visible tattoos. They weren't necessarily handsome or ugly and could easily be forgotten within seconds of passing anyone on the sidewalk. They were also two of the most skilled and efficient killers that Perry had ever known. They were elite warriors of the 1st Special Forces Operational Detachment - Delta, or simply Delta Force. They'd served under Stan before he'd been re-assigned to 7th Group. Thomas and Samuels were both highly experienced in hostage rescue and counterterrorism, as well as reconnaissance and direct-action missions against high-value targets. When Stan's superiors at the CIA insisted that Perry have some real operatives to back him up, Thomas and Samuels were Stan's first choice. Three years ago, they'd happily packed their bags and left Fort Bragg to serve once again under Lt Col Sheppard.

Perry stood in the doorway, staring at Thomas. Thomas took a step forward, and nose-to-nose, stared back. It took thirty seconds before Perry, with a disgusted look on his face, stepped aside.

Thomas shouldered past Perry and walked into the dining room.

"What's with Samuels?" he asked. "Is he claustrophobic or just have better manners?"

"You know he's not cleared to your level."

"But you are?" asked Perry.

"Yes. They just read me in on your satellite program."

"And how do I know that?"

"You don't need to. I'll do all the talking."

"Fine, but technically I'm not cleared either, they took my TS/SCI away and it's not my program anymore."

Perry knew he was delaying the inevitable but had to at least try to hold on to his new life.

"It doesn't matter. You signed the paperwork," Thomas said. "You can still go to jail if anything I tell you leaves this room."

"Well, I can guarantee it won't because I don't care. Say what you have to say and get out."

Thomas smirked. He knew Perry well enough to see through the bluff. He pulled a Marlboro cigarette pack from his shirt pocket, opened the top, flipped a small switch inside, and placed it on the table.

"It's a high-power, broadband RF jammer," he explained. "Every cell phone, GPS, radio, Wi-Fi, and garage door opener within 100 meters is completely disabled."

"Great!" Perry said. "Let's give away our position to anyone else smart enough to geolocate a hostile emission in this neck of the woods."

"Not likely, but we took additional precautions. There's only one cell phone tower out here, so no one at the phone company can triangulate our position. You need at least three towers to get an accurate fix."

"It's only two but go on."

"We've also timed our arrival. For the next thirty minutes, the Russian and Chinese SIGINT satellites lack a clear line-of-site to our position. For backup, we have a second jammer synchronized to this device. We placed it out on a Coast Guard cutter that's sitting five klicks offshore. Any possible geolocation results are going to be skewed. It'll show our position as two kilometers south of here, in the middle of the ocean."

Perry wondered why they were taking so many precautions. Curious where this was going, he relaxed his shoulders and gestured for Thomas to take a seat at the table.

"Sounds like overkill to me, but okay, let's hear it."

"A week ago, during the final testing of our new USA-245 satellite, an anomaly was detected. The operators were positioning the sensor payload to observe the Mount Etna eruption in Sicily. They were going to use it to test the DE countermeasures system.

"That's a good idea. Who came up with that?" Perry asked.

"It doesn't matter," Thomas said. "As the ground swath of the sensor swept towards the mountain, the thermal shutters slammed shut."

"So, what's the problem?" Perry said. "That's what they're designed to do."

"I know, but the swath hadn't reached the volcano yet. The shutters activated 100 kilometers too soon."

"It sounds like a boresighting issue, but you don't need me to tell you that."

"No, that was the first thing they checked. They re-calibrated the sensors and tested them several times. It's not a boresighting issue. The sensors are dead on. Then they pointed the sensors back at the spot on the ground where they'd gotten the shutter activation. Nothing happened; they couldn't repeat the anomaly. Everything worked as it was supposed to. They were about to blow it off as some unexplainable glitch except for two things."

"Go on," Perry said.

"One of the operators in the control room remembered reading a while back about a strange series of electromagnetic events. They'd occurred on the northern coast of Sicily. He did a quick internet search and pulled up some old news articles. He calculated the position and compared it to our anomaly. The locations coincided exactly. It was in the village of Canneto di Caronia."

Perry asked, "What is the second thing?"

"Your PIT sensor was triggered."

"What?"

"The controllers were focused on testing the visible and thermal cameras. Your PIT camera wasn't scheduled for testing and calibration for another week. But the operator had it turned on anyways. He was collecting and storing the PIT data automatically; it was just free running in the background. After reading about the Canneto incident, he got curious. He pulled up the PIT data stream and correlated the location and time. Your camera received a huge signal that triggered the shutters at the exact moment the sensors passed over Canneto."

"That's impossible! Nothing triggers the PIT except the tags."

"I know, but it happened. We need to find out why."

Perry was born with a dangerously curious nature. His career fed that hunger, straddling the fields between science and engineering, between research and development. His mind was wired to solve mysteries. He needed more data.

"Tell me about these incidents in Canneto."

"It's a small Sicilian village on the north coast of the island. It has a population of 180 or so," said Thomas. "It made international news fifteen years ago when some unexplained fires broke out inside the homes of residents. Over a few weeks, it was reported that a television, a stove, and a vacuum cleaner had burst into flames. One person, a scientist according to reports, was said to have observed an unplugged electrical cable ignite right in front of him. In response, the Italian power utility, ENEL, cut off the town's power supply. But the outbreaks continued. A state of emergency was imposed, and part of the village was evacuated. Later investigations were completely inconclusive, and the whole matter died a slow death. There is not much to go on. Here's a newspaper article that discusses the highlights."

Thomas pulled out a copy of the article and handed it to Perry.

There are many ways for evil to arrive, but perhaps only one way to get rid of it: exorcism. That about sums up the collective psyche of this stone-filled village perched above the sea after a series of puzzling electrical shorts, unexplained fires and smoky outbursts struck in nine houses, displacing 17 families.

First to explode was Nino Pezzino's television, two days before Christmas.

Fuse boxes then blew in houses all along the Via Mare. Air-conditioners erupted even when unplugged. Fires started spontaneously. Kitchen appliances went up in smoke. A roomful of wedding gifts was crisped. Computers jammed. Cellphones rang when no one was calling, and electronic door locks in empty cars went demonically up and down.

Before long, the mainly Roman Catholic populace professed to see the hand of the Devil at work, turning their postcard-perfect paradise into a place possessed of evil, embers, and ash.

As Mr. Pezzino put it, "Whoever believes in the good believes…

Perry crumpled the paper into a ball.

"Hand of the Devil? Is this a joke? Did Stan put you up to this?"

He threw the crumpled article into the trash can and said, "Get the hell out of here, Thomas."

"Franklin, I assure you this is no joke. We're dead serious."

Thomas got up from the table and called outside. "Samuels! Bring me the files."

Thirty minutes later, Thomas, Samuels, and their jammer were gone. All that remained was a USB drive with reports, news articles, and conspiracy theories surrounding the Canneto events. They also left behind a folder containing an old-fashioned computer printout of the PIT data stream. In the modern day of electronic espionage, a stack of paper and a fireplace was often the best technique for counter-surveillance.

Perry picked up the folder with the long list of times, locations, and camera parameters. He walked out the front door of his cottage and down to the rocky shoreline. It was cold. The few oak, birch, and maple trees had shed their colorful leaves a week ago. What remained was a vast green forest of cedar, pine, and fir that thrived on the rocky coast. A stiff breeze blew from the south. Perry watched the waves crashing against the house-sized boulders lining the shore, plumes of white foam erupting into the air. He smelled the salt, the seaweed, and the clam flats. His heartbeat slowed, and the tension in his shoulders and back melted away. He heard the gulls in the distance and the sand and the rocks rustle as the waves ebbed and flowed. A metallic rattle reached his ears. He knew what it was before he even looked. Farther down the shoreline, in a small cove, a dingy was moored to a rusting steel chain, its bow rising and plunging with the swells. He walked out onto a boulder and stood on the same spot he had many times over the last 40 years. In the distance, passing in front of Squirrel Island, was a Coast Guard cutter with the familiar bright orange slash across her beam. She looked to be heading back to her slip at Boothbay Harbor.

Perry sat on the rocks and opened the folder, holding the papers firmly in the wind. The twelve pages of data were completely unfathomable without the knowledge of how and why the data stream was produced. Perry scanned through them. It was unquestionably clear; a detection and tracking event had occurred. That was the beauty of his design. There was nothing left to interpretation; it couldn't be fooled. He'd been studying the data for fifteen minutes before noticing something odd. One of the lines of data represented the health parameter of the satellite's power source. The radioisotope thermoelectric generator, or RTG, used thermocouples to convert the heat generated by the radioactive decay of plutonium-238 into electricity that powered the various electronics on the satellite. The health parameter in the data stream predicted the lifetime of this radioactive power source. At the exact time the PIT camera recorded a detection, the lifetime of the RTG fell from 36.7 years to 34.2 years.

That's impossible, Perry thought. *There must be something wrong with the data stream.*

He stood up and walked back home to carefully read the reports stored on the thumb drive. He didn't believe any of the stories about Canneto di Caronia. They lacked credibility. Electrical fires don't randomly break out without a cause, and no causes were reliably identified. Scientific theories abounded: bad house wiring, nearby electric train tracks, static electricity, and Mount Etna itself. Maybe underground lava flows had caused the release of highly flammable methane or even carbon disulfide gas, which auto-ignites below the boiling point of water. Then there were the fanatics and conspiracy psychos: a sign from the Devil, a sign from God, a secret weapon test. Perry was leaning toward the final category: a hoax!

But now he questioned his PIT data from the KH-11 tests. Thomas had verified that every one of their tracking assets was accounted for, and none were even remotely close to Sicily. Could it really be a glitch in the system? Complex systems always have glitches. It's unavoidable. All you can do is manage them as best you can and press on. But his camera couldn't be fooled. It was the only thing that brought him some feeling of accomplishment, some satisfaction in life, something that balanced the price he'd paid: the loss of his wife, and the alienation of his children. Perry did not want to go back into the field again. It had been all too costly to his personal life, and besides, there were no two ways around it, they'd put him out to pasture. He typed another email.

Hey Stan,

I looked at the data. I don't see anything jumping out that would explain these odd results, but you might want to have your guys run some diagnostics on the RTG. It looks like you had a power glitch. That might have caused the shutters to close. Either way, I'm not interested in going back into the field. You're on your own with this one.

Perry

He reread the email several times. He was split. It was the right thing to do for his personal life, but he needed the challenge, the adventure, the danger of being out in the field. He was being called to serve once again, and he was having a difficult time saying no.

He turned away from the computer and looked up at the pictures of his family, of his ex-wife, parents, and his two girls that still rested on the fireplace mantel. He turned back at the computer and clicked SEND.

That evening, Perry was cutting into a medium-rare filet that he'd blackened on the grill when his phone rang. Glancing across the table, he saw the word "Unknown" on the small screen. He let it ring four times before answering.

"Hey Franklin, it's Stan."

"I figured it was you."

"Why's that?"

"Because you don't know how to take 'no' for an answer."

"Yeah, or maybe, cause you're livin' like a hermit, and I'm your only friend."

"I'm just sitting down to dinner…"

"I'll make it quick. Will ya at least come down to DC so we can talk? If you're still not interested, we'll figure out somethin' else."

"I already told you. I'm not your guy anymore."

"There are some things ya need to know that even Thomas isn't cleared for. Jus' meet with us. What's the harm?"

"The harm is me losing what little bit of peace I've built here."

"I know, you're right," Stan said. "But it's jus' a meetin'."

"I'm sick of all the crap, Stan. I'm finally happy..."

"Happy? That's bullshit, and ya know it. If we don't git this under control, your life's work is goin' up in smoke."

For the last 20 years, Perry had worked in research and development for the Defense Department and then transitioned to the CIA. He was an expert in the art of tracking people who didn't want to be tracked. He'd also been happily married for that 20 years and had raised two daughters with Julie. Except that Julie had done all the raising. A year ago, Perry's world unraveled. Over a few months, he'd lost his kids to college, his job because of one failed mission, and most importantly, his wife. After nursing him back to health, Julie had packed her bags one morning and told him, "Franklin, I'm sorry, but there's got to be more to life than spending the rest of my days with you."

He'd always been a wanderer, a disciple of the journey, and his career fed that hunger. It's what cost him his marriage. Working with Special Forces and the Intelligence Community, his job had carried him all over the globe, fielding state-of-the-art surveillance and reconnaissance technologies. The game was intense and high paced, leaving little time for a wife and family. It was a high price to pay and if he had to do it over again... well, he probably would. After his forced retirement, Perry decided to become a freelance photojournalist, specializing in adventure travel. It wasn't all that new for him; he'd been doing it all his life. He'd written a few articles for some magazines and received a few awards for his photography. But, if he was honest with himself, he missed the action, the adrenalin rush of running operations in hostile parts of the world.

"I'll tell ya what," Stan continued. "I'll buy ya lunch. What's the name of that expensive place over by the Mayflower Hotel, where you always liked to eat?"

"Le DeSales," Perry said.

"Yeah. Come on down. After our meetin', I'll take ya there for lunch. My treat."

"I'll take the meal," Perry said. "But I'm not promising anything. And make sure there's someone at the airport to pick me up. I've gotten spoiled up here. I don't want to deal with the traffic."

"Great! I'll even do ya one better. I'll tell Samuels to let ya play with the siren."

"You're an asshole," Perry said.

"There's a plane leavin' out of the Pease Air National Guard PAX terminal in Portsmouth at 0630 tomorrow morning."

"Okay."

"Oh, I'll also have the PIT camera set up for ya. We'll need to demonstrate it to some folks in the meetin'.

"Whatever."

"See ya in the mornin'... and Franklin?"

"Yeah?"

"Thanks."

Perry showered and slipped on a pair of hiking pants and a shirt before going to a small safe bolted to a concrete pad he'd poured between the floor joists in his closet. He pressed a button and placed his index finger on the small window next to it. His thumb glowed with red light and he heard the familiar whir of the internal mechanism. Pushing his 40-caliber Beretta aside, he grabbed his loaded 9mm Glock and an extra 10-round magazine. The Glock was not standard issue. The caseless, frangible bullets were designed to prevent forensic investigators from tracing the bullet back to its owner. The steel barrel and receiver had been replaced with high-strength ceramic-polymer duplicates, and the trigger mechanism was an electronic switch. This would not have been enough to prevent detection by the latest airport scanning technology. But, when inserted into a specially designed compartment hidden inside his bulky laptop, it virtually disappeared. Perry had never used the prototype weapon in the field. He was not a warrior, but because of his unique skills and the dangerous places he visited, the powers that be insisted he become skilled in defending himself. Now, after many years of carrying a weapon, it had become a habit, even for a meeting in DC. Also inside the gun safe were three passports. He left behind the brown US government and the black diplomatic passports he'd neglected to turn in and grabbed the blue tourist passport, along with an envelope containing two-thousand Euros in small bills. *Just in case*, he thought to himself. He stuffed them into his pocket and locked the safe. After pulling on his trail shoes, he grabbed a fleece jacket from the hook by the door and headed out with his small pack slung over his shoulder. Perry looked just like any other Gen Xer going on vacation.

The air outside was cold and dry, the temperature close to freezing. He threw his gear into the back of his BMW. It was a twin-turbocharged, all-wheel-drive MX5 SUV. A special-order he'd splurged on after his divorce. The day it was delivered, he pulled the MX5, Turbo, and X-Drive emblems off the car. The only indicators of its uniqueness were the width of its oversized snow tires and the looks on the faces of other BMW owners when he pushed the accelerator to the floor. He loved the idea of having a car that looked like it belonged to a soccer mom, drove like a high-performance sports car, but could easily haul a bunch of camping gear into the snowy backwoods of Maine. It made him look stable.

The early morning sun was rising when he pulled out of the gravel driveway. After the divorce, his home and a small, early-retirement pension were all he had. He'd given everything else to Julie. The BMW was his only liability; everything else he owned free and clear.

An hour later, he arrived at the Portsmouth airport and maneuvered the BMW over to a grey aircraft hangar, several blocks from the main passenger terminal. Perry walked through a doorway with a small sign mounted over the top: US Military PAX Terminal - Authorized Personnel Only.

"Hi, Anita!"

"Hey, Mr. Franklin! I haven't seen you in a while. Where are you off to?"

"I have a meeting in DC."

Anita typed Perry's information into the DOD computer.

"The flight to Andrews will be boarding in fifteen minutes."

"Great!"

"You're still Category I?" she asked.

"I think so, at least for this week."

"Let's see… yup, you are good to go. Give me a few minutes, and I'll print your boarding pass."

Anita studied the computer for a few more seconds and typed at the keys.

"Mr. Franklin, it looks like they also have you booked on a flight to Sicily."

Chapter 2

Day 1

Perry walked across the terminal at Joint Base Andrews and found Samuels waiting for him at the door.

"So, now you're a taxi driver?" Perry asked.

"Only while you're on our side, Franklin. So, don't get used to it."

They walked out into the heat. It was late October and DC was 20 degrees warmer than Ocean Point. Perry removed his jacket and climbed into the black Ford Expedition. As soon as he sat he sensed the difference. There was no slight shift in the suspension from his added weight and the outside sounds of traffic and airplanes were silenced. He pounded a foot on the floorboard. It struck with a thud.

When Samuels climbed into the driver's seat, Perry said, "What gives? This is up-armored, but the windows look stock."

"It's a new type of glass," Samuels said. "It's the same thickness as the original windows but it'll stop small caliber rounds all day long."

"That's comforting," Perry said.

Samuels headed north on Suitland Road. Perry pulled his laptop from his bag and studied the PIT data for the tenth time. Locked away in the back of his head were the entire schematics and software code for the camera. From whatever angle he approached the problem, he couldn't reconcile the test results with the design of the system. It just seemed impossible. He was deep in thought when he felt something disorienting. He looked up just in time to see the Expedition pass the entrance ramp to 495 South.

"Where are we going?" Perry asked. "You should've jumped onto 495 South."

"We're not going to Fort Belvoir. We're going to Liberty Crossing."

"I thought we were going to the KH-11 Operations Center?"

"Just doing what I'm told," Samuels said.

When they arrived at Liberty Crossing, Samuels parked the car and led Perry to the security gate. They emptied their pockets into a tray and fed it through the x-ray machine. Perry pulled a card from his wallet and walked through the metal detector. The alarms rang and a hefty security guard blocked Perry's path.

Waving the medical card in the guard's face, Perry said, "Metal rods, lower back."

The guard studied the medical card and nodded. He waved a hand-held wand along Perry's belt line until it beeped and then signaled him to pass.

Several minutes later, Perry stepped into a large conference room on the 6th floor. He hesitated for a second. Sitting at a long mahogany conference table across from Stan were two men dressed in dark suits.

Stan stood up and walked over to Perry. "Hi, Franklin! Glad ya could make it."

Perry shook Stan's hand while looking at the other two men. "Good to see you. This isn't what I was expecting."

"Come sit," Stan said. "I've set up the PIT camera over in the corner and plugged it into the overhead projector. It's pointed at our Somalia site."

Perry sat next to Stan. "What's going on? I thought this was a worker-bee meeting."

"It's a little more than that," Stan said. "Oh, and there's some nanotubes sittin' in a vial over there on the table."

"I saw them," he said, having catalogued every detail of the conference room as soon as he stepped through the doorway.

Stan turned to the men seated at the table. "This is Perry Franklin, the inventor of the PIT technology. He was also one of our best field agents. Franklin, this is the deputy director for national intelligence, Mike Sheehan. He's runnin' the show."

DDNI Sheehan didn't rise to shake Perry's hand; he simply nodded.

"Mr. Sheehan," Perry said. "I understand through the grapevine that you're the one who decided to put me out to pasture."

"Mr. Franklin. I'm sure you understand, your injuries were quite serious. The CIA had no business sending an untrained, inexperienced operative like you on a mission like that."

"Sir," Stan said. "Franklin had a perfect record. He was our best man."

"Not anymore," Sheehan said.

"Yet, here I am," Perry said. "And I charge a lot more as a freelancer."

"I understand," the director said. "I hear your calendar's been quite full lately."

"And this is retired Brigadier General Bill Lewis," Stan said. "He's the director of NCPC."

"Mr. Franklin. I hope you've been enjoying your retirement," said General Lewis. "We appreciate you joining us."

"Honestly sir, I didn't see much of a choice. Either with my retirement or this meeting."

Bill Lewis had retired from the Air Force when he was 51 years old. His 25-year career in the military was atypical. He was a scientist, a physicist, who'd joined the military after receiving his Ph.D. from MIT. Reaching the rank of brigadier general was unheard of for someone who hadn't served as a combat pilot. His specialty was the counter-proliferation of nuclear material, and he was very good at the job. Lewis was a tall, handsome, charismatic man, with a friendly smile and a warm heart, but that was not the key to his success. His ability to make sound executive decisions under immense pressure was what got him his star. In his line of work, millions of lives were at stake, and he had little patience for emotional arguments or self-serving politicians. Where other officers used aggression, intimidation, manipulation, and politics to get what they wanted, Lewis used logic and indisputable scientific facts, with a high dose of probability theory and bullheadedness, that allowed him to sell his decisions (and himself) up the chain of command.

"This is a very delicate situation," Lewis said. "What we discuss here is classified at the highest level."

"Yes, sir, I understand. What's going on? I haven't worked for you nuke guys ever since the PIT technology took off. This isn't what I was expecting."

"You'll learn soon enough." General Lewis looked at Sheehan and then back to Franklin. "For the sake of everybody's clear understanding, I'd like you to review in layman's terms just how this PIT technology works."

"That I can do," Perry said. "But, it's important to point out that we don't completely understand the physics behind our technology. There are a lot of theories but little direct proof."

"We understand," Lewis said. "Just get on with it."

"Okay, well, we've developed a camera that can detect a special type of neutrino. As you know, neutrinos are subatomic particles that, up to this point, had been too elusive to capture except with multi-ton detectors buried deep underground."

"Why is that?" DDNI Sheehan asked.

"Most neutrinos are electrically neutral, with extremely low mass compared to other particles. Since they have no electric charge, they're not affected by electromagnetic forces that act on charged particles such as electrons and protons. Since they have no mass, they're not affected by gravity or other nuclear forces."

"Mr. Franklin, please keep this in layman's terms for the director," said the general.

"Sure. Let's consider light radiating from an incandescent lightbulb. To produce that light, we run electricity through a filament, it gets hot and releases photons, and the photons bounce all over the room. We absorb these photons of light using our eyes or a camera, and we convert this energy into information that we see as an image. Now, what if our eyes or our cameras were made out of clear glass? What if they were completely transparent to light?"

"Well," said Sheehan. "I imagine the energy would just pass right through."

"Exactly," replied Perry. "If we couldn't capture the light, we wouldn't be able to measure it, to see it. We'd be blind."

"Okay, so that's what's happening with the neutrinos?" Sheehan asked. "They pass right through us?"

"Exactly. They pass right through normal matter, unimpeded. That's why they're so hard to detect. In fact, 65 billion solar neutrinos are passing through every square centimeter of Earth, every second. Through every rock, every tree, and every person. Except for some enormous and expensive detectors, everything is completely transparent. And even those giant detectors can only capture one in 10 billion particles."

"So, it's kinda like trying to catch minnows in a chain-link fence." General Lewis added. "They just swim right through."

"That's a good analogy," Perry said.

"But your new camera here can see the neutrinos?" asked DDNI Sheehan, motioning to the PIT camera in the corner.

"Not normal neutrinos. We're detecting a different type of neutrino. They're called Majorana neutrinos. They can be detected because, in theory at least, they have some mass. Enough mass that we can catch them and measure them and, as with many inventions, it was developed by accident. Under one of your programs, General Lewis, I was designing a camera for detecting nuclear materials at long ranges. If the project had been successful, we would have been able to mount these cameras on some of our low-earth-orbit satellites to track the proliferation of radioactive material, anywhere around the world."

"Which," Lewis said, "was a complete failure."

"Not a complete failure. We detected normal neutrinos emitted during radioactive Beta decay, but only at ranges of a few meters."

"But," Stan interjected. "You did develop somethin' just as useful."

"Yes, during the development of the camera, I invented a technique for manufacturing gold-encapsulated nanotubes of thorium-fluoride. I was planning to use them to collect and focus the neutrinos being released by radioactive materials. By focusing the neutrinos down to a tiny area, there'd be enough density for me to see them."

"But that's not what happened," Lewis said.

"Right. It turned out the nanotubes had some unique properties of their own. During our experiments, we observed some rather strange results that correlated with a theory developed by the Italian physicist, Ettore Majorana. Back in 1937, he predicted that neutral spin-1/2 particles could be described by a real wave equation and... "

General Lewis cleared his throat loudly. "Mr. Franklin, do you possess the capability of getting to the point?"

"Oh, sorry, I tend to go on about Ettore Majorana. Few people appreciate his genius. Let me just say that the physics for our technology is based on theories developed by Majorana. No one had the capability to prove his theories back then. The technology just didn't exist."

"Until now," Stan said.

"That's right. Recent advances in nanotechnology gave us the tools. You need to understand, the size of these tubes are at the molecular level. They are invisible. Let's go back to the light bulb analogy. Instead of a regular incandescent light bulb that uses a hot filament to produce photons that we can see, let's consider a fluorescent lightbulb. In a fluorescent light, we use electricity to send electrons through a glass tube filled with mercury vapor. The electrons cause the mercury vapor to ionize and emit photons just like an incandescent lightbulb. But there's a problem. It's ultraviolet light, and UV light is invisible to the naked eye. It's not very useful when you want to read the newspaper. But if you coat the inside surface of the glass tube with a phosphor powder that glows bright white when radiated with ultraviolet light, voila! You have a light bulb. This is kind of what's going on with the neutrinos and the nanotubes. Think of the normal neutrinos as UV light. It doesn't matter if they're coming from the sun or being emitted from radioactive material here on Earth, we can't see them. My nanotubes are like the phosphor that converts invisible light to visible light. In our case, when the nanotubes are bombarded with normal neutrinos, they emit heavier Majorana neutrinos. These neutrinos can be detected with our camera, at very long distances."

Stan spoke up. "Franklin, I think we need to get more to the point about why we asked ya here."

Sheehan interrupted, "Why doesn't your camera work for detecting nuclear material?"

"It does work, just not at distances beyond a few meters. The number of neutrinos released during radioactive beta decay is just not enough to overcome the background noise created by solar neutrinos. It's like trying to find a needle in a haystack, except it's not a needle, it's a specific piece of straw in a haystack."

"The Majorana neutrinos are easier to find?" Lewis asked.

"Exactly. With the camera I developed, I can see the Majorana neutrinos emitted by the thorium-fluoride nanotubes. We've gone from using an underground, multi-ton facility capable of capturing only one in ten billion neutrinos to a hand-held camera capable of detecting about one in a thousand, at least as far as the heavier Majorana neutrinos are concerned."

General Lewis said, "But something is missing. You're producing neutrinos, correct?"

"Yes, the interaction between the incoming neutrinos from the sun and the thorium-fluoride encapsulated in the nanotubes causes a conversion and re-emission of these Majorana particles. The cool thing is that because there are so few of these new particles out there in nature, I can see them from thousands of miles away. It's like looking at a lighthouse in the dark. You can see them at huge distances."

"But you said you needed nuclear material to produce them? That's a bit dangerous, isn't it?" the DDNI asked.

"No sir, thorium-fluoride is only mildly radioactive," Perry explained. "Along with the neutrinos being released, thorium-fluoride emits alpha particles, but they are completely blocked by the gold layer."

Perry picked up the small liquid-filled flask from the table.

"This is what they look like."

Everyone leaned closer, peering at the contents of the bottle.

"It looks like Goldschläger, that liqueur with the gold flakes in it," Sheehan said.

"Exactly. Like I told you earlier, the nanotubes are microscopic, they're the size of molecules, but for a specific scenario we disguised them as exactly that, Goldschläger."

"What scenario is that?" Sheehan asked.

Perry unscrewed the top and brought it to his lips.

Stan yelled, "Franklin! Don't do that!"

Perry ignored him. He drank the entire contents and placed the empty vial back on the table.

"We've used this on suspected terrorists," Perry said. "Disguised as Goldschläger. It's completely harmless and takes about a week or so to work its way out of your system. If you ingest it in its pure nanotube form, instead of these larger flakes, it gets absorbed right into your body, and takes years to work its way out."

"You can drink that stuff?" the DDNI asked.

"Sure. The thorium-fluoride is poisonous, but it's completely encapsulated in the gold, which is inert."

"So, you're tagged now," the general said.

"Yes, sir. The solar neutrinos passing through my body interact with the tubes, turning me into a Majorana neutrino beacon. Any of our cameras can track me for the next week or so."

Perry focused his gaze on Sheehan. "You can even watch me shit it out and follow it all the way to the Potomac."

Sheehan gave Perry a stern look but didn't reply.

Perry turned to Stan. "You said the camera is set up?"

Stan reached over and turned on a digital projector sitting at the center of the conference table. An image appeared on a screen mounted to the wall on the other side of the room.

Lewis asked, "What's this?"

"It's a live image coming from that camera over there."

Perry pointed to a camera mounted on a tripod standing in the corner of the conference room. It was aimed down at the floor. Perry walked over and waved his hand in front of the lens. A corresponding hand appeared on the screen. Then he flipped a switch on the camera. A red dot immediately appeared on the screen, as if someone was aiming a laser pointer at the carpet.

"Gentlemen, what you see here is a kilogram of the thorium-fluoride nanotubes."

"We're looking right through the floor?" Sheehan asked. "Downstairs?"

"No sir, not downstairs, it's in the desert. In Somalia, actually. We have assets over there tasked with collecting intel on Al-Shabaab."

"Somalia?" the DDNI asked.

"Yes, sir. About 8000 miles away. As far as these Majorana neutrinos are concerned, the Earth is completely transparent. We've developed special lenses using the same thorium-fluoride tubes to focus the energy onto our detectors. The only time we have any problems tracking our assets are when we're looking directly at the sun. Then our cameras are overwhelmed with energy. As you may know, we installed a camera on the last KH-11 satellite you just launched. With that camera, you can pinpoint the exact location of your tagged targets, anywhere in the world."

"That camera in the corner can see your tags at 8000 miles?" Sheehan asked, his expression skeptical.

"It all comes down to size," Franklin said. "That camera can see a kilogram of nanotubes at 8000 miles. To find a smaller amount, like what I just drank, we need much larger optics. The PIT camera on the KH-11 we just launched has huge optics and can track me at a range of about 300 miles."

"Okay Mr. Franklin," Sheehan said. "I think we understand what we're dealing with."

"Maybe you understand, but I don't. I thought I was here to figure out what caused the PIT malfunction. You haven't told me why you're both here. The program was transitioned to our CIA's Covert Ops Directorate three years ago. We have nothing to do with nukes anymore."

Lewis continued looking at the wavering red dot on the screen and said, "Let me ask you a hypothetical. What would happen if you produced these new Majorana neutrinos in a larger quantity and they happened to be directed all in the same direction? Could they do any harm?"

"No," Perry said. "As I already explained. The earth is mostly transparent to neutrinos, even these heavier Majorana neutrinos. They pass through everything except my thorium-fluoride. We're being showered with trillions of neutrinos as we stand here. It takes hours before a single neutrino interacts with an atom in our body."

"What if it was a very large quantity? What if a high-intensity beam of your Majorana neutrinos was pointed directly at the Goldschläger you just drank? Would they interact?"

Perry looked at the three men and stared.

What the hell's going on? he wondered. *They already know the answers to these questions. Even Stan's uncharacteristically quiet.*

"Well, technically, yes," he continued, at a more cautious pace. "You can interact with them, but the process is inefficient. It takes a massive amount of the heavier neutrinos, much more than what we're being hit with from the sun."

"Maybe trillions per second?" Lewis asked. "All compressed into a high-energy beam?"

"It would have to be a pretty narrow beam to concentrate enough energy to cause a reaction," Perry said. "As some of you already know, we tried to create a concentrated beam like that. We used a nuclear reactor at NNSS to get the energy densities we needed but ran into severe instability problems we couldn't overcome."

"What if someone did overcome those problems?" Lewis asked. "Just for argument's sake. What if we created a high-intensity beam, maybe a meter in diameter?"

That's it, Perry thought. *They've made progress at the NNSS.*

"Just a minute," Perry said. He reached in his pocket for his phone before remembering he'd given it up as soon as he entered the classified facility. He walked over to a computer sitting by the camera, opened the calculator app, and typed.

Looking back over his shoulder, he asked, "At what range, no, forget it, it's columnated, like a laser, it really doesn't matter."

Perry already knew the answer but didn't let on. He typed some more numbers, rubbed his head, and mumbled to himself, "Well, that wouldn't be very good at all."

"What?" the general asked.

Perry turned to the group.

"Well, okay, so, neutrinos are the highest energy particles we know of in the universe. But, one particle at a time, they're harmless. That's because they're small and they lack charge. They're neutral, so they don't interact very much with other forms of matter, like us. But, if we're talking about Majorana neutrinos, in high enough densities, when focused onto anything that might be able to absorb the neutrinos, like my nanotubes, ahhh, not good at all."

"What do you think would happen?" Lewis asked.

Perry said, "If you hit my nanotubes with a beam like that, they'd most likely meltdown, releasing the thorium-fluoride as a very hot, poisonous gas, not to mention the molten gold. If that happened while it was in your body, it would be a prolonged, agonizing death."

"Exactly, Mr. Franklin," Lewis said. "That's why this is a very delicate matter, and that's why I'm here. Your PIT technology can be turned into a weapon, and since this is nuclear radiation we're talking about, it falls under my purview."

"A weapon? You've got to be kidding! Producing that many Majorana particles, in a narrow beam like that? We've already tried. It's impossible. It's like trying to turn a flashlight into a high-energy laser. We just don't have that kind of technology."

Lewis turned to Stan and nodded.

"Franklin," Stan said. "Somethin's happenin' in Sicily, and we don't know what. We just happened to stumble across a neutrino emission strong enough to shut down your camera. And, there's somethin' else we haven't told ya. They ran more tests on the PIT," Stan explained. "They haven't picked up any more signals from Sicily or any of our stockpiles. Nothin'. Your camera appears to be fried."

"I thought that's what the shutters were for," said Director Sheehan. "To prevent something like this from happening."

"Exactly sir. That's why we believe it's a heavy neutrino beam," Stan said. "It passed right through the shutters. Nothin' can slow it down except Franklin's nanotubes."

Turning to Franklin, Stan said, "Our guys did some calculations too. The thermal energy required to destroy your camera, well, that's where the 10 trillion particles per second came from, and that's per square centimeter."

"You think someone is turning this technology into a weapon?" Perry asked.

Lewis replied, "Yes. And if they've developed a PIT camera like yours, they'd know exactly where to point it."

"They could fry every ounce of nanotubes we've produced, every camera we've built," Perry said.

"Exactly," Stan said. "Including that Goldschläger ya just drank."

Perry walked into Le DeSales. It was an unassuming French restaurant sitting on a side street halfway between Dupont Circle and Farragut Square. He navigated through the lunchtime crowd and found Stan seated at a small butcher-block table in the back corner. Perry walked over and sat.

"I can't believe I'm letting you pull me back into this shit."

Stan shrugged, "I had no choice, but let's not talk shop. How are your girls?"

"They're fine. They're both at UMass in Amherst. They don't talk to me much."

"Because of the divorce?"

"Yeah, they took Julie's side. Guess I can't blame them."

"Franklin, they still need their Dad. Don't let'm slip away."

"I know, you're right. It's hard. Most days, I just want to climb into a hole."

"We've all been through it. It'll git better. Are ya seein' anyone?"

"Not by a longshot. I've taken a vow of abstinence." Perry smiled. I learned the hard way; I just don't get the whole relationship thing."

"Yeah, I felt the same way after my divorce. If it weren't for the sex, I'd a turned gay."

Perry laughed, "Yeah, me too."

"But, hey," Stan said. "Now I've got a great woman. Brenda is the love of my life, and I thank God every day she came into it."

"I'm happy for you, but I need time... maybe start with a pet."

"I hear Sicily has some beautiful women."

"About that, Stan. I have no interest in going to Sicily. And what the hell? You could'a told me ahead of time about the nanotubes."

"How was I supposed to know you were goin' to drink the stuff?"

"It was a setup."

"Look, it's highly classified, I couldn't tell ya anything until we got you into McLean. And, we shouldn't be talkin' about it here. Just drop it."

"Fine, but why do you guys want to send me? You've got plenty of people that can do this."

"You're right," Stan said. "Yur the best at deploying your tech, but that's not what this is about. We could'a sent Samuels or Thomas. For some reason, Sheehan insisted on you. That was strange. He acted like he knew nothin' about the technology but knew enough to ask for ya by name."

"They probably want a civilian out there in case it all goes to hell. They'd throw me under the bus in a heartbeat, let me rot in some Sicilian prison for the rest of my life."

"I don't think it's quite that bad. Sheehan doesn't know what the hell he's doin', but Lewis is a good guy, and he's been doin' this for a long time. We're workin' directly for him now, at least until we git this all sorted out. Lewis has unlimited resources when it comes to countering threats. We just need you and yur camera to do a little pokin' around. Nothin' ya haven't done before."

Perry leaned in close enough to make his point. "Not interested."

Stan grabbed Perry by the front of the shirt before he could sit back. He whispered, "Franklin, I know that dead Saudi girl is messin' with yur head. It was a huge mistake. But it wasn't yours. Yur not to blame. Those guys never should have pulled the trigger without a positive ID from you."

"I could have stopped them!" Perry said as he reached up and squeezed a pressure point between Stan's thumb and index finger.

Stan grimaced and released his grip. "It's over," he said softly. Ya almost died tryin' to save her. And right now, you have a chance to save a lotta good people. If this technology really can be used as a weapon, I can't think of anyone better then you to figure out how to stop it. We need ya."

Perry, surprised by the intensity of his own anger, said, "Let's order!" and motioned to the waiter across the room. "I want to start pushing this stuff through me as fast as I can."

"That reminds me," Stan said. He reached down beneath his chair. "I got ya a few presents."

Stan handed Perry a small plastic bag. Inside were two new iPhones still in their boxes.

"They're encrypted and already set up with local accounts in Sicily. Our phone numbers are preprogrammed. All ya gotta do is turn them on when ya need us."

"What's this?" Perry pulled a bottle of clear liquid from the bag and read the label. "Magnesium citrate?"

"Yeah! It's great stuff. Gotcha the lemon flavor. Used it before my colonoscopy a couple months ago. It'll have ya thoroughly cleaned out in a few hours."

"I can't fucking believe you guys!" Perry said. "I think I'll take my chances with the molten gold burning its way through my guts."

"Order as much as ya want. This meal's on the government."

"You're another reason I question my judgment in relationships."

It was mid-afternoon when Stan dropped Perry off at Andrews AFB. Stan got out and pulled a Pelican case from the trunk.

"Here's the PIT camera."

"You're assuming I'm going?"

"I know you are; ya can't help it."

Perry looked over at the terminal and back at Stan, who was now smiling at him.

"This is going to be a quick turn and burn. I'm not screwing around over there."

"That's all we need. We booked ya on another Space-A flight. There's a C-5 transport waiting for ya that'll connect through Rota, Spain. The aircrew's been briefed to stick to their normal routine. You're high priority. There'll be no diversions."

"Okay."

"And, Franklin, security keeps putting papers on my desk, complainin' that ya haven't turned in yur Glock or yur passports. Did ya bring them?"

"Just the Glock."

"Well, turn the damn stuff in when ya get back. I'm gettin' into hot water over it."

"Good luck with that. I'm a civilian. You've got no authority over me."

The Lockheed C-5 Galaxy was the largest military transport aircraft in the US Air Force. It stood over six stories high, and its length was fifty feet shy of a football field. With a maximum takeoff capacity of close to one million pounds, it could carry two M1 Abrams main battle tanks or six AH-64 Apache attack helicopters or 15 Humvees. Today, it was carrying only one high-value load, a 185-pound civilian.

Perry climbed the long set of boarding stairs and ducked through a small hatch in the side of the C-5. The interior was dark. There were no windows. He took a moment to let his eyes adjust before finding a seat. Unlike every other military cargo plane, the C-5 had a dedicated passenger compartment. It was perched three stories off the ground, above the massive cargo bay. Instead of the typical nylon-strap benches pinned to the side of the fuselage, it contained 73 wide, well-cushioned, high-backed seats. Aside from the lack of windows and the disconcerting fact that all the seats faced backward, he could easily imagine he was sitting in the first-class section of a commercial flight.

Nine hours later, Perry was walking through the terminal at Rota Naval Air Station, or NAS, in southern Spain. It was 0800 hours, 2 in the morning back in Ocean Point. He walked out the "Arrivals" side of the PAX terminal, turned left and walked back into the "Departures" side.

A half hour later, Perry was following twenty Marines as they climbed up the C-17's narrow steps leading into the fuselage. The crew chief walked over and introduced himself.

"Welcome aboard, Mr. Franklin. I'm Sergeant Hernandez. We've been waiting for you."

"Thanks for holding the flight," Perry said.

"No problem, sir. It gave the rest of our passengers a few more hours to enjoy Rota before their tour in sandland. Have you flown on a C-17 before?"

"Yes, several times, not the most comfortable of aircraft, is it?"

"Not at all," said Hernandez as he led Perry down the narrow pathway between strapped-down cargo and the curved side of the fuselage. He unfolded a stiff, nylon bench seat built into the side of the aircraft and handed Franklin some earplugs. Perry untangled the 6-point harness while the crew chief read the safety placard out loud. Thirty minutes later, the plane was airborne, heading for the middle of the Mediterranean Sea.

Perry unbuckled his harness and laid down across the stiff nylon web seats. He wanted to catch a few hours of sleep. Even on the relatively comfortable C-5, sleep had eluded him. Now his mind was racing. The last time he'd flown on a C-17, he was strapped to a medical transport stretcher, heading from Saudi Arabia to Landstuhl, Germany, and the largest US military hospital outside the continental US. His pain was so severe that the fentanyl dripping into his IV might as well have been saline solution. A year later, he still remembered the six-hour flight in excruciating detail, as well as the events that had led up to it. He had a sinking feeling in the pit of his stomach that it was happening all over again.

Chapter 3

A Year Ago

The Makkah Royal Clock Tower was part of a government-owned complex of seven skyscraper hotels located in Mecca, Saudi Arabia. The central tower, containing the world's largest clock face, was the third-tallest building on earth. Franklin closed the circuit panel mounted on the wall of the small alcove by the elevator shaft on the 74th floor. He calmed his breathing and listened for the soft drone of the elevator. He heard the distinctive slap of the cable. Three seconds later, the droning stopped, and the elevator dinged. He was already moving. Three steps, a quick turn to the left, five strides toward the now closing stainless-steel doors and a sidestep through the narrow opening. The prince's two bodyguards slammed Franklin against the door of the elevator. But it was too late, he was inside.

Although many of his colleagues suspected otherwise, Franklin wasn't a sociopath. And unlike the rest of his team, he wasn't a killer. He was a geek, who possessed an innate ability to separate his emotions from his intellect. That one simple trait, along with his eidetic spatial memory, made him one of the CIA's most effective field agents. The fact that he designed, built, and fielded the most advanced tracking technologies in the world was an added benefit.

The prince spoke rapidly in Arabic and the two men released Franklin.

"I apologize for my companions," he said. "They are a bit zealous in their duties."

"No problem," Franklin replied, brushing the wrinkles from his suit. "I didn't mean to startle them."

"I suspect you were more startled than they," said Mohammad bin Saud, the crown prince of Saudi Arabia. "This is a private elevator. It was not supposed to stop on this floor."

Franklin scanned the two bodyguards head to toe. They were stocky Arabic men, weighing in at over 100 kilos each, without counting their bulletproof vests. The bulges on the sides of their suit jackets were long. Starting from just under their armpits, the concealed weapons extended down the right side of their rib cages, ending just shy of the hems of their jackets. Franklin couldn't identify the make and model, but that was of no consequence, such weapons were useless in tight quarters. With a feigned look of nervousness, he scanned their faces a second time. The man on the prince's left had several scars on his face. Some were older, almost disappearing under his dark complexion. Other, newer scars, had a pink hue. Their locations corresponded with the bony protrusions of his eyebrows and cheekbones. He had a crooked nose and a scar on his lip. He looked relaxed, almost amused. It was literally written all over his face. He underestimated people. He had a problem learning from past mistakes. The guard couldn't imagine a threat from someone as unassuming as this pasty-white American businessman. The guard standing to the prince's right had more intelligence. His eyes bore down on Franklin, waiting for the slightest glint, the slightest gesture that he wasn't who he appeared to be. The guard's shoulders were tense, his knees slightly bent, and his left hand was hidden under his jacket. A knife, Franklin assumed. The perfect weapon in this environment.

Franklin was a pacifist, but a well-trained one. He decided if the situation went wrong, the stupid guard was the first to go. It would be quick, easy, and completely unexpected. He'd crouch and roll in, using the prince to shield him from the other, more alert, guard. He'd position himself such that the stupid guard's upper right leg was only inches from the karambit blade concealed in Franklin's belt buckle. A quick slice where the thigh meets the groin, would sever the femoral vein and artery, as well as the saphenous nerve, causing the leg to collapse. The opening left by the descending guard would give him room to retreat behind the prince as the other guard, already in motion, attacked from the front. Another quick slice and the prince's left carotid artery would spray blood into the face of the pursuing guard. The shock value alone would give Franklin the half-second he needed to plunge the karambit into the back of the guard's neck, severing his spinal cord. But that was but a simple mental exercise.

Franklin wasn't looking for a fight. He doubted he'd even survive the fight. There were too many variables to ensure a positive outcome. Even if he succeed in killing the three men, more of the prince's security detail were waiting for them 55 floors below him. Franklin only wanted to confirm what he'd already deduced. He spotted the two skinny legs standing behind the more intelligent guard. Franklin stepped casually to the left, as if making room for the prince to exit. The teenage girl wore a hijab over her head and shoulders. It did little to conceal the flushed skin, the red eyes and nauseous expression on her face. Mohammad's daughter was highly intoxicated.

"I'm very sorry to interrupt your highness," Franklin said with a nervous jitter in his voice. "I'll get off at the next stop."

"I am afraid that will not be possible," said the prince. "My security staff is very strict. Any deviations from protocol must be dealt with directly."

"But, but... I have an urgent meeting to get to, I'm already late."

"I apologize again for the inconvenience. I'm sure you understand."

Franklin turned and frantically pushed at the numbered elevator buttons. None of them lit from his touch.

Franklin was standing in the elevator because the powers that be wanted to send a message, a strong message. Saud and his personal assassination team, or Tiger Squad, would not be tolerated on the international scene. Saud had been warned. He'd been cajoled. He'd been threatened. He'd been bribed. Yet, he continued to indiscriminately eliminate his adversaries one-by-one. If he'd kept these murders limited to the Arab world, the US would have turned a blind eye. That was not to be. Saud had stepped over the line. He'd orchestrated the elimination of a naturalized US citizen, Mamut Kalem, a US congressman from the great state of New Mexico. Kalem was a distant member of the Royal Family, who'd been exiled from Saudi Arabia decades ago because of his progressive views and attempts to democratize the country. Until recently, he was a very vocal and influential critic of Saud's ascension to the throne.

Kalem's death on a ski slope in Taos had looked like an accident, but, because of Franklin's tracking technology, the intel folks knew differently. Abdul Zahir, Saud's closest bodyguard and Tiger Squad member, had been tagged with Franklin's nano-tubes a year earlier. He was being tracked in realtime by a sophisticated network of airborne and ground based surveillance platforms. The fact that he was enjoying a ski vacation in Taos hadn't raised any red flags. He'd often traveled to the US with Saud's contingent, and even bad actors needed a vacation. What the intel community was not privy to, was the fact that Congressman Kalem was on the same ski slope at the same time as the Saudi assassin. By the time the congressman's broken body was discovered in a snowbank hours later, Zahir was on a private jet flying at 40,000 feet over Mexico.

Franklin found kill missions distasteful. He believed that good intelligence could solve any political problem without bloodshed. But he was a realist. He knew they may never get the intel they needed. So, to that end, he compromised. Instead of using big bombs, killing conscripted foot soldiers and innocent civilians, his group specialized in surgical strikes. They were responsible for cutting the head off the snake. He did his job, his only job, which was to tag and track bad guys. His special forces' counterparts took care of the rest, and they had developed an excellent plan to end both Saud's and Zahir's lives.

Franklin and his team had arrived in Mecca, Saudi Arabia, a week earlier, under the pretense of attending a conference. Their mission: to tag Mohammad bin Saud. Once accomplished, he'd turn his back and walk away, knowing that sooner or later, Saud and Abdul Zahir would be eliminated in a single, anonymous and bold stroke. The problem was that the crown prince, already targeted by the Muslim Brotherhood, had a security team befitting a king. Aside from his security team, no one at any time, day or night, knew of the prince's precise location. Except, of course, right now. Franklin knew precisely where he was as he stared at one of the most powerful and deadliest men in the world.

"Please, there is nothing to be concerned about," Mohammad said. "We will have this all settled in no time. What is your name, and what brings you to our wonderful city?"

"Ah, ah, I'm Perry Franklin. I'm here for the SPIE Computer Engineering conference downstairs."

"Well, Mr. Franklin. Just relax. My men will have you back at your conference in no time."

Franklin nodded and looked back at Saud's daughter.

"If you don't mind me saying, your young companion does not look well."

"This is my daughter, Munira. Don't mind her. She has misbehaved today."

"How so? If you don't mind me asking."

"Not at all," he said as he turned towards his daughter. "The whole world can see what happens when our laws are broken."

"She's so young," Franklin said. "How could she possibly break…"

"By drinking wine behind my back."

"Oh, my," said Franklin. "By the looks of her, it appears she drank the whole bottle."

"That was her punishment," the prince said. "She'd only taken a sip. I decided natural consequences are the best lesson. I instructed her to finish what she had started. She had drunk almost half the bottle before the vomiting. What a waste of good wine."

The night before, Franklin had injected his nanotube tags into the bottle of the prince's favorite wine, a 1988 vintage Domaine De La Romanée-Conti Grand Cru. The inert nanotubes were tasteless, odorless, and completely undetectable by the prince's official taste tester. The tagged bottle of wine even passed inspection when wanded by a Geiger counter, a precaution the prince's security chief put into place after the Russians used radioactive polonium-210 to assassinate one of their defectors, Alexander Litvinenko. It was general knowledge that the prince had an evening habit of drinking a couple glasses of wine before dinner, even though the consumption of any type of alcohol in Saudi Arabia was forbidden.

Franklin stood quietly, running alternative scenarios in his head while the elevator descended quietly to the lower level parking garage. This young teenager had ruined their mission. They'd been following Abdul Zahir for weeks, and he was now in Mecca. Franklin and his team were just waiting for the right opportunity. Sooner or later, Zahir and Prince Saud would be in the same spot at the same time. All they had to do was tag the prince, sit back and wait while their airborne assets tracked their targets. When the two tracking signals converged, and were isolated from innocent civilians, the MQ-9 Reaper pilot sitting in a control station at Creech Air Force Base , Nevada, would press the launch button. He had failed and needed to cancel the operation immediately.

Franklin felt the elevator stop. As soon as the doors slid open, the two bodyguards grabbed his arms.

"Hey! What the hell!" he protested.

"They will take you to our security office and run a background check." said the prince. "Good day, Mr. Franklin."

Franklin watched as Saud, his daughter, and the rest of his security detail walked towards a line of five waiting limousines. Saud spoke angrily to his daughter in Arabic and pushed her toward the lead vehicle. One of his guards opened the rear door of the limo, and Perry stiffened. There, sitting in the rear passenger seat, waiting for the teenager, was Abdul Zahir. Saud yelled more commands directed at Abdul while gesturing towards his daughter. Abdul nodded in agreement and pulled the girl into the car. The lead vehicle headed out of the garage, leaving the prince and the rest of his contingent behind.

The two guards led Perry through a doorway and down a long corridor. They entered an office and dropped Perry into a hard steel chair.

"Your passport, please," said the more intelligent guard.

"Sure," he said. "No problem. Can we just speed this up. I really need to get going."

He handed his passport to the guard, who sat down at a desk and started typing on a computer.

Franklin pulled his phone out of his jacket. He had to cancel the mission. They had a straightforward set of coded messages. "coffee?" meant the mission was a go, "coffee." meant hold, and "coffee!" meant abort. Before he could press the send button, the dull-witted guard grabbed the phone from Perry's hand.

"What?" Perry asked. "I can't even send my colleagues a message that I'm running late?"

The guard looked at the message suspiciously and said, "Coffee! That's how you tell them you are delayed?"

"Well, yeah! I'm letting them know I stopped for one of your awesome Arabic coffees. I love the cardamom you guys add, it really smooths it out."

Perry reached for the phone, but the guard slammed it on the desk. They spoke more Arabic, and the guard at the keyboard picked up Perry's phone and plugged it into the computer.

Perry panicked. He pictured the drone pilots looking at the two red dots on their monitors, so close together, they were practically one. He knew there was a very high likelihood that Saud's daughter was being sent home for her misbehavior, and Perry knew precisely where their Mecca residence was located. He pictured the long, deserted highway that led to it. That would be the spot. He looked at his watch. Seven minutes had passed since the limo left the garage. He recalled the surface streets and intersections between here and the highway. He calculated the remaining time the driver needed to reach the outskirts of the city. He had maybe eight minutes left before the young woman's life came to an end. He knew Samuels and Thomas would eventually find him but there wasn't enough time. He had to do something, and he had to do it now. Adrenaline pumped through his bloodstream; he felt his heart gallop. He was losing his cool. Franklin prided himself on his ability to stay calm in any situation. He leaned back in his chair and stretched his legs, letting out a long, slow breath. He placed his hands across his waist and watched as the two guards scanned the contents of his cell phone.

Franklin couldn't stand violence, but he wasn't going to let an innocent girl die because of him. He pressed the release on his belt buckle, slid the three and a half-inch curved blade from its concealed sheath, and exploded forward. He caught the dim-witted guard entirely off-balance. As the guard fell towards the computer, Franklin reached around and in one smooth motion severed his jugular vein. The second guard was fast, way too fast for his size. He grabbed Perry's right wrist with one hand and Perry's throat with the other. He rose from his chair, lifting Perry up off his feet. The man twisted and bent forward, flipping Perry further into the air and over his shoulder. Perry crashed backwards onto the metal chair he'd just been sitting in. He felt a sickening crunch as the guard's weight landed on top of him. His back exploded in pain. The guard stood up and Perry fell to the floor. A second later, he fell into darkness.

Perry didn't regain consciousness until he was being wheeled across the tarmac at Taif International Airport.

"Don't worry, Franklin, we got ya," said Samuels. "You did it. We got the sons-a-bitches."

Perry was in too much pain to respond. They wheeled him up the ramp of the C-17 and were airborne five minutes later, heading for Germany and the best military trauma surgeons in the world.

Chapter 4

Day 2

Perry walked into the Sigonella terminal, pulled out one of the iPhones and turned it on.

"Franklin!" said Stan. "Did ya make it okay?"

"Yeah, just landed in Sigonella."

"Great! So, we've set up a cover story for ya. We're populating Nat Geo with some of your articles and pictures. Hope ya don't mind, we pulled them off your computer at the house."

"You've broken into my house already?"

"No, no, relax. We just hacked your computer from a remote terminal. Ya really should have unplugged it from the wall before leavin'."

"I'll try to remember that."

"We also modified your history of working for the government. It was too difficult to hide everything, there's too much data out there. We just made it a little more benign. You were a public relations guy that used your background in physics and engineering to transition government technologies to the private sector. You worked for the Tech Transfer Office at the US Army Aviation and Missile Command. Now that you're retired, you're a photojournalist writin' about travel and adventure."

"Sounds like you've got me all figured out."

"We got ya covered."

"I'm heading out to pick up a rental car. Then I'll drive over to Canneto.

"Okay, but don't forget to stop at the Mount Etna Observatory. That's your cover story. Yur doin' an article on the eruption and the impact Mount Etna's has on Sicilian culture. I made an appointment for ya to meet with the director this afternoon. Don't be late."

"Will do, I'll check back with you in a couple days."

Perry walked over to a woman sitting under a sign labeled "Information Counter."

"Can you tell me where I can find a cheap rental car?"

"Si`, signore. There are the Europcar and Budget franchises right here at the airfield, and if they do not have any cars available, there is another just outside the main gate. But their cars are wrecks. Most of the time, they are returned by tow trucks."

"Thanks, grazie, signora."

Perry left the terminal and headed for the main gate. It was a bright, warm, sunny afternoon. Mount Etna sat clearly on the horizon directly north of him, the snow-covered mountain sending plumes of steam billowing into the sky. Perry loved the mountains and felt a brief pang of loss as he looked northward. He and Julie had spent many weekends camping in the White Mountains of New Hampshire: hiking steep trails, swimming in frigid streams, and making love under the trees.

"Stop that!" he said out loud.

Exhaustion was making him nostalgic. He needed some sleep.

Perry walked out the front gate of Sigonella NAS and crossed the street to the small rental car agency the woman had warned him about. Seeing no one in the lot, he headed for a small trailer with sliding glass doors. Slipping inside, he dropped his case and backpack and called out.

"Hello! Anybody here?"

Hearing no reply, he walked to the far end of a narrow hallway and pushed a partially closed door open. There, sleeping on the couch, was an elderly man, dressed in a crisp white shirt and dress slacks. The man's eyes opened at the sound of the squeaking door.

"Excuse me, signore," Perry said. "Buongiorno, mio nome è Perry Franklin."

The man blinked a couple times and said, "Signore, it is siesta. We are closed. Per favore, come back later."

"I'm sorry. I didn't realize but I need a car right now."

"You Americans are always in such a hurry. Slow down, signore. Relax."

He stood up, held out his hand and introduced himself while guiding Perry back to the front office.

Roberto was a short, barrel-chested Sicilian, with a thick mane of white hair. He had deep creases and acne scars on his face, reminding Perry of a snow-capped Mount Etna. He wanted to take a photograph of the man to capture the details of his face but decided against it. He had work to do.

Roberto sat at his desk and motioned for Perry to sit.

"Okay, signore Franklin, now that you have woken me, how can I be of service?"

"I need to rent a car."

Roberto pulled a rental contract from his desk, his pen poised to start writing, and asked, "How long would you like it?"

"Oh, I don't know. Can I just bring it back when I'm done?"

Roberto put his pen down.

"Signore, we keep close track of our cars. A breakdown far away can be costly for us to retrieve. Most of my customers make reservations ahead of time and know when they will return. Maybe you try Europcar or Budget."

Perry sat back into the seat. He'd studied the many differences between cultures and knew the Sicilians were social people, very family-oriented. They preferred to make friends, not customers.

"When I'm traveling," Perry said. "I like to use the local services as much as possible. We use a phrase in the States... think globally, act locally."

"This is a very good philosophy, Mr. Franklin. Would you like a coffee?"

"Very much," Perry said.

Roberto turned to a side table and flipped a switch on a small espresso maker.

"Tell me, signore Franklin, what brings you to Sicily?"

"I'm retired from the military and I've always wanted to see Sicily."

As Roberto poured two cups of espresso, he recommended places to visit: the wine regions, the northern shore, Mount Etna, Palermo. Then he opened a side drawer to his desk.

"You are a good man, Mr. Franklin. I can see it." He gave a quick wink. "I have one car you can take for as long as you like, I'll charge you, oh, say 800 euros for one month. Half payable in advance. But you must check in with me from time to time to let me know you, and the car, are okay."

Perry replied, "That sounds reasonable."

Perry pulled some cash from his pocket and counted out four 100 euro notes. After signing the rental paperwork and finishing their coffee, they walked out to the parking lot. Roberto led Perry to a small, white Fiat sitting in the back of the lot. It was covered in dust. The plastic front bumper was cracked, and the back bumper had a hole in it the size of a 45 caliber bullet. Both the left and right rear fenders were pushed in about an inch, obviously from someone trying to squeeze through a narrow passageway, and the passenger-side mirror was broken. Looking inside through the driver's door window, Perry saw that it had over 200,000 kilometers on it.

"This is exactly what I'm looking for," he said. "I suspect the 400-euro deposit will cover any mishap, including total destruction."

Roberto shrugged with a smile.

Neither Franklin nor Roberto bothered to fill out the little diagram on the rental form indicating past damage. The unspoken deal was apparent, just return it in one piece. Perry threw his Pelican case into the small trunk and dropped his backpack onto the back seat. He climbed in and started the engine. It belched a cloud of thick black smoke and then purred like a kitten. Except for the faint knocking he heard when he hit the throttle, it was perfect for complete immersion into the Sicilian countryside.

"Is this a diesel?" Perry asked.

Roberto said, "Si`! It is very efficient car."

Perry reached out the side window and shook his hand.

"Thanks! I'll take good care of your baby."

Roberto folded his hands in mock prayer, and Perry was off.

The exhaustion mounted as Perry drove ten kilometers east to the second-largest city in Sicily, Catania. Exiting the highway, he was enveloped in a sea of ancient buildings built of dark stone. Since he'd been unable to sleep on the airplanes, he spent most of his time researching the history of Mount Etna.

Palermo might be the largest city in Sicily, but Catania, an ancient port city sitting at the base of Mount Etna, had the unique distinction of being buried by lava a total of seventeen times in recorded history. The Sicilian name of the original village was Katane, which meant "grater" or "flaying knife." Other translations were "harsh lands," "uneven ground," "sharp stones," or "rugged soil." Perry thought these translations were justifiable. Each time the city had been rebuilt, they had used the very material that had destroyed it, the black-lava basalt.

It was 1515 hours when Perry parked his car at Piazza Roma. He walked across the tree-lined street and headed east on Viale Regina Margherita. A block later, he spotted the small travel office of Antica Corte Viaggi e Turismo il Salotto dei Viaggi, aka, the Ancient Court Travel Agency.

During his career with the NCPC, and later with the Agency, Franklin had traveled extensively throughout Europe, the Middle East, and Southeast Asia. Whether he traveled undercover or not, he rarely booked accommodations ahead of time and refused to let the Agency secretary book them for him. He'd had too many close calls. He preferred the flexibility of being able to make last-minute changes to his plans and the security of knowing that an adversary couldn't predict a time and place of his whereabouts. Perry always slept better when he avoided brand hotels, choosing local accommodations instead. The tourist hotels were notorious for having special rooms for foreigners, outfitted with upgrades such as microphones, video cameras, and monitored internet connections. But that wasn't going to be a problem this time. There were no big brand hotels where he was going.

Perry walked up to the solo travel agent sitting behind her desk.

"Good afternoon, signora. I need a place to stay."

"Buongiorno signore, my name is Maria Parisi."

She stared patiently at Perry.

"Oh! Scusi, mi chiamo Perry Franklin."

"How very nice to meet you, signore Franklin. Where would you like to stay? We have some beautiful vacation rentals right here on the beach."

"I'm looking for something near Canneto di Caronia."

"Oh! Well... Are you sure? That is not very popular..."

"Si`! I'm quite sure."

"There is only one hotel there, the Hotel Za' Maria. It is right in the center of the village. Let me..."

"Do you have anything on the mountainside, that looks out over the ocean?"

"If you do not mind my question, what brings you to Sicily?"

"Not at all," Perry replied. "I'm a photojournalist. I'm here to write an article on Mount Etna. The recent eruption has renewed interest in the area. I want to explore the history of Mount Etna and its effect on Sicilian culture."

"But where you want to stay is very secluded. There is not much to see or do in that area."

"You know Maria, I've found that the people you stay with are so much more important than the location or the speed of the internet. Don't you agree?"

"Of course."

"If you can just find a nice, quiet place, I would be delighted."

Maria nodded. "I will make a few phone calls. How long will you be staying?"

"I'm not sure yet, at least a week, maybe longer."

Maria picked up the phone and dialed a number pre-programed into the phone. She talked for a couple of minutes while watching Perry from the corner of her eye.

Perry noticed her staring and wondered if she'd not been pleased with his direct approach. He reminded himself to slow down and take it easy. The Sicilians need to be treated with respect. A little bit of tact can go a long way here.

Maria hung up and said, "I have booked you into a wonderful old casa con camere in Canneto. It has a magnificent view of the sea. I am sure you will appreciate its beauty. You will be their only guest, and they will take very excellent care of you."

"Thank you so much, signora. I'm sorry I was so abrupt."

She smiled. "Non c'è problema. You will find Sicilians enjoy very much this moment."

"How much is it?" Perry asked.

"You will pay 55 euros per night. With the local taxes and my small commission, the total is 433 euros for one week. If you need to stay any longer, simply tell your host. All I need is a passport and a credit card."

"Do you mind if I pay cash?"

"Ma certamente, but I will still need a copy of your passport."

Perry handed Maria 450 euros and his tourist passport.

"Please, keep the change for your effort."

"Grazie, signore Franklin. I will write directions to the Casa Rurale. It can be difficult to find."

Maria copied his passport, gave it back to him, and wrote the directions on a piece of paper. She folded the paper in half and wrote a phone number on top.

"If you have any problems, please do not hesitate to call this number."

Seeing Maria's smile, Perry assumed the number was hers.

"Arrivederci signora Parisi. It was a pleasure meeting you."

After he walked out the door, Maria picked up the phone again. She pressed another speed-dial number as she studied the copy of Perry's passport.

Perry walked back towards the plaza and found Piazza Roma 2. Going by the date on the cornerstone, the large, three-story building was two hundred years old, but the Romanesque stone porticos, with massive square columns and circular arches made it look older. The Osservatorio Etneo del Istituto Nazionale di Geofisica e Vulcanologia was the local observatory that carried out research, monitoring, and surveillance of Mount Etna. He had a few questions and needed to build his cover story. With the enormous plumes of smoke and steam still billowing into the clear blue sky, it was an excellent excuse to explore Mount Etna. But that wasn't his objective. He needed to find the source of an anomaly that had taken out his PIT sensor. And that was 100 kilometers northwest of the mountain, in the small village of Canneto di Caronia. He walked into the stone building and up to the front desk where an elderly woman sat at a computer.

"Buongiorno. I'm Perry Franklin. I have an appointment with Dr. Gerard."

"Buongiorno signore Perry, we have been anticipating you. Per favore, come this way."

Perry followed the woman back to a laboratory filled with racks of instruments. A large black man in a lab coat sat at a stainless-steel workbench, hunched over a microscope.

"Dr. Gerard, Mr. Franklin is here to see you."

The man straightened and stood. Sam Gerard was six and a half feet tall and weighed at least 250 lbs. His commanding presence contrasted with a warm, inviting smile. He greeted Perry with a handshake that enveloped Perry's hand.

"Mr. Franklin, I am so glad you come to visit us."

"My pleasure. Thank you for taking the time on such short notice."

"We thrive on short notice. That is why we are here. Our monitoring stations are used to predict volcanic activity, but even at our best, Etna gives us little time to prepare."

"I understand last week's eruption killed a local farmer," Perry said.

"That was a tragedy," said Gerard. "Etna is reasonably predictable as far as volcanos go, and its activity, although impressive, has rarely caused catastrophic damage."

"How often have people died because of an eruption?" Perry asked.

"The last time was about 30 years ago. Another case of being in the wrong place at the wrong time. A local couple was killed when Etna spewed large volcanic bombs of molten rock into the air. The magnitude of the eruption had been accurately predicted days before and had led to the closing of tourist facilities on the south side of the mountain. The couple had decided to pit probability against reality when they climbed a knoll at the base of the mountain. Very unfortunate."

At almost 11,000 feet, Mount Etna was the highest active volcano in Europe outside the Caucasus. It was also the highest peak in Italy south of the Alps. Etna covered an area of 459 square miles with a circumference at its base of 87 miles. This made it by far the largest of the three active volcanoes in Italy, being about two and a half times the height of the next largest, Mount Vesuvius. Only Mount Teide on Tenerife in the Canary Islands surpasses it in the whole of the European/North African region.

Gerard continued. "The farmer killed last week was a vignaiolo. I knew him. He had a small vineyard on the northeast side of the mountain where he made a wonderfully unique wine. Sergio was struck by a single rock that had been ejected from the eruption. A freak accident. He was over 10 kilometers away."

"That's terrible," Perry said.

"Yes, very sad. So, Mr. Franklin, what exactly can I help you with."

"Well, I'm writing an article from the perspective of Mount Etna's effect on the whole social fabric of Sicily. As you had just said with the vig-ne-olo…"

"Vignaiolo… winemaker!" said Gerard.

"Vignaiolo. You said he made a unique wine. Is it because of the volcano?"

"Oh, yes. Etna creates a micro-climate with perfect conditions for growing grapes, and the volcanic soil adds a subtle mineral flavor."

"That's exactly the type of story I'm interested in. But, as far as how you can help, I'm also interested in the physics, or I guess the volcanology, of Etna."

"Yes, volcanology is a well-known branch of science, and it will serve you well to study one of the numerous books on the subject…"

"But what is it that makes Etna unique?"

"You mean, besides it being the largest active volcano in Europe?"

"Exactly," Perry said. "Besides that."

"Well, Etna is not that unique in a geophysical sense. It is a common type of stratovolcano. Its lava flows relatively slowly because of its high viscosity, so there have been amazingly few deaths caused by its eruptions. People can simply walk away from it."

"Assuming they don't get hit on the head with a rock."

"There is always that, but obviously the odds of being hit by a flying rock 10 kilometers away are low. One unusual thing though is the extent and size of the lava tubes created by these flows. Monti Nebrodi, the mountain range north of us, has some remarkably long tunnels that were formed hundreds of thousands of years ago, some of which have been mapped all the way to the northern coast."

"I'd never heard of them," Perry said.

"You would not. It is very dangerous to enter them; they collect poisonous gases. The government has done a good job of keeping the locations of the entrances protected. The tunnels are all sealed off now. If you do not mind, please leave that information out of your story, they have nothing to do with our culture and it only endangers people."

"No problem." Perry said, but didn't need the warning. His whole career in nuclear counter-proliferation, and then more recently with the CIA, revolved around his drive to keep innocent people safe. Some might have called it patriotism, but they would have been wrong. He made no distinction between protecting innocent American lives or the innocent lives of others. It was all the same to him. The tough part was deciding which lives to save, and which had to be sacrificed for the greater good.

Perry spent the next hour talking with Gerard while getting a tour of the facility. After taking numerous pictures and notes, Perry and Gerard parted with the promise that he'd send his article to the Institute for fact-checking, which was never going to happen.

Perry maneuvered the Fiat around the base of the mountain, glancing up occasionally at the steep volcanic slopes. He was heading north-west, taking the most direct, if not the quickest route to Canneto. He needed time to think, and the mountainous back roads with their steep drop offs and hairpin turns were sure to keep him awake. The added benefit was avoidance of the surveillance cameras set up at the highway toll booths.

Perry was halfway to Canneto when his personal cell phone buzzed. He glanced at the screen. The caller ID displayed, "Do Not Answer!" It was Julie. She needed something. A faucet was leaking, the lawnmower wouldn't start, a light bulb needed changing. Perry was still grieving, and her calls left him feeling used and angry. He tried avoiding the 'honey-dos', but he just couldn't. Even after he'd moved to Ocean Point, he'd drive the few hours to Boston to take the dog to the vet or fix her car. Perry asked her not to call. But, she couldn't help it.

"Please, I know I shouldn't, but just this once?" she'd ask.

Perry finally took matters into his own hands. He changed her name in his contacts list from "Julie Franklin" to "Do Not Answer!" It worked; it was the final reminder that turned him away from the darkness.

Perry ignored the call and pressed harder on the pedal, pushing the Fiat, taking the corners with a squeal of the tires. He was moving into unfamiliar territory, but the more he pushed, the more his mood improved. He was on the SS289, a narrow, winding road that bisected Nebrodi National Park. The arid, dusty farmland that surrounded the base of Mount Etna had given way to forested mountains. The temperature dropped dramatically, and he felt as if he were back in Maine. He turned off the A/C and rolled down the windows. The sweet scent of pine permeated the air. On a rare straightaway, he pulled the piece of paper from his pocket and glanced at the directions the travel agent had given him. The words were written in Italian.

"What was she thinking?" he wondered.

He grabbed his phone, then dropped it, swerving to miss an oncoming car speeding out of the next curve.

Seeing a small dirt road up ahead, Perry downshifted and turned. The road led to a clearing with a panoramic view of the northern coast of Sicily and the deep blue Tyrrhenian Sea. He stopped and admired the scene for a few seconds before searching for his phone. Finding it wedged between the center console and the passenger seat, he dug it out and dialed the number.

A woman's voice answered. "Pronto!"

"Maria, this is Perry Franklin, your directions, they are written…

"Ahhh! Mr. Franklin. I am Christina LaTorre."

"Christina?"

"I will be your host during your stay in Sicily."

"Oh! Okay. I'm calling to get directions. The travel agent wrote them down in Italian and…"

"No problem Mr. Franklin, our home is in the mountains, a few kilometers south of Canneto. It can be difficult to find…"

"I'm good with directions," Perry interrupted.

"I will have someone meet you at…"

"Just get me pointed in the right direction and I'll find you," Perry said. "I'll be arriving at Canneto in about forty minutes."

"Mister Franklin, please stop at Hotel Za' Maria. It is right in the center of town. You will not miss it. I will have my Uncle Leo meet you there, and you can follow him up the mountain to our villa."

"That's not necessary. Just give me the address… and please call me Perry or Franklin. Mister Franklin makes me feel like you're talking to my father, and he's dead."

"Ahhh… Mister Franklin, from your accent, it appears that you are an American. We Sicilians use surnames when conversing with strangers. It is a sign of respect. You are to be a guest in our home, and my uncle will meet you at the hotel in forty minutes. Please call back if you have any trouble finding it."

"But I…"

His cell phone beeped. Christina had disconnected. Something about her manner was disconcerting. He suspected this woman was going to get under his skin. He hoped Uncle Leo was friendlier.

Perry turned the car around and was heading back to the main road when he suddenly stomped on the brakes. In a cloud of dust, the car skidded to a stop. Inches in front of him was a huge black boar; the animal must have weighed 300 pounds. As it crossed the driveway, five babies scurried out of the bushes after her, all of them completely ignoring him, like a train passing through a busy intersection. In all his travels, he'd never seen wild boars before. He put the car back into gear and drove down and out of the Nebrodi Mountains.

Reaching the coastline, Perry took a left onto State Road 133 and opened the little Fiat up. Twenty minutes later, he pulled into a cobblestone parking lot across from the Hotel Za' Maria.

Christina was right, Za' Maria was hard to miss. It was a large, sprawling hotel with two arched doorways and a curved wall of glass on the upper floors, all landscaped with palm trees and bougainvillea blooming with bright red flowers. The hotel didn't fit. Canneto could barely be called a town or even a village. The place was more like an intersection with old adobe buildings, shabby garages with tractors parked inside, and a few dozen beach-side villas. Perry saw a train track that ran right through the center of the village, but there wasn't any train station. Across from the hotel, close to where he'd parked, a steep road headed into the mountains.

I bet I could find signora LaTorre's casa rurale just fine, he thought.

Weaving his way around a few customers sitting at tables on the covered patio, Perry walked into Za' Maria's main lobby. The inside was filled with luxurious mahogany furnishings, brass fixtures, white marble floors, and ornate columns supporting a high, curved ceiling. Off to the left, behind a chrome display case filled with bread and pastries, a barista stood. He was operating a polished stainless-steel espresso machine. A puff of steam floated up between him and the machine.

"Buongiorno," Perry said. "Uno doppio espresso e... e... what is that down there?"

Perry pointed to a golden, crusted sphere in the glass case. It looked like a round, handball-sized fritter.

"That is arancini, signore. A rice croquette made with white wine risotto. It is filled with mozzarella, prosciutto, and tomato sauce. Molto delizioso!"

"'ll have one of those."

"Excellent choice, a double espresso, and arancine."

"On second thought, make it a double cappuccino..."

The waiter frowned for a split second then recovered.

"I know, I know," Perry said. "Sicilians don't drink cappuccinos in the afternoon."

"Si`, signore. It is too much weight... too heavy. Breakfast only. "

Perry carried his coffee and arancini out to the tree-lined patio and sat down at a marble-topped cast-iron table. Several older men sat at the table next to him: smoking cigarettes, drinking beer, and laughing. Two were dressed in suit jackets and ties; the third wore farmer's overalls and work boots. He assumed they were friends enjoying an afternoon break before going back to work. He pictured the farmer heading back to his field, but the suits - they just seemed out of place. Where would they go when they went back to work? On the other side of him, he noticed a couple of high school girls dressed in Catholic school uniforms. One was drinking a foamy, white, creamy soda while the other was stuffing the remainder of a small cannoli into her mouth. They were both staring out at the street as if waiting for a ride. Perry watched people on the sidewalk come and go. Cars passed by with horns occasionally beeping and a hand waving out the window. For a little out-of-the-way place, he thought the town quite lively.

Five minutes later, Perry heard the unmistakable low rumble of a Harley Davidson. He turned toward the street and watched as the motorcycle came down the mountain road. All eyes were on the bike as the rider pulled up to the patio. The Harley Road King was beautiful, meticulously cared for, with chrome shining brightly in the sunlight and a custom, silver and black paint job that hadn't a scratch or speck of dirt on it. On the fuel tank, where the classic Harley Davidson emblem would have been, was an airbrushed painting of pearlescent white angel wings cradling an elaborately detailed Roman Catholic cross, as if the wings were hands holding the cross up in sacrifice. The rider, fully dressed in leather, pushed out the kickstand and dismounted. Embroidered on the back of his jacket were the same wings and cross. In a smooth, quick motion, he pulled off his helmet and stepped onto the patio. The man looked about 60 years old. He had dark hair cut close to the scalp, olive skin, a broad smile, and a starched white clerical collar. The priest walked up to the elderly men and patted the farmer on his back. They all began talking at once, greeting each other and laughing at something the rider said. The farmer offered him a seat. The biker priest declined with a wave of his hand and pointed to a pack of cigarettes. One of the well-dressed men fished out a cigarette, handed it to the priest, and lit a match.

Even the schoolgirls seemed excited to see him. One stood and walked over, speaking to him in rapid Italian. Perry strained to listen, determined to gain some understanding of the language. Much as he tried, he couldn't figure out what they were saying. The only word he deciphered was "monsignor." Perry had no idea if the schoolgirl was talking to him about church or his motorcycle or something completely different. It was all a bit odd, but he decided he liked the place. Seeing a young teenager mix so casually with the elders wasn't a common sight in the US. He liked being in this close-knit community, even as an outsider.

Perry sat back and enjoyed his coffee as life in the small village continued around him. He wondered about his lodging and the uncle coming to meet him. How would the uncle recognize him and how difficult could it be to find the villa in the first place? It's not like they didn't use addresses. He glanced up at the Nebrodi mountain range south of him. Several zig-zagging roads appeared and disappeared through the trees. He decided to give up trying to control the situation, something his ex-wife Julie had consistently complained about. He relaxed his tense shoulders, took another sip of coffee, and sank into the comfortable surroundings. He let the sounds of unfamiliar conversations and village life wash over him like cool water from a mountain stream.

The monsignor finished his conversation with the men and said goodbye to the schoolgirl with a pat on her head. Then he trained his dark eyes on Perry. He smiled, revealing even, white teeth as he approached Perry's table.

"Signore Franklin?"

"Si`!" Perry sat up quickly.

"I Leo LaTorre."

"LaTorre? Christina's uncle? Excuse me, Monsignor. I didn't realize."

"Si`! Per favore, mi chiamo Leo."

Perry stood and shook Leo's firm hand.

The monsignor pulled out a chair and motioned for Perry to sit back down. "Per favore, finish caffe."

For the next few minutes, the two men sat at the table, struggling to communicate. Perry had scraped together a few Italian phrases from an app he'd downloaded but they were of little help with the rapid-paced language. And Father Leo's English was just too primitive to get anything meaningful across. So, they smiled politely and studied each other. Perry felt awkward. Leo's eyes seemed to bore into him as if reading his secrets. Perry had never met a Catholic priest that rode a Harley before, even in America. He had little to go on in sizing up Christina's uncle. When Perry drained the last of his coffee, Leo waved his hand and nodded towards the mountains.

"Guess I passed the test," Perry said.

"Not yet," Leo said, adding a smile for good measure.

"Very funny," Perry said. "You speak English, don't you?"

"I speak many languages."

Perry signaled toward the barista who was serving more coffee to the three older men.

"I haven't paid yet," he said, pulling some euros from his pocket.

Leo put a hand on Perry's arm and shook his head.

"Geno!" he called to the barista. "Per favore!" The priest pointed to the coffee and empty plate and then to himself.

The barista called back. "Si` monsignor, va bene."

Leo nodded to Perry. "We go."

The monsignor straddled his Harley and fired up the engine, the low rumble echoing off the surrounding buildings. Perry got back into his banged up Fiat with as much manliness as he could muster and fired up the small 4-cylinder diesel. They were soon heading straight up the mountainside.

Perry was a fast and confident driver. He'd driven in third world countries all over the globe, where traffic laws existed only as a suggestion. He felt completely at ease driving through dust storms in the Egyptian desert or monsoons in India with water up to his headlights. He even enjoyed the charge of stopping within a pebble's width of another car's bumper, mimicking the behavior of the locals in pretty much every third-world city on the globe. His reflexes, along with his knowledge of sports cars, gave him an edge over other field agents, but the steep ride up the Sicilian mountainside was making his heart race. His knuckles were bone white as he negotiated the narrow mountain roads, trying to keep up with the biker priest. They wove around steep hairpin turns that repeated in quick succession. Several times he thought for sure his driver's side mirror was going to shatter as an oncoming car barreled down the mountain. There were some spots too narrow for two vehicles to pass. He assumed the rule was first come, first served, but soon learned fastest in, fastest out was the rule. He gunned the Fiat up the mountainside as the Harley up ahead banked sharply through the curves and accelerated on the short straightaways. Before reaching the top of a long, narrow ridge, Perry caught up just as the Harley and its rider went over the edge. Perry panicked, slamming on the brakes. Slowly rolling up to where the bike had disappeared, he saw an old iron gate. It was open. Attached to the entrance gate was a sign, "LaTorre".

Chapter 5

Day 2 (Continued)

The sound of Uncle Leo's motorcycle spilled in through the open kitchen window. Christina finished drying the pot she was holding and hung the towel in a neat fold over a wrought iron hook by the stove.

Nonna, Christina's grandmother, walked up to her and ran her wrinkled, arthritic hands through her granddaughter's curly black hair. Christina kissed Nonna's hand.

"Non ti preoccupare. Mi prenderò cura di questo," she said, giving her grandmother's shoulder a soft squeeze.

Nonna was the matriarch of the LaTorre family, and although Christina was all grown up, she still treated her granddaughter like a child. Christina loved Nonna more than anything in the world, even though her protective nature aggravated her at times. Christina walked out of the kitchen and stopped for a second in the alcove by the front door. She stood in front of a beveled mirror, pushed her long hair back over her shoulders and straightened her collar. Christina's smooth, toffee-colored skin glowed, her cheeks still flushed from working in the warm kitchen. Her bright green eyes, framed by thick black eyelashes, blazed with intelligence. Most of her suitors were attracted to her soft, sensual body, but they soon discovered she had little patience for men who couldn't challenge her mind. She was

39 years old, and the only sign of pending middle age was a slight furrow in her brow from years of study. She brushed white flour from the front of her designer jeans, slipped on a pair of leather boots, and walked out the front door.

Perry was getting out of the car when she approached.

"Buongiorno signore Franklin. I am Christina LaTorre, welcome to our home."

Remembering their conversation on the phone, Perry bowed slightly before saying, "Buongiorno signora LaTorre, it's a pleasure to meet you."

When Christina offered her hand, Perry took it gently, raising it halfway to his lips. She pulled away with an abrupt tug.

Turning to the back of the car, she said, "Please, let me help you with your luggage."

"No need, signora," Perry smiled. "That I can handle that on my own."

He reached into the back seat of the Fiat and removed his backpack, deciding to leave his equipment case in the trunk until he got a better feel for the place.

"Very well," she said, heading for the house. "Let me show you to your room."

The LaTorre home was perched on the side of a mountain overlooking Canneto di Caronia. The front of the house faced north, delivering a panoramic view of the Mediterranean. Six kilometers to the east was the ocean-side city of Marina de Caronia. On the horizon, far off to the west, was Cefalù, over 40 kilometers away. The LaTorre's land was terraced into the rocky mountainside. Their house, built of huge blocks of limestone, stood two-stories high. Three gabled windows protruded from the traditional red-tiled roof like sentries watching for approaching ships. A horizontal line of rough-cut timbers ran across the exterior wall. Perry assumed they supported the second floor. He knew little of Italian architecture and couldn't tell if the house was 50 years old, 100 years old or 200 years old. The structure simply looked old.

As they walked towards the house, she said, "Mr. Franklin, if you do not mind my asking, what brings you to Sicily?"

"Ask all you want. I'm here to do an article on the recent Mount Etna eruption."

Perry noticed a catch in her stride, a slight stiffening of her posture. Christina was uncomfortable with Mount Etna. He'd expected her to ask why he decided to lodge so far from the volcano. Instead, the two walked the remaining distance to the front door in silence.

When they stepped into the dimly lit alcove, Christina said, "Please, leave your shoes here."

Perry slipped off his trail shoes, thankful that he'd worn his wool socks, the ones without holes in them. They placed their shoes under the mirror and walked into the central part of the home. To the left, Perry saw a large living room with a leather sofa and chair facing a stone fireplace. Several bookcases lined the wall. To the right, a formal dining area with dark mahogany furnishings and framed family photos hanging on the walls. The floor was covered with a terracotta tile laid in a spiral-shaped pattern that undulated throughout the rooms. The walls were covered with white-washed plaster that showed the uneven sweeps of the mason's trowel. The room had a feeling of permanence, of antiquity, of lives spanning generations.

Perry gazed up at the ceiling. "That drawing is amazing. How old is that?"

Both the living and dining room ceilings had broad, colorfully painted frescos of Jewish religious scenes. At least he assumed they were Jewish, based on the presence of a menorah in each scene.

"Are they not beautiful?" Christina said. "My uncle Leo was remodeling these rooms eight years ago. The plaster was peeling from the ceilings. When he began scraping, he found those underneath. They are over five hundred years old."

"This house is 500 years old?"

"Yes. These two front rooms. The rest of the house has slowly grown in size over the centuries."

"It's amazing!" Perry said. The house was warm and inviting even if the host wasn't.

"Our home was originally built by a Jewish family sometime in the mid-1400s. Jewish Sicilians were a tenth of the island's population back then."

"Why would anyone want to cover them up?"

"They were plastered over as part of what you Americans know as the Spanish Inquisition. In 1492 King Ferdinand II proclaimed the Edict of Expulsion. After the Edict was announced, the Jews had to choose between leaving the island or converting to Christianity. This family obviously converted."

"Hard to imagine. While Ferdinand and Isabella were sending Columbus off to discover the New World, they were at work destroying the Jews."

"Yes, it is quite sad. The Inquisition erased almost all evidence of the Sicilian Jews. Luckily, there are treasures such as these frescos left behind."

The two of them stood for a few moments looking at the beautiful scenes depicting farm life and religious ceremonies in the 1400s. Perry had a passion for architecture and knew that the typical house in the US wouldn't be standing in 500 years.

"Come, Mr. Franklin. I will take you to your room."

"They just don't build houses like this in the United States."

"No, you Americans appear to be more interested in profit and power, while we value permanence."

"Maybe," Perry replied. "But we're also interested in innovation and freedom of expression and we have far less corruption than you do here in Italy."

"You will do well to remember that this is Sicily, Mr. Franklin, not Italy."

"Oh, I'm aware of your island's unique history, signora. In fact, you exported some of your culture to America. We call them the Mafia."

Christina started to respond but her Uncle Leo walked in through the front door.

"Hai presentato Perry alla mamma?" he said, pointing at a door at the back of the room.

Christina visibly chafed at the idea but dutifully led Perry through a narrow passageway and into a brightly lit kitchen. It faced west, the setting sun sending shafts of light through the open window over the kitchen sink. At the table, with her back to the brightly lit window, sat an elderly, silver-haired woman. The sun's rays fell on her wispy hair, shrouding her face in a glowing halo. Her skin was translucent and wrinkled like tawny crepe paper. The long shadow of the woman's silhouette ran across the kitchen table and spilled down onto the terracotta floor.

Nonna was wielding a knife, trying to cut through a yellow squash sitting on a thick, wooden cutting board. Perry knew by the amount of force she was using that it was hard to slice. Her hands trembled as she struggled to push the blade down.

"Nonna!" Christina said. With a gentle motion, she pulled the knife from her grandmother's hands and placed it out of reach at the far end of the table. Then she walked up from behind and wrapped her arms around her grandmother's tiny frame.

Looking up at Perry, Christina said, "This is signore Franklin."

"Buongiorno signore Franklin," Nonna said. "Welcome."

"Mr. Franklin, this is my grandmother, signora Isabella LaTorre."

"Signora LaTorre," Perry bowed slightly. "I'm very pleased to meet you. You have a beautiful house... una... bella... casa," he pronounced slowly.

97

"Grazie, per favore. Benvenuto. Puoi chiamarmi, Nonna."

Christina frowned.

"What did she say?" he asked.

"She said welcome and to please call her Nonna."

"Tell her I'd be delighted, but only if she returns the favor by using my first name, Perry."

Christina moved forward to face them both and said some hasty words to Nonna that didn't sound at all like the correct translation, but he did hear her say 'Perry.' He guessed Christina was giving her grandmother some instructions on proper introductions. When her grandmother replied tersely, it was clear that Nonna ran the family.

Nonna smiled and motioned for him to sit down next to her.

Christina motioned for Perry to exit. "Mr. Franklin, please. Let me show you to your room; you must be tired."

"I'm not tired at all," he lied. "But, thanks for your concern."

Perry propped his backpack against the wall by the door and sat across from Nonna. He liked this woman the moment he'd seen her. She was an old soul. It was impossible to describe in words; he only felt it.

Nonna reached across the table to pick up the knife, and Perry's hand descended onto hers. He gently touched the knife and she released it.

"Let me help," he said, sliding the scarred cutting board over to his side of the table.

Christina, realizing she had been outvoted, said, "You should wash your hands."

"Oh, sorry, what was I thinking?"

Perry jumped up from the table, went over to the old soapstone sink, and turned on the faucet.

"Would you like a cup of coffee?" Christina asked, with a hint of apologetic guilt. There must be some goodness in a man so authentically kind to her Nonna.

"That would be perfect!"

"I know you Americans drink it, how do you say, weak?"

"Ms. LaTorre, the stronger, the better. Is this soap?" he asked, picking up a blackish-green object somewhat like a bar of soap.

"Si`. My uncle makes it from old olive oil."

"Really?" Perry asked, studying the bar closer. "You can make soap out of olive oil?"

"Of course."

Perry wondered where Leo found time to do such labor-intensive chores like remodeling the house and making soap. He'd imagined monsignors as full-time men of the cloth, not men of the earth. He finished washing his hands and returned to the table. Perry placed the knife on the yellow gourd and looked at Nonna. She shook her head and guided his hand over just a fraction of an inch and nodded. He pushed hard and cleanly cut off a 1/4-inch slice. Perry and Nonna smiled at each other, and he kept slicing.

Christina watched as this man swept Nonna off her feet and her protective instincts took over. *Why would a journalist look for lodging this far from his subject? Mount Etna is over a hundred kilometers away. Why had he not replaced his worn and weathered backpack sitting in the corner? Do not Americans buy hiking equipment like they buy their gadgets, always eager to own the latest? And he arrived in an old, dented Fiat. Was he poor or just cheap? And do not people who fly across the world make reservations sooner than a few hours before their arrival?*

Christina heard Perry and Nonna laugh, without either of them saying a word. She knew one thing for sure; she was not going to let this American get too close to her family.

She pulled a small espresso maker down from a shelf, filled it with water from the sink, and opened a fresh tin of coffee. She brought the tin to her nose, inhaled the rich nutty scent, and tried to relax. She filled the filter, placed the espresso maker on the stove, and watched as Perry and Nonna worked at the table.

"Mr. Franklin, what made you decide to stay so far away from the volcano? Would it not be easier to write your story if you were closer?"

"I'll be taking plenty of pictures over there, but I'm not as much interested in the recent eruption as I am in the history of the volcano: the geology, its impact on the regional soils, farming practices, the people and cultures that evolved around it."

"That is quite an ambitious undertaking."

"Yes, if I were some kinda researcher, but I'm looking to capture the essence of Sicily, in words and pictures. I want to describe a millennium of geologic and cultural history in anecdotal stories, from farmers to fishermen, hotel clerks to potters, from volcanic scientists to politicians."

"The essence of Sicily? What an interesting approach," Christina said.

She filled three small porcelain cups with the espresso, carried them and a bowl of sugar over to the table, and sat down.

"Still, it appears to be a huge project."

"That's for sure. I don't pretend to think I can capture it all, but I will capture something, and I already know it will be special. I'm starting with the geology, and that, in answer to your question, is why I'm here in Canneto."

"Well, I am sure you will be successful with your study of rocks, but how do you plan to learn anything about our culture when you do not speak Italian?"

"You ask the perfect question. In fact, I'm looking for someone to help me," Perry explained. "Someone who knows the area and can translate for me. Maybe you can recommend someone?"

"At such short notice? This is a rural area; finding a good English speaker will be difficult."

Nonna interrupted their conversation to ask Christina to translate. Christina described their discussion for a minute, then Nonna seemed insistent that Christina say something to Perry.

Christina shook her head. "No, no, che non è importante!"

Perry looked confused. "What does Nonna want you to say?"

"Nothing. It is not important."

"How do you happen to speak such excellent English?" Perry asked.

"I am a humanities professor at the University of Messina. I teach many of my classes in English."

"Well, your English is perfect, and you teach humanities? That's a broad field; you must have an area of interest."

"If you must know, I have a Ph.D. in cultural anthropology."

"Wow! You must know a lot about Sicilian culture..."

Perry wondered if he should ask. He wasn't sure he even liked her or if he'd be able to work with her. But she was stunning, and there was something else, something hidden behind the formality.

"Mr. Franklin, I have a wonderful job. I am only taking a short vacation during harvest season. I am not interested in being your translator."

"Oh! No, I wasn't suggesting... I'm just at a disadvantage. I try to study the country I'm visiting, but this assignment was very short notice. I didn't have an opportunity to learn as much about Sicily as I'd like. I always try to pick up a little of the language before going to a new place."

"I understand," Christina said. "Learning a language when you are older can be difficult."

"Excuse me!"

Christina laughed. "I do not mean it that way, I mean as an adult, it is difficult. I was taught English at a young age. My parents were academics as well and started my English education when I was three."

"Your parents made a good choice. I wish mine had done that. Where are your parents now?"

"They are deceased," Christina said softly.

"Oh, I'm sorry, I shouldn't have pried."

"That is quite alright; they died a long time ago. I was still a child. Let me show you to your room?"

Perry had finished slicing the vegetables for Nonna, and his coffee cup was empty; he had no more reason to stay.

Nonna nodded to him with a smile. "Grazie, signore Perry. La mia casa è la tua casa."

Christina said, "Nonna says…"

"That I understood," said Perry.

Christina led Perry up a wide flight of black stone stairs built into the side of the fireplace.

Perry knew that, just like in Catania, the basalt stones were from Mount Etna. Right in front of him, another connection between the volcano and the people of Sicily. Too bad his real assignment had nothing to do with either. He didn't know why, but he suddenly felt guilty for lying to Christina. But the stakes were too high to let feelings take over.

At the top of the stairs, Christina headed down the hallway to a corner room right above the dining room. Opening the door, she led Perry into a large bedroom filled with antique furniture. The bed rested high off the floor on four heavy wrought iron legs. The ivory porcelain accents on the iron headboard and footboard were chipped and worn in places. There were north-facing louvered patio doors, framed in white lace curtains, and a window on the west wall where light from the setting sun poured in. Christina swung the patio doors open, revealing a panoramic scene of rolling mountains, vineyards, olive groves, pastures, and the sea beyond.

"This will be your room."

"Molto buono," said Perry.

"Also, I will need your passport. It is a requirement," she said. "We must keep track of our foreign visitors."

Perry pulled his passport from his back pocket and handed it to Christina.

"No problem. Here you go," he said.

"I am sure you are tired from your trip. I will leave you in peace. Let us know if there is anything we can do to make your stay more comfortable. We eat the evening meal at 2100 hours, that is 9 p.m. You are welcome to join us."

"I have some jet lag. Despite all the coffee, I suspect I'll sleep through the night, but thanks for the invite."

"Very well."

Christina handed Perry a key to the room and left. She walked downstairs and through a narrow doorway that led to her small home office. Sitting down at her desk, she placed Perry's passport on the glass flatbed of her scanner. She opened her laptop and typed.

```
Andreo,
Please run a full security check on
our new guest. Attached is an image of
his passport. Something is odd. He just
arrived, but I cannot find any
immigration stamp of him entering
Sicily or any other EU country in over
a year.
    Christina
```

Chapter 6

Day 3

The smell of frying ham woke Perry from a deep sleep. He glanced at his watch.

"Shit!" he said. He'd slept 13 hours.

He jumped out of bed, got dressed and went outside to his car. The blue sea sparkled from the gentle breeze blowing from the west. Large, billowy, bright-white clouds floated far off on the horizon and closer to shore, small fishing boats were spreading their nets. Perry pulled the Pelican case from the trunk, removed the camera and looked through the viewfinder. He flipped on a switch and slowly scanned the camera east and west.

On the outside, the digital camera looked like an expensive Canon 5D outfitted with a low-cost Rokinon 500mm/F8 mirrored lens. Professional photographers would have admired the 5D but scoffed at the cheap telephoto lens, but in an abrasive volcanic environment, they would have understood. It was the perfect choice for taking pictures around an active volcano. The lens was practically disposable. But looks can be deceiving.

Perry pressed a small button on top of the camera and a bright red square lit up inside the viewfinder.

"Well, I'll be damned," he whispered. "What the hell is that?"

The flashing red square hovered over a small patch of ocean to the northeast, just a kilometer offshore.

Perry returned the camera to the car and went inside.

Perry was a pragmatic engineer, an experimentalist, not a theoretician. He had to see it to believe it. He was also one of those lucky individuals who, as a child, knew what he was going to be when he grew up. At the age of five, he was dismantling kitchen appliances and electrical outlets with a butter knife. At the age of eight, he was wandering into the forest behind his home, spending hours getting lost, climbing to the tops of trees and navigating his way back home. His mom, a single parent, found it impossible to keep track of him short of locking him in his room. That didn't work either. One day, after he had been locked in his room for some serious act of deconstruction, she opened the door and it fell off its hinges. After that, she gave up.

During high school, Perry worked for Chuck, a local locksmith who'd recognized his talents. He'd told Perry's mom, "There's no lock this kid can't open." He learned the trade and he learned it very well. The locksmith paid him wages equaling a professional's and his customers were so pleased they never questioned the age of the expert. Perry's expertise also became common knowledge to another group of people, people that paid much higher wages than Chuck's customers. After a few episodes of opening doors after-hours, Perry realized that the pay didn't outweigh the risks. That's when he walked into an Army recruiting office.

"I want to join the Army, it's either that or jail."

The recruiter was skeptical but ran Perry through a series of aptitude tests. The next day, after completing the scoring, the recruiter sat down with Perry and his mom. Perry was only 17 years old and needed her permission.

"Mrs. Franklin, I've got some good news and some bad news. Which do you want to hear first?"

"Tell me the bad news, I'm completely against this. There's a war going on for Christ's sake! But he's convinced me he's joining, either this year or the next."

"Okay, well, to put it bluntly, Mrs. Franklin, your son completely sucks at English and verbal communication."

"Really!" she said with a shred of hope. "Will that keep him from joining?"

"Actually, no. This is the Army Ma'am. But don't worry, he's not going to war, not if he doesn't want to."

Perry and his mom looked confused.

"Mrs. Franklin, Perry's math, mechanical, and spatial skills are completely off the charts. He can do whatever he wants in the Army."

Perry's mom knew that he was a bit odd when it came to these types of skills, but she had no idea how odd, as she had no one to compare him to.

Perry said, "I want to go to engineering school."

The recruiter sat back and leafed through a series of pages in a loose-leaf binder sitting in front of him.

"Look, Perry, you need to understand, you should be going to college, not joining the Army."

"I know, but I can't afford it. That's why I'm joining, so I can get the GI Bill."

"Okay, well here is what we've got. It's a great fit. I can send you to the Army School of Engineering. They have a Power Plant Technician School that is first rate. It's the best we can do. It'll teach you both mechanical and electrical engineering and it requires a lot of math."

"Cool!"

"Perry, I'm also going to pull a few strings. After you graduate, I want to send you to the 163rd Military Intelligence Battalion. It's a combat battalion and it specializes in photoreconnaissance. It's very hands-on and they need smart, versatile people like you. They spend a lot of time out in the field and they need good technicians that can keep the equipment running."

Perry's mom heard the word "combat" and flared up.

"But you just said he wouldn't have to go to war!"

"No Ma'am, he doesn't, at least not during his three-year commitment. The 163rd just returned from a tour in the

Middle East. They won't be going anywhere for a few years. They're stationed at a remote airstrip near Fort Hood, Texas. The only things out there to be afraid of are rattle snakes and the occasional pissed-off armadillo."

The day after graduating high school, Perry held up his hand, said the oath, and began his career in military intelligence. After basic training he attended the Army School of Engineering at Fort Belvoir, VA. He graduated at the top of his class, achieving the highest score in the history of the school. He spent the next few years learning all there was to know about mechanics, electronics, optics, and photography. When his military commitment ended, he enrolled at the University of Massachusetts in Amherst and four years later, had a BS in Engineering. His professors encouraged him to continue with grad school, but Perry had had enough of academics. A month after graduating, he was working for the military again: designing, building and operating the most sophisticated imaging technologies known to mankind.

Perry walked into the kitchen, where he found Nonna standing at the stove, struggling to fry eggs. He watched her shaking hands succeed in flipping the eggs, but not without breaking the yokes. When he pulled the kitchen chair out from the table, Nonna turned with a start.

"Ahhh, buongiorno, Perry."

"Good morning, Nonna," he replied.

Christina walked through the back door carrying a large bowl of freshly washed apples, pears, and figs.

"Please have a seat," she said. "We normally serve breakfast in the dining room, but my grandmother insists you eat here in the kitchen with us."

"I'm honored," said Perry

"She is also trying to make an American breakfast for you. How do you like your eggs?"

"Whatever way you're having them."

Christina looked over at Nonna and the frying pan. "Then scrambled eggs you will have."

"Your uncle is not eating with us?" he asked.

"He is at the church preparing for the festivities. He will return at lunchtime."

"I need to ask him about where to charter a boat. What festivities?"

"This is a busy time for him. Today is All Saints Day and tomorrow All Souls Day."

"You mean, like Halloween?"

Christina said, "No, in Sicily u juornu rii muorti, or day of the dead, is a sacred time. Our children wake up hoping to find a treat from relatives who are dead but not forgotten. The 'muorti' bring presents of toys and sweets. The tradition serves to strengthen our family bonds, linking our children to family members who have come and gone."

"Sounds a lot nicer than our cheap costumes and trick or treat."

"Yes, it begins at dawn with a Mass, offering prayers and alms for the deceased. After Mass, families visit the graveyards to pay tribute to the faithful who have gone before them. At the cemetery, the graves of family members are decorated with chrysanthemums and candles."

"It all sounds very respectful. But, I'm not religious."

"I understand," she said. "The tradition is slowly dying away. There are fewer and fewer of the faithful, even here."

Spooning a large helping of eggs and fried prosciutto onto his plate, she asked, "Do you not believe in God?"

"Oh, on the contrary," Perry said. "I do believe in a higher power."

"Is that not what you Americans call 'new age' thinking?"

"New age? No, in fact, it's an ancient belief. You're an anthropologist. Why is it that every known human civilization, every aboriginal tribe, on every continent, believes in some type of higher power? Some force of nature, or independent of nature, that can't be seen but permeates everything around us. Is it some evolutionary trick, some survival mechanism?"

"That is a very good question that I do not have a good answer for," Christina said.

"Neither do I, but the more scientists learn about the structure of the universe, the more they are amazed at what we don't know or can't understand. Many scientists believe there is some higher order of thinking out there, somewhere, beyond our grasp. Whether it's true or not, I think it's ignorant of people to completely deny the possibility that some higher entity exists."

Christina said, "You seem passionate about this topic."

"Oh, sorry. I can get carried away with people thinking they know all the answers, either for or against organized religion. No disrespect to your uncle."

"None was taken. But perhaps you are confusing your spirituality or higher power with organized religion. There is a big difference."

"You're right. They are on opposite ends of the spectrum."

"Signore Franklin, they are not at opposite ends of the spectrum, they are complementary. The scripture surrounding organized religion is a foundation from which we can grow, from which our beliefs can evolve to hopefully a higher level of understanding. You might argue that the Christian, or any other religion's dogma, is too rigid, too ancient, too outdated but that is just a matter of degree. All of our religions evolve, just not as fast as some people like."

"I agree. I was simply trying to say our American Halloween never made a whole lot of sense to me."

"Nor me," Christina replied.

"Signora LaTorre. Since your uncle is busy, maybe you can help me. I want to take some pictures of the underwater rock formations off your coastline. I'd like to charter a dive boat for the day. Can you tell me where I might find one?"

Christina looked concerned. "No one dives in these waters; it is not safe."

"I can take care of myself. Can you point me in the right direction?"

"You will need to drive all the way to Cefalù. It is two hours west of here. That is the closest port, but I doubt you will find a boat."

"Would you mind calling the marina for me?"

Christina stood up in an act of dismissal. "Signore Franklin, I do not know who to call. You must understand, our community is different from yours. You will need to drive to the port yourself and find someone to talk to."

"I'm going to have a tough time explaining what I need with the few words I know of Italian. I need an interpreter."

"I am sure you will manage," she said abruptly.

Perry was an experienced diver and knew how difficult it could be to dive in unknown waters. He needed to cover a lot of territory and being able to communicate with the skipper was important. Relying on some old Sicilian sea captain's command of English wasn't going to cut it. He decided to try a different tack.

"Ms. LaTorre, I simply don't understand you. From the first moment we talked on the phone yesterday, you've acted as if I'm some pariah. Is it because I'm an American or are you like this with all your guests?"

"Mr. Franklin, is it too much to ask for civility? This is not a hostel. You are a guest in our home, and I expect you to have manners."

"I might not have the Sicilian manners you want," he said. "But I'm trying very hard to be friendly. If you are going to run a guest house, I think you might want to lighten up on your expectations about how foreigners should behave and load up on some of that civility yourself."

Perry stared at Christina, thinking her response could go either way. She'd either kick him out of the house or lighten up. He hoped he'd played the indignation card enough to draw out any shred of empathy she might be keeping under lock and key. He didn't have the time to go searching for another place to stay. He watched as Christina's shoulders softened.

"Perhaps I have been too abrupt with you," she said. "In fact, I am uncomfortable around strangers. I always have been. This guest house is the invention of my grandmother and uncle. I am at the university most of the year and rarely interact with guests."

"Well, I certainly can see why. Can we maybe drop the formalities? I'm going to be around for a week or two and I'd like us to get along."

"Very well," Christina said. "I shall try."

"Thanks, maybe we can start by having you use my given name."

"I suppose, but only when we are in private."

Perry smiled, "Are we going to be doing things in private?"

Christina pointed at his chest. "That is why I do not like Americans."

Perry laughed. "I'm sorry, you're right."

"I will be less formal," she said. "But your suggestive American humor will not take you very far."

"I'll keep that in mind."

"I will make a few phone calls to see if I can find a dive boat for you. When would you like to go?"

Perry's phone buzzed and he glanced at the screen. Stan, calling for an update. Perry pressed the 'Decline' button and said, "As soon as possible, and I'll need dive equipment."

"This is a holiday weekend. It will be difficult to find a boat."

"I appreciate the effort, thank you, Christina."

She forced a smile. "You are welcome, Perry."

Perry finished his breakfast, returned to the front yard of the LaTorre household, and hit the 'Call Back' button.

"Hey, Stan."

"Franklin! It's 'bout time ya called in. What's goin' on?"

"Hey, I've been here less than 24 hours. Give me a break."

"We don't have time for you screwin' around. People are gittin' anxious. Have ya found anything yet?"

"Yeah, I'm in position, and I've picked up the signal. Strangest thing though, it's underwater, a kilometer offshore."

"Can ya get closer to get a better look?"

"It's going to take a couple days. I need a boat and it just happens to be a holiday. It's All Saints Day or All Souls Day or something like that. The whole place is shut down and I can't get close to the signal without a dive boat."

"We need an answer now. Do you understand what kinda impact this is goin' to have on us?"

"Yeah, Stan, I understand."

"Good. Git your shit squared away. ASAP."

"Goodbye, Stan."

Perry looked back towards the house in time to see Christina turn away from an upstairs window. *What is she doing in my bedroom?* he wondered.

Chapter 7

Day 3 (Continued)

It was 9 a.m. when the president's chief-of-staff ushered DDNI Sheehan into the Situation Room. Located on the ground floor of the West Wing, the room held a long oak conference table that filled the small space. The lower half of the walls were paneled in a burled red mahogany. The top half held six large flat-screen monitors and two digital neon clocks, one on each side of the conference table. In bright red numerals, the clocks displayed local DC time, Zulu/UTC, and presidential time, the time at the president's current location on earth.

"Have a seat right here, Mike," said Joe Davis. "The president will be with you shortly."

Several minutes passed before Davis returned with the president.

"Joe, you can leave. I need to talk to Mike in private."

"Sir, it would be appropriate to have DNI Gonzales here."

President Blake looked at Davis without saying a word.

"Yes, sir," Davis replied and left the room.

At 55, President James Blake was tall and lean. He had a sharp chin and bushy eyebrows shielding dark-blue eyes that had the unsettling ability to lock onto his prey and, if disappointed, just as easily destroy. He'd been a Republican senator from the great State of Indiana when he decided to throw his hat into the presidential primary ring. He was a dark horse, but the other candidates all but shot themselves in the foot. Stumbling over themselves trying to pander to their constituents, they diluted their message to the point where everyone looked the same. For better or worse, Blake's positions never faltered. He was pro-gun, pro-life and pro-religion. He didn't give a damn about any of those issues, but he knew what it took to win. He was also a pro at planting the seeds of hatred through fake news, conspiracy theories, and outright bribing of anyone who could pave his way to the top. One of his favorite sayings, voiced only within the confines of his inner circle, was, "Half the people you meet on the campaign trail will have an IQ of less than 100. Those are easy pickings."

"Mike, it's been way too long since we've talked. How's Betty? We've missed seeing her on the campaign trail."

"She's fine," Sheehan said. "She decided to move back to Mississippi, to be closer to the grandkids. She sends her love."

"Well, tell her 'Hi' for me. Now, I still want to get you that Director of National Intelligence job for all your support, but you know how the politics work around here."

"I understand, sir. When you hear what I've been doing this last year, I'm sure you'll rethink the 'politics.' The DNI's getting old. In fact, she's downright archaic. I've never seen anyone so cautious when it comes to national security."

"It is what it is, Mike. I can't fire Gonzales without another shit storm of accusations about me interfering with the workings of our intelligence community. They all love her. So, what's so important?"

"It's about the PIT program. Gonzales briefed you on it last week."

"Yeah, the broken spy satellite. Is it fixed yet?"

"Well, no, it's a little more complicated than that. You might remember, we're using this PIT technology for our tagging, tracking and locating operations. They call it TTL.

I've had some of my people experimenting with it, looking for other applications. Started right after you put me in the DDNI slot."

Blake asked, "Does DNI Gonzales know what you're doing?"

"No, sir. We've been keeping the security really tight."

"God damn it, Mike. Why do you put me in these positions? She should have…"

"Please, hear me out. This is huge."

The president studied him. Sheehan was almost drooling.

"What?" the president asked.

"Our folks at NNSS. They've discovered something very unusual. It's going to change the world."

"NNSS?"

"Our nuke folks at the Nevada National Security Site. They've been working for General Lewis at the NCPC, trying to understand the physics behind the PIT technology."

"Get to the point, Mike."

"They've figured out how to produce a high-power beam of these Majorana neutrinos, the same neutrinos we're detecting with the PIT sensor. And, if they point this beam at nuclear material, they can break it down."

"That doesn't sound good," said the president.

"No, sir," Sheehan said, "They did some calculations. If we radiated a nuclear warhead with a beam of these heavy neutrinos, it would destroy the warhead in a matter of minutes."

Blake was silent for several long seconds.

"You're telling me if someone pointed this beam at one of our nukes, they could destroy it?"

"Yes, Mr. President, but it's not that simple. NNSS is using one of their nuclear power plants to generate the kind of neutrino energy they need. A device like this would weigh over fifty tons. And you'd have to point the beam with extremely high accuracy. That would be very difficult considering the size. And, you'd have to know exactly where the warheads were, like within a half-meter or so."

"Okay," said the president. "Let's say someone did have this capability. How can it be countered?"

"There's no way to stop the beam, sir. They're neutrinos. They pass through everything except the nanotubes used in the PIT technology and dense nuclear fissile material. The phaser Howell is building… "

"A phaser?" the president interrupted. "Like in Star Trek?"

"Yes, sir," Sheehan said. "We've been moving forward with this."

"What the fuck are you thinking?"

"Jim, don't you understand what we have here? This phaser can destroy every nuclear arsenal in the goddamn world. We can knock out every nuke before anybody realizes what's happening."

The president shook his head. "That's crazy. People will die from radiation exposure."

"Most of these warheads are in heavily shielded bunkers," Sheehan said. "My guys did the calculations. No more than ten thousand people would be killed."

"Ten thousand? Are you insane?"

"Where is your perspective, Jim? We killed well over 100,000 civilians in the Iraq war, and they weren't even a direct threat to us. We are talking nuclear disarmament."

"It would be an act of war. One wrong move, one hint of what we're doing, one missed warhead and they'd have no choice but to launch a strike."

"At who?" Sheehan asked. "Nobody would know where it's coming from."

"This is too dangerous, Mike. What if something went wrong? What if someone found out?"

"No one is going to find out," said Sheehan. "We're going to severely compartmentalize this project. I've already put the wheels in motion to clean up the loose ends."

"What loose ends?"

"The PIT program. There are too many people involved. They're going to figure out what's happening."

"Mike, this is a high-risk game... "

"Don't you understand?" Sheehan asked. "Someone else already has this technology. That's how the PIT sensor was taken out. If we don't do it, someone else will."

The president shook his head.

Sheehan said. "Jim, if this works, you'll go down as the greatest president, no, the greatest person in history."

Blake was silent. He thought back, to earlier in the morning, when he'd swung the Oval Office terrace doors open only to hear a throng of protesters. A blow-up skunk was floating in the air with his face on it. It had gotten to be a common occurrence. Hardly a week went by without the left-wing fanatics concocting another excuse to protest. Sooner or later, he was going to show them what real power was all about.

"Mike," said the president. "What do you need to pull this off?"

"Two things, sir: a lot of money and one of your Ohio-class nuclear subs."

"Okay, but it's your job to make sure no one, and I mean no one, knows what you're doing. I will always have plausible deniability. Make sure your NNSS people understand that."

"I will," Sheehan replied.

"What about Lewis? You said NNSS reports to him."

"I transferred him out of the program last night. He doesn't know about their latest results."

"What about the CIA team in Sicily?" Blake asked.

"Once they find the machine that's doing this, we'll grab some of the scientists and destroy the facility."

"That's a sovereign country, Mike. It would be an act of war."

"They took the first shot, sir. They fried our PIT sensor to keep us from seeing what they're up to. We have the right to retaliate."

"You'll have to do it clean," said the president.

"Yes, sir. If Sheppard or any of his people give us trouble, well, they don't call it 'black ops' for nothing."

"I don't want to hear about any of this, Mike. If this all goes to shit, you're the one taking the fall. Do you understand?"

"I understand," Sheehan said.

"Oh, and you're right."

"About what?"

"I think it's time our DNI considers an early retirement. Our whole intelligence community is going to need a new skin; I'm sick and tired of them nosing in my business."

"I thought you might begin to see it my way. We are, after all, talking about nuclear disarmament of the entire world."

The president looked across the Situation Room at a world map covering the far wall. He'd had it installed soon after his inauguration.

"Not the entire world," said the president.

Stan ran up the stairs instead of taking the elevator. His office at the Liberty Crossing Intelligence Campus was on the first floor of the LH1 building. General Lewis' was on the fifth. He performed this daily ritual to get a little exercise. His usual fitness routines had suffered ever since he'd taken on this assignment. Whenever he was in the building after hours, Stan went a step farther; instead of running, he'd climb the inner railings of the stairwell to the top floor, timing his ascents, trying to beat his record. A few minutes later, out of breath and a little flushed, he walked into the general's outer office. Nancy was familiar with his routine.

"He's not here Col. Sheppard," Lewis' secretary said. "He's been…"

"What? I ran up here for nuthin?"

"I'm afraid it's more serious than that," she said. "General Lewis has been reassigned, immediately."

"What do you mean? I was just talking to him yesterday."

"It happened last night. He packed up and left first thing this morning."

"Where to?" Stan asked.

"He didn't say."

Stan shook his head and turned back towards the door. "Unbelievable."

"Oh, and Col. Sheppard."

He looked back at Nancy.

"DDNI Sheehan told me to tell you to go to his office as soon as you come in."

"Yeah, I'm already plannin' that."

Stan burst into Sheehan's office.

"What the hell's goin' on?" Stan said.

"I'm sorry, sir," Sheehan's secretary said, standing behind Sheppard. "He wouldn't stop."

"That's fine; I was expecting him. Close the door, please."

After his secretary left, Sheehan folded his hands on his desk and asked, "Is there a problem?"

"Ya know damn well there is! Ya don't cut the head off an operation without a single bit of notice or coordination. That's how ya get people killed."

"I'm going to cut off more than the head of this operation if you don't calm down."

"Ya don't have a clue!" Stan said. "We have hundreds of agents in the field, we have operations on hold, we have a broken satellite, and we have Franklin in Sicily. What do ya think…"

"General Lewis has been reassigned to a critical mission, and you are fully capable of running this operation without interference from your superiors."

"What mission is more important than…"

"That's none of your business. Calm down and get me up to speed on Franklin's progress. That's an order."

Stan realized he was butting his head against a brick wall.

"Yes, sir," he barked, his eyes squinting with anger. "Franklin is on station and has detected the neutrinos. It appears the source of the emissions is in the ocean, off the coast of Canneto. He can't zero in on the location without a dive boat, and that will take a couple days."

"Underwater? How can the facility be underwater?"

"It's too soon to tell. We don't even know if it's a man-made source or some natural phenomena. Or the camera is just fuckin' broke and we're puttin' together some doomsday scenario to explain it all."

"In case you've forgotten Sheppard, that is our job. We assume the worst-case scenario and we counter it! So, tell me, can there be an underwater facility?"

"That's next to impossible. Somebody would notice. It would be a huge undertakin', take years, if not decades, to build. Ya wouldn't be able to keep a secret like that."

Sheehan nodded, already seeing the logical conclusion to this conversation.

"Unless," Stan said slowly. "It was mobile."

"I've heard enough," Sheehan said. "Is there anything else I need to know?"

"No, sir. We'll have more answers in a couple days, when Franklin gits closer to the source. I've scheduled one of our other KH-11 satellites to keep an eye on him. If he finds the source, we'll have the location."

"How can you track Franklin without a PIT sensor?"

"We're usin' conventional tech. Franklin's handheld camera is too classified to just let loose in the field. It has a built in GPS chip that transmits its location. We'll use the coordinates to guide the KH-11's imaging sensor."

"Fine. Report back when you have something more concrete to tell me."

"Yes, sir."

"And Sheppard. It goes without saying. Anything and everything you think you know about this operation is strictly between you and me, nobody else. You report directly to me. Do I make myself clear?"

Stan turned his back to Sheehan and walked out of the office.

"Perfectly," he muttered.

Chapter 8

Day 3 (Continued)

Perry adjusted the settings on his camera and looked through the viewfinder again. Using the camera's GPS, rangefinder and the tripod's azimuth and elevation scales, he calculated the position of the strange anomaly. But the angles were wrong. They didn't make sense. He put the camera away and returned to the villa to see if Christina had any luck finding a boat. He found her sitting at the kitchen table with Nonna.

"Vieni signore Perry, siediti, siediti," said Nonna.

"I took the liberty of making your bed while you were outside," Christina said.

"Oh, thanks, but you don't need to. I can take care of that."

"We do this for all of our guests."

Nonna picked up a plastic jug and poured a deep-red liquid into a juice glass. She slid it across the table to Perry.

"This wine is made of grapes from our garden," Christina said. "It is our final container from last year's harvest. We will be opening our new barrel from this year's harvest in a couple weeks."

"Ahhh," he said. "An excellent year. But it's not even afternoon, yet."

"What do you mean 'not afternoon'?"

"I guess the saying loses something in translation. It's a joke about only alcoholics drinking before noon."

Christina shook her head.

Perry raised the small glass to his nose and inhaled deeply. He took a sip and swished the liquid around in his mouth before swallowing. Then he took another sip.

"Wow, that is very good for a new wine."

"Technically, a new wine is from the same year as the harvest," Christina explained. "But yes, I think it is excellent."

They were enjoying the wine along with some fresh baked bread and cheese, when they heard the rumble of Uncle Leo's Harley. Several minutes later, Leo walked through the back door, dressed in well-worn blue jeans and a flannel shirt.

"Greetings, signore Perry," Leo said, giving Nonna and Christina a two-cheeked kiss.

Perry raised his glass, "Saluti Father. Traditional robes for a Sicilian priest?"

"I change at the church. I go to my garden now."

"My uncle loves to spend time with his plants," said Christina. "It is his therapy."

Christina spoke some quick Italian to Leo. He frowned for a few seconds, looked at Perry, then nodded his head.

"You come see garden?" he asked.

"Actually, I just came in to see if Christina had found…
"

"Go," she said. "We will talk later. There is plenty of time."

Perry followed Leo out the back door and into a large courtyard surrounded by high stone walls. Over their heads, on a wooden trellis, were vines as big around as his arm; they shaded the entire courtyard from the late morning sun.

"Vieni, seguimi… come, follow," Leo said.

They walked to an iron gate at the rear of the courtyard and stepped under a stone archway.

Leo saw the amazement on Perry's face. He bent over and pulled some small weeds growing under a bush filled with cherry tomatoes.

"You like garden?" he asked.

Perry had pictured a small plot of land with a few rows of vegetables. It was nothing like that. Several lush acres of tropical greenness stood before him. It looked like a botanical garden.

"It's amazing, how do you find time for all of this? Ah... dove... il... tempo? It's huge." Perry said, spreading his arms wide.

"There always time for love, signore Perry."

Perry and Leo spent the next half-hour wandering through the garden. There were small groves of orange and apple trees. Farther on were trees filled with avocados, lemons, limes, and grapefruit. Leo identified each one in Italian. Perry practiced the words then told Leo the English translation for potatoes, onions, carrots, tomatoes, green bell peppers, and small, skinny red peppers.

"Caution," Leo explained. "Molto piccante."

There were banana trees, squash, lettuce, arugula, and some strange fruits that Perry couldn't identify. He heard honeybees buzzing around figs dripping with sticky nectar. They walked along a stone wall that separated the land from their neighbors. The priest stopped several times, pulling leaves from what looked like weeds at the base of the wall. He rubbed the leaves between his hands and brought them to Perry's nose.

"Oregano!" Perry replied.

Leo seemed to enjoy Perry's company. He walked from plant to plant, pulling leaves and asking Perry to identify each aroma. After Perry pronounced the name in English, Leo responded with the Italian for thyme, timo... fennel, finocchio... mint, menta... basil, basilico... lemongrass, citronella.

Eventually, walking back toward the house, they found Christina and Nonna picking tomatoes.

"Christina, this is unbelievable," Perry said.

She smiled with pride. "This is their love, their life. Leo and Nonna spend most days out here tending to the garden.

You are lucky; we are having a late harvest this year. You may pick as much as you want, whatever you like."

Perry looked over the garden. "I wonder how many ingredients I can squeeze into one meal."

Christina laughed, translated for Nonna, and listened to her reply.

"Nonna says that she will cook you a wonderful dinner. Just pick your favorites and bring them to the kitchen."

"That I will do, but you said you make your own wine. Where are the grapevines?"

"You didn't see them? They could have hit you in the head."

Perry scanned across the garden.

Christina said, "The vines shading our courtyard. The grapes have been picked already. They keep our patio cool in the summer."

As they approached the entrance to the courtyard, Christina pointed at a tree as big around as Perry's waist. He recognized the leaves and spotted several more trees running along the stone wall, their branches reaching up and over into the courtyard.

"Wow!" Perry said. "They're huge. I didn't realize grapevines grew so thick."

"They are ancient," Christina said.

She led Perry to a small, weathered wooden door built into the wall of the courtyard. She lifted the latch and swung the door open, signaling Perry inside. As he stepping into the darkness, the musty aroma of rich, damp earth washed over him. The light from outside filtered onto a cobblestone floor. Perry's eyes slowly focused on the dimly lit room. In the corner were baskets of potatoes and onions. Hanging from the rafters were ropes of plaited garlic, papery white and tinged with purple. Christina pointed to the back wall where a giant oak cask rested.

"We picked the grapes a month ago. Maybe you will still be here on November 10th. That is when Sicilians open their wine barrels."

Uncle Leo leaned in through the doorway. "Signore Perry! Come."

As Perry turned to leave, he noticed something odd: a solid wrought iron door. It looked out of place from its surroundings. It was relatively new and had a solid paddle lock on it. He assumed they must have expanded the cellar. *But why lock it?* he wondered.

Leo grabbed Perry's arm and pulled, "Come, you must see."

Stepping back into the courtyard, Leo led him over to a large brick barbecue built into another one of the stone walls inside the courtyard.

"I finish building last week. Sicilian men no cook in the home, I barbecue like you Americans. You try."

Perry was in awe of this family. He'd never been exposed to this intensity of gardening, or this type of multi-generational family so deep-seated in tradition but riding Harleys and wanting to barbeque like Americans.

"I'd be honored," he said.

Perry and Christina returned to the kitchen and she started making phone calls. Her first conversation was short, and she immediately called a second number. Perry listened, understanding little, except for one word. Christina had said it several times. 'Pericoloso.' He'd seen the word several times on traffic signs. It meant dangerous.

Christina hung up and turned to him.

"This is not easy. I spoke to a friend who is a fisherman. He said that few people dive the waters off Canneto. They are too treacherous. There are many caves and currents caused by volcanic hot springs. You could be drowned or cooked alive. A dive boat is difficult to find."

Franklin was a certified divemaster and had dove with the Navy SEALs in a variety of rough conditions. His work had required it. Many times, ingress to his targets required submersibles and long swims underwater to a rugged shoreline. He loved the ocean and the adventure, the only times he didn't were in freezing conditions. That just made

Joseph W. Foster

him miserable. Diving the October waters of Sicily with the threat of warm springs to soothe the chill seemed more like Club Med than 'pericoloso.'

Perry raked his fingers through his hair. "I'll take my chances," he said. "I need to make this happen. I'll drive down there myself."

"I do not understand why it is so important that you have to risk your life," Christina replied.

Perry shrugged his shoulders. "What can I say? I love my work."

"Well, you certainly cannot go alone. If you find a boat, you will need someone who can communicate with the captain."

Perry smiled at Christina.

"No! I am not taking you to Cefalù, and I hate boats!"

Perry pointed out the window. "Look at the water. It's flat as a pond. All I need you to do is explain to the captain where I need to go. Please?"

Christina needed to be in control of this situation. She did not want this supposed photojournalist getting anywhere close to those volcanic vents, but she could not convince him otherwise.

"Very well," she agreed. "I will go with you. We will drive over tomorrow morning."

"I was hoping to dive first thing in the morning. Can we drive over today?"

"Today?" Christina said. "I told you. Today is All Saints Day. I need to be with my family tonight. Tomorrow is the best I can do."

Perry calculated the time needed to drive to Cefalù, find a charter boat, rent equipment, and motor the boat back to Canneto for his dive.

"I don't think we have time," he said. "It will take several hours just to motor the boat back here from Cefalù. How about we drive over there tonight after your family gathering?"

130

"Nonna would not like me spending a night away from home with a stranger. I do not understand why you are in such a hurry."

"Oh, come on. You're a grown woman, and I'm not a stranger, and your grandmother likes me. I'll gladly pay you for your time."

Christina laughed. "That helps. She will love to hear I will be paid to spend the night with you."

Perry laughed back. "You're right, I really am an ugly American."

"Yes, you are. I will let you know later tonight."

"Fair enough."

It was late afternoon. Perry was sitting at a small wooden desk in his room when he heard the knock at his door. Quickly folding his navigation charts of the coastal waters, he said, "Si`! Come in."

Father Leo swung the door open.

"Signore, Nonna e me like you come for a special occasion."

Perry said, "Christina mentioned this is All Saints Day."

"Si`, e All Souls Eve. A very special day."

"Molto bene," Perry said, pointing to his clothing. "How should I dress?"

"Is good. We depart 1800 hours."

Perry needed to spend more time preparing for his dive trip but thought a trip into town might prove useful, and he didn't want to disrespect his patrons - he might be needing more of their help.

It was a few minutes before 6 p.m. when Perry walked downstair wearing the best clothes he could pull from his backpack: black hiking pants, a grey safari shirt with half a dozen pockets, and a pair of Crocs, the only black shoes he had. When Christina walked in from the back of the house, his eyes grew wide. Christina wore a long black satin dress

131

trimmed with lace. Around her neck hung a pearl choker and a white lace shawl covered her shoulders.

"Wow, you look... that's... quite beautiful," he said. "Your dress, I mean... it's nice."

Perry had never seen a woman smile and frown at the same time.

"Where are you going?" Christina asked suspiciously.

"What? Didn't Leo tell you? I'm your date for the night."

Christina turned immediately and stormed out of the room.

Perry heard Christina and Leo talking in rapid Italian and Nonna's softer voice coming from the kitchen. He didn't understand a word, but Christina's intention was clear. A few minutes later, all three walked into the living room.

"It appears that my Nonna and Uncle Leo neglected to inform me that our new guest will be accompanying us to our VERY sacred family plot on a VERY sacred day of the year. You are most welcome to join us."

Perry figured Nonna was playing matchmaker and was willing to go along if it helped his mission.

"Come," said Leo as he headed for the front door.

Christina eyed Perry and said, "Un minuto."

She left the room and returned a minute later.

"Here is one of my uncle's suit jackets. It will help cover that ridiculous shirt of yours."

Perry feigned indignation and slipped on the jacket as they walked out the door.

Perry assumed that Leo would turn the family's small Opel left to go down to Canneto. Instead, they turned right and headed higher into the mountains.

"Where are we going?" asked Perry.

"To our ancestral village," Christina answered. "San Pier Niceto. It is where our family plot is located."

In true Italian fashion, there were only two throttle positions on Uncle Leo's automobile. Completely 'up' and completely 'down.' Leo piloted the vehicle through the hills and curves with a finesse that came only from a lifetime of familiarity and a lifetime of faith in the afterworld. Perry held tightly to the back of Leo's seat while Christina held a relaxing conversation with Nonna. Their nonchalance was comical. Leo reached for the radio knob as the sheer drop-offs passed by, inches from the vehicle's tires. He turned up a classical tune.

Perry muttered to himself, "This is crazy."

Christina asked, "What was that?"

"Just saying a blessing to all the saints," he said.

Christina smiled. "How sweet of you."

She returned to her conversation with Nonna as Perry tightened his grasp onto the back of Leo's seat.

They drove through the mountains for the next half hour, steadily moving inland. The sun had set, and the sky was completely dark as small hamlets whizzed by. When they rounded another curve, San Pier Niceto appeared out of the darkness. The town was built into the mountainside. He saw the streetlights and people under them walking in small groups.

Leo maneuvered the Opel through the village's narrow passageways and up onto a knoll on the far side of town. They slowed as their headlights illuminated a long concrete wall. It was old and crumbling, paint flaking like curled leaves hanging onto a winter tree. Chunks of concrete had fallen away exposing rusted rebar. Two ornate light poles stood guard on either side of a large wrought iron gate at the far end of the wall. Small groups of people, all dressed in dark suits and dresses, made their way toward the entrance. Leo parked in a small, gravel parking lot on the other side of the street and they silently joined the procession.

Burning luminaries were strung along the foundations of the vaults and were secreted in small alcoves filled with fresh flowers. The polished marble and granite mausoleums danced in the light of a hundred flickering flames. The dim light illuminated the names and portraits of the deceased.

Shadows jumped back and forth as the evening breeze swept up the mountain. The same breeze that threatened to extinguish the flames brought a musky sweetness, an earthiness from the vineyards and fruit orchards below. Perry had never seen anything like this. He'd wandered through plenty of graveyards and mausoleums during his travels, but only as a tourist, in the bright light of day. Not like this, not a place alive with families, flowers, candles, the soft murmur of hushed voices and gently placed feet. Christina was right; he didn't belong here. This was too personal, too connected, too foreign. He wanted to go back to the car. Nonna and Christina walked ahead and stopped to talk with some friends. A hand grabbed Perry's elbow.

"Come," said Leo. "You see my family."

Leo guided Perry to the entrance of a large burial chamber at the back of the cemetery. He swung a miniature version of the main gates open and soft light drifted out of the vault. Leo motioned for Perry to enter and he stepped inside. All three walls, left, right, and rear, contained 2-foot by 1-foot facias of stone, all engraved with names, some even with portraits. Most of the surnames on the tombs were Germanni.

"This is Nonna's family," Leo said.

"I don't know what to say; it's... it's... inspiring and beautiful and sad all at the same time."

"Yes, it is a special place. It teaches us about life, how sweet and short and sacred."

Leo pointed to one of the crypts. "This is my grandfather, Salvatore. He fought in the resistance against the fascist and the Nazis. He was a great civil engineer; he could build anything."

Pointing to a crypt at the right of his grandfather's, he said, "And this is my great uncle, Marco. He was a fascist. He fought with the 429th Coastal Battalion against General Patton's Army when they came ashore in Gela. An American soldier's bullet killed him. My grandfather and

Uncle Marco hated each other for what they were doing but loved each other."

"What about your father's family, the LaTorres?" Perry asked. "Where are they?"

"They are from Messina. Come, let us join others," Leo replied. He turned, stepped toward the doorway and stopped abruptly.

"Don Tumeo," Leo said.

A heavyset, elderly man stood at the entrance to the small crypt. He was dressed in a tailored pinstripe suit and wore a fedora. His complexion was dark and rugged, as if he'd spent a lifetime of hard labor in the fields or on the sea.

"Monsignor," the man said, bowing to Leo. "You are well, I hope?"

"Si`," said Leo, bowing back. "And yourself?"

"Perfetto."

They stared at each other for several seconds before the man said, "And your friend?"

"Oh, excuse me. Please, this is signore Franklin, a guest of ours."

"Perry, this is Don Tumeo. We grew up together. Here, in San Pier Niceto."

The Don eyed Perry suspiciously but took Perry's hand.

"I understand you are an American," he said.

"You'll have to excuse us, compadre," said Leo. "The women are waiting for us."

"Of course," said the Don.

As they walked across the courtyard, Perry asked, "Who was that? And how did he know I was an American. I hadn't even opened my mouth."

"Don Tumeo is a very important man here in Sicily. Word spreads quickly."

"I don't know if I should be honored or scared. He seemed a bit rough around the edges."

Leo nodded. "It is no secret. Don Tumeo is the most powerful leader of the Cosa Nostra here in Sicily."

Perry stared at Leo. "And you are friends? How can a man of God be friends with… "

"Signore Franklin, you have a lot to learn about Sicily," Leo replied.

When they caught up with the women, Perry pulled Christina aside.

"What is wrong?" she asked.

"Nothing, I just wanted to say I'm sorry."

"For what?"

"I didn't understand. This is something extraordinary. I shouldn't have come. I don't belong here."

"Then maybe I was wrong. I think this was perfect."

Perry asked, "What do you mean?"

"Maybe you understand a little more about us."

Christina turned back to the small group.

"Oh, by the way," Perry said. "Did you get permission from Nonna to venture out tonight?"

Christina turned and said, "Yes, apparently she has become more liberal in her elder years. I heard a hint of debauchery when she said it was fine with her."

"As I said, she likes me."

"Maybe you should have her spend the night with you instead."

"I gladly would if she spoke a little more English, signorina."

"It is signora, not signorina," Christina said. "I am as old as you."

"You're married?"

"No. Signora is also used in formal business settings and with older women, regardless of their marital status. Signorina is used to address a very young woman unless, of course, she is married."

"I stand corrected."

"We can leave as soon as we get back to the house," she said.

"Thank you."

Christina turned away again to join the group and Perry said, "Oh, Christina."

She stopped and looked back again.

"Tonight… when we're all alone… just the two of us… do I use signora because you're an older woman or because our sleeping arrangement is a formal business affair?"

Perry had accomplished something he hadn't realized he was trying to do. He'd embarrassed her. Christina hesitated for several seconds. Seeing her expressions change by the second, he thought he'd gone too far. She stared back at him; her lips set firmly. After what felt like an eternity, she smiled, then laughed out loud, drawing stares from the many families in the small courtyard. She shook her head, turned and walked away, saying, "In your dreams, Franklin. In your dreams."

It was just past 10:00 p.m. when Perry and Christina entered the outskirts of Cefalù. He maneuvered the Fiat through the narrow, crowded streets and pulled into a parking spot highlighted by yellow painted lines.

"No! Not there." Christina said. "You will get a parking ticket. That is for the residenti, the residents."

"How am I supposed to know that?"

"You are not. You are a foreigner."

A minute later, he found a white-lined parking space and parked the car.

Grabbing their backpacks, they walked down a gently sloping side street heading towards the water. There were few streetlights, and Christina searched the dark shadows on either side of the street.

"We should have just driven here in the morning, or at least made reservations for the night," she said nervously.

Perry replied, "I need to start early. I'll be making several deep dives. They have to be spaced out over the day to avoid getting the bends. And, I hate making reservations at someplace I haven't seen first."

"You did not see my home before you made a reservation."

"You came highly recommended," he replied. "I'll know better next time."

"I will as well," she replied.

Reaching the shoreline, they walked along a wide promenade that paralleled the beach. Sago palms and magnolia trees lined the busy street on the beachside; cafes, pizza shops, and small family-run hotels lined the other. They searched for a half-hour, checking at each pension they found. The rooms were fully booked. Stopping to rest, they leaned their backpacks against a low stone wall. In the light of the full moon, the surf glowed as waves crashed against the base of the wall. Across the walkway, at a dimly lit outdoor cafe, sat a middle-aged couple watching them.

"I told you so," Christina said. "We should have found something ahead of time."

"I didn't realize how busy the town would be."

"It is a popular area for tourists."

The man sitting at the cafe stood up, said something to the woman he was with, and crossed the small street separating them.

"Buonasera," he said. "You look lost. Can I help you find something?"

"We were hoping to find a pension for the night," Christina explained in Italian. "But all seem to be full."

"You need to check with Allison," he said. "She will find a room for you. Just walk straight up this street to the other side of the church; when you get there turn left. Look for the apartment with all the plants outside; you cannot miss it."

Christina thanked him and they followed the man's directions.

They did miss it, several times. They searched down several side streets, eventually finding themselves at the deadend of a long alley. Overflowing trash cans lined both sides of the lane and an animal was skittering through the debris. The buildings were three stories high, creating the feeling of a deep chasm in the earth.

"Must be a long weekend with all this trash lying around," Perry said to break the silence.

"Non mi piace questo," Christina said nervously.

Christina dropped her pack to the ground. Perry could barely see in the dark but knew something was wrong. Her eyes darted back and forth, there was fear in her voice. Her feet seemed anchored like stone. He'd seen it before, hell, he'd felt it before. She was having a panic attack.

Perry stepped in front of her and said, "Look at me."

She looked at him. "I am not taking another step! We are lost."

"That's fine," he replied calmly. "There's no rush. Your house is only a couple hours down the highway. We can go back."

She looked around nervously. He put his hands on her tense shoulders, pulling her attention back to him. As soon as he caught her gaze, he looked up at the narrow strip of sky above the rooftops. Christina's gaze followed his.

"Look at those stars," he said. "It's such a beautiful night. Let's go back and take a walk on the beach. Don't you love the sound of those waves and that cool ocean breeze? This is a little piece of heaven you have here. I love Sicily."

Christina relaxed enough to remove Perry's hands from her shoulders. She took a few breaths and said, "Perhaps you are right. I do not know why I get so scared." She shook her head. "Stupid."

"It's not stupid. Fear can grab hold of you. I've been there. We might not be standing here in a life or death situation, but that reptilian part of our brain doesn't care one damn bit. You just need to give the logical part of your brain a few seconds to catch up. It knows you're not going to get shanked in this dark alley."

Christina nodded in agreement. "Yes."

"Well, that's a first. You're agreeing with me."

"Only partly," Christina said. "If anybody is going to get shanked, it will be the ugly American."

"Ha! See? The logic's kicking in already. Come on," he said.

Perry headed back down the alley. "Grab your backpack, and let's go back toward the beach. We'll either find someplace to stay or drive home."

They had retraced their steps only a few meters when Perry saw someone enter the far end of the alley. The silhouette paused for a second and then walked directly toward them. Perry stopped and put his hand out, signaling Christina to wait. The stranger's footsteps tapped hard on the cobblestone and echoed off the high walls. The person seemed in a hurry to get to them. Perry slid the backpack off his shoulder and let it fall to the ground.

They're wearing hard street shoes, he thought. *They'll be slippery on this cobblestone. Goddamn it! What the hell am I doing standing here in a deserted alleyway. Most people are right-handed,* he remembered. *Step to their right to avoid. This is crazy!* he thought. *I really am going to get shanked by a stranger, and Christina's going to have a freaking meltdown.*

Perry shifted his left foot forward, centered his body weight, and waited.

A woman's voice broke the silence. "Excuse me! Signore, signora!"

Perry stared as the dark silhouette transformed into a raven-haired, voluptuous, middle-aged woman in high heels. She was dressed in an evening gown and wore a long black jeweled necklace. Her dress' deeply-cut neckline displayed enough cleavage to turn the head of every adult male in town and half the females. Perry's anticipation transitioned from being attacked to being propositioned.

"You are looking for a bed?" the woman asked.

"What?" Christina asked. "No! We are not interested…

"I will be your host for tonight."

"Yeah, right. I don't think so," Perry said.

Allison laughed. "You no understand signore. My name is Allison. My beautiful friends at the café, Peter called right after he talked to you and explained there were two lost souls wandering the streets looking for a bed for the night. When you did not appear, I worried. It is easy to become lost on these dark streets. I wish there were more lights."

Christina, visibly relieved, said, "Buonasera Allison, mi chiamo Christina e il mio amico americano è Perry. Thank you for rescuing us."

Christina didn't appear at all surprised by the Sicilian hospitality that brought a woman out into the dead of night, searching for two wandering strangers. Especially a beautifully dressed woman who was obviously pre-engaged with other pursuits.

"Meraviglioso! Come!" Allison said. "We must hurry. I have left my guests alone."

Perry and Christina walked fast to keep up with the beautiful, well-heeled woman clicking her way down the alley. Allison led them the short distance to her apartment and quickly ushered them inside. Walking into the kitchen, she introduced Perry and Christina to a couple of her party guests who were pouring themselves fresh drinks. She then led them upstairs. Unlocking a door at the end of the hallway, they entered a dimly lit room.

Spreading her arms wide, Allison said, "I have but one room left. But is large and beautiful and two comfortable beds. I push them together for you."

Christina frowned and talked to Allison in rapid Italian. Perry had a good idea what she was saying.

Allison shook her head apologetically.

Christina appeared to agree reluctantly and they both turned back to him.

"Signore Perry," Allison said. "The room is L-shaped. If you please move this bed over the other side of room, we will all be satisfied."

"Maybe you two will be, but I'm not sure I want to share the..."

Allison interrupted with a smile. "I am a terrible host to my dinner guests. I must return to them. You can either sleep with the signora or you can sleep with me. It is your choice."

Perry wondered if she was serious but said nothing.

"Va bene!" she said with a wide gesture of her hands. "Once you two have made yourselves comfortable, please, come downstairs and join our party. We love to have you."

"Grazie, Allison," Christina replied. "But I will unpack my luggage and go to bed early. It has been a long day."

"Prego!" Allison said, handing Christina the key and walking out.

Perry and Christina looked around the large room in awkward silence. The travertine tiled floor was worn down and uneven from centuries of use. In one corner stood two richly upholstered wingback chairs separated by an antique Queen Anne side table and ornate brass floor lamp. Against the wall by the door was a large curved dressing table with beveled mirrors and a dozen small drawers. Perry walked over and opened the French doors that led to a small balcony overlooking the water. The sheer white curtains drifted inward with the breeze, along with the voices of the dinner guests.

Perry asked, "Are you okay with this? It's not exactly what you bargained for."

She nodded. "I am fine, but please do not tell anyone. I will be humiliated if Uncle Leo or Nonna found out."

"No one will ever know."

"I am serious; you do not tell a soul."

"Your secret is safe with me."

After Perry and Christina slid his bed over to the other side of the room, Christina started unpacking her night clothes from the backpack.

"You see?" Perry said. "Everything turned out alright. There was nothing to be afraid of."

"Do you think I did not see you drop your backpack in the alley and…"

"Okay, okay, we don't need to go there." he said. "I think I'll go take Allison up on her offer."

"For dinner, or to sleep with her?"

"I'm still thinking," he said as he walked out the door.

As soon as Perry left, Christina pulled out her phone.

Chapter 9

Day 4

The early morning sun slowly lit the eastern horizon as Perry walked along the quay. He passed several old fishing boats and heard the purr of a small outboard bouncing off the concrete walls of the breakwater. Seconds later, a dark blue, wooden dory appeared around the quay's northeastern point. The fisherman piloted the craft slowly, leaving the large swells of the open ocean behind. He steered into the light chop of the harbor and headed toward a fishing dock where a row of small, colorful boats were bobbing in the water. A woman stood at the end of the dock, waiting.

Perry walked back the way he came, keeping pace with the boat's slow progress. The fisherman killed the engine and drifted the few remaining meters toward the woman. Standing in the center of the boat, he tossed her a line. She was securing it to the concrete piling when Perry noticed her wedding ring. He stopped and watched them for a few minutes.

The woman looked happy, seeing her husband return safely from the sea. Perry knew no sane person ventures out on the ocean without a healthy dose of fear. The sea's too unpredictable, too powerful. The couple moved efficiently, like choreographed ballet dancers. The fisherman balanced in the center of the small craft as it rocked back and forth in the waves. Bending and lifting, he tossed baskets of fish to the outstretched arms of his wife. Her toes hung off the weather-beaten edge of the pier as she took hold and swung each one ashore. Their well-practiced dance with the sea, the boat, and each other matched their expressions; relieved to be back home, together, after a good night of fishing.

The couple talked gently… about the catch, maybe the weather or the upcoming day. The words didn't matter. Perry knew those same words had been spoken a million times. His thoughts drifted back to the dark alley: Christina's fears, his own fears minutes later and the unexpected arrival of Allison. Perry thought about something he'd read in a philosophy book about there being only two real emotions: love and fear. Every other human emotion was simply a response to love or fear. Anger, desire, hate, compassion, greed, empathy, competition, jealousy, joy, violence, sacrifice… they were all reactions to fear or love. He imagined that the fisherman and his wife lived a simple life, balanced between the sea and their home, their loves and their fears. Taking a small craft out into the sea was a risky endeavor. Being the wife of a fisherman was a risky endeavor. *Why do they take such risks?* he wondered. *And why am I even here? Was it love or fear that brought me to this island?*

He'd woken early and decided to let Christina sleep. Now he wished he hadn't, wished he was sharing this moment with her. There was something about her, her family and her home, that felt so familiar. He wondered why he turned into such an asshole when he was around her. From now on, he decided he was going to be nice.

The coffee Perry was carrying had gotten cold, but he continued to drink it as he walked back toward the shoreline. Halfway there, he noticed a familiar white and blue dive flag flapping at the bow of a boat. As he got closer, he saw the open transom and the mounting saddles for scuba tanks along the sides.

"That's it, just what I'm looking for."

In big black letters on the hull was the name: Narcogen Nitrosis. Perry laughed and scanned the shoreline. He spotted the small building. It had another white and blue dive flag flapping on a pole outside the front door. Above the door, hung a sign: Narcogen Nitrosis Dyve Senter

He walked over and tried the door. Finding it locked, he glanced at his watch. It wasn't even 0700 so decided to head back to Allison's.

❖

Perry climbed the stairs in time to find Christina walking down the hallway. She had a large bath towel wrapped around her and another wrapped around her head. She smiled at him.

"Buongiorno signora Christina, did you sleep well?"

"Surprisingly well, thank you, I must have been exhausted."

"I am glad… sono contento."

"I did not hear you come in last night," she said. "Assuming you did return."

"I was only gone for a couple of hours. For some reason, I was quite tired myself. Why don't I go downstairs and make you some coffee? That way, you'll have some privacy to get dressed."

"You know how to make real Italian coffee?" she asked.

"You might be surprised to know I've been making real Italian coffee for the last twenty years, every morning."

"Wow. There is hope for you, signore Perry."

"I'd like to think so. Would you like a cappuccino or espresso?"

"A cappuccino with a little sugar, please."

"I'll be back in fifteen minutes. Is that enough time?"

"Perfetto."

An hour later, Perry and Christina were standing outside the Narcogen Nitrosis Dyve Senter.

"Will you explain to them I'm an underwater photographer and I'd like to hire them for the day? Here's a chart. I've circled the areas I'd like to go to."

Christina looked and immediately recognized the locations. She shook her head.

"Perry, I told you before, this is not a safe area. The volcanic vents can be dangerous."

"I know what I'm doing. I've dove on vents before."

She shook her head and they walked into the dive shop. Christina approached the young man behind the counter. As they spoke, the dive shop owner said, "no" repeatedly.

Christina turned back to Perry. "He said he is booked. He cannot possibly spend the day over by Canneto."

"Paying customers on a Monday? In November? That's hard to believe."

Christina shrugged.

The young man heard their conversation and in perfect English said, "I agree, we are usually very slow this time of year, but we had a group book our boat for the entire week. They telephoned just yesterday."

Christina said, "Grazie, we will have to wait until later." and ushered Perry out the door.

As they walked away from the shop, the man opened the door and called after them.

"Wait! I just remembered. I saw a dive boat pull into the docks this morning. I'd never seen it before. You might want to see if they have some time to take you out."

Perry called back, "Thanks; we'll go check."

"The boat is green and white with a red stripe down the side," the divemaster said. "You cannot miss it."

"Perry, we do not know who this person is."

"Stop worrying. A dive boat is a dive boat."

They headed down to the pier, the same pier where Perry had watched the fisherman and his wife.

"That's funny," he said. "I walked down here earlier this morning while you were sleeping. I don't remember seeing any other dive boats beside the Dive Center's."

Three-quarters of the way along the pier, they spotted the other boat. It had a dive flag flying from the mast. A shirtless man with black, curly hair and tattoos stood on the stern coiling a dock line. Perry was terrible with faces and names and words but had an uncanny knack for remembering scenes, any kind of scene. He could recall the smallest details of buildings, trees, roads, vehicles, and especially boats. He loved boats. They reminded him of home.

"This wasn't here two hours ago."

"Maybe he keeps it somewhere else," Christina said. "Or maybe he was out fishing."

Perry pulled 500 euros from his pocket.

"I doubt he'll have any paying customers, but just in case, here, take this and don't take 'no' for an answer."

Before Christina could call to the captain, he looked up and greeted them in English. "Hello!"

Perry replied, "You speak English?"

"Un po."

"I'm Perry, and this is signora Christina. I want to go diving. Can you take me out for the day?"

Christina translated for Perry, and the man replied.

"I Captain Simon. I take you diving."

Simon looked to be in his early thirties and in excellent shape. He had a six-pack torso and bulging biceps. He wore a three-day-old beard and had full-length tattoos running down his arms depicting scenes of Roman gods and a coliseum. After a few minutes of negotiating in Italian, Christina handed Simon 300 euros.

Perry said, "Meet us back here at ten, and we'll head out."

Christina added, "We will need tanks and gear for the both of us."

"Both of us?" Perry said. "I thought you hated boats."

"I do, but I love scuba diving."

"But you said it's not safe."

"I am going with you. You are not diving alone, and I know this coastline better than this stranger you just hired."

As she walked away, Christina wondered how a dive boat could mysteriously appear right after her people had booked every single boat within a hundred kilometers. She needed to come up with a better plan.

Christina helped Simon stow the gear while Perry checked his camera. As soon as Simon started the engine, she untied and coiled the lines holding the boat to the dock. Minutes later, they were in the open ocean, motoring at full speed towards Canneto.

Over the din of the engine, Perry said, "You seem pretty comfortable around boats."

"Just because I do not like something does not mean I am not competent to do it."

"You mean like how good you've been taking care of me?"

Christina thought for a second. "I cannot tell if you are serious or trying again to be humorous."

"I'm serious, signora. You might be uptight about us Americans, but I appreciate everything you've done for me. You've been a molto gracious host."

"It is signora, now?" Christina asked. "You must want something."

"Your cynicism will get you nowhere," he said.

"Since there is nowhere I want to be going with you, I guess that is no problem."

"You never quit, do you?"

"Perry, I do not like boats. I do not like diving in dangerous waters, and I do not like your cavalier attitude. Am I supposed to be behaving in some special way?"

"As I said, thanks for helping, and I'll try harder to be more… more… Italian."

"I think you mean Sicilian, but either way, I do not particularly like Sicilian men, either."

"Oh," Perry said. "It all makes sense now. You don't like boys; you like girls. I should have…"

"No!" Christina interrupted. "I like men. I am just partial to men who treat me as an equal, who have a gentle, soft side, are respectful and intelligent."

"And there's not a single Sicilian man…"

"They think they are so masculino, they act so condescending to women."

"Every one of them? I find that hard to believe," Perry said. "Maybe it's just a certain type of woman that gets their Roman gladiator blood pumping."

"What are you trying to say?"

"You know what I'm saying. Do I have to spell it out for you?"

"Please."

"Christina, you are an intelligent, successful woman. You have a loving family, you're kind-hearted, and the few times you smile, you radiate a beauty that lights up the whole damn room. But I'm getting the feeling you don't have any male friends… or boyfriends… or lovers. Why is that?"

"That is not your business."

"Do you disagree with anything I've said?"

Christina turned and looked at the horizon.

"No."

"Then why don't you have any male friends?"

"I like my freedom."

"You think having a relationship will take your freedom away?"

"Absolutely, men are just so… controlling… abrasive."

"Look, I've only known you for a few days, and I want to be honest with you. But I don't want to overstep my bounds."

"Please. You have not held back on any of your opinions so far."

"Okay. If I thought you were just some hard-ass, I wouldn't bother to say anything. You're not fooling anybody with this act you're putting on. I see how loving you are with your family. It's not that you don't like men…

I think it's because you're afraid of them. You're afraid of getting your heart broken, of being vulnerable. Maybe it's because of your parents dying. Or maybe some man broke your heart. Whatever it is, you've strapped on a suit of armor. I think that's why men react to you in such an abrasive manner. They can see what's hiding behind that armor, and they want to strip the layers off."

Christina's eyes glistened as she stared at Perry. She abruptly pulled her sweatshirt up over her head and slipped out of her jeans. Underneath, she wore an athletic-looking, one-piece, dark red bathing suit, cut seductively high on the thighs and low on the neck.

She was gorgeous. The soft curves of her hips and full breasts did little to hide the fact that she was in excellent shape. Her smooth legs had well-defined calves and muscular thighs. Her broad shoulders hinted of long-distance swimming.

She reached for the scuba suit lying next to her.

"Aren't you going to say anything?" he asked.

Putting the scuba suit in her lap, she looked at him. "And you hide your vulnerability behind a crude sarcasm."

"Touché!" Perry said. "Don't we make a fine pair."

"We are not a pair," she said.

"You know what I mean. I know you'll take this the wrong way, but I can't help noticing. You must workout. A lot. Are you a swimmer?"

Christina laughed. "Does that line work on American women? Because it is not going to work on me."

"I can't even make a simple observation?"

"Yes, I swim a lot," she admitted. "I used to compete in triathlons. That was some time ago. Now, I just enjoy swimming. It is a way to relax, to stay centered."

Perry nodded and turned away as she slipped into her wetsuit.

He removed his camera from the Pelican case, along with a clear plastic housing. He opened the housing and carefully installed the camera. After spreading a small bead of silicone grease along the neoprene O-ring, he clamped it shut.

"That will do it," he said. "This housing is good for a depth of 30 meters. We'll get some great pictures."

"Some of these vents run a hundred meters under the seafloor."

"Well, we certainly aren't prepared to go that deep," Perry replied. "This will be quick; all I need are a few good pictures of the openings. Why didn't you tell me you were familiar with these vents?"

"I did not want to encourage you. This is not a good idea."

"Yet, here you are, ready to risk life and limb. If I didn't know better, I'd say you were a closet adventurer."

"I do not understand. A what?"

"You crave adventure, but you're too afraid of the dangers. It's the Indiana Jones effect. You're an academic, but you teach anthropology, a profession that has the potential to take you to some exciting, possibly risky places?"

"Maybe."

"Most of the time," Perry continued. "You live a boring life, standing in front of a classroom of students, writing academic papers, doing research in the stacks, but when the opportunity arises, like the dive boat this morning, you can't resist. All in the name of saving me from myself when you don't even like me."

Christina laughed, "You might be right."

Perry picked up his camera, pressed a few buttons, and scanned the eastern horizon. He saw the open ocean straight ahead and Canneto slightly to the south. They were still an hour away, but there was a weak signal. *We're getting close,* he thought. He pressed another button and saved the image as well as the azimuth and elevation angles from the camera's internal GPS.

"What do you see?" Christina asked. "Can I take a look?"

He put the camera down and reached back into the Pelican case.

"Here's another camera, not as good but completely waterproof. You can use it if you like."

"Okay."

As she watched him take several pictures of what appeared to be an utterly open ocean, she wondered why he did not want her to handle his camera. She thought it strange but resigned herself. She just wanted to keep track of his movements and, if needed, guide him away from sensitive areas.

"Will you ask the captain to move to the next coordinate?" he said.

"The next?" she said. "We have not arrived at the first one."

"I've gotten what I need."

"We are not diving at that location?" she asked.

"No, I'll be zeroing in on the spot soon."

"What spot? It is open ocean."

"Oh, yeah, my camera can pick up heat signatures," Perry lied. "I can get a rough idea of where the vents are by the slight variations in surface temperature."

Christina went to where Simon stood at the helm and pointed on the chart to where Perry wanted to go next. Simon nodded his head and turned his vessel ten degrees to the south. She was worried. The points Perry had first indicated on the chart were safe but now he was deviating from the plan.

Simon's boat was heading east by southeast at 12 knots. Christina watched Perry as he continued to scan the waters with his camera. Every time he snapped a picture, she estimated the pointing angle of the camera and looked back at the chart. She pictured imaginary lines drawn from the boat's position to where Perry was looking, and a image slowly emerged.

That's impossible, she thought. *How can he know?*

Christina pulled out her cell phone and quickly typed a text message: SHUT IT DOWN! SHUT IT DOWN IMMEDIATELY!!! She pressed SEND. The small progress bar at the top of her screen crawled from left to right. Thirty seconds later, a red message appeared: "UNDELIVERED." She checked the signal level. The indicator dipped from a single bar to no bars.

"Merda!"

"What?" asked Perry.

"I just remembered something vital that I needed to do today. We might have to shorten our trip."

"Shorten? We're just getting started!"

"I am so sorry."

"Look, we're already out here, and I have a good idea where we need to go. Here. Let me see the chart."

She reluctantly handed him the chart.

Perry pulled a pencil from his pocket and drew a circle on the chart three kilometers directly south of their position, straight towards Canneto.

Handing the chart back to Christina, he said, "Have the captain go here and drop the anchor. We'll be in 40 meters of water. That'll give us about five minutes of bottom time. We can head back afterward. Better yet, we can drop you off on the beach at Canneto if that helps. You can have your uncle pick you up."

Christina looked at the chart, at the circle Perry had drawn, and her heart raced. The location was the exact spot, the only spot, they had to avoid. And Perry was right. The boat would get there quick enough and only 15 minutes were needed to dive down and come back up. How could she protest? How did he find that exact location? It was impossible.

Ten minutes later, Simon dropped anchor. They were a kilometer off the beach, directly in front of Canneto. As soon as the anchor was set firmly in the sandy bottom, Simon killed the engine and called out, "Signore Perry, Christina, you are free to go."

Perry lifted Christina's tank and vest and helped her slide the straps over her shoulders.

"Are you okay?" he asked. "You seem distracted."

"I am a little seasick. I will be fine once we go into the water."

"Okay, well, let me know if you need to come back up. We'll make this as quick as possible."

While Perry donned his equipment, Christina tried her phone, again. They were closer to shore now and she had a small amount of signal. She quickly resent the message, then deleted the text from her history.

Perry strapped on his weight belt, double-checked his equipment, and stepped off the transom into the water.

When he surfaced, he reflexively tapped his head to signal he was okay and called to Christina. "Will you hand me my camera?"

As Christina handed him the camera, she flipped on the power switch. She saw it for only an instant. A bright flash of red appeared on the display screen.

Perry saw her confused look and swore to himself. He thought he'd turned the camera off. He hoisted himself halfway out of the water and grabbed for it.

"I got it," he said.

She withdrew the camera from his grasp and considered 'accidentally' dropping it onto the hard deck. But in the waterproof housing, it probably wouldn't have any effect. She reluctantly handed it to him.

"Thanks! I'll meet you at the anchor line and we'll descend together. You'll feel better as soon as we get under the waves."

"Okay," she said.

Perry released enough air from his buoyancy compensator, or BC, to lower him below the water's surface. He kicked his fins hard through the water. Reaching the bow, he grabbed the anchor line. With the other hand, he scanned the camera across the bottom, watching for the telltale red flashes on the screen. He needed to locate the signal while he was still close to the surface, so his GPS could record the exact location. Once submerged, the GPS would be useless. In an instant, he had what he was looking for. Half of the watery scene in his viewfinder was awash in red.

He scanned back and forth, trying to measure the size and shape of the signal. But as quickly as it appeared, it vanished. He tried different camera settings, he scanned larger and larger arcs, but the signal was gone.

Perry was about to snap a picture of where he thought the signal had been when the boat's engine rumbled to life. A second later, the anchor rode was torn from his grasp, and he tumbled forward. Looking up quickly, he saw the bow accelerate and rise, just before crashing down onto his head. The impact knocked Perry's mask and regulator from his face, pushing him deeper underwater. He saw the spinning prop an instant before he felt another crushing blow. His legs went numb and everything went silent. He felt frozen in time, disoriented, as if he were an astronaut floating in deep, black space.

Christina was sitting on the stern, making final adjustments to her gear while trying to figure out how to stop Perry. As she tightened the strap on her mask, she saw Simon look at his cell phone.

Just can't live without them, she thought.

Simon turned toward Christina. He had a stern expression on his face. He watched her closely as his hand moved towards the ignition switch. When he started the engine, she knew instantly what was about to happen.

Christina yelled, "No!"

She lunged towards Simon, but the boat's strong acceleration and her heavy scuba tank slowed her down. She felt the impact, the crunching, and heard the motor stall.

When the engine stopped, the boat's acceleration stopped, but Christina's forward momentum didn't. Simon

157

was large and strong but hadn't anticipated Christina's strength and speed. Her added weight from the scuba equipment took care of the rest. He tried to step away from the steering console, but it was too late. They collided. The impact carried them both over the side rail. Simon fell backwards with Christina above him. When he hit the water, his speed slowed. Christina, tumbling through air, didn't. The top of her tank struck Simon's face a crunching blow. His nose broke instantly, and several teeth were knocked out. He was barely conscious.

Christina didn't hesitate. She hadn't inflated her BC yet, so she sank like a rock. She kicked hard towards the back of the boat while stuffing the regulator into her mouth, clearing the water out with one smooth motion. Ten meters behind the stern, she saw a steady stream of bubbles in the red-tinged water and dove straight down.

Perry's back and head throbbed. He had trouble seeing but knew he was sinking. His ears were about to explode. He tried kicking, but his legs were useless. He tried inflating his BC, but there was no change in his descent rate. He equalized the pressure in his ears and looked up towards the retreating surface. He saw a blurry trail of rising bubbles. The tank had a leak. At this depth, the air wouldn't last long. He searched for his regulator but found only a severed hose bleeding precious oxygen. He grabbed his backup regulator, pushed it in his mouth, and took a long, deep breath.

Christina kicked quickly towards the bottom, following the trail of bubbles. She saw something moving, something translucent. It oscillated back and forth, drifting toward the bottom. At first, she thought it was a jellyfish, but when she got closer, she recognized the shattered pieces of clear acrylic plastic, what used to be the housing for Perry's camera. She kicked harder.

Perry landed gently on the bottom, a thin layer of silt rising as if welcoming him to his final resting place. He continued to watch the rising bubbles as he tried to figure out his best course of action. His legs had transitioned from numbness to screaming fire. He'd taken a good hit to the spine. He couldn't think clearly. He'd taken a hard blow to his head as well, and at this depth, nitrogen narcosis would be taking its toll.

Why can't I surface? he wondered.

He tried swimming with his hands and made feeble motions with his legs. He glanced at his depth gauge, 60 meters, almost 200 feet. He couldn't spend more than a minute at this depth without suffering decompression sickness, if he didn't drown first. His air wasn't going to last that long.

Christina saw the bottom approaching and spotted Perry lying on his side. Seconds later, she landed on her knees next to him. A slight tinge of blood, bluish-green at this depth, clouded the water around his head and lower back. Confusion filled his eyes. She smiled, but with the regulator in her mouth, a sneer was all she could manage. She moved to rub his injured head, but he batted her hand away. When she offered Perry her backup regulator, the confusion ended. He discarded his own regulator and pushed her's into his mouth. Christina reached around and unstrapped his tank, seeing large gouges on the lower end of the thick aluminum. She straddled Perry's chest, wrapping her legs tightly around him. He struggled for a second before realizing what she was doing. She pressed a button on her vest, filling her BC. They rose, slowly at first, then faster. As they neared the surface, she bled off air to slow their ascent.

At three meters below the surface, Christina neutralized their buoyancy. They hovered weightlessly in the water. She knew they had to take a safety stop to prevent decompression sickness. She looked to see if Perry was still breathing. She watched him take long, slow breaths. *At least that camera is out of commission,* she thought. But her heart hurt. As she watched Perry floating below her, she realized that she cared for him.

v

Simon struggled to stay on the surface. He was severely hurt. Blood clouded the water and he couldn't see out of his left eye. He had to get away before Christina returned; he was in no condition to fight her. He had a splitting headache, and he felt nauseous. Swimming to the back of the boat, he climbed onto the swimming platform and tumbled onto the deck. He sat up and looked down to see a steady stream of blood coursing down his chest. Crawling to the helm, he pulled his cell phone from the cubby hole and pressed the green button twice.

"Andreo, it is me. I am injured, but do not worry, the American is lying at the bottom of the ocean."

"..."

"Yes, I am sure. I felt the prop tear right through him. I struck him so hard, I stalled the engine."

"..."

"The girl? I do not know. She disappeared under the surface. A real pity though, I could have had fun with her."

"..."

"Si` signore! Mi dispiace, signore. Right away. I will send my coordinates and stay submerged until I hear the boat approach. I have air for about 60 minutes."

Simon climbed down into the cabin and looked in a mirror to assess the damage. His nose was visibly crushed and bleeding profusely. His left eye had swollen shut. He had deep lacerations on his cheek, and when he probed, he felt pieces of broken bone. Simon pulled out his medical kit and used waterproof bandages to staunch the bleeding as best he could. Then he slipped into his wet suit, hung his face mask around his neck, and headed back up to the deck. Lifting a floor panel at the back of the boat, he reached down and opened a 3-inch seacock. Seawater immediately poured into the bilge. Simon restarted the engine, put the boat in gear, and pushed the throttle all the way forward before setting the autopilot for due north. He felt a severe vibration and realized he'd damaged the prop when he'd run Perry over. Using his marine radio, he sent a digital message of his GPS coordinates to Andreo, the head of security. Immediately after pressing the SEND button, Simon rolled over the side of the fast-moving vessel and crashed into the water.

Perry and Christina heard the boat's engine start. A half-minute later, the rpm increased, and the sound ebbed into the background. Christina released her leg hold on Perry and pulled him up to her. Grabbing the buckle to his weight belt, she released the last thing holding him underwater. They rose slowly to the surface.

When they reached fresh air, Perry spat out the regulator and yelled, "What the fuck just happened!"

"How much are you hurt?" Christina asked. "I thought you were dead."

"Are you hurt?" he asked.

"Me! You are the one who got run over by a boat. I am fine. You have a terrible wound on your head. Let me see your back."

Perry moved his legs but not without stabbing jolts of pain running up his spine.

Christina released her hold on him and unbuckled her own weight belt, letting it follow Perry's to the bottom. She turned Perry around.

"Your lower back is bleeding," she said.

"The bastard's leaving us out here!" Perry said, watching the dive boat in the distance. It was headed due north at full speed.

"This was no accident," she said. "He was trying to kill us."

"What?"

"If I had not landed on him, I think he would have finished the job. He had a crazy look in his eyes. I tried to stop him. When we fell overboard, I landed on top of him."

"How did you find me?"

"There was a stream of bubbles coming up so fast I thought Mount Etna had erupted again."

"I'd still be down there if it weren't for you."

"Well, it is not over yet. We still have some swimming to do."

They looked over at the distant shoreline while Christina removed her tank and BC.

"It's not that bad," Perry said. "We have the whole afternoon."

Christina nodded. "But can you swim?"

"I'm going to have to."

Perry reached over and put a hand behind Christina's neck. She didn't resist when he pulled her toward him and hugged her.

"You're shaking," he said.

She nodded, "I was terrified."

Perry hugged her tighter and then kissed her on the lips.

Christina pulled away but not before returning the kiss.

"I think you have a concussion," she said.

"Yeah, you might be right for once."

"Perry, I am right most of the time. I told you this was a bad idea. How are your legs? Do you need me to pull you?"

"No. I'm good."

"Okay, let us go before Simon changes his mind."

Christina swam toward the beach and Perry swam slowly after her.

After an hour of swimming, Perry and Christina reached the shallow water. He had to stop several times to rest, but every time Christina offered to pull him, he refused. They came ashore west of Canneto, close to a small beach. At the far end was a tiki hut bar. Perry's legs and back had loosened up with all the exertion, but they still throbbed, and he had a splitting headache.

Christina stood in the shallow water and waited.

"How are you feeling?" she yelled.

"I've been better."

He tried standing but lost his balance.

"I don't think I can walk."

Christina swam back to him.

"Just lie back and let me pull you ashore."

When Perry resisted, she grabbed his jaw in one hand and said, "Lie down!"

"Okay, okay," he replied.

Christina wrapped her arms around him and dragged him to shore, his heels carving two tracks in the wet sand. She lowered him to the ground and said, "I will go borrow a phone and call an ambulance."

"No! No, don't bother. I'll be fine. My back just needs a little time to recover."

"Perry, you just swam a kilometer. Your back is fine. It is your head I am worried about. You may have a concussion."

"Yeah, well, you know what they do for concussions, don't you?"

"No"

"Nothing. Bed rest is the only treatment. They'll put me in a hospital gown with my ass hanging out and make me lie in bed all day. They'll watch my behavior, and if anything strange starts happening, they'll cut a hole in my skull to relieve the pressure."

"It sounds like you have done this before."

"Yeah, and I'm not doing it again. Could you just call someone to take us back to your place? I'm going to need to rest for a while. And pain killers, lots of pain killers."

"Very well. We can always call the ambulance if your behavior becomes stranger."

He managed a weak smile. "Thanks."

Christina took a second opportunity to check for other injuries.

"Oh my, Perry! Your suit is ripped open. You have a terrible gash on your lower back. It is still bleeding."

"I told you it hurt."

"How did you swim so far? We need to get you off the beach. I will be right back."

"Christina!"

"Yes."

"Please, no police."

"Why? We need to call them. Tell them what happened."

"Let's just say I have some paperwork issues with immigration that I'd rather not get into."

"That does not sound important right now, but okay."

Perry didn't know that Christina had no intention of calling the police.

She peeled off her scuba suit and ran up to the tiki hut. Two minutes later, a small van was heading down the beach. Christina and a well-tanned man in surf shorts and a Grateful Dead T-shirt jumped out.

Christina called out, "I found a friend. This is Steve. We spend time together when I come down here to the beach."

"I didn't picture you as a beach person," Perry said. "I'm not sure I can handle any more surprises today."

"Do not worry, no more surprises. We will have you in your bed in less than fifteen minutes."

"Good, but before we go, will you cut this scuba suit off me. I'm getting pretty hot in here."

Steve pulled a folding knife from his pocket. "I got ya covered, mate."

"You speak English?"

"Better than you do, Yank. I'm from Australia."

Christina kept her promise. They pulled into her driveway ten minutes later. She, Steve, and Leo helped Perry out of the van and up the stairs to the bedroom. They cleaned up his head and back wounds using butterfly bandages for the most severe cuts. Then they gave him a healthy dose of painkillers.

"Thanks for all the nursing," Perry said as he lay back in bed.

"Perry, while we were cleaning your back wound, I could see a metal rod."

"Yeah, I had back surgery last year. If it were not for those rods, the prop would have cut me in half."

Perry thought back to his last mission and the young Saudi girl that ended his career.

Chapter 10

Day 5

Perry squinted from the afternoon sun streaming in through the open window. He'd just woken up. His head and back throbbed. He swung his bare legs over the edge of the bed and stood. A jolt of electricity shot down his spine. He jerked, knocked a water glass from the bedside table, and fell back into bed.

"You stupid son-of-a-bitch," he said to himself. "Why do you let yourself get into these situations?"

He heard footsteps rushing down the hallway and his door swung open.

"Are you okay?" Christina asked.

"Yeah, couldn't be better."

"You do not sound better. You must stay still."

"I found that out the hard way. I need to go to the head. Where are my clothes?"

"I will get you something to relieve yourself."

"What time is it? How long have I been out?"

"It is 2 p.m.," she answered. "You were sleeping for almost 24 hours."

"I don't remember much after you put me to bed. In fact, most of yesterday is a blur. I remember sinking to the bottom of the ocean and you saving me, but there are some gaps. What did you give me?"

"It was probably the Ambien. Amnesia is one of the side effects. We wanted to make sure you did not move for a while. I am sure your memory will clear up."

"Well, I guess it worked, but for future reference, you shouldn't give sleeping pills to someone with a concussion."

"Thank you. I will know better next time one of our guests is run over by a boat and refuses to go to the hospital."

Christina walked out and returned with a red terracotta vase.

"Here, this is the best I can find."

Perry swung his legs off the bed and tried to stand again, but Christina pushed him back down.

"You know that is not a good idea," she said, handing him the vase.

"Fine."

"Do you need help?" she asked.

"Yeah, right. I don't think so."

"Nonna has made you something to eat. I will be back."

"And coffee please. I'm going through caffeine withdrawal."

"Okay. But not until you have eaten and drunk some water."

"Yes, Mother."

Perry was in and out of sleep for the rest of the day. It was 3 a.m. when he finally climbed out of bed. He grabbed one of the burner phones from his backpack, turned it on, and waited. A minute later, the screen lit up showing eight missed calls and five messages. He dialed Stan's number.

"Perry! Where the hell have ya been? We have a team out searchin' for ya."

"Weren't you watching us?"

"Not anymore."

"Why not?"

"We lost the GPS signal from the camera. I was watching the satellite imagery in realtime. It looked like everything was going smoothly up til ya anchored. We saw some kinda scuffle and the boat took off. It headed due north at max speed. Without the tracking signal from the camera, we decided to follow the boat. It took about 20 minutes before we realized you weren't on it. We steered the satellite sensor back to where ya had anchored but couldn't find ya."

"Stan, he tried to kill us. He ran me over for Christ's sake. I can barely walk. If it weren't for Christina and those steel rods in my back, I'd be dead, or at least paralyzed."

"Are ya alright?"

"I'll be on my feet in a couple days, but the camera is toast. Without that, the only lead we have is that dive boat. We have to find it, find that captain."

"We already have."

"What?" Perry asked.

"The boat sank. We couldn't tell if you or anybody else were still on it."

"What about the captain?"

"We don't know where he is, but our team is on station."

"How'd they get there so fast?" Perry asked.

"We lucked out. We had a fast attack sub close by with a SEAL team on board. They were doin' some exercises in the northern Med."

Perry ran the scenarios through his head.

"He must have opened a seacock," Perry said. "Then set the autopilot to due north and jumped ship. If we could swim ashore, he could have. Check your track log. If the boat's speed steadily slowed, that's a sure indication it was taking on water."

"Hold on, let me check."

Perry heard Stan shouting orders in the background. Thirty seconds later, they had their answer.

"You're right, that's exactly what happened."

"So, Simon was probably in the water with us."

"Why would he do that?" Stan asked. "Why take that risk?"

"To make sure we were both dead?"

"But he didn't come after you," Stan replied. "He coulda run ya over again with the boat or swam after ya and finished ya off. And what about Christina? He even left a witness behind to tell the story."

"Christina thinks she hurt him pretty badly. He probably wasn't thinking straight."

"She seems like one tough lady."

"That's for sure. But someone put a lot of effort into this. Planting that dive boat at the right place and time. This was a well thought out plan, even if it did fail. I think it's a lot bigger than just one boat captain."

"We'll try to find some answers. Where are you? What's goin on."

"I'm back at the LaTorre house."

"Can you still operate, complete the mission?"

"Right now, I need a couple of days off my feet. My head feels like it's going to fall off every time I move, and my back is killing me."

"Okay, well hold tight. We'll git a new camera to you as soon as we can get it assembled. If that boat was a setup, how did they know what you were up to? You said you tried a dive shop first?"

"Yeah, but they were booked up and pointed us to the dive boat down at the pier. Damn it, Stan! I knew something was wrong. That boat wasn't tied up there two hours before."

"Who knew you were there? Who knew you were lookin' for a dive boat?"

"Plenty of people. I wasn't trying to keep it quiet; it was part of my cover. I'd had Christina make some phone calls. I'd told guests at the place where we'd spent the night in Cefalù. It could have been anybody. Just send in a team. This is a lot bigger than a one-man operation."

"We will, but it's not goin' to be easy. We can't just send assets into Sicily."

"Why the hell not?"

"It's Sicily, Franklin! Our guys would be spotted in a heartbeat. It's a tight-knit island. Everybody knows everybody. It's one huge damn family over there."

"I'm going to end up dead if you don't do something."

"I understand, but you're not the only one in danger. If this technology gits compromised, if someone else figures out how to track our targets or our assets, some good people are goin' to die."

"I know."

"Well git some rest and git better."

Perry spent the next hour reviewing his actions since landing at Sigonella. He came up with a dozen different scenarios where he could have been exposed, but none of them were certain. The one thing he couldn't understand was why'd they try to run him over but not Christina? He needed to talk to her; one word to the police and she could expose their whole operation.

Christina was in a heated argument with her uncle when Perry limped into the kitchen.

"What are you doing up?" she asked. "You should not be walking."

"I'm fine. I just need to move. I've been awake since three this morning."

"Sit down," Uncle Leo said. "We talk."

Perry had already planned his cover story, his second cover story. He sat down slowly at the table.

"Uncle Leo is insisting we call the police," Christina said. "He wants this man found and punished. I told him about your wishes not to call."

"If I understand," Leo said. "You are illegal alien."

"I assure you, I'm not an illegal."

"Perry, we checked your passport," said Christina. "You have no stamp of arrival into Sicily, or any other country for that matter. How can this be?"

Perry had screwed up. He'd been in such a hurry and so jet-lagged that he'd forgotten to get his passport stamped back in Rota. The military was lax about official immigration paperwork because their soldiers were automatically covered under international agreements. The few civilians that traveled on military aircraft had to be proactive in getting their passports stamped.

Perry went with his training. Tell as much of the truth as possible. Hide only the most critical pieces.

"I'm sorry, I haven't been honest with you. I'm not doing a story on Mount Etna and Sicilian culture. I'm investigating Canneto di Caronia."

"What?" Christina feigned surprise.

"I'm sure you know about the strange events that happened here fifteen years ago, the unexplained fires and... "

"Oh no, Perry. You are not one of those conspiracy fools, are you? I thought we were done with them. That was so long ago."

"There have been some recent unexplained events, and I've been sent to investigate."

"What events?" Leo asked.

"We have very sensitive low-frequency antenna arrays that track movements of ships in the Mediterranean. They're no secret to anybody, all our European counterparts know about these underwater sensors. We picked up some strange anomalies a couple of weeks ago that we triangulated back to Canneto. We don't know if the Mount Etna eruption had anything to do with it or if it's some deliberate attack on our tracking system, but we need to find out. It's preventing us from monitoring the ship traffic."

"How does that explain passport?" he asked.

"A simple oversight. I flew into Sigonella Naval Air Station on a military aircraft. They're very relaxed about proper immigration procedures. I forgot to get my passport stamped."

Christina knew the eruption had caused some disturbances. But it was her technology that was disturbed, not Perry's. She also knew it would have no effect on low-frequency antenna arrays. Perry was lying.

"Perry," Christina said. "If what you said is true, there is no reason not to call the police."

"Look, you don't want another bunch of quack scientists coming out here trying to find devils, ghosts and goblins, do you? The fact that these anomalies happened so close to All Souls Day is just going to make it worse. Besides, I talked with my boss; they said the interference has stopped, they're back online again."

"You appear to recover without permanent injuries," Leo said. "We wait."

"Thanks, and I'm so sorry about all this. I should have been more honest about why I'm here."

"Yes," Christina said. "And I was just beginning to trust you."

"I know."

Father Leo stared at Perry for a few moments. "This does not explain why someone tried to kill you," he said. "You almost have my niece killed!"

"I know and I'm sorry. I can't explain what happened out there."

"You should go back to bed," Christina said. "Get some sleep."

Perry tried to object, but she and her uncle made it clear that it wasn't a request.

After he left the kitchen, Leo said. "We are in trouble. Something must be done."

"Si`," Christina agreed. "He is lying. The Americans can detect the radiation."

"But how can they possibly have the technology?" Leo asked.

"I saw it with my own eyes. Perry's camera can see the neutrinos. If his camera can detect them, just imagine what one of their spy satellites can detect. The Americans have made huge advances in nanotechnology. They have caught up with us."

"That is very hard to believe," Leo said. "The chances of a satellite orbiting 300 kilometers above us looking down at our exact position are astronomical."

"Not if we have a volcano erupting in our backyard. The whole world knows about it. Everyone was watching it; we have been under a magnifying glass for the last week."

"Maybe they detected us from an airplane."

"No," Christina shook her head. "I had one of our people check the air traffic control radar plots at the Palermo airport. There was not a single track of an airplane within twenty kilometers of the beam."

Leo replied, "We must shut down the project while the Americans are here."

"We will require another week to repair the damage caused by the eruption. We will re-orient the BiniSphere, so it points straight down. It will be more difficult for them to find us. We will transmit the beam straight through the center of the earth and out into space somewhere in the South Pacific."

"They are going to find us eventually," Leo said. "There will always be stray emissions from the main beam. Even if we are pointing straight down."

"Actually…" Christina paused for a moment. "I think we have a little time."

"Why?"

"Two reasons," Christina said. "If their satellite can see us, if it can track us, they would already have our exact location. And, if they had any understanding of what we were doing, they would not have sent one person to search for the source. They would have sent commandos on a battleship."

"What is the second reason?"

"We were transmitting megawatts of neutrino energy into space. What do you think would happen to their satellite if it looked straight down our beam?"

"You are right," her uncle said. "Their camera would have been destroyed."

"Exactly," Christina said. "And the Americans have no idea why or how that happened. So, they sent someone to quietly investigate."

"You said Perry's camera was destroyed in the accident. He will need to wait for a new one before continuing his search."

"But what do we do then?" asked Christina. "We will not have the repairs completed in time."

"We need a diversion," said Leo. "Can you distract Perry until the repairs are finished?"

"Of course. That will be easy."

Leo thought for a second. "Do you realize we are having the final piece to our puzzle delivered right to us?"

Christina nodded. "I do. If we had his camera, we would be fully operational."

"But there is one other problem we are not addressing."

"What is that?" she asked.

"The boating accident was no accident."

"Si`," Christina nodded. "Someone else is involved."

"I need to talk to Don Tumeo. He can track it down."

"Be careful, Uncle. I do not trust him."

"Do not worry, he is on our side."

Stan had been sitting outside of Sheehan's office for 30 minutes when Emily said, "The deputy director is free now, you may go in."

Stan walked through the door to the inner office.

"Stan! Good to see you. Come have a seat."

"Yes sir."

"I read your email on Franklin's progress. That was a close call, I'm glad he's okay."

"It was sir. As I'd told ya before, we need to git one of our teams in there. It's too dangerous, Franklin's not qualified for this."

"I understand, but it's too risky," Sheehan said. "We can't take the chance of exposing more people to this."

"We need operators in there."

"It's too classified," Sheehan said. "We can't risk anyone else finding out."

"My guys are the best, and they already know what's goin' on. And they know how to keep their mouths shut. Does the Director know… "

"That is not your business, Sheppard. You might be Army, but you report to me, presidential orders. I handle the chain of command. Do you understand?"

"Yes sir, but there's a high risk of this blowin' up in our faces."

"I understand. Now sit down. The reason I called you into my office is to talk about these neutrino emissions. In your report, you said Franklin picked up the location from several different angles. Isn't that enough to triangulate on the source?"

"Yes, based on the look angle of the KH-11's PIT sensor just before it was destroyed and Perry's observations, we've calculated the emissions to be about a kilometer off the coast of Canneto and about 120 meters below sea level with a CEP of 200 meters."

"CEP?" Sheehan asked.

"Circular Error Probable," Stan said. "It's the errors in the measurements. There's a 50 percent probability that the location of the emissions is within a radius of 200 meters."

"50 percent? We need to be more accurate than that."

"I've been considerin' the idea that we might be dealin' with a submarine, but the water is only 60 meters deep. That means the source is another 60 meters deeper, 200 feet under the seafloor."

"200 feet? That's impossible. You stood here in my office the other day and said no one could build something like that without us knowing it?"

"I know sir. Either our geo-location numbers are wrong or, more likely, we've had a huge intelligence failure in Sicily."

"Unless, as you said before, the neutrino emissions are completely organic, natural," Sheehan said.

"True, but strong enough to fry a camera orbiting the earth? That's highly improbable."

"If we rule out everything else, then the improbable becomes probable."

"We haven't ruled out anything. Ya know yourself just how much our intelligence services had suffered at the hands of you politicians. Our human intelligence capabilities are still recovering, and all the focus has been in the Middle East," Stan said. "All we know for sure is that Franklin verified there are neutrino emissions. I suspect there is someone behind it."

Sheehan wanted to keep Sheppard in the dark as much as possible so he continued to sow doubt, using Stan's own words against him.

"But it might be natural. We're dealing with a very volcanic area, and there's a lot we don't know about those Majorana neutrinos."

"You're forgettin' one thing, sir."

"What?"

"The dive boat. Why send someone to kill Franklin if it were just some natural occurrence?"

"Maybe someone learned about them and wants to exploit it," Sheehan said.

"Then we've gone full circle. Franklin's all alone. We need muscle in there."

"What do you suggest?"

"We leave Franklin on station at the farmhouse. He's picked up the emissions right from the LaTorre's front yard. He'll set up 24-hour surveillance and contact us as soon as he zeros in on the source. Next, we send in a team. We tell them nothin' bout the PIT technology. It's merely a counter-surveillance operation to ensure Perry and our technology are safe from pryin' eyes. They'll be operators though. As soon as we zero in on the source of these hostile emissions, they'll have orders to take it out. Then everybody comes home."

"That's it?"

"Yes, sir."

"I thought you wanted Franklin out of there, immediately."

"I do, but more importantly, I don't want him runnin' around the countryside riskin' anyone else finding out about the camera. It's too dangerous. If there are some scientists there who have figured out a way to weaponize these neutrinos... well ,that's bad news all around."

"Okay, I'll send a team in."

"That's what I hoped you'd say. I've already put my guys on call this..."

"Negative! I'll send my own team in."

"What team? With all due respect, sir, this is my operation, my people. They're the best in the..."

"That's an order, Stan. This isn't your operation anymore. I'll have my people take care of it. Tell your guys to stand down."

"That doesn't make any damn sense."

"Do I need to remind you who's in charge?"

"No, sir."

"Good. You're dismissed."

After Stan left, Sheehan called his secretary into his office.

"Get the Alpha and Bravo Team Leaders in here ASAP. I've got work for them."

"Yes, sir."

Ten minutes later, two men walked into Sheehan's office.

Cal Atwood was 39 years old. He was short and squat. He had light skin and blonde hair he kept Marine short. In past times, it would have been a clue to Atwood's profession, but men's hairstyles had changed. Combined with his unshaven face, and the many tattoos on his arms, he could blend in with many of the millennials. Bravo Team leader, Greg Meyers, was a tall, dark man with a thick black mustache. He was in his mid-forties, and it was apparent he'd been in a few firefights in his time. Meyers had shrapnel scars on his face and arms and burn scars on his right ear and the side of his head. He carried himself with authority, seeming to flaunt his battle wounds by wearing short-sleeve shirts and close-cropped hair.

"Your missions are a go," Sheehan said. "Atwood, get your guys on the next flight to Sicily. I want you on station within 24 hours."

"Yes, sir."

"Meyers, set up round-the-clock surveillance on Sheppard and be ready to act on a moment's notice. He's getting too close and too suspicious. As soon as we get some accurate intel, he's finished."

"Will do sir. We'll be ready."

"You're dismissed, and if you screw this up, both of you might as well start running. I've got a lot more guys who would love to replace you."

Chapter 11

Day 6

The Alpha Team commander yelled over the din of the lumbering C130's engines. "Wheels down in 10. Get your gear ready."

The three other men nodded and moved their gear to the rear of the airplane. A few minutes later, the plane banked into its landing approach, lowered its flaps and slowed its airspeed. The cargo ramp started dropping several seconds before the C130 touched down at Sigonella NAS. It was 0200 hours, the NAS was asleep. The aircraft stopped at the end of the runway, where a small Toyota van was parked.

Atwood and his men, all dressed in casual Chino pants and sport shirts, were contract civilians. They specialized in conducting covert, direct-action missions outside the standard chain of command. They were secretive, exceptionally well trained and utterly unidentifiable except as four friends spending a week deep-sea fishing and drinking on Sicily's northern coast. After loading their bags of gear and themselves into the van, Brett asked, "Are you finally going to provide some mission details. It's hard to navigate when I have no idea where we're going."

Brett Martinelli, who went by DJ, was responsible for navigation, communications, and driving. He was a tall, lanky 35-year-old man of Mediterranean descent. Martinelli had olive skin, dark bushy eyebrows, and a permanent 5 o'clock shadow. Outside of the Scandinavian countries and the Far East, he could blend into any local population.

"Ok, here's the mission," Atwood said. "We have a rogue CIA agent named Perry Franklin who's teamed up with some unsavory scientists here in Sicily. These people committed an act of war last week by taking out one of our satellites. Deputy Director Sheehan didn't give me many details except that this is a high-priority nuclear counter-proliferation mission. Millions of lives are at stake. We need to capture the perpetrators, eliminate Franklin, and destroy their facility."

Garret, the team's sniper and surveillance expert, said, "This is fucked up. No mission planning? No rehearsal? What's our infil and exfil strategy? Are we urban or rural?"

Garret was 38 years old when he retired from the Army's 7th Special Forces Group. That was two years ago. He was a bear of a man. Standing six-feet, four inches, he had broad shoulders, a narrow waist, and skin so black he virtually disappeared during night operations. He could easily bench press 400 lbs., but was agile and quick and very, very patient. Ideal characteristics for a sniper, despite his size. He'd been an Army Ranger and had trained incessantly in unconventional warfare, special reconnaissance, direct-action, and counter-terrorism. The rest of the team were all prior military as well but had not been special operations. His three teammates had been trained in covert operations by the CIA's Special Activities Division and Garret had had a difficult time transitioning to their more informal ways of taking action against our nation's enemies. They were all initially part of the division's Special Operations Group, or SOG, a CIA department responsible for high-threat military or covert operations that the US government did not wish to be overtly associated. But his team had been released from government service soon after the new administration made sweeping changes to the US' counter-terrorism rules of engagement. In an instant, they all became contract professionals, where many of the strict rules that had separated them from the monsters they pursued had simply been thrown out. They were now under contract, working directly for the deputy director of national intelligence, Mike Sheehan. Garret hated working for him. Sheehan had little military experience and none in the intelligence community. He was a hack of a politician and Garret knew he wouldn't last long. But the money was triple what he'd been making in the Army, for doing essentially the same job: pointing and squeezing a trigger.

"Stop bitching," Atwood told Garret as he opened one of his cases. "All you need to know is they're all bad guys, every one of them. If someone gets in our way, we eliminate them, it's that simple. There are too many American lives at stake."

Atwood pulled out a hermetically-sealed mylar bag and ripped off the seal. He removed three folders and handed one to each of his men. The air around them had a faint acrid odor.

"Operational security is paramount on this mission. I've done all the planning. You'll find everything you need to know right there in those folders. Memorize them. The folders will slowly disintegrate into ashes."

Gregory, the team's medic and demolitions expert, eyed the front and back of the papers and brought them to his nose. Gregory, or Doc, as the rest of his team called him, was of average height and weight. He had red hair and freckled skin and seemed to have a permanent sunburn, even when they executed long missions in the more northern latitudes. Gregory was also, surprisingly, the second strongest man in the team, next to Garret. He had strength and endurance, making him a formidable opponent when he and Garret took their red force-blue force training a little too seriously; often ending up in an all too aggressive wrestling match on the ground. They had both grown up poor in Southern Appalachia and just didn't like each other.

"It smells like peroxide," Doc said.

"The oxygen in the air is already reacting with it. It'll start smoking in about a half-hour."

"Good to know since I've got 20 kilos of C4 under my seat. Are you sure we brought enough?" Doc said sarcastically.

"Relax. We all know you can put a match to that stuff without it going off." Atwood said. "Hell, I started a campfire with it last time I was in Pakistan."

"Whatever," Doc replied. "But this sure is a lot of explosives."

"We don't know how big this facility is," said Atwood. "We'll be prepared."

Brett drove the van out a small gate at the end of the airfield that had been conveniently left unlocked for their departure.

"Head northeast on 417," Atwood commanded. "Then take the A19, towards Palermo. We'll be at our observation post in two hours. As soon as we get to the OP, set up a perimeter. Garret, you and Brett will need to install some eyes and ears inside the LaTorre household. I want to know everything that's being said in that place. Martinelli, you're the only one that understands Italian, you'll be on the headset, 24-7."

"Roger," Martinelli replied.

Max Howell was sitting in his temporary quarters aboard the *USS Rhode Island*, currently moored at the General Dynamics Electric Boat Division's pier in Groton, CT. The sequestration of the sub had been a lot easier than he'd expected. All it took was one call from President Blake to the president of Electric Boat. Over the last few years, GDEB had received tens of billions of dollars in contracts from the US Navy. Blake made it crystal clear; those contracts were all in jeopardy. In less than five minutes, the naval chain of command had been bypassed and Naval

Reactors, the people with cradle-to-grave responsibility for all naval nuclear propulsion matters, had been sidelined.

Max wiped sweat from his forehead as he poured over the new design changes. His workstation had three large monitors mounted to the far bulkhead, each displaying various schematics of the new systems being installed on the sub. The modifications to the existing hardware were marked in bright fluorescent colors to track the multitude of changes required for his team to install the world's first nuclear-powered phaser.

The Ohio-class ballistic missile submarine was being tended to by a select crew of skilled machinists, pipe fitters, electricians, and nuclear technicians. Each team member was read into the program, the fake program, and sequestered for the duration of the mission. They were stripped of all electronic devices and were under heavy guard. There would be no communication whatsoever with the outside world. But working 12-hour rotating shifts, 7-days a week, gave them little time to think about it. They were all Navy servicemen, or prior-service contractors who were accustomed to this kind of treatment. And they knew they'd be well rewarded: the sailors with extra leave and accelerated promotions; the contractors making three times their typical hourly pay plus bonuses, if the tight schedules were met. The cover story was the installation and testing of a passive reactor cooling system that reduced the sub's acoustic signature by an order of magnitude. The device used subatomic particles to carry the thermal energy from the reactor out to the surrounding water, eliminating the need for noisy pumps and turbulence-producing cooling ports in the hull. It was a good story but a complete fantasy. Only a handful of Howell's people knew what was really happening or how dangerous it was. No matter how they modified their design, there was still a risk of the phaser going unstable.

Max's phone rang. Welcoming the distraction, he picked it up on the first ring.

"Howell here."

"Max, it's Sheehan. Where are we? How much longer?"

"We're on schedule, sir. We're installing the PIT sensor as we speak, and we've retrofitted our prototype to handle the increased power from the subs nuclear reactor. Another week and we'll start bringing systems up to see how well it works."

"Great news, I'll let Blake know. When will we be operational? We need the system up and running ASAP. There's shit happening in Sicily."

"A week after that, but remember, we can't be close to land when we fire this thing up. I still don't have the stability problem solved."

"Don't worry about that. We're going to grab one of the scientists down there and deliver him right to your doorstep."

"What if he doesn't want to talk?" Howell asked.

"They always talk, Max. Sooner or later, they always talk."

Chapter 12

Day 6 (Continued)

Simon stood outside the tall, wood-paneled office door and knocked. The left side of his face was swollen black and blue, and five angry stitches held a puckered, two-inch-long gash on his cheek together. He'd undergone surgery the day before to straighten his nose, now splinted and taped. White gauze and dried blood clogged his nostrils. An agonizing ten seconds passed before a command came from the other side of the door.

"Enter!"

He turned the bronze doorknob and walked in.

Don Tumeo stood at his massive mahogany desk. His dark brown eyes bore into Simon's as he held a small glass of Vergine Marsala.

He took a sip and said, "Come here. I want you to meet someone."

Simon saw a pair of legs dressed in black trousers and polished shoes sticking out from under a tall wingback chair in front of Don Tumeo's desk. As he approached, the stranger stood.

"This is Monsignor Leo LaTorre, the uncle of the woman you almost killed the other day."

"Monsignor! I had no idea. I am so sorry…"

Simon reached out and took Leo's left hand. He bent forward to kiss the monsignor's gold and diamond signet ring; a gift given to him by the Pope himself.

Simon saw it coming but had no time to react. Leo pulled his left hand back a split second before his right fist landed hard and fast on the bridge of Simon's nose.

The boat captain's head snapped back and he fell to the floor. Blackness filled his vision with unbearable pain. He struggled to push himself up off the cold tile and got to his knees. Blood poured from his ripped stitches, down his face and onto his shirt. The taped splint had torn away from one side, and his nose sat at an odd angle, shifted to the right. It felt as if slivers of glass had penetrated his forehead.

Leo removed a clean white handkerchief from his lapel pocket and wiped Simon's blood from his hand.

"Stand up!" Leo ordered.

Simon stood. Losing his balance, he grabbed for the chair back and waited for the next blow.

Leo said, "Your Don insists that he punish you, punish your family, by eliminating you from this earth. I personally believe that he would not be punishing your parents but doing them a great service. He would be removing you and your stupidity from their family line."

Simon, afraid to speak, nodded.

"You were very fortunate," Leo said. "My niece appears to have inflicted sufficient punishment on you by herself. Her actions are the only reason we will spare your life."

"Thank you, Monsignor LaTorre, Don Tumeo. I am very sorry for the confusion, I thought…"

"You thought?" the Don said. "You were given a specific job, and that did not include the elimination of anyone, including the American."

"But sir, he was too close… I was under strict orders not to let him…"

Simon saw the fury in the Don's eyes and stopped.

"You left that woman out there to die!" he yelled. "Do you not know who she is, how important she is to all of this? Leave, before I change my mind."

"Yes, sir."

Simon turned and headed quickly for the door. The Don and Father LaTorre watched as Simon ripped the swinging splint from the side of his face.

Don Tumeo called back to him. "Simon!"

He stopped and turned, dread returning to his face. "Yes, sir."

"Leave your nose as it is. Do not go back to the surgeon. It will serve as a reminder of the monsignor's compassion."

"Yes sir," he mumbled and walked out the door.

Don Tumeo said, "I'm very sorry, Father, for what happened. Somewhere, our communications had broken down. My head of security, Andreo, was informed by one of our travel agents that someone suspicious had arrived, coming in through Sigonella. When your signore…" The Don searched for a note on his desk.

"Franklin," Leo said. "Perry Franklin."

"Si`, signore Franklin. The man you introduced me to at the cemetery. There was something off about him. That is why Andreo instructed signora Parisi to book him into your casa, as a precaution… so you might keep an eye on him. Andreo performed a background check and found that this Franklin had worked for the government, doing what, we could not determine, but he had retired from civil service a year ago. That was odd. Retired government workers do not fly into Sigonella on military aircraft, only active duty and retired military have that privilege. When we learned of his intention to dive near Canneto, we called Simon."

"I had already reserved every dive boat within 50 kilometers," Leo said. "We had it under control."

"I know that now. Simon is new and very good at what he does. He had strict orders to avoid your underwater portals. When he realized too late that he had anchored right on top of one of them, he panicked. He had no idea Christina was one of ours."

"Christina is not one of yours!" Leo said sternly. "She never will be. You will stay away from her."

"Calm down, calm down, Monsignor. We are all on the same side. Christina had no business escorting this American around. She is too valuable, and he is too dangerous."

"Under normal circumstances, I would agree, but signore Franklin is much more than what he appears to be. He might hold the secret to our problem."

"What problem?"

"That is none of your business. The point is, he must not be harmed, and if any harm comes to Christina, it will be more than your boat captain who will be eliminated."

Don Tumeo was a powerful man in Sicily. He did not like being threatened but knew Leo had the authority to carry through on his actions. There was no room for mistakes, for any of them. They were too close. The Mafioso chief walked to his office door and opened it.

"I think we are finished here. We will take no further actions without communicating with you first."

"Good," said Leo.

"I believe you know your way out."

Leo walked out of the Don's office, across the polished marble foyer, and through the front doors, into the bright Cefalù sunlight.

Chapter 13

Day 7

Perry studied the high-resolution overhead imagery of Canneto. It was a series of time-lapse images collected over several days by one of their satellites. He was looking for anomalies: strange traffic patterns, hidden entrances, anything that would give him a clue as to what was going on. His phone rang.

"Stan, it's about damn time," Perry said. "I'm going stir crazy over here."

"How are ya feelin'?"

"Still stiff and a splitting headache, but besides that, I'm fine."

"Good. Look, the camera is on the plane headin' for Sigonella. Are ya okay to pick it up this afternoon?"

"What time does it land?"

"1530 local."

Perry looked at his watch. 1000 hours.

"I'll be there."

"Oh, and we found the boat."

"Good! Did you learn anything?"

"You were right, the guy scuttled it," said Stan. "There was nothin' pointin' to who owned it. It had fake registration numbers."

"Not surprising."

"We've already sent in a team."

"You mean I can get the hell out of here?"

"No, they're just for keepin' you safe. You won't even know they're there."

"Are you kidding me?" said Perry

"You don't need to do anything, just stay put at the LaTorre house. You're in a good over-watch position. Set up the camera and keep lookin' out over the water. Once you've pinpointed the source, we'll have the team investigate."

"I guess that works. But tell your guys to stay close."

"Franklin, they're not my guys."

"What?"

"Sheehan is worried about security. He sent one of his black teams."

"His contract guys?" Franklin asked.

"Yeah, I don't like it either. Something is fishy, and I'm goin' to find out what."

"Okay, well, forget what I said about keeping them close. I'll be safer without them."

"Yeah, no kiddin', but I have no control over it. They'll be watchin' ya. Okay, I gotta go. Text me when ya have the camera and yur back on station."

"I will."

Christina walked out to the terrace a few minutes after he'd hung up the phone.

"Perry, Nonna is making a salad for lunch, and then I need to go back to the university to..."

"Okay. That's fine. I need to drive over to Sigonella to pick up the new camera."

"Your camera? We have plenty of good camera stores here in Sicily. Why have one shipped into your military base?"

Perry didn't answer.

"Because it is not just a camera, right?" she continued. "It detects the signals interfering with your antenna arrays."

"Maybe."

"I will go with you. You should not be driving. You are still recovering from a concussion and back injury."

"I'll be fine, and you said you need to go back to the university?"

"You seem to think you have a choice," she replied. "The university can wait."

Christina leaned Perry forward and checked the bandages on the back of his head and lower back. He winced when she prodded the wounds.

"How is your back feeling?" she asked.

"Better," he replied.

"Very well, we will go after lunch. I will drive so you can relax."

Perry and Christina arrived at Sigonella at precisely 1530 hours.

"If you don't mind," Perry said. "Pull into the car rental lot across from the main gate. The guard won't let you through without filling out a bunch of paperwork. I'll drive over to the terminal to get the camera. It's not far."

Christina drove the car onto Roberto's rental lot, parked, and they got out.

"I'll be right back," he said as he slipped into the driver's seat.

Perry drove across the street and flashed his ID at the military guard standing at the front gate. Ten minutes later, he pulled back into the rental car lot, parked the car and walked over to where Christina was talking to Roberto.

Christina switched from Italian to English.

"It was completely shrouded while driving in," she said to Roberto.

"The afternoon sun burns off the clouds quickly," Roberto replied. "Signore Franklin. Nice of you to check-in. I was worrying that my little bambino was not going to be returned."

Roberto patted the dented fender of the Fiat.

Perry laughed and said, "Somehow, I find that hard to believe."

"I was just talking with your beautiful girlfriend here about…"

"She's not my girlfriend," Perry said.

"Okay," Roberto winked. "We were talking about the Mount Etna eruption. It was very dramatic."

They all looked northward at the giant plume of white smoke still billowing from the mountain.

Perry said, "I hear you can climb right to the top."

"Yes," Christina replied. "But who would ever want to?"

"You've never been there?" Perry asked.

"Never had the desire. It is a volcano. They explode."

Roberto said, "You really must go. It just erupted last week."

"That is not very convincing," she said.

"C'mon," said Perry. "What's the odds of it happening twice in a row."

"No," Christina said.

Roberto continued. "It is quite rare. All four cones erupted at the same time. "

Perry looked at Christina with a gleam of excitement in his eyes.

"No! I do not want to go. Besides, you are in no condition to be driving up a mountainside, let alone hiking to the top."

"That's fine," Perry said. "I'm just picking on you. Let's get back to the house."

Christina was in no hurry for Perry to return to Canneto. They still needed another day to complete the repairs on the BiniSphere.

"I had been hoping to visit a vineyard on the north slope of Etna on the way back. A friend of the family produces a wonderfully intense, earthy wine. We stock up on it every year."

Perry didn't see any harm in the little detour.

"That I can agree with," he said.

After saying goodbye to Roberto, they drove northeast through Catania and headed north on the A18. The volcano rose into the clouds west of the highway, while the blue Mediterranean Sea glistened at the bottom of the craggy slopes east of them.

Halfway between Catania and Messina they exited the A18 and headed west toward the northern slopes of Etna.

The Patria Azienda Vinicola was a sprawling stone winery surrounded by hundreds of hectares of vineyards. Perry and Christina drove through the wrought iron gates and parked in the empty parking lot. A worker walked up to the car and spoke to Christina.

"What's wrong?" Perry asked.

"No problem," Christina said. "He was just informing me that the tours have closed for the day. I told him my American friend and I were hoping to purchase a couple cases of wine. He has gone to collect Mario."

"Mario?"

"Yes, he is the son of the owner. We were close at one time, a long time ago."

"So, you actually did have a boyfriend."

"Is that so shocking?"

"Well, you're certainly pretty enough," Perry said. "I just wonder what kind of man can withstand you."

"You are such a smooth talker."

They were just getting out of the car when Mario came bounding around the corner with a broad smile on his face.

"Christina!" he yelled. "It has been too long." He ran up and hugged her tightly.

Mario was a tall man with a dark complexion and bright blue eyes.

"I understand you have an American friend with you," he said, turning to Perry.

"Si`," Christina said. "This is Perry Franklin. He is staying with us for a short time."

"Signore Franklin, a pleasure." Mario shook Perry's hand tightly and slapped him roughly on the back.

Perry winced but kept a tight smile on his face.

"Perry, this is Mario Finocchio. We went to school together. Our families have been friends for generations."

"Have you ever been to a winery before?"

"I've been to a wine bar," Perry said. "Does that count?".

Mario laughed.

"Come, signore Franklin. Follow me. Let me show you how it is all done. Then we will sample some of the best vino in Sicily."

The three of them walked across the yard toward a sizeable ancient barn. A truck and trailer, parked just outside the front door, was feeding a large hopper hundreds of pounds of the dark blue grapes.

"We are right at the end of our harvest season. These grapes over here are of the spumante variety. They are from one of our highest vineyards, where the cool night air of Mount Etna extended their maturity until now. Most of our grapes were harvested a month ago."

"I never would have guessed that you could grow grapes in volcanic soil," Perry said.

Mario continued. "Here is where it all starts. The grapes from our vineyards are brought in on trucks and dumped right into the top of this destemming machine."

Perry and Christina looked down into the large trough where an auger was spinning.

"After the stems are removed, the crushed grapes, what we call the must, are poured into the fermentation tanks."

Mario led them into the barn where they found a dozen tall stainless-steel tanks with pipes and hoses heading off in all directions.

"The fermentation process takes several weeks, then we transfer the wine into oak casks."

Mario led them down a set of stone stairs where a cool, moist air enveloped them. At the bottom, they entered a dimly lit, cavernous room. The walls were volcanic and lined with huge wooden casks. Perry heard water dripping nearby.

"This is where we allow the wine to mature," Mario said. "Our reds stay in these casks for up to 3 years."

"This is amazing," Perry said. "You excavated this cellar right into the volcanic rock."

"Si`. But remember, it was not me who excavated this. It was my great-grandfather who dug this cellar by hand over 150 years ago. The rock is very porous, and there are natural springs that keep it wet. The porosity enhances the evaporation of the water, which provides a cooling effect. Come!"

Mario led them to the other side of the cellar where they found a bare wall unobscured by the oak casks.

At the base of the wall was a small grotto filled with water.

"Look at the colors in the wall," Mario said, pointing to striated bands of earthy black, brown, red and orange that created a rainbow effect.

"Each color represents a different eruption, a different lava flow," Mario explained. "You are looking at thousands of years of volcanic history."

"The wine itself," Christina added, "is an expression of the minerals, the flora and fauna of our present conditions. All integral to the mountain. Even the micro-climate here has such a significant effect on the quality of the wine. It is all a living, breathing organism."

Christina looked intensely at Perry. "Do you understand?" she asked. "The mountain and the people of this region are inseparable."

Perry nodded.

"Come, Christina! You are always so serious," Mario said. "Let us go to drink and be merry."

Perry leaned over to Christina and said, "Is he always like this? Or has he been drinking the profits?"

"A little of both," she said. "He was born into a wine family, that explains it all."

They walked out of the barn and over to a stone building with a large veranda.

"Go sit down," Mario said. "I will return shortly."

The warmth of the day had given way to a cool breeze flowing down the mountainside.

Perry sank into a lounge chair and let out a long sigh. "This feels nice."

"It is amazing, is it not?" Christina said as she sat next to him. "The more the vines struggle to eke out their precarious existence, the higher the quality of wine. As Mario said, the cool air washing over the grapes slows their ripening. The climate, the unique environment, the basalt rich soil, the minerals, they all help to create its unique quality, its terroir. There is nothing like it in the world."

"Like many Sicilian things," Perry said.

Mario returned with several bottles of wine and three glasses.

"Nonna will come in a minute with a few antipasti," he said.

"You are always so accommodating," Christina said. "I only wished to purchase a few cases to take home."

"For you, I would stop the world," he said.

Christina rolled her eyes and leaned toward Perry as Mario went to work uncorking the bottles.

"He can be so dramatic," Christina said.

"I can hear you, mia cara," Mario said, and they all laughed.

Mario poured a chilled Etna Bianco Patriainto into the stemmed glasses.

They inhaled the aroma of citrus fruit and spice and soil. Perry knew before it even touched his lips that this was going to be good.

He took a sip, savored the taste, and his eyes opened wide.

"Wow."

The three of them spent the next two hours tasting the different varieties of wine while grazing on a constant stream of appetizers that Mario's nonna kept supplying from the kitchen.

The sun had already set when Christina finally said, "We should start heading home."

Nonna interrupted quickly. "Sciocchezze, amore mio, tu e il tuo amico passerete la notte. Troppo buio e hai bevuto troppo."

"Si` Nonna, hai ragione, grazie," Christina replied.

"What did she say?" Perry asked.

"That it is too late to go home, and we have had too much to drink. She insists that we spend the night."

"I suppose she's right. Should you call your Nonna to get permission?" he chided.

Christina laughed. "I do not think that is necessary. I do not understand why, but you seem to have her on your side. It is my uncle you should be worried about."

"Yeah, I don't think he likes me very much."

"Either way, they are not at home tonight. My uncle took Nonna to visit family in Catania."

"Come," said Mario. "You stay the night with us. Let me show you to your room."

"Rooms, Mario," she replied. "We are not a couple."

"Oh! Scusami. I just assumed, "

"Yes, I am sure and I am getting tired of people assuming."

Mario laughed. "Then there is hope for me yet!" and he waved a hand for them to follow him.

Mario led them to a small, stone guest house separated from the main house. On the ground floor was a simple kitchen and living area with a terracotta-tiled floor. Sitting in the center was a solid wooden table with a multitude of scars, and areas worn down in the center from chopping and slicing. The white porcelain gas stove against the wall was chipped and worn in places. An iron spiral staircase in the corner led them up to two tiny bedrooms and a bathroom. Mario entered each room and swung open the shutters, letting a fresh breeze blow through.

"It is not very elegant, but it is comfortable," Mario said. "There are linens on the shelf downstairs. Please make yourself at home."

"Thank you," Christina said. "You are still an amazing man."

"Ahh, amore mio, then why did you leave me?"

"Leave you? Please, Mario, you knew we had no future. You are tied to this land and I will never… "

"I understand, perdonami my insensitivity."

Christina nodded, and Mario bid them goodnight with a wink and a smile.

"Good luck, signore Franklin," he said. "You will be needing it."

After Mario left, Perry asked, "What was that all about."

"Nothing important, just old wounds," she answered. "Speaking of wounds, how is your back?"

"It's fine," Perry said.

"Lie down and let me look."

Perry loosened his pants, lay face first on the bed, and flipped his shirt up.

"Oh, it has been bleeding. You really should have had it stitched."

"It will heal up; it just needs a little more time."

"Well, if you sat still for a few days it might. Let me have your car keys. I will go get the butterfly bandages."

Christina walked to the car and popped the trunk. Inside was the Pelican case. She opened it, finding Perry's new camera nestled into the black foam cutout. Remembering what she had seen when Perry was operating the camera on the dive boat, she removed it from the case, unfolded the display and turned it on. The screen lit up, ran some diagnostics, and then an image appeared. Christina scanned the lens quickly north, towards Canneto. Nothing. She adjusted the settings until she could increase the sensitivity and then relaxed. *They must have finished repairing the leak,* she thought. Then the screen saturated bright red, *What is that?* she wondered. She scanned the camera back and forth. Whenever she got close to the trunk of the car, the screen went completely red. She put the camera down and searched the Pelican case. Hidden behind the foam insert in the lid were five zip-lock packets. They each contained a gold powder. She waved one in front of the camera lens, and it flashed red again. *This is impossible!* she thought. *Our people are using a huge particle accelerator to produce heavy neutrinos, and here they are right here, in powdered form.* "Unbelievable," she said out loud. She slipped two of the packets into her pocket, returned the camera to its case, and closed the lid.

When Christina returned with the bandages, she found Perry on his feet. He was looking at a plaque hanging on the wall in the bedroom. He read it out loud.

"A spreading bay is there, impregnable

To all invading storms; and Aetna's throat

With roar of frightful ruin thunders nigh.

Now to the realm of light it lifts a cloud"

Christina recited the remaining words from memory, "Of pitch-black, whirling smoke, and fiery dust,

Shooting out globes of flame, with monster tongues

That lick the stars; now huge crags of itself,

Out of the bowels of the mountain torn,

Its maw disgorges, while the molten rock

Rolls screaming skyward; from the nether deep

The fathomless abyss makes ebb and flow."

201

Christina thought about Mount Etna and the small packet of powder in her pocket, streaming neutrinos out into the universe.

"It is by an ancient Roman poet named Virgil. He wrote it around 20 BC. It is the first written documentation of Mount Etna erupting."

"It's beautiful," Perry said. "But, it has so much darkness at the same time."

"I think there is something that we love about the darkness," she said. "It brings comfort. Nonna wrote it down and gave it to me a month after my parents died. I still have the letter in my bedroom drawer."

"Why would she do that?" Perry asked.

"It is not something I wish to discuss."

"Why not?"

"It is none of your business," she said. "Go lie down so I can change your bandage."

Christina pulled the blood-soaked bandage from his back and cleaned the wound with alcohol.

"I was thirteen years old," she said.

"What?" Perry asked.

"When my parents died."

"Oh, I'm very sorry."

"The newspapers wrote that they should not have been there, that they should have known better."

"Been where?" Perry asked.

"On Mount Etna, while it was erupting."

"Wait!"

Perry struggled to roll over, but Christina pushed his shoulders back down into the mattress.

"Those were your parents that died almost thirty years ago? Up on Mount Etna?"

"Si`, please stay still," she said as she applied the fresh butterfly bandage. "The news articles said they were out hiking, that it was a freak accident. That was not entirely the truth. We were looking for mineral samples."

"We?" Perry asked.

"Yes, I was there."

"I had no idea. The director said nothing about you being there."

"The director?"

"Of the Mount Etna Observatory. I interviewed him the other day, before I came to stay with you. He'd explained that it had been 30 years since someone died because of an eruption."

"Dr. Gerard did not know," she said. "What they were doing was a secret. It was kept undercover. No one even knew I was with them. It was reported that they were just out sightseeing."

"But they weren't?" Perry asked.

"No, they were scientists, collecting samples of a special mineral that was being ejected by Etna. I was a strong-minded teenager. They did not want me to go, but I insisted. I wanted to help."

"Most teenagers would have been wanting to do the opposite," Perry said.

"I was a curious child, they encouraged it. They eventually gave in and let me come along. When we arrived, I ran up the mountain ahead of them, searching for the minerals. They yelled for me to stop, but I did not hear them. The roar of the volcano was deafening. By the time they reached me, we were too close to the lava. We turned around and began hiking back down. That is when there was another explosion. My mother and father saw the magma flying through the air. They both jumped on top of me."

Christina finished applying the new bandage to Perry's back and got up from the bed.

When he rolled over and sat up, she turned her back to him and unbuttoned her blouse. She let it slide off her shoulders to the floor. On the right side of her back, just below her bra strap, was a red burn scar the size of a giant hand.

"This is all that happened to me," she said softly. "They were not as lucky. It was not quick. They were in agony for a long time."

Perry walked over to Christina and wrapped his arms around her.

Her words were muffled as she spoke into his chest. "That is why I could never be with Mario. His whole family, his whole world is centered on Mount Etna, on these vineyards. Even here, fifteen kilometers away from the summit, my heart pounds in panic."

Tears rolled down Christina's cheeks. She wiped them away and said, "I do not know why I am telling you this. I am being foolish. This is what happens when I have had too much to drink."

"Not at all," he said. "It's good to talk about it."

Perry led Christina to her bedroom and had her lie down. He pulled off her shoes, covered her with a blanket, and sat next to her.

Placing a hand on her scar, he whispered, "It was a terrible accident. I lost my mom when I was very young. In a car accident. My dad never remarried."

She nodded, her head against the pillow. "I have never recovered from it. I know it was a long time ago, but it seems like just the other day. I am terrified of that mountain."

They had been silent for a few minutes when Perry said, "Back home, in Maine, one of my neighbors, Mary, has a Doberman Pinscher. She must keep him locked up because he terrorizes the neighborhood. He's killed two cats and a dog and bitten a neighbor down the street, so she put up a tall fence to keep him in the back yard. My wife, my ex-wife, Julie, has a little Chihuahua named Allie. A couple years ago, when we were still together, we were sitting out on the front porch drinking our morning coffee. Allie was sitting on Julie's lap. It was one of the few times I wasn't working. It was a beautiful morning, very peaceful, until all hell broke loose. Mary's Doberman came charging around the corner of our house and headed straight for us. It was growling; its teeth bared. As soon as Allie saw the Doberman, she jumped out of Julie's lap. I thought for sure Allie was a goner. Her tail was wagging. She was yapping and jumping and ran straight for the Doberman. My heart just sank. That dog was going to tear Allie to pieces, and I knew I'd never get to her in time. I leaped out of my chair while Julie calmly sat there, taking another sip of her coffee. It was surreal. Like watching a train wreck as the person next to you enjoys the show. I had jumped off the porch when I saw the Doberman turn tail and run straight back towards his own yard. That dog's chain-link fence was six feet high, and in one bound, it reached the top and jumped down to the safety of its pen. Allie ran to the fence, hopping back and forth, barking, trying to get the Doberman to come play. I couldn't believe what I was seeing. I looked back at Julie. 'What the hell just happened?' I asked."

"Julie laughed and said, 'When Allie and that Doberman were puppies, they were the same size and they played together. Then Mary took the dog to get his ears clipped. When he came back from the vets, they were playing again. Well, Allie couldn't resist those bright white bandages. She latched onto his bandaged ear with her sharp teeth and would not let go. That Doberman screamed to high heaven, jerking his head back and forth, but Allie held on tight. When I heard the ruckus, I ran out and separated them. Mary was so upset, she never let them play together again. That was a big mistake on her part. On the rare occasions they come face-to-face, the Doberman either cowers behind Mary or runs back to its pen. As big and fierce as he is, he's never forgotten that encounter. The fear of that little Chihuahua has never gone away.'"

Christina, with her back still turned to Perry, thought for a moment and said, "So you are saying I am the harmless little Chihuahua that could confront the mountain if... "

"No darling," Perry said, reaching up and running his fingers through her hair. "You're not the Chihuahua, you're the Doberman. Mount Etna is the Chihuahua."

Christina rolled over and looked at Perry.

He said, "In the grand scheme of things, Mount Etna is pretty damn harmless. We're a lot more likely to die in a car wreck on these freaking mountain roads of yours then at the hands of Mount Etna. You were hurt terribly at a young age and never learned to have faith that it wouldn't happen again. Like the Doberman, you never had a chance to experience anything other than intense pain. You never returned to the mountain."

"Do you think the Doberman was so vicious because of that one incident?"

Perry shrugged his shoulders. "Fear's a funny thing. It can be irrational. We all have these episodes buried in our past. Fear of water, fear of strangers, or heights, or abandonment, or dogs. Just a single incident at a young age, and your neurons get locked into a pattern of anxiety that lives long after the real threat has disappeared. How you react to that anxiety, fight or flight, just depends on the dog, or the person, or the circumstances."

"I guess you are right," Christina said. "I feel like I have been locked in that fear my whole life."

"Yeah," Perry said. "Maybe that's why you avoid close relationships. Like that Doberman, you can be pretty abrasive at times. Maybe it's because you're afraid of the pain of losing another relationship. Isn't that what anxiety is all about? Anticipated pain?"

Christina nodded her head.

"In fact," Perry continued, "I'm surprised you haven't kicked me out of your bed yet."

Christina elbowed Perry hard in the ribs.

"Ouch!"

Christina sat up. "That is what you get for trying to take advantage of a drunk woman with your bullshit."

Perry laughed, "It almost worked, didn't it?"

"Go to bed."

"Buonasera," he said. "And thanks. I had a nice time today."

"Me too."

After Perry left, Christina lay in bed wondering what Perry was afraid of. What was he avoiding with his sarcasm? Why did he break the mood so quickly?

She pulled one of the small packages of gold powder from her jeans pocket and held it up to the light.

And what in God's name is he doing with this, she wondered.

Chapter 14

Day 8

It was 8:35 the next morning when Perry and Christina pulled into the driveway. As they unloaded the cases of wine, Christina said, "Thanks for last night. You were an absolute gentleman."

"You're welcome. I know I'm an ass most of the time, but I like to think that when things get real, I can rise to the challenge."

"Well, I wasn't going to say anything about that since you were being so polite." Christina hip-checked Perry as she lifted a case from the trunk.

"I really wish you'd stop doing that."

"I am sorry. I did not realize how much pain you are still in. Let us forget about the wine and get you to bed. I think you still need more time to heal."

"That's a good idea," Perry said. "Will you grab the case with the camera. I don't want to leave it in the car."

"Of course, but promise me you will go straight to bed," she said.

"I promise, but please back off. I'm a grown man. You're not my mother."

Christina shook her head and walked away.

"Then get your own camera," she said as she walked away.

Perry unpacked the camera and set it up outside the terrace doors of his bedroom. Using landmarks on the shoreline and the camera's GPS, he aligned the viewfinder to center on the bare expanse of ocean where the dive boat had been anchored. Activating the sensor, he expected to see the familiar red glow he'd seen the other day. There was nothing. He adjusted a few parameters on the screen, increased its sensitivity but didn't find the signal.

Hmmm, that's strange, he thought.

He walked into his room, opened his laptop, and ran a geo-referencing program, typing at the keys until he found the correct coordinates for their safe house in Somalia. He went back to the camera and pointed it 12 degrees down towards the floor and rotated it southeast to a bearing of 132 degrees true. He looked in the viewfinder.

Nothing! he thought. *They sent me a broken camera.*

He grabbed the burner and held down Stan's speed dial number.

"Franklin," Stan answered. "Did ya…"

"Stan! What the hell! The camera isn't working."

"It was workin' fine when it left here. We calibrated it and tested it."

"There's no signal, even when I point it at our stash in Somalia. Nothing!"

"Point it at the Pelican case," Stan said. "We sent ya five packets of nanotubes in case ya need them."

Perry put the phone on speaker and went back out to the balcony. He leveled the camera and swung it around, towards the bedroom. The viewfinder immediately saturated red.

"Got it!" he said. "But why can't I see the stash in Somalia?"

"I don't know. I'll check into it."

"What do you want me to do?"

"Stay where you are and keep monitoring that spot on the ocean. That must be where the beam came from. This is important Franklin; we need to know the exact coordinates as soon as possible. Whatever it is, we're goin' to take that sucker out."

"Okay, I'll set up the automatic alert on the camera. It'll monitor that area 24/7. As soon as it gets a hit, the camera will text me the coordinates. Have you heard anything more about Sheehan's goons being on station?"

"No, I'm afraid I'm out of the loop on that one. If I were you; I'd assume they're there and ready to pounce as soon as ya send me the coordinates."

"Okay, when I detect a signal, you'll be the first to know."

"Great, check in with me every 24 hours, so I know ya haven't been run over again."

"Fine, and Stan, find out what happened with the stash in Somalia."

"Will do."

Perry hung up the phone and went back to his laptop. He pulled the coordinates for several other depots around the world. Repositioning the camera to the new coordinates, he searched for the nanotubes methodically. Croatia, Korea, Kuwait... none of the locations trigged the sensor.

Something is wrong, he thought.

Perry knew he couldn't search the entire surface of the earth for his nanotubes. It would be like looking through a soda straw. It would take forever. He repositioned the camera to the flat piece of ocean just off the shore and programmed it to send alerts to his cellphone.

I guess I'll just sit back and wait. Let Stan worry about the rest. That's his job.

Perry walked to the bedside table and grabbed some more painkillers. His head throbbed. He'd been pushing his recovery too hard.

A few hours later, Christina knocked on Perry's door, and walked in.

Eying the camera and tripod just outside the terrace doors, she said, "Come down to the kitchen and eat something."

"No thanks," Perry said. "But I do need to move a little bit. My back muscles are tightening up from all the sitting and driving. I think some walking will help loosen me up."

"That is a very good idea."

"Yeah, as long as you don't run me over with a truck or something."

"I do not own a truck."

"I guess I'm safe then."

"I can always borrow one," she said. "But, I am going to the farmers market to buy some groceries for Nonna. You are welcome to come if you want to walk around."

"Perfect. Let me take a shower first. I'll be down in 15 minutes."

"Come down whenever you are ready."

Returning from the shower, Perry checked the settings on the camera one more time. The heading was off several degrees and the clamp locking the tripod head was loose.

How did I screw that up? he wondered. Must be the pain pills.

He readjusted the azimuth, locked the tripod head tighter, and headed downstairs.

Perry and Christina strolled along the crowded market street in Cefalù. The voices of the vendors called out, "CALAMARI FRESCA!!" and "PREZZO DI LIQUIDAZIONE!!" Their announcements were mixed with the hum of mopeds and the laughter of children as they ran through a maze of customers, vegetable crates, and baby strollers. Everyone was looking, bartering, and searching for that special ingredient for the evening meal. The sheer variety of what was to Perry "exotic foods" kept the two of them tunneling deeper into the crowd. They came across clams barely submerged in their shallow basins, spitting streams of water across the table. There were huge, white pig legs lying on the bloodied butcher's block and freshly caught swordfish with their foils pointing into the sky. Cheeses. There must have been 50 different varieties. Wet mozzarella balls wrapped in cloth and tied with a reed of dried grass. Hard, aged blocks of dark orange and yellow with names he couldn't pronounce. They spent an hour wandering the stalls, smelling herbs, watching people, squeezing warm freshly baked bread, sampling olives. Perry followed Christina as she shopped in the mass of confusion.

"There're so many vendors," he said. "How do you know which ones to trust? Especially when buying pork or chicken. The meat is just sitting out there in the open. Wouldn't it be better if we went to a grocery store?"

"We have trusted these vendors for centuries," Christina said. "If a large store sells you something less then fresh, you might stop patronizing them. But it will not put them out of business. They are huge, they have tens of thousands of customers; they can weather the storm of occasional poor quality. If one of these small vendors sells you bad meat, they are finished. Everyone knows each other here; the word spreads fast and their livelihood goes away in an instant. These vendors do not just sell safe food, they sell the best. They compete every day, that is what keeps them in business. The big stores have less competition, they can get away with more inferior products than our friends here. And, the money I am spending right now… it stays right here in the community… it does not go into an investor's pocket in Naples or Rome."

"I never looked at it that way. It's very different in the US. We certainly have higher-end stores that offer freshness and quality, but here in Sicily, it seems like a way of life, for everyone, not just for those who can afford it."

Perry and Christina finished shopping and found a small alcove at a cafe overlooking the water. They put their grocery bags down and ordered a bottle of Chianti and antipasto. The waiter brought assorted cheeses, fresh bread, olives and olive oil. The two of them sat alone at a large stone table with an awning protecting them from the afternoon sun. They sipped their wine while watching a small sailboat tack back and forth in the harbor.

"The sounds of the market seem to be ebbing," Perry said.

Christina looked at her watch. "It is almost 1300, riposo."

"Riposo?" he asked.

"Yes, siesta, we call it 'riposo'."

"I didn't hear your Uncle Leo or Nonna this morning."

"They are still visiting family in Messina," she replied. "They will be back tonight."

"We have the whole house to ourselves?" he winked.

"The wine must be having an effect on your perception of reality."

"It's the painkillers," he said. "I get more bang for the buck with each sip of wine."

"Bang for the buck?" Christina asked. "I am not familiar with that term."

"It's a colloquialism. It means you get more for your money."

"Perry... there is something I have been meaning to ask you."

"What?"

"That day in the water, before swimming ashore."

"Yeah?"

"Why did you kiss me?"

"What are you talking about? I never kissed you."

"Okay, that is what I assumed."

"I kissed you?" he asked.

"Yes, but that is alright. You were confused. It was just a little bizarre."

"I'm sorry, I don't remember much. I hope I didn't offend you. I'd actually decided that morning to be more respectful of your kindness. You've done nothing but help

214

me ever since I got here, and I feel as if you've somehow accepted me into your family."

"It is fine, and yes, contrary to my behavior towards you, we are very trusting people. You will do well not to forget that next time you consider lying to us."

Perry looked away. His thoughts drifted to his cottage in Ocean Point and his family. His parents, grandparents, great-grandparents, all making a living from the sea. He felt homesick but realized he had no home. There was the family cabin, but no more family. His parents had passed, he had no brothers or sisters. His wife had left, and his kids weren't talking to him. He'd never set down roots because he loved adventure, leaving his family behind for the next mission, the next experience, with a drive to dominate and overcome any obstacles. As he sat there in a beautiful cafe, in a beautiful town, on a beautiful coastline, next to a beautiful woman, he was scared. And this kind of fear wasn't familiar to him, it was deep down inside of him, and he wanted it out.

"I'm going to make you a promise as long as you agree to one thing," he said.

"What?"

"I'll never lie to you again as long as you don't ask about my work."

"What type of promise is that? What are you offering in return?"

"Ahhh… I just told you, honesty?"

"You must make a promise to be honest? Are you joking?"

"Well, what do you want?"

"I want you to behave yourself for as long as you are with us. I do not want my family in danger because of your misdeeds."

"Misdeeds? What mis…"

"Perry, honesty goes without saying. In return, I will not ask about your work. I do not even care about your work."

"Fine, I promise to be a true and honorable gentleman as long as I am with you."

"I expect nothing less."

"So, to start out on the right foot... I need to tell you something."

"What?"

"I do remember kissing you."

Christina laughed. "I knew it, you ass! You were not that confused."

"Christina! Your language. What would your uncle say?"

"He would say I should have left you on the bottom of the ocean where you belonged."

She stared closely at Perry. "Are you feeling alright? You look pale."

"I'm fine. It's just the wine and the medicine."

"Let us go back home," she said. "I have what Nonna needs and it is time for riposo."

"I'm feeling tired myself. I must be assimilating."

"In a good way?"

"I'm not sure."

Perry slowly made his way upstairs and sat stiffly on the bed. Christina followed him into the bedroom, kneeled and pulled off his shoes.

"Stand for a second," she said. "Let me remove your pants."

"I'm not an invalid. I can do it."

She looked up at him and said, "You just cannot let anyone help you, can you?"

"Sure, I can."

"You are so blind... "

"Fine! Take off my pants," he said, standing up in front of her. "I know you've been wanting to get into them."

Christina stood quickly and slapped Perry so hard he fell back onto the bed.

He looked up at her in shock. The words had just slipped out. He hadn't thought about how she'd react. Although getting walloped in the face wouldn't have been one of his guesses.

"What are you so sensitive about," he asked.

"It is insulting when you talk to me in that way," Christina said. "You promised an hour ago to treat me with respect."

"It was just a joke! What am I missing?"

"Love, Perry, that is what you are missing."

"Love? Are you kidding me? We just met."

"I am not talking about romance. It is about caring for and respecting others. More importantly, in your case, it is about letting others care for you, as I am caring for you now, a complete stranger, because that is what we do."

Christina sat on the bed next to him.

"You are not comfortable with someone caring for you, so you make a crude joke out of something sacred in our culture. Americans are so wrapped up in being independent and self-sufficient. You worry that by letting me care for you, you will owe me. And you do not like that. You do not like that I saved you out there in the water. You do not want to owe anybody, especially a woman. That would make you weak. So, you resist. You have to twist it into something that it is not, so your delicate ego is not damaged. That is why you kissed me out there in the water. Do you know Americans have the highest divorce rate in the world? In the world, Perry! Why is that?"

"I don't know."

"Maybe you should think about that. Why did your wife leave you after all those years?"

"I don't know."

"You are not stupid. You know why."

"She said I was never around, that my work was more important than her."

"After twenty years? Suddenly, you were not there for her?"

217

"That's what I said. I had just retired. I was there for her."

"You were there, physically," Christina said. "Maybe, that is when she finally realized."

"Realized what?"

"That you would never be there for her."

"You don't know what you're talking about," Perry replied.

"Maybe she compensated by pouring her love into your children... for 20 years. Then they left for college and were replaced by you."

"You know nothing about my marriage," Perry said. "We had intimacy; we had a great sex life..."

"Your interpretation of intimacy is wrapped around sex, and that is fine, that is the way men are. But you need to realize, women are different. We need someone to care for, and I can see right now, you would not let her care for you. Just as you do not want me to care for you. But caring is in a woman's nature, especially for Sicilian women. We are nurturers; you men are warriors."

"I'm not sure all women would agree with that," he said.

"Of course not, we are all individuals. The masculine and the feminine, the warrior and nurturer live in all of us. I'm talking about human beings, as a species. We are over a million years old, and we have evolved to be masters of the world. That evolution, or higher power, or grand scheme of God's, however you believe we came about, resulted in you and me, here, right now. A man and woman, and we are not the same. We play complementary roles, balanced roles, the yin and the yang of Eastern philosophy."

"I'm sorry, but all this sociology, anthropology, whatever you call it, you're losing me. I was only making a joke."

"No, you were not. You were deflecting. You are not stupid. You understand exactly what I am telling you. You are fighting because it cuts too deep."

"Okay, okay," he said, throwing his arms up. "I just need to let you care for me. It is in your nature. Go ahead, take my pants off. I'll play nice."

"You are close, very close," she said, putting a hand on his leg.

Perry looked confused.

"I do not need you to let me care for you," she continued. "I was doing just fine without you."

He threw his hands up. "Then what, God damn it!"

Christina stared into his eyes. "It is about you. Letting yourself be cared for, be loved. Do you not see the difference? It is about letting go of any expectation that you have to return the favor, that you have to do anything at all except receive."

Perry looked away from her probing eyes. He knew she was right. He didn't like letting people in. He tried to manage them by staying in control, by staying on top. Perry felt uncomfortable sitting on the bed with Christina looking at him. She was in his space.

He shook his head. "I can't. I don't know how."

She said, "Then, I will show you."

Christina stood and grasped his hands.

Perry stood up and Christina unbuttoned his shirt and slid it off his shoulders. She threw it to the floor and knelt. She unbuckled his belt, unbuttoned his pants, and pulled them off. When she hooked her fingers into the waistband of his shorts, he resisted. She gently moved his hands away. Perry knew she was trying to make a point, so he let her. After Christina removed his shorts, she stood up.

Christina looked into his eyes, stepped back, and deliberately gazed at him, scanning slowly from head to toe.

"How does it feel?" she asked.

He made a brooding expression as he stood naked in front of her.

She reached behind him and pulled the covers back. Placing her hands on his shoulders, she guided him down to the bed, gently pushing him back until he was lying flat on the soft mattress.

He tried reaching for her, to hold her arm, to do something in response, but she gently laid his hands back on the bed. They were silent for a full minute.

"What do you hear?" she asked.

"What?"

"The sounds. Listen."

Perry listened for a second. "Well, besides my heart beating out of my chest, I hear some birds outside and... I hear a breeze in the trees."

"Good, keep listening, and I want you to stay still, do not move."

"Okay, but..."

"Shhh..." she said. "Relax."

Christina walked out of the room, and he soon heard water running in the bathroom. A few minutes later, she returned with a porcelain basin filled with steaming hot water and a small towel. She set them onto the bedside table and sat next to him.

After dipping the small towel into the water, she said, "Close your eyes."

He closed his eyes.

"What do you smell?" she asked.

He thought some more. "Well, there's some type of flowery scent coming in through the window. There's also a very slight scent of manure, from the garden, I guess, and... the steam from the water, that's strange, I can actually smell the water."

"We have had that ability for a million years," she said. "Why is it so strange?"

Perry was wondering about that question when the warm towel was spread across his face. He felt the sting on his cheek from where she'd slapped him, but it felt wonderfully pleasant everywhere else. He made a conscious effort to relax.

Christina slowly bathed him. He occasionally reached for her or attempted to move to make it easier for her, but each time she stopped him. She'd push his hand back down to the bed and remind him not to move. Perry opened his eyes to look at her, to look at the ceiling, to do anything to distract himself.

"Keep your eyes closed," she said. "Just relax. I need nothing from you."

He consciously willed his hands to remain still.

Christina finished bathing him, and the warmth of the wet towel slowly transitioned to a chill spreading across his body.

With his eyes still closed, he said, "Can I cover up now?"

"Not yet, just relax into the coolness. How does your back feel?"

"Wow," he said. "The pain is gone."

"Because you let go."

He looked at her. "But I'm still feeling exposed."

Christina put her hand over his eyes. "Just feel the coolness on your skin. Pay attention to your other senses. Do not move, just relax."

"I'm trying, but I feel like I'm in the doctor's office about to get a prostate exam."

"I am going to take care of that for you. Will you trust me?"

Perry exhaled in reply. He heard Christina pick up the washbasin and leave. He listened to her footsteps as she walked down the hall to the bathroom. He heard water pouring and the rattling of a towel rack. His thoughts drifted to the scent of the fresh air blowing in through the window. He could smell the stone and the wood of the house, feel the softness and warmth of the bed under him, and the chill and tightness of his skin as the light breeze raised goosebumps across his legs and arms.

Christina stood in the bathroom, not knowing what to do. She'd had little experience with Americans but had developed an opinion and it was not complimentary. Americans were rough, unkempt, unsophisticated. They had little appreciation for family, the land, tradition, and culture, all the things that made life worth living. All they cared about was work and success and money... and sex. But there was something adventurous about Perry, something exciting and seductive. Why was she repulsed but attracted to him at the same time?

Christina feared the physical: boats, Mount Etna, dark streets, and heights. Perry seemed fearless in all those matters, but that was of little consequence. He was afraid of emotions. He feared intimacy, attachment... dependence. By maintaining control of his surroundings, he protected himself... *from what*? she wondered. *From himself?*

She had watched while bathing him, watched his expression as he finally relaxed. She looked at herself in the mirror and spoke the words out loud.

"If you want to make a difference in this world, you must take risks, be vulnerable. I am no different than him."

But she knew he was different. He was a man, a warrior, and they have a language all their own. Christina hung up the towel. She knew what needed to be done.

Perry listened as Christina walked back into the room. He not only heard her, he could smell her, the subtle muskiness of her body, the scent of her hair. She was close, very close.

Christina stood at the foot of Perry's bed, watching him. She saw his nostrils flare. She felt a hint of panic but pushed on.

"Are you going to trust me?" she asked.

"Yes," Perry replied, his eyes still closed.

"Will you remain completely still?"

"Yes."

"Do you promise?" she asked.

"Yes."

"Okay, then you can open your eyes."

Perry opened his eyes.

Christina stood before him adorned with a warm smile on her face. She was completely naked. Her hair was spread across her broad shoulders, her chest was tanned and sprinkled with freckles from the summer sun. Her breasts smooth, white, and flawless. She had a soft, round belly and firm hips that flowed down to muscular legs.

Perry sat up.

"You said you would not move," she said.

He relaxed back into the mattress, his initial look of surprise transforming into something that almost looked like fear.

"We all get pleasure from giving," she continued, "It is in our nature. But receiving a gift is a lot more difficult, especially for someone like you."

Christina and Perry's gaze remained fixed on each other. They were going down a path that scared both of them.

Despite his stillness, parts of him were responding to his heightened senses; her voice, her scent, her body excited him, he was rising.

Christina ran a soft hand along Perry's leg. She placed her left knee on the bed and slowly swung her right leg over, straddling him. She sat on top of him, hip-to-hip, and looked into his eyes. Perry couldn't help himself, he had to move, but with each attempt, she just smiled and shook her head.

"Wait," she said.

Christina put her hands on his shoulders and slowly rocked her pelvis back and forth. She swayed for several minutes, feeling his hardness increase, the pressure sending a chill up her spine. She continued to rock in slow arcs while watching the passion build on Perry's face. His once cold skin had dampened with perspiration, and he had a smile she had not seen before. It was joy.

She lifted herself slightly, arched her hips a bit further, and he slid inside.

Perry began to thrust, but when he saw the look in her eyes while shaking her head, he stopped, and let the pleasure engulf him. He'd never experienced anything like this. She was slow, loving, warm, and strong. The chill he'd felt was replaced by a fire inside aching to escape. He wanted to take her, possess her, control her. He wanted to thrust hard and fast until she climaxed and then, only then, would he let himself go. But she had simply said, "Not yet," and he didn't. He lost track of time as the light in the room slowly faded.

At one point, Christina climbed off and retrieved a bottle of water from the bureau. She opened it, took several large swallows, and climbed back on top of him.

"Would you like some?" she asked.

Perry nodded.

She poured the water into his open mouth.

"Are you hot?" she asked.

"It has gotten a bit warm in here," he said.

She poured a slow stream of water down his chest, spreading the wetness with her hand.

"How is your back feeling?"

"It's actually stiffening up a bit."

"Would you like me to stop?"

"Hell no."

"It is going to end very soon… if you are ready."

Perry's nodded. "I understand what you are doing. And you are right, I can be a bit closed off. I'm putting myself in your hands."

"Well, that is not the only thing you are in."

Perry smiled, looking down to where they were joined.

She leaned forward, put her hands on each side of his face, and stared into his eyes.

"You're in my heart… you're in my mind… and you're in my body."

Perry stopped smiling.

"This is what I am trying to show you."

He choked, "I know… and I'm sorry for the way I've been acting."

Christina nodded.

They both knew Perry wasn't just apologizing to her. He was apologizing to his ex-wife, his children, and himself.

Christina ran her fingers through his hair. "Let yourself be cared for, to be loved. I know it is hard, but it is the only way to be happy."

"You're scaring the hell out of me."

"Me too," she said.

Christina started rocking again, this time faster, with greater urgency.

"Perry?"

"Yeah," he said.

"You can move now."

Christina's eyes never left Perry's as she rode him. She increased her pace, and he matched each thrust with his own. When she saw he was ready, Christina stopped and squeezed. Perry let out a moan that could have been heard from the back garden, but he never took his eyes off her. Christina's body stiffened and shook, a look of ecstasy washing across her face. A minute later, she lay on top of him. Their lips met with a tenderness that was without hunger. They kissed slowly, savoring the feel and the taste of each other, foreign and familiar, as if returning from a long trip and stepping across the threshold of home.

Christina's eyes snapped open when the floorboards creaked outside Perry's bedroom. A flood of emotions ran through her. She pulled the covers to her neck and looked over at the open door. Uncle Leo stood there, shaking his head. He nodded in a gesture to come downstairs and walked away.

Perry stirred when she climbed out from under the covers, but he was sound asleep. The pain meds and afternoon wine were doing their work. She slipped Perry's shirt over her nakedness and ran back to her room to dress.

Christina walked into the kitchen a few minutes later. Nonna was at a cupboard putting away some homemade desserts, given to her during her visit to Messina. Leo was pouring himself a glass of wine.

"I thought you were not returning until tomorrow," she said.

"We were worried about you," Leo said. "We decided to come back early."

"I can take care of myself," Christina said, her face flushed, her eyes watery.

"Obviously. And you have him right where we want him," he said. "Good work."

"I am sorry," Christina said. "I was not thinking, please do not…"

She looked over at Nonna, wondering if he had told her.

Leo saw that Christina was on the verge of crying. He put an arm around her and smiled. "I am having fun with you, mi amore. He is a good man, and the Lord knows you have not been with a good man for quite a while."

"It is not what you think, Uncle. He just…. he just needs someone…"

"Someone like you, I suppose. My only concern is how do you think he is going to react when he finds out you have been interfering with his work? He is going to be angry. He is going to think you are a whore who seduced him just to distract … "

Nonna raised her voice in a way they had not heard in some time.

"Leo! How dare you talk to her like that! You fool. You got her into this mess, and now you are going to condemn her because she has fallen in love."

"Nonna, do not be silly," Christina said. "I am not in love, I just…I just got carried away."

"Then you are both fools."

"You are right, Nonna," Leo said. "I apologize to both of you. I like him and it is none of my business who you bed, but he is dangerous. We must remember our priorities.

We are almost operational. If you can discover how his camera works, our project will be complete."

"We can just steal it," Christina said.

Leo shook his head. "No, we are lucky the Americans only sent one man to investigate something they do not understand. If their second camera disappears, they will know something is not right. They will send a team of people, and I guarantee they will not be scientists."

Christina nodded. "You are right, and I have spent too much time with him. I must get back to work. I am incorporating some new calculations into my design. If they are correct, I will be able to increase the output power of the BiniSphere by a factor of five and still maintain beam stability."

Chapter 15

Day 8 (Continued)

Alpha Team had set up their observation post in a deserted frantoio sitting near the top of a hill, a half kilometer southwest of the LaTorre homestead. The crumbling building was overgrown with vegetation and could barely be seen from the road. Rotting timbers and broken pieces of terracotta tile littered the main floor along with a growing pile of guano from the birds and bats that called it home.

Atwood had planned their mission days earlier. After identifying the location of their OP, he'd meticulously mapped their primary escape route. There was only one road leading to and from the LaTorre's house. It began in the center of Canneto and meandered south, into the Nebrodi mountains. Several kilometers past the LaTorre's home, the road split into a maze of one-lane dirt tracks that continued up and over the top of the mountain range and down the other side. This was their primary escape route. When the orders came, their goal was stealth and speed. If their mission didn't go as planned, which was usually the case, the local polizia could only intercept from the north. Heading south, into the mountains, would give his team the time and distance they needed to avoid a confrontation.

Martinelli removed his headset and signaled his team leader.

"Hey, you need to come read this."

Atwood walked over and looked at the laptop Martinelli had been typing on. He read Leo and Christina's translated conversation.

"Well I'll be damned," Atwood said. "Get Sheehan on the line."

❖

Stan reached across his desk and picked up the receiver of his secure phone. He punched in an access code and then the lead engineer's phone number at the KH-11 Operations Center.

"Johnson here."

"Dave, it's Stan."

"Hey, how's it going? Franklin making any progress in Sicily?"

"That's what I'm callin' about. Can we switch to a secure call?"

"Certainly."

Both Stan and Dave pushed a button on their phones, and an electronic voice announced, "Encryption activated."

"What can I do for you?" Dave asked.

"You know anything bout the caches of thorium-fluoride nanotubes we've stored away? When Franklin was testing the new camera, he pointed it at the Somalia stash but didn't find them. Then he checked the other locations. Nada. Have we relocated them?"

"Sorry Stan, we've been told to stand down. Since the PIT sensor is fried, we have no way of supporting any of your ops."

"That doesn't make sense, Mike. We're buildin' more PIT cameras as we speak. It won't take that long."

"I know. That's what I'm thinking too, but it came down from the top. Sheehan pulled the plug. You'll need to talk to him to find out what happened to the tubes."

"Look, I need you to… "

"Keep me out of it, Sheppard. I was told to shut up and forget all about the PIT technology. Since your sensor has gone to shit, I'm doing just that. You need to stand down as well."

Stan heard the click of the phone connection.

Well that's a strange reaction, he thought, as alarms sounded in the back of his head. Something was going on, and no one's talking. His next call went to the basement. Samuels picked up on the first ring.

"Yeah, Boss."

"Get Thomas and come up here. I've got a job for ya."

Five minutes later, Samuels and Thomas were standing in Stan's office.

"What's up?" Thomas asked.

"This might be nothin', but I need you to follow-up. The caches of tubes have been pulled outta the field, and somethin' just doesn't feel right."

"What's the big deal?" Samuels asked. "They do that kind of stuff all the time."

"It's the way they did it. No one gotta heads up. They did it behind our backs, and as soon as I started askin' questions, I was directed to stand down. I'm goin' to call Howell next, but I suspect I'm going to get the same run around."

"What do you want us to do?" Thomas asked.

"Grab one of the cameras and find out where those tubes went. Search every location we know of."

"Yes, sir. We'll get right on it."

"Oh, and be ready to deploy in a heartbeat. I'm worried about Franklin. We might need to pull him outta there quickly."

"Will do. We'll be ready."

The DDNI packed his briefcase and logged off his computer.

Walking out of the office, he saw Emily answering the phone. He shook his head and waved goodbye.

"I'm sorry, Deputy Director. It's Dr. Howell on Line 2. He says it's urgent."

Sheehan looked at his watch. It was 4:15 p.m. He picked up the receiver and pressed Line 2.

"Howell, what do you need? I'm busy."

"I just got off the line with Sheppard."

"Sheppard? How did he know to call you? What have you been telling people?"

"Nothing sir. He wanted to know if I had anything to do with the missing caches."

"That's faster than I thought. I planned for this to all be over by the time Sheppard's people figured out they were missing."

"What would be over?" Howell asked.

"Forget it. I'll take care of it."

"Deputy Director, is there anything I should know about what's happening? "

"You've got nothing to worry about Howell, stay on task. Have you finished the modifications to the Rhode Island?"

"The captain has been giving me a hard time, but the General Dynamics folks have been toeing the line just like you said. What did you say to them that…"

"That's none of your concern, Howell. When will you be ready?"

"In three more days everything will be installed and ready for testing."

"Well hurry up, we're getting short on time here."

"What about this scientist you found. Have you captured him yet?"

"It's not a him, it's a her. We've intercepted a communication. They're calling the facility a 'BiniSphere,' and it appears that our PIT camera is the only thing keeping them from being operational."

"We need her," Howell said. "How long will it take to bring her back here?"

"The problem is Sheppard and Franklin. We need to shut them up before we take her. They'll make too many waves. Did Sheppard give you any idea what he's going to do next?"

"No, sir. I told him it was none of his business, to stay out of it. But he does have a reputation for being a bulldog with a bone. Especially when he thinks his guys are at risk. You need to talk to him."

"I'm going to do more than just talk to that son-of-a-bitch," Sheehan said and hung up the phone.

"Emily, get Sheppard on the line ASAP."

"Yes, sir."

❖

Stan took the Langley exit ramp off the George Washington Memorial Parkway. He had turned left, heading towards home, when his phone rang.

"Yes sir," Stan said. "I understand. I'm on my way."

He made a quick U-turn and took the entrance ramp back onto the parkway for the fifteen-minute drive to the deputy director's office. His phone rang again.

"Hey, Thomas, what have ya found?" Stan asked.

"The nanotubes, every last bit of them."

"That was fast! Where are they?"

"They're at the Electric Boat docks in Groton. Samuels and I are up here right now."

"In Connecticut?" Stan said. "What's goin' on?"

"There's a lot of activity, day and night. They're doing something on board the *USS Rhode Island*. The company line is that it's being upgraded with a stealthier propulsion system."

"The *Rhode Island*? I've been on that boomer."

"That's where the nanotubes are, and there's more," Thomas said. "We set up surveillance on the top floor of the Electric Boat Engineering Building. I have a buddy that works here. Our credentials got us in the front door, and he paved the way for some office space. We can watch every single dick coming and going from the ship. Samuels just spotted your buddy, Dr. Howell."

"Howell? I just talked to him. I thought he was at the Nevada site."

"Judging by the number of people working on that ship, this is a major modification. I doubt he's the one in charge. Our security clearances gave us access to the sub, but only the outside. The inside's locked up tighter than a witch's twat. I was able to talk to some of the crew, though. They claim they're reducing the acoustic signature using sub-atomic particles."

"Sounds like they've learned somethin' bout these nanotubes that they don't want to share with us." Stan said.

"Yup, this is a lot bigger than some TTL operations."

"Okay, well I've just been called to Sheehan's office. He wants a face-to-face."

"What do you think that's all about?" Thomas asked.

"One of two things. He's goin' to read me in on this fiasco or fire my ass. Just in case, I need you and Samuels on station in Sicily, immediately. This might be the last command I give ya."

"Will do. We can be wheels down at Sigonella in 15 hours."

"Do it! Set up over-watch on Franklin and be careful of Sheehan's team. They're already on station, watchin' and waitin'."

"Roger."

"Take a seat," Sheehan said as soon as Emily led Stan into his office. "Emily, close the door on the way out."

"Yes, sir."

As soon as they were alone, Sheehan said, "Sheppard, how long have you been in the Army?"

"Twenty-two years, sir. Why do ya ask?"

"I'm wondering if it's time for you to retire."

"Retire? No way, I'm havin' too much fun."

"Fun? That's the way you feel about this job? Fun? I'm not sure you're taking this job seriously."

"I'm doin' a damn fine job, sir, doesn't mean I can't enjoy it."

"You call going behind my back doing a damn fine job?"

"I don't know what you're talkin' about," Stan replied.

"I'm talking about the nanotubes! Do you think I wouldn't hear about you talking to our station chiefs about the caches?"

"Well sir, last I looked I was part of this team, and my job is to be prepared to deploy those tubes at a moment's notice. I have a man in the field as we speak who needs direct support from my team. Why wasn't I told about it? "

"Because you didn't have a need to know Sheppard. I also know you've been keeping your team on standby."

"No harm in bein' prepared with contingencies."

"Not after I gave you a direct order to stand down," Sheehan said. "You're in direct violation of my orders, and you are hereby relieved of your duties. You'll step away from this or face the consequences. That's an order."

"Sir, I'm a Lieutenant Colonel in the United States Army. You'll need to go through my chain-of-command with written orders."

"Your career's at stake, Sheppard. Get out of my office."

Sheppard was barely out the door before Sheehan picked up his phone.

"Bravo Lead here," came the reply.

"He's not playing," Sheehan said. "Your mission is a go, and remember, it's critical that it looks like an accident. He's got too many friends here on the Beltway."

"Yes, sir. It will take a couple days to execute the…"

"I told you to be ready at a moment's notice!"

"Sir, Sheppard's being very cautious. He knows he's being watched."

"Just get the damn job done Meyers! As soon as you've accomplished your mission, Alpha Team will engage their target."

"Yes, sir."

Chapter 16

Day 9

It was after lunch by the time Perry made his way down to the kitchen. Nonna was at the counter, preparing a lunch of assorted cheeses, meats, and freshly baked bread.

Perry was drinking a glass of Nero-d'Avola wine when Leo walked in a few minutes later.

"Your back feel good?" Leo asked.

"Si`, molto grazie." Perry spread his arms and shrugged. "No Christina? She's okay?"

Leo replied, "Si`, si`, she go to university. She has a lot of work to do. Many people depend on her."

"I hope I'm not causing any problems."

"Si`, you are problem."

"I am very sorry."

"You are guest. We take care our guests. But you," Leo looked at Perry sternly, "too much care."

"I really didn't mean for it to go so far…"

"There is limit to... "

"Look, I really appreciate...“

In perfect English, Leo said, "Signore Franklin! Stop interrupting me. If any harm comes to my niece because of your actions, if you hurt her in any way, I will kill you."

Perry looked stunned.

"We Sicilians have a reputation, and it is well deserved. We protect our families. Do you have any doubt of what I am telling you?"

Perry shook his head.

"If anything happens to my Christina, you will disappear from the face of this earth."

Perry nodded. "I understand."

"Good. Then also be at ease, if you behave properly, we will treat you like one of our own."

Perry was thoroughly confused. How could Leo talk in such polar opposites, a man of God? Perry felt like a child being scolded by his father, loved and threatened at the same time. He feared for his life while being strangely drawn to this family.

Perry nodded. "Thank you, I will work hard to gain your trust."

Trying to diffuse the tension, he scanned the walls covered with aging pictures of the LaTorre's life: courtyard weddings, distant vacations. One photo, stained and sepia-colored, caught Perry's attention. It showed a young couple standing in front of the LaTorre home arm-in-arm. The picture had a vague familiarity to it.

Leo noticed Perry's stare and said, "That is Nonna, and my father, Bini LaTorre."

"Ahhh, okay. He looks so familiar, as if I'd seen him before. Would it be rude if I took a picture of it?"

"Of course not."

Perry pulled out his cell phone, but before he could take the picture, Leo stood up and put his hand on Perry's shoulder.

"You see this picture over here?"

Leo pointed to a younger image of himself sitting proudly on a burnt-orange and chrome motorcycle."

"Yes."

"I bought it brand new."

Perry looked closer. "Wow, that's a '69 Honda CB750. The first 'superbike.'"

Leo nodded, "Molto Buono! You know motorcycles. It was my first. I was only 20 years old."

"Well, I'm certainly familiar with this beast. It's a true classic. I bet you wish you still had it."

"Come!" Leo said.

Leo's face looked almost childlike as he led Perry out the back door. They walked through the courtyard and over to a detached garage. Leo lifted the ancient iron latch and swung the wooden doors open. There, nestled amongst an array of tools, farm implements, and empty wine casks, was his Honda CB750. Perry's eyes fell on the sleek bike with its powerful in-line 4-cylinder engine that could propel it to over 120 mph; extremely fast by 1969 standards.

Leo moved a few boxes out of the way and wheeled it out into the sunlight. An avalanche of dust and dirt slid off the bike.

"It hasn't run in years."

Leo pointed to the original wiring harness with its burned insulation and frayed, dead-end wires.

"I have installed a new, ahhh, I don't know the English words, bobine di accensione and candele di accensione."

Leo pointed to the ignition wires and spark plugs.

"But I know so little about mechanics and nothing at all about electrical wiring."

Perry stepped closer and gestured. "Do you mind?"

"No, look."

Perry got down on his knees and probed deep under the fuel tank, pulling on more loose wires and spider webs. He removed the side cover and saw that the battery had melted.

"Wow, the wiring and battery look like they've been through a fire, but the rest of the bike looks fine."

"Si`," Leo said. "It is strange how this happened. I cannot explain it."

"Could it have anything to do with those unexplained events that happened in Canneto fifteen years ago."

"Ah, yes." Leo laughed. "The Devil in Canneto."

"You don't subscribe to that Father?"

"Yes, that is when the motorcycle was damaged, but no, I do not believe the devil had anything to do with it."

239

Perry straddled the 750 and kicked down on the starter lever several times.

"Well, it's not locked up, and you have compression. Shouldn't be too hard to get it running."

Without another word, Perry walked back into the garage and looked around. He spotted a toolbox sitting on the workbench. Doing a quick inventory, he saw it was well enough equipped. There were no discussions of what their plans might be for the rest of the day.

"Do you have any fresh gasoline?"

"Si`," Leo said.

"Okay, I'll be right back, I need to go into town for a few things."

Leo looked confused as Perry walked away.

Leo cleaned up the bike and brought his toolbox out into the daylight. He removed the fuel tank and headlight assembly, exposing most of the melted wiring. Two hours later Perry returned with several spools of colored wire, electrical tape, a box of small crimp-on connectors, a digital multimeter, and a motorcycle battery. He went right to work.

Another hour and they had reinstalled the fuel tank, added fresh fuel and hooked up the battery. When Perry opened the fuel valve that led to the carburetors, fuel poured from the bottom of the bike.

"Stuck floats," Perry said. "Typical for a carburetor that's been sitting this long."

He turned the valve off, unscrewed the four carburetor bowls and tapped the floats up and down to free the needle valves. He reinstalled the bowls and turned the fuel valve.

"No more leaks," he said. "Let's give it a try."

Perry turned the ignition switch to "ON", and the motorcycle jumped forward.

He quickly turned it off.

"The starter switch is shorted."

He grabbed the multimeter and began troubleshooting.

"Looks like it's the starter solenoid. I think the contacts are stuck; it's another common problem."

"It will be challenging to find a replacement here in Sicily," said Leo.

Perry grabbed a wrench and banged on the side of the solenoid a few times.

"Put the transmission in neutral and try it again," he said to Leo.

Leo rocked the shifter lever until he felt it settle in between first and second gear and turned the ignition switch to "ON." The bike remained silent and still.

"Okay!" Perry said. "Close the choke and hit the starter. Let's see what happens."

As soon as Leo pushed the start button, the bike sputtered, spit and backfired. Leo held the starter switch down, while Perry put his hand on each of the four exhaust pipes.

"You can stop," he said. "Two pipes are getting hot, and two are cold."

Perry pulled the plugs and showed Leo that two were wet and cold and two were dry and warm.

"You're getting fuel to all four cylinders, but two plugs aren't firing. You have a bad ignition coil, or the wiring is messed up."

Perry pulled the fuel tank again and inspected the two black ignition coils mounted underneath. He found the problem, a broken wire going to one of the coils. He repaired the wiring, checked the firing order, and replaced the fuel tank.

When Leo pressed the start button, the bike roared to life. The open, straight exhaust pipes immediately echoed the pedigree of the machine across the mountains. Leo hit the throttle hard, over and over, as the sound roared through the valley, a symphony of Japanese engineering. They both had huge grins on their faces.

Leo leaned towards Perry and yelled over the roar, "This first time she runs in fifteen years!"

Garret had taken up a forward position several hundred yards from the OP, on the side of a small knoll west of the LaTorre homestead. He'd dug a slight depression into the rocky ground underneath the broad leaves of a wild caster bean tree. His position was perfect. He had an unobstructed view of the western side of the LaTorre house and a clear line-of-sight of the approaches from the road. He'd been lying there for 78 hours: sleeping, urinating, or eating only when their surveillance bugs indicated the household was asleep or empty. He watched through the scope of his Barrett M107A1 50 BMG semi-automatic as Leo and Perry rolled an old motorcycle out of the garage. The sun was setting, and the mountain shadows soon obscured his target. He switched from his rifle scope to his spotting scope. Using a special adapter, Garret attached his night vision monocular to the Leupold 12-40x spotting scope and adjusted the focus. He continued watching and worrying that something was seriously wrong with this mission.

Garret spoke into his comms. "Hey, guys. Franklin's got the bike running."

"I don't get it," Gregory said. "We've been watching this douche bag for days. He acts like he's on vacation. I'm ready to bag him, grab the girl, and get the hell out of here."

"I hear ya," Garret said. "This guy doesn't have a care in the world. Hard to believe he's a traitor."

"It takes all kinds," Atwood said. "We're just going to do what we're told. Remember, the woman is our first priority. Got it?"

A double click came through the comms.

Leo shut off the ignition and they reinstalled all the parts they'd removed. They filled the tires with air, tested the brakes, checked the oil and rolled it out onto the narrow road. Leo climbed on, started it, popped it into gear and took off like a rocket, the rear tire shooting loose gravel at Perry's legs. He banked the 750 into the first of many curves.

For the next twenty minutes, a high-pitched reverberation of exhaust pipes echoed off the hillsides as Leo shifted through the gears. The bike roared up, down and across the narrow roads that ran along the ridgeline. Five minutes later, Leo pulled the bike into the driveway.

"Perry! Go!" he yelled.

Perry climbed on and shot off into the twilight. Having traveled the roads several times, he knew every curve and straightaway in intimate detail. Even with no headlight, he hit the throttle hard and the cold mountain air rushed by. The bikes responsive acceleration brought a thrill as narrow, dark, winding road blurred as he sped by. Perry rode into a different consciousness. His usually focused, analytical, scientific mind had completely shut down. He was in-the-moment, on-the-edge. For a moment, he thought about Christina, imagined her holding on tightly behind him, screaming with joy and fear as they banked into another curve.

When Perry returned, his cheeks were numb, his ears ringing, and a permanent grin had spread across his face. He barely heard Leo's words over the sound of the engine.

"Sigaro, whiskey"

They rolled the bike back into the barn, closed the doors, and walked to the back of the house.

While they smoked their cigars and toasted an 18-year-old Macallan single malt scotch, Perry looked into Leo's bright eyes. He felt it in his own heart, too. An old motorcycle, its electrical system damaged by the same strange phenomena he'd been sent to investigate, carried him the final steps into the LaTorre family.

Chapter 17

Day 10

Perry jerked awake when Christina opened his door.

"What are your plans today?"

"What time is it?" he asked, rubbing his head and two-day-old stubble.

"It's 7 o'clock. Have you ever picked olives?"

"I can honestly say I've never picked an olive in my life."

"Today is your opportunity."

Perry shook his head. "Sounds exciting but I can't. I need to work."

"I thought you said your camera operates automatically. It will text you when it picks up a signal."

"It does but… "

"Come. It is not like we are going very far."

"Alright," he said, "let me go use the bathroom first."

After Perry left, Christina went out to the balcony, and nudged one of the feet of the tripod.

Fifteen minutes later, they stood next to each other looking at the grove of several dozen small trees arranged in four neat rows. His warm breath hit the chill air and clouded as he spoke.

"These are olive trees?"

"Si`."

Christina dropped a nylon net to the ground, reached up, and picked a dark purple berry from a branch just above their heads. She rolled it between her fingers, the cold juices dripping down into her palm. She squeezed it firmly and the olive pith shot into the air. She took Perry's hand and rubbed the juices onto his palm.

"Feel it?"

Perry rubbed his hands together.

"Wow! I had no idea there was so much oil."

"An olive contains about fifteen percent olive oil."

Christina raised her index finger to Perry's mouth. "Taste it."

Perry licked her fingertip. His face screwed into a sour grimace.

She laughed. "The oil tastes wonderful, but olive water is one of the bitterest things you will ever taste. That is what the pressing is all about. Separating the oil from the water."

Perry dropped the stack of baskets he'd been carrying and asked, "So how do we get started?"

"It is easy. First, we spread the net out underneath the tree."

They went to work unfolding the net and spreading it around an olive tree.

"Pass me one of those small hand rakes in the basket."

Perry grabbed the plastic rakes and handed one to Christina.

"We just pull the rake through the branches like this."

She reached up and raked through the branches as if combing a giant's rough hair. Olives, small branches and leaves fluttered down to the net. Perry caught on quickly and began combing. It took several hours of work. By the time they were finished, they were scraped and bloodied from the constant onslaught of branches. But, it was good, satisfying work. They collected the last batch of olives from the net and poured them into the remaining basket.

"Do you not feel great?" Christina asked.

"Yeah, now that you mention it, I actually do. Funny, considering how covered I am with scrapes and bruises."

"Wait until you taste the final product. Shall we load the baskets into the van and go for a ride?"

"Okay, but can I at least take a shower first, and maybe have a little breakfast?"

"You are such a girl," Christina said.

They spent the next few minutes loading a dozen baskets of olives into a small Toyota van used for such things and headed inside.

Christina ran up the stairs ahead of Perry and said, "I will meet you downstairs in fifteen minutes."

"Okay."

Perry stood at his bedroom window, looking out over the LaTorre property. He wondered once again how he'd gotten into this situation. Christina was acting as if they'd been together forever, as if they were husband and wife or brother and sister or best friends, or something he couldn't quite figure out. She hadn't made a single sexual advance toward him since the other day. She seemed at peace with their... their... whatever it was. He was far from being at peace. He needed to do something, anything, to get beyond this cliff he was standing on. He grabbed his towel and headed for the bathroom.

Steam had filled the room, completely fogging the shower door. Christina was washing the bark and twigs from her hair when she heard the door creak. She tensed for a second then realized who the visitor must be.

"Has it been fifteen minutes already?" she asked.

Perry replied, "I lost track of time."

She swung the shower door open and found him slipping out of his clothes.

Perry stepped in and enveloped her in his arms, his cold skin contrasting nicely with the hotness of the shower. He guided her back against the rear wall and kissed her, hard.

"A girl am I?" he asked.

Christina smiled and wrapped her arms tightly around his neck. She pulled herself up and wrapped both legs around his waist.

He whispered in her ear. "What? No foreplay?"

"What do you think we have been doing all morning long?"

"Picking olives?" he asked.

She nodded and pulled a stray leaf from his hair.

"You're a strange woman," he said and kissed her again.

After breakfast, Christina tossed the keys to Perry. "Maybe you should drive."

He pulled the van out of the driveway and turned south, soon passing the overgrown path leading to the abandoned frantoio.

Christina said, "Ages ago, before I was born, there was an olive press right here on the right. The olive industry has grown so much since then that larger, more efficient frantoios replaced the smaller, family-owned businesses."

They drove farther into the mountains, with Christina occasionally indicating which way to turn at an intersection. For the most part, they were silent.

Fifteen minutes had passed when Christina said, "Tell me more about this fancy camera of yours. How does it work?"

"Didn't we make a deal the other day, that I behave myself and you don't ask me about my work?"

"Ha! You have already broken that deal."

"What do you mean?"

"You slept with the monsignor's niece!"

"What! You were the one… "

"Do you really think that is going to save you?"

"How's he going to find out?"

Christina smiled.

Perry remembered Leo's lecture the day before and figured her uncle already knew. And what was the harm in telling her? Christina was an anthropologist, not a physicist. She'd never understand how the camera really worked.

"Fine, but I really don't think you'd understand the physics."

"Well, maybe you can keep it very simple," Christina replied. "So my little brain will not be overwhelmed."

"I didn't mean it that way. It's just complicated."

"I am not asking you to design it for me. I just thought it would be something to talk about during the drive."

"This is just between us, okay?"

"Perry, you already told me why you are here, and I have not told anybody."

"In simple terms, it detects a certain type of electromagnetic radiation."

"You already told me that. But how? Electromagnetic signals cannot travel through water."

"How do you know that?"

"It is not rocket science. Everybody knows why submarines use sonar, not radar, to navigate."

"Well, I invented a new type of nanotechnology, and it's used in the camera. It can detect radiation outside of the normal boundaries of physics."

"You invented it?" Christina asked. "I thought you were just some kind of field technician or something."

"No, I'm more like an engineer," he said, regretting the conversation had ever started.

"An engineer? You promised you would not lie to me."

"I didn't lie. I told you not to ask me about my work, and that's my work. I'm an engineer, for the government."

"What kind of engineer?"

"Look, I shouldn't have said anything."

"What kind of engineer?"

Perry didn't answer, his eyes locked onto the road in front of him.

"Perry!"

He mumbled, "Nuclear."

"Nuclear!"

He nodded his head.

"Are you telling me your nanotechnology is detecting nuclear radiation in Canneto?"

"No, no, it's nothing dangerous. It's naturally occurring and very small. I use nanotubes to detect very, very small signals."

"But how can that interfere with your underwater antenna arrays if it is so small?"

Perry lied. "We don't know. That's what we're trying to find out. Can we drop it?"

"Fine!" she answered.

Five minutes later Christina said, "Take a left at that driveway with the frantoio sign. Slow down! You are going too fast."

Perry took a sharp left, and the van slid sideways.

"What frantoio?"

"See the big barn way up there up on the hill? That is where we are going."

Perry drove to the barn and parked next to several small trucks.

"Come on, let us go."

Entering the dark, expansive interior, they were enveloped in the aroma of fresh olive oil. Off to the left, several elderly farmers sat in overstuffed lounge chairs next to a stone fireplace. To the right, a younger man tended to some machinery. Another man was operating a forklift. He picked up a huge red plastic bin filled with olives. He maneuvered the container over to some more machinery and poured the green and black olives into a hopper. A dark-skinned woman dressed in blue jeans and a flannel shirt walked over and greeted Christina. They talked for a minute, then Christina said, "Perry, this is my close friend, Arianna."

"It's a pleasure to meet you, signore Perry."

"Boungiorno, Arianna. What a wonderful name!"

"Thank you."

"Do you know what it means?"

Arianna looked confused.

Christina said apologetically, "He is American."

"Ahhh, si`. I believe it has something to do with virtue."

"Yes," Perry said. "It comes from the Latin word 'Ariadne' which means utterly pure."

Christina said, "I did not know you were so scholarly."

Perry laughed. "It's just a coincidence. The name of my first sailboat was Ariadne, and she was an utterly pure sailing vessel. That was twenty years ago. Now I'm crossing paths with another Ariadne, and she's creating the utterly pure essence of the Mediterranean, virgin olive oil."

"I did not know you were a sailor, another surprise."

"That was a long time ago."

"No more sailboats?"

"No, I sold my last one during the divorce."

"Oh, that must have been hard."

"Actually, no. The divorce changed me; the sailing wasn't the same anymore."

Christina nodded, "I guess I can understand. What was her name?"

"Julie."

Christina poked him in the arm. "Not your wife, your last boat."

"Oh, sorry, Freeflight."

Christina tilted her head, looked at Perry and then at Arianna.

"What?" Perry asked.

"Freeflight?" Christina asked.

"Yeah."

Arianna said, "And your first boat was Ariadne?"

"Yeah, why?"

Christina replied, "You got what you asked for."

"What are you talking about."

Arianna said, "Ariadne and Freeflight, pure freedom."

Perry was surprised he'd never made that connection. Neither one of his boats had been named by him, they were the original names when he'd purchased them.

Arianna continued, "If you do not mind me asking, did the divorce set you free? Are you on a journey looking for pure freedom?"

Perry exchanged an awkward look with Christina.

"Maybe it is a journey you are both taking," she added.

They stood in silence for a few seconds.

"Enough!" Arianna said. "Let us go press some olives."

It was almost lunchtime when they returned from the frantoio and Perry parked the van next to the LaTorre's garage. They climbed out and walked to the back to unload.

"You are quiet," Christina said.

"Yeah, I've been thinking."

"What about?" she asked.

"It's not important."

"Say what is on your mind."

"I've been thinking about us and where this is going."

"Us?" Christina asked. "What do you mean?"

"What's going to happen when I'm finished here?"

"Perry, there is no us."

Christina picked up a couple of the tins and walked quickly towards the back courtyard.

He grabbed a couple more and followed. She led him to the wine cellar, where she stacked the tins on an old pallet sitting next to the wine barrel. Perry did the same. When Christina turned to leave, he stepped in front of her.

"I do not want to talk about it," she said. "You have your life and I have mine."

"You are so full of it. You lecture me about not letting anyone in, but you're doing the exact same thing. You're so afraid, you've holed yourself away into this fortress of a home. It's like you're still living with your parents. How often do you go out into the world?"

"I go out many times," she said.

"Well, you put us Americans down, but you've never been to America. Have you?"

"No, but... "

"I bet you've never even been outside of Italy."

"I have, but I do not need to leave Sicily to be happy."

"Are you really happy?" he asked.

She shrugged her shoulders.

"It seems like you've poured all your love into your family, and there's little else outside of that besides your work. You even chose a profession where you can just sit back and observe mankind from your ivory tower, like some kinda princess."

"Perry, you do not understand. I cannot leave here, and I cannot be in a serious relationship with you."

"Serious? You don't think this is serious?" he asked. "It feels pretty damn serious to me. We almost died together, and you can't hide what you feel when you look at me."

"Perry, please." Christina felt claustrophobic in the small cellar and tried to walk around him.

He grabbed her arms and pulled her toward him.

"Please stop," she said, lowering her gaze to the earthen floor.

He put his hand under her chin and lifted her head gently.

"Before I came along, when was the last time you were with a man?"

"A while."

"How long?"

"Eight years."

"Eight years? Wow! I had no idea."

"Well, now you know. And I really do not want to talk about it."

"Okay," he said. "Sorry I brought it up."

Perry realized this was just as serious for her as it was with him.

"Look," she said, "Maybe it is this warrior, nurturer, male, female thing we talked about the other day. There is nothing out of the ordinary about you being nervous about emotional risks or me being afraid of physical risks. We just fit inside the mold."

"I guess," Perry said. "But, I'm probably more adventurous than the average male, at least physically."

"Maybe so, and I guess, from your viewpoint, I might have been more adventurous with you, in a different way."

"That's for sure, God, I couldn't believe how you just climbed on top…"

"Yes, I know, you do not need to go into details. I surprised myself. But we are only talking about matters of degree, we are still living our predetermined roles."

"Ha!" Perry laughed. "Leave it to an anthropologist to take all the fun out of it. But do you hear what I'm saying? You haven't exactly been putting yourself out there into the real world."

"You are right, very right. I like to get up on my high horse and analyze everybody, but in some ways, I cannot relate."

"There's nothing wrong with that except that maybe you should allow yourself to go through a little therapy yourself," Perry said. "Maybe next time it's going to be you lying naked on the bed looking up at me."

"I do not think there is going to be a next time. We have gone far enough. This needs to stop."

"Yeah, right. You're going to stop after going eight years without…"

Christina punched him hard in the arm and walked out of the cellar.

"Damn, I think that's going to leave a mark," he called after her.

They carried the last of the olive oil into the cellar and placed the tins on the pallet before another word was said.

"Look," Perry said. "I'm sorry I brought it up. I know this isn't easy for you. I barged in here last week and upset this beautiful life you've set up for yourself. Who am I to question it? Hell, I wish I could live like this. It's, it's, intoxicating!"

Christina wrapped her arms around Perry and kissed him before laying her head on his chest.

"Would it be okay if we just take it one moment at a time?"

"You do realize that's exactly why you're so intoxicating, why all of this is so intoxicating," he said, spreading his arms wide. "You Sicilians live so much in the moment."

He wrapped his arms around her and gazed around the ancient cellar.

"Christina?"

"Yes."

"I can't help it. My curiosity is killing me. What's that door for?"

Perry was staring at the back wall, at the locked wrought iron door he'd noticed the other day.

"It is nothing, just another storage area," she said. "We keep it locked because my uncle stores his hunting rifles there."

Christina grabbed Perry's hand and pulled him out of the dark interior.

"I am hungry. Let us find something to eat, amore mio."

"My love?" Perry asked, his eyebrows raised. "Really?"

"Do not go crazy," she replied. "We say that to everyone."

Chapter 18

Day 10 (Continued)

Howell stood on the deck of the *USS Rhode Island*. He was still arguing with the sub's commander, Captain Wainwright, when the VH-60N executive transport helicopter flew low over their heads. The modified UH-60 Black Hawk flared, sank to the ground, and landed on a small square patch of grass adjacent to the pier. Seconds later, Sheehan emerged from the interior.

Howell and Wainwright walked down the gangway and met Sheehan on the pier.

"Commander!" Sheehan said. "Weren't the president's orders clear enough? You are to do exactly what Howell tells you to do, the fate of the country is at stake."

"This is insanity!" replied the commander. "With modifications of this magnitude, you don't go operational without months of sea trials. This is a nuclear submarine!"

"Well, right now, it's my submarine! If you want to remain commander, you damn well better do what the president ordered."

Wainwright's face turned red and he balled his fists.

Sheehan said, "Wainwright, I know exactly what I'm doing here. Do I have to remind you that I helped design that nuclear power plant of yours? I know every square inch of that reactor and that propulsion system."

"We should at least unload the nukes, for God's sake," said the captain. "There're over a half million people within the blast radius of a single missile."

Howell turned to Sheehan. "He's right, sir. It's too dangerous. If something went wrong, we could… "

"You're talking about removing 24 ballistic missiles," Sheehan said. "How long would that take, commander?"

"We don't have that capability here, sir. We need to steam down to Kings Bay in Georgia. Once there, it would take ten hours per missile."

"Exactly! In other words, we don't have time for this."

Wainwright had heard enough. He marched away from the two civilians and back up the gangway to his ship.

"What's the status of the phaser?" Sheehan asked.

"We're close. Four more days and we'll be operational."

"Good, the longer this stretches out, the more risk of being exposed."

"That reminds me," Howell said. "We got a report of a couple of new guys asking questions. We don't know how they gained access."

"You allowed outsiders on the ship?"

"No, no, nothing like that. They were on the pier. All they got was the company line, modifications for a stealthier propulsion system."

"Who were they?"

"We don't know, but we got them on our surveillance cameras."

"Let me see."

Howell led the Deputy Director into the security shed and asked the guard to pull up the footage from two days ago.

"God damn it!" Sheehan said. "Those are Sheppard's men, Thomas and Samuels. They must know the nanotubes are here. It won't take long before they put two and two together. Howell, if this ship isn't underway in four days, it's more than your career that will be over."

"Yes, sir, but we still have the stability issues. We haven't been able to surpass 10 percent power without the reactor core going supercritical. There's some type of feedback loop between the phaser and the reactor. I don't understand it. The reaction is transitioning from a negative to a positive coefficient of reactivity."

"Howell, in twenty-four hours I'm going to serve one of those Sicilian scientists to you on a platter. And I guarantee she'll be talking up a storm by the time you get her. She'll solve your problem. Now get back to work."

It was just past noon when Alpha Team's satellite radio emitted a burst of static and the DDNI's voice crackled.

"Alpha Team Lead, are you there?"

"Damn it, Gregory!" Atwood said. "Send it directly to our headsets. We don't need that kind of noise giving away our position."

"Sorry!" he replied.

Gregory pressed a couple buttons on his comms unit, and the director's voice switched to everyone's integral headset.

"Can you hear me?" the deputy director asked.

"Loud and clear," Atwood said.

"The mission is a go. We're waiting on one target here in the States to be eliminated and then it's your turn. Bravo Team will contact you as soon as Sheppard is down. Then you need to execute immediately."

Garret keyed his mike. "Sheppard? Sheppard who?" he asked.

"Who is that?" Sheehan asked.

"It's Garret," Atwood replied.

"Tell him to shut up and forget that name. It's none of his business."

"Yes, sir," Atwood replied.

"Eliminate Franklin and everyone else that gets in the way, except for the Christina woman. She's high priority, we need her back here ASAP."

"Will do sir. We'll execute as soon as we get the call. What about all this ordnance for taking out the facility?"

"It's underwater but there must be a land entrance. If you can get to it, take it out. If not, we'll send one of our fast attack subs to finish the job."

"Roger."

"And the camera!" Sheehan said. "Grab the camera! We can't let it get into their hands."

"Yes, sir."

After hanging up with Alpha Team, Sheehan contacted Bravo Team Leader.

"Bravo here."

"What the hell is taking so long?" Sheehan asked.

"We're following the target right now, sir. He appears to be heading home."

"Eliminate him. I don't care if it looks like an accident or not. Contact Alpha Team as soon as you've completed the mission."

"Yes, sir."

Garret continued to watch the villa through his scope but was distracted. He'd seen his share of enemies and this guy Franklin wasn't behaving like one. And, waiting for a target in the States to be eliminated… that went against a lot of federal laws. The DDNI had no authority to conduct DA missions on US soil. He barely had the power to conduct operations outside the US. And the name 'Sheppard' made him very nervous.

Garret turned off his headset and pulled his company-issued sat-phone from his pocket. He still remembered Stan's cell phone number.

"Sheppard, here."

"Stan, it's Garret. How you been doing?"

"Garret? Wow man, it's been forever. I'm doin' okay. What about you?"

"Just not the same on the outside but making big bucks."

"Yeah, I heard ya went to work for some kinda mercenary defense contractor. Good for you!"

"Hey, I can't talk long, I'm in theatre. I just need to ask if you're into any kinda deep shit."

Stan looked at his rearview mirror and the black SUV that had been tailing him for the last few days. He said, "It's the same deep shit I'm in every day."

"I hear ya, but I just heard a name over the grapevine, and I just had to check."

"What do ya mean?"

"You know I can't tell ya much. Just needed to check. It's a DA mission, and the name Sheppard came up."

"Well, it's not me. I'm in the States. In fact, I'm in DC right now runnin' an op."

"That's the problem, Stan, that's why I'm calling. The DA op is in CONUS."

"What! You've got a kill mission in the States? Garret, what the fuck are you…"

"No, no, no. It's not my mission. It's a second team. I heard your name, and it just sent up some warning flags. Stan, my target just doesn't look right, he doesn't fit the profile."

"Where the hell are you?" Stan asked.

"You know I can't tell you that."

"Garret!"

"Sorry man."

"Fine, then tell me this. Are you eating a lot of fuckin' cannolis?"

The line was silent.

After a few seconds passed, Stan said, "Ya need to get the fuck outta there, right now Garret."

"I can't, I'm with a team. I can't even tell you who the hell we're working for, but they're high up the food chain, very powerful people. You need to take care of yourself. I gotta go, bye."

"Hold it! One more question."

"What?"

"Yur target. Is it an American or a Sicilian?"

"American, bye," and Garret disconnected

Stan immediately dialed Perry's number.

"Hey Stan, still nothing."

"Forget it!" Stan said. "You need to leave, now!"

"What? I'm finally getting comfortable. "

"The team Sheehan sent to watch over you, they're not a rescue team, they're a kill team. I just got a call from their sniper. You need to get the fuck out of there, right now! Don't even pack yur bag. They'll know you're boltin'. Just grab the camera and go."

"Kill team? What the hell are you talking about? Why would they want to…?"

"Don't argue, just do it."

"What about Christina and her family?"

"The best thing ya can do for them is git the hell outta there. They'll be collateral damage if you don't move. Now!"

"Collateral damage? You mean, I'm the target?"

"Yes, get out! Go to that Hotel Za' Maria. I've told Thomas and Samuels to meet ya there. We can't risk sendin' them in to git you. It would tip them off.

"Okay."

Stan disconnected just as he pulled into his driveway. He scanned the perimeter of his house and looked up and down the tree-lined street. The black SUV was gone. Pressing the button clipped to his visor, he waited as the carriage-style garage doors slowly swung open.

Stan had built the doors himself. After doing four tours in Afghanistan and one in Iraq, he couldn't sleep unless he felt secure. He suspected it was PTSD but refused to acknowledge how strong a hold it had on him. He'd replaced the vertical rolling doors as soon as he and Brenda purchased the house. The new doors were sheathed in consumer-grade wood paneling, inside and out. They looked just like any other garage door on his suburban street. But sandwiched in between the wood panels were 3/8"-thick steel plates. The layered doors were mounted to a welded 3" box-channel frame using four industrial-size hinges on each side. Stan had performed similar modifications to his front and rear entryway doors. They were already constructed of steel sheathing over a 2"-thick, solid wood core. All he needed to do was install the same steel box-frame and industrial hinges as he had with the garage, and flip the doors, so they opened out instead of in. His walls of steel wouldn't stop a high-velocity round, but that wasn't the point. Criminals, or SWAT teams for that matter, hoping to surprise their victims, always chose the easiest and fastest route of entry: a battering ram or pry bar against a front or rear door, or an up-armored vehicle running through the garage doors. Serious criminals could always find a way into a house, but Stan concealed his modifications enough that the assailants wouldn't know to try anything other than the easiest and quickest way in. The noise and time wasted on the thwarted attempts to enter would be all Stan needed to prepare an adequate defense. In addition, he'd installed infrared security cameras with thermal motion detection and geofencing. He could access the images in realtime from his cell phone, and in the case someone came to his front door, an image of the visitor was automatically displayed on his phone without any actions on his part.

As soon as the garage doors closed, Stan got out of his car and walked over to a pegboard wall filled with woodworking tools. Pulling on the edge, he swung the panel open, revealing a small handgun safe. He punched in the code and heard the familiar whining of the internal mechanism. The safe's door popped open. Stan kept a more extensive array of weapons locked in a larger safe inside the house but always wanted to have access to a second location, just in case. He pulled off his suit jacket, strapped on a shoulder holster he'd retrieved from the safe and slid his .45 caliber Glock 21 into the pocket of the holster. He felt the familiar weight of the sidearm against his side, nestled right under his left arm. His tension eased slightly.

Okay, I've got to call Brenda, he thought. *Tell her not to come home after work. She's gonna to be so pissed, but she knew what she'd signed up for when she married me.*

Meyers watched Stan's garage doors slowly swing shut as they passed his house and pulled to the curb. They stopped two houses down on the far side of the street, affording them a broad view of the residence and surrounding yards.

"This is perfect," said Meyers. "A home invasion gone wrong. Duke, Sam, leave your high-powered shit behind and use your silenced sidearms. Cover the back and I'll take the front. Butch, set up the .338 in the back seat and cover us. You'll have a clear line-of-sight out the rear window."

Butch lowered the rear window halfway and crawled into the back of the SUV. He unlatched the case carrying his McMillan TAC-338. The high-powered sniper rifle had a 27-inch, 1-9.35″ twist barrel chambered for the mighty .338 Lapua Mag. Attached to the top of the barrel was a Leupold Mark 4 3.5-10x40mm LR/T Illuminated scope. The rifle was way overkill for the less than 100 meters range he'd be operating at, but it was better to be safe than sorry.

"I'll go knock on the front door," Meyers said. "If he's stupid enough to open it, I'll plug him. Butch, if he comes to the door but doesn't open it, on my signal, blow out the deadbolt. Use your suppressor and keep the muzzle inside the truck. That'll reduce the report enough to give us some time to egress. As soon as you destroy the lock, I'll plow right through the front door and put him down. If he bolts out the back, he's all yours guys. Sam, grab the empty duffel. After he's down, we go in, grab anything that looks expensive and pull his wallet. Oh, and weapons, he's got to have some lying around. The cops will think it's some gangbangers stocking up on supplies."

Butch raised his weapon, sighting on Stan's front porch. The others pulled on nitrile gloves and screwed suppressors onto their sidearms.

Butch said, "He's got a security camera."

"Damn! Okay. Set up the dazzler on a tripod and narrow the beam all the way down. We'll blind the camera."

Butch pulled a B.E. Meyers GLARE MOUT non-lethal laser from its case and mounted it on a small tripod. The laser caused temporary blindness, disabling a human target without permanent injury. It also worked quite well at blinding visible and near-infrared sensors, such as those used for home security systems.

"He'll probably have one at the rear door as well," said Sam.

"Use your balaclavas to hide your faces. Let's move out."

Butch readjusted the barrel of the TAC-338 on the back-seat headrest while the other three exited the vehicle.

Stan walked in through the pantry door and headed upstairs while speed dialing Brenda's phone. He needed to grab his go-bag and head for the cabin. He'd meet her there. Stan froze halfway up the staircase. The familiar sound of her phone drifted down the stairwell.

Stan slipped his Glock from the holster and crouched. Then he heard her familiar voice on the phone.

"Hey, Darling. What's up?"

"Brenda?" He called up the stairs.

A second later, she appeared around the corner, her eyes opening wide when she spotted Stan's weapon.

"Oh my God! What are you doing?" she said as she jumped back in surprise.

"What are ya doin' home?" he asked as he bounded up the stairs.

"Stan! Put that gun away. You're scaring me."

"Where's yur car?" he asked, slipping his gun back into its holster.

"It's at the shop, I told you yesterday there was no school today, so I was going to take care of that recall. They... "

"We need to git out of here!"

"What are you talking about?"

"No questions. Move! I'm in danger, and you shouldn't be anywhere near me. We have to go."

Stan grabbed Brenda's cell phone and ran down the hall to the bathroom. He removed the porcelain lid to the toilet tank and dropped both Brenda's and his own phone into the water. He then ran to the closet and grabbed the go-bag he kept on the top shelf. It contained a change of clothes for him and his wife, a set of passports, four burner phones, new credit cards and plenty of cash in both dollars and euros.

Brenda was still standing in the upstairs hallway with a look of panic on her face when he exited the bedroom.

"Come on, darlin. It's going to be alright. We just need to git in the car and go."

"Okay," she said.

Stan grabbed her hand and took the first step down the stairs when the front doorbell rang.

They both froze.

"Shit!" Stan said. He'd made himself blind as soon as he dropped his phone into the toilet tank.

"Hold on," he yelled downstairs. "I'll be right there."

Stan knew that if it were a threat, they would have been watching and knew he was inside the house. He needed to act as if it were just a typical morning. He wanted the assailant to stay right where he was.

Stan handed Brenda the bag and whispered, "Go into my office and lock the door behind you. I'll let ya know as soon as I git rid of whoever's at the front door."

He didn't want Brenda to be any more alarmed than she already was, but as soon as he told her to go to the safe-room, she stiffened and shook her head.

"No! You come with me. Don't go down there."

The safe room was another one of Stan's construction projects designed to protect the occupants before reinforcements arrived.

He knew it wouldn't hold up to an onslaught of a professional team. It was just supposed to give him more time.

If he engaged the kill team and lost, he knew they'd egress immediately, if there were no witnesses.

"Okay," he said. "I'll go with you."

Stan pushed her down the hallway to his office located just above the garage. Guiding her inside, he quickly closed the door behind her.

"Stan! What are you doing! Don't do this," she yelled from the other side of the door.

"Don't worry, just lock the door. I'll be right back."

He'd installed a bolt latch that locked from the outside just in case he ran into such a situation. He was sure glad he did. The doorbell rang again, and Stan ran down the stairs.

"I'm coming!" he yelled. "Keep yur shirt on!"

Reaching the front door, Stan unholstered his weapon, put his left hand on the deadbolt, and turned the lock.

The smack of the .338 caliber round impacting Sheppard's front door lock made Meyer's ears ring. He felt the sting as shards of metal and wood pierced the exposed skin on his face, but he didn't have time to inspect the wounds. He took two running steps and lunged for the door. The right shoulder of his 220-pound body struck just above the shattered lock. The door stopped his forward momentum instantly. His head, still moving forward, struck the steel doorframe with a sickening crack. He stumbled back, shook his head, and made another running start. Before he reached the door, it erupted with bullet holes, and slowly swung out towards him. At first, Meyers thought Butch was trying to help him by riddling the door with rounds, but when the pain started, he realized that wasn't the case. A second later, he fell to his knees, another second and he was flat on his back, a few more seconds passed before his heart stopped.

Stan was lying on the floor, adrenalin surging through his veins. His heart was pounding and he was dazed. But he'd been trained well over many years. He'd instinctively raised his weapon and brought his left hand up to cup his right. He'd pulled the trigger three times before realizing he had no left hand. Blood gushed from his wrist, and his arm felt like lead. Single-handed, he fired the Glock four more times. The front door swung open, revealing a large dead man lying on his porch. Stan rolled to the side and struggled to his feet. The next attack would come from the rear. Anyone left at the front of the house would think long and hard before exposing themselves in his doorway. With a stream of blood trailing behind him, Stan entered the kitchen. He heard bodies crash against the back door. He sent seven rounds through the door and the walls on either side before the Glock's bolt locked open. He pressed the release button and the empty magazine tumbled to the floor. Tucking the Glock under his left arm, he retrieved a fresh magazine from his shoulder holster, slammed it into position, released the slide, and fired four more rounds through the back door. He waited. It was quiet. All he heard was the ringing in his ears and Brenda pounding on his office door. He looked at the blood pooling on the floor and felt light-headed.

Tourniquet! he thought.

He pulled off his tie and wrapped it tightly around his wrist. He was working on the knot when the blackness enveloped him. His feet slipped on the blood, and he fell. His head struck the corner of the kitchen counter.

Butch walked up to the front entrance of Stan's home, knelt and pulled the cell phone from Meyers' jacket. The only link back to the Deputy Director was the phone. He stepped over Meyers' body without an ounce of resignation. He'd hated the narcissistic asshole since the day they'd met. Holding his service weapon steady, he eyed the steel hardware surrounding the front door and nodded in appreciation.

Dammit! This guy was waiting for us, he thought. Then he spotted the blood-soaked entryway. *But that son-of-a-bitch sure wasn't expecting me.*

When he heard the pounding, Butch crouched low and aimed his weapon at the top of the staircase.

"Help! Help! Somebody help. I called the police. They're on their way!"

Butch relaxed. If his target were upstairs, he wouldn't be letting his wife give away their position. He followed the blood trail toward the back of the house. Entering the kitchen, he found Stan in a puddle of blood with a bullet hole in his head. Wondering where his other teammates were, he looked toward the back door. A dozen or so bullet holes let narrow shafts of light filter in. He went to the door, unlocked it and pulled. It didn't budge. *Stupid!* he thought and pushed. It opened a few inches before thumping against something. He pushed harder, slowly opening the door. On the other side were his remaining teammates. One was obviously dead, judging by the gaping hole in his neck. The other, Duke, was groaning, holding his hand to his stomach. Blood poured around his fingers. Butch heard distant sirens to the east.

"Sorry mate, you know the deal. I gotta get outta here."

Butch raised his silenced semi-automatic and put a round into the center of Duke's forehead.

Chapter 19

Day 10 (Continued)

"God damn it!" Atwood said. "Call Sheehan, tell him what happened. Then you need to head for the hills. Check in with me in a week."

Atwood hung up the phone.

"We're on! It was a complete fuckup back home, but the target is down. It's time to take Franklin out, just don't kill the girl. Get into position."

The team went into action. They slipped on their gear and checked their weapons. Atwood ran out the back door of the abandoned building and turned east while Gregory and Martinelli headed north, down the ravine, toward the approach road to the LaTorre home. Garret remained at his over-watch position with the .50 cal.

Atwood took the longest to get into position. He used the cover of the ravine to work his way up toward the garden on the southwest side of the LaTorre's property. From there, he'd be able to watch the back door and the west side of the house. Gregory and Martinelli would cover the approach road on the north-east side and Garret had the north-west. Perry and his girlfriend would be caught in a deadly crossfire.

Atwood keyed his comms while climbing the hill behind the LaTorre's home.

"This is team leader, activate the jammer."

Gregory reached into his backpack and pulled out a small black box with an antenna protruding from its side. He flipped the toggle switch. A dim red light glowed. Back at the OP, the jammer they'd set up started broadcasting a powerful signal, blocking all cell phone communications and radio frequency bands used by the polizia. The only working comms in the valley were the team's radios and the few remaining landlines that had gone out of fashion years ago.

Gregory and Martinelli ran up to the last curve before the LaTorre home. Martinelli removed a spike strip from the pack. They'd planned this spot carefully. Garret had a clear line-of-site to their position. The narrow width of the road at that point, combined with the high cliffs on one side, and the steep ravine on the other allowed them to shut down any northern approach to the homestead completely. They stretched the spike strip across the narrow road and anchored it securely. They had little concern for the southern approach since it led further into the mountains. Traffic was non-existent and it would take the polizia fortyfive minutes to respond from that direction. They would be long gone by then.

Perry pulled his camera off the tripod and threw it into the Pelican case. He retrieved his Glock from under his mattress and slipped that into the waistband of his pants. He ran out the bedroom door, down the stairs and headed towards the front of the house, then stopped. He couldn't just disappear, he had to say something.

Christina was working on her laptop when Perry burst through the kitchen door.

"Hi!" she said, closing the computer quickly. "Come, have some coffee."

"Ahhh, I can't, I have to go."

"Oh?" She eyed Perry's case with suspicion. "Where are you off to?"

"I just need to take some more measurements. I'll be back later."

"Okay, maybe we can go to... "

"Sure," he said as he turned and walked out the door.

Christina saw the distress in Perry's eyes and worried that he had seen too much. She knew she should not have been working on her computer with her back to the door. Deciding to go after him, she got up, went to the front entranceway, and slipped on her shoes. That is when she heard the reports from a hunter's rifle, a common occurrence this time of year.

She twisted the front door handle and it blew open in a shower of wood splinters.

Garret was regretting every second of this assignment as he watched the front door through his Nightforce rifle scope.

The door opened and Franklin walked out.

Garret clicked his comm. "The target's heading for his car!"

"Shit!" Atwood replied. "Take him out!"

Garret centered his crosshairs on Franklin's chest but hesitated. He couldn't pull the trigger. His gut instincts were screaming at him. Don't do this, he said to himself. He shifted his aimpoint and squeezed. A moment later, the 50 BMG round hit the center of Franklin's Pelican case. It exploded from his hand. The bullet exited the case and shredded the right rear tire of the Fiat. It punctured the steel wheel rim and harmlessly bounced to the ground. Garret's second round sliced past Franklin's right shoulder, piercing the lower-left corner of the rear windshield before punching through the driver's seat at center mass. It entered the dashboard via the AM/FM radio. A few seconds later, a stream of engine oil and water began pouring onto the ground. Garret moved the crosshairs to the LaTorre's old van and put another round through the its engine. Franklin wasn't going to be driving into the hands of his two teammates. Garret needed to herd him back into the relative safety of the stone house. He moved on to the heavy wooden door of the LaTorre's home, put a pound of pressure on the trigger and waited. There was a high probability that Christina would come running out to investigate. His Barrett might be suppressed, but there's only so much you can do to silence a 750-grain bullet traveling at 2800 feet per second with 14,000 foot-pounds of energy. It wasn't long before he saw the handle move. He raised the crosshairs to the top frame of the door and squeezed the trigger.

Perry was walking to the car, trying to decipher what he had just seen on Christina's computer. Displayed on the right side was an electrical schematic, on the left were long lines of software code. She'd been using MATLAB, a design tool used by scientists and engineers. He traced the connections and symbols in his mind and realized it was some type of control loop. The image of the control loop disappeared the instant the Pelican case was ripped from his hand. He heard the crack of the supersonic round. He felt the pressure from the second round passing inches from his head and two distant, muffled booms from a high-powered rifle. He drew his weapon and turned back towards the direction of the sound just in time to see the front door of Christina's home explode open.

"Christina!" he yelled.

Running back to the house, he found her laying on the floor, blood oozing from several wounds on her face and chest. She sat up with a dazed expression and looked at him. When she saw the look of concern on his face and the Glock in his hands, her confusion changed to fear.

"What happened?"

"Someone's shooting at us," he answered.

Perry slammed the door shut and slid the large iron latch closed. He remembered Christina telling him a week ago, when he first entered the home, that the door hadn't been locked in over 50 years. If he'd had the time, he'd have felt ashamed. He pulled her to her feet.

"We need to get out of here. Where's Nonna and Leo?"

"Leo is at the church. Nonna is visiting family."

"Good. We need to move. We're dead if we stay here."

"What is happening?"

"These are professionals, they're trying to kill me, and there's no stopping them."

"How do you know this?" Christina asked, eyeing the handgun Perry was carrying.

He grabbed Christina's arm and looked straight into her eyes.

"You're going to have to trust me! They're American para-military, and they know exactly what they're doing. Is there any other way out of here besides this door and the rear courtyard?"

Christina pulled her arms out of Perry's grasp. "I am not leaving; I must call the police."

Christina removed her cell phone from her pants pocket and dialed 112.

Perry ran to the windows and closed the large wooden shutters. They wouldn't stop the assault team, but they'll at least slow them down. After latching the shutters, he headed for the kitchen.

Christina ran after him. "My phone is not working. There is no signal."

"They're jamming the network."

"Jamming? Who does that?"

He closed and latched the rear door. "We need more weapons. Are there any in the house?"

"No."

Christina went to the sink and washed the blood and debris from her face.

"Get away from the window!" he yelled.

Perry yanked her from the window and inspected her face.

"They're just minor cuts," he said as he pulled a wood splinter from her face. "We need to get out of here."

"We cannot go out there," Christina said. "It is too dangerous, and this house is a fortress."

"It won't stop them. We need a way out of here. It's our only chance."

Atwood stopped in midstride. Their plan to hit the front and rear doors simultaneously was gone. The element of surprise was gone. He repositioned himself in the garden with a clear view of the courtyard door. He decided to let his team hit the front. They'd work their way in and hopefully flush his targets, through the courtyard and out into the garden. Anyone beside Christina or his men coming through that archway were dead.

"Mobile!" Atwood said. "What's your status?"

"Garret missed his target, Franklin's inside. We've already spiked the road 30 meters down from the driveway, and we're moving in fast."

"Roger. I'm in position in the garden. Use flash-bangs at the front. I'll wait for them to come running out the rear. Garret, if you can manage to hit the broadside of a house, start blowing holes through that damn place, I don't want them feeling like it's a safe haven in there."

"Will do."

Two carabinieri were sitting on the Hotel Zia patio eating lunch when they heard the muffled gunshots rolling down the mountainside.

Although technically a separate branch of the Italian armed forces, the Carabinieri were the national police of

Italy. They operate parallel to local law enforcement, like the state police in the US.

The sergeant said, "It is probably Giermo again, shooting at the feral pigs raiding his garden."

"He knows he is not allowed to do that," said the junior officer, sliding his chair back and standing up from the table.

"Let the Canneto polizia handle it this time," said the first. "Let us finish lunch."

Another, more extended volley of gunfire echoed down the mountain, and the two officers looked at each other.

"That is not Giermo's shotgun," the sergeant said.

They both jumped from the table and ran for their squad car.

Fist-sized chunks of stone and concrete exploded through Christina's kitchen. Glass broke and the shattered frame of the kitchen window crashed into the sink.

"There's only going to be one outcome if we stay here," Perry said.

Then they heard the explosion.

"They're coming in through the front door."

Christina grabbed his hand. "Okay, you win, we cannot stay here."

More shots rang out and the house seemed to shake in response.

"We need to go to the wine cellar," she yelled over the din of a kitchen cabinet being torn from its mounts. Shattered china poured onto the floor.

Perry remembered what Christina had said earlier about Leo's hunting rifles. He ran to the kitchen door and crouched down low. Christina followed close behind. As soon as he swung the door open a volley of automatic fire thudded into the rear wall, high above their heads.

"Stay low," he said. "The courtyard walls are blocking their field of fire."

277

They ran in a low crouch to the wine cellar built into the side of the hill and entered the musty interior. He closed and locked the massive iron door and switched on the single light dangling from the ceiling.

"Are you okay," he asked.

She nodded.

He brought his fingers up to where the top of her right breast was exposed and pulled a large sliver of glass from her flesh. Christina winced.

"We'll be okay for now," he said. "It'll take a little time for them to clear the house, but they'll find us sooner or later. Let's grab your uncle's weapons and see if we can escape into the garden."

Christina hesitated.

"Come on, we can't wait," Perry said. "Where are they?"

She looked over at the door in the back wall of the cellar.

"Where's the key?" he asked.

She nodded toward the wine barrel. "It is in the bung plugging the top of the wine barrel. Pull it out, and you will see a slot where the key is hidden."

Perry retrieved the key from the barrel.

Christina grabbed his arm. "I need you to promise me something."

"I'll promise you anything if you can get us out of here."

"I am serious," she said, squeezing his arm tighter. "I am trusting you with something more important than either one of us. I would rather we go out there and die than have you reveal what you are about to see."

"I have no idea what you're talking about, but I swear. Whatever it is, it stays with us."

"Okay, and I want you to remember something."

"What!" he said impatiently.

"No matter what happens, I love you."

"What?"

Christina pushed him toward the iron door at the rear of the cellar.

"Hurry," she said.

Perry slid the key into the lock and looked back at Christina. He saw the concern on her face, but also something else, a vulnerability. Was it because of what she'd just said? Whatever it was, he knew that he'd never break his promise to her. He turned the key, removed the padlock, and swung the door open. What he saw on the other side stopped him in his tracks.

The explosion echoed across the mountain. Garret scanned his scope back to the front of the house in time to see Martinelli and Gregory rush through the doorway. Martinelli's voice cracked over the comms. "We're in."

Scanning back toward the kitchen, he saw Perry and Christina exit the rear of the house and run through a door built into the courtyard wall. He knew they were trapped. There wasn't much else he could do.

"Garret!" Atwood called. "Watch the approach road. We're making too much Goddamn noise down here. Find these people and wrap it up! We need to get out of here."

Atwood ran through the archway at the rear of the courtyard and heard the clang of metal on metal. He slid to a stop, crouched and swung his H&K to the right. He spotted the steel door to the wine cellar.

"DJ, Doc.," he said. "Sweep the first floor of the house and come out the back. I'm holding here in the courtyard."

"Roger!"

"Garret, how we looking?"

"The approach road is clear, but it's not going to stay that way. We need to get out of here, fast."

"We're not leaving until this guy is down and we have the girl. Take out anybody coming up that road."

"Roger."

Garret scanned the road down the mountain. Nothing. Then he scanned back to the right, past the house and up the hill. Near the top, he saw a flash of red. It was a small car, similar to Perry's, coming slowly down the mountain. It was uncharacteristic. Everyone he'd seen had been speeding through these Sicilian hills like it was a roller coaster. It was halfway to the house when he spotted the occupants. Two elderly women.

"Lead, we got a red Fiat with two women approaching from the south. I'm letting them pass.

"Roger," came the reply.

He continued watching until the vehicle pulled to the side, just above the LaTorre's garden.

What the hell, Garret thought.

The car pulled across the road, reversed a few feet, and then forward a few feet. When it was finally pointed back from where it came, the passenger door opened.

"Shit!" Garret said out loud.

"Lead! It's the grandmother! You need to get the hell out of there. She's coming in through the garden."

"Roger," Atwood replied calmly.

Nonna leaned over and kissed her sister on the cheek. "Addio, il mio amore."

She grabbed her bag from the backseat and opened the car door. The scents from her garden filled the air and she inhaled deeply. Citrus, garlic, and fig. And another scent, something she couldn't identify. An acrid smell, with a hint of sulfur. *"Was Leo burning leaves again?"* she wondered and shook her head. She carefully made her way down the stone steps and headed for the courtyard. She was wondering what she might make for dinner when she noticed the ripe tomatoes hanging from their branches. A tomato sauce, she decided, with the fresh pasta she had in her canvas bag. Nonna picked a half dozen plump tomatoes, pulled some garlic out of the soil, and grabbed a handful of basil that grew like a weed along the base of the courtyard wall. She imagined the wonderful aromas that would soon fill the kitchen and smiled. She was still smiling when she stepped to the archway and saw the armed man standing inside.

Garret couldn't see inside the courtyard; the stone walls were too high. He watched with horror as Nonna made her way through the garden, stopping several times to pick vegetables. She turned and stepped toward the entrance to the courtyard. A split-second later, she fell silently in a heap. He watched in silence as Atwood walked up to the body, poked it with his boot, and looked up towards Garret. Garret immediately centered his crosshairs on Atwood's chest. He had just started to squeeze the trigger when Atwood disappeared back into the courtyard.

Chapter 20

Day 10 (Continued)

Christina led Perry into the cavern, turned on the overhead light and locked the door behind her. She walked over and pushed a button on the wall next to the elevator shaft. A whirring sound of spinning gears and motors rose up from below, and a moist breeze blew out of the opening. Thirty seconds later, a large freight elevator emerged from the shaft.

"You need to explain what's going on," he said.

"Remember, you promised," she said.

She slid the rusted mesh gate up and they stepped into the elevator. Christina pushed another button and the elevator descended.

Perry's ears popped and he felt the temperature decrease. The smooth, dark basalt walls passed by as the elevator continued to descend. Reaching the bottom of the shaft, the elevator stopped.

"Where are we?" he asked.

"110 meters below sea level."

Perry knew one thing for sure, this place and this woman were somehow connected to the source of the Majorana neutrinos.

Christina lifted the elevator gate and led Perry down a long corridor. It was wide enough and tall enough to drive a dump truck through. The dark, rough-cut basalt walls contrasted starkly with the polished, grey concrete floors.

High overhead was an array of pipes, multi-colored cables, and ventilation ducts. The earthy scent of the elevator shaft had been replaced by clean, dry, sterile air. She walked over to an electric golf cart parked against the wall and unplugged the charging cable.

"Get in," she said. "It is a long walk."

As soon as Christina sat down, the dashboard lit up. She pushed a button under an icon shaped like a sphere, and the cart took off. For several minutes, the autonomous vehicle drove through a maze of corridors. It required no input. It steered itself around pallets of machinery and stopped at every intersection to avoid traffic.

"You know why I'm here, don't you?" asked Perry.

"The original tunnels were created by lava flows thousands of years ago," she answered. "We cleaned them out and added more tunnels as our research progressed."

"What research?" he asked.

She looked Perry in the eyes. "I think you already know."

The corridors grew busy with what looked like scientists, engineers and technicians, all heading in different directions. Turning down another corridor, they reached a deadend. On the far wall was a large double door with a keypad to one side.

"Less than 100 people know where this facility is, or that it even exists. We used the construction of the highway tunnels to mask our efforts. The elevator was disguised as a ventilation shaft for the highway," Christina said. "Many others at other facilities are involved but have no idea of the extent or purpose of our facility."

"How are you involved with this?"

"It is a type of particle accelerator," she said. "I will show you."

Christina punched a sequence of numbers and held her eye up to a retinal scanner. The lock buzzed and they walked in.

Perry stopped at the doorway and looked up. "A particle accelerator?"

"We call it the 'BiniSphere.'"

The polished stainless-steel sphere in the center of the room dwarfed the suited workers standing next to it. The BiniSphere stood at least 20 meters high, filling the underground cavern to capacity.

"It is the largest, heaviest, and most accurate sphere ever built," Christina explained. "It is also the most powerful particle accelerator known to mankind, or in our case, unknown to mankind, and it is built for only one purpose, to put Ettore Majorana's theories into action."

"You know about Ettore?" Perry asked.

"My parents tried using a nuclear reactor to provide the neutrinos, but it proved too unstable. The beam could not be controlled, it created a feedback loop with the reactor. They almost died when they turned on the benchtop model. It self-destructed. Luckily, no one was injured. We switched to a new particle accelerator design but did not have the technology to shrink it to this size until the world discovered cryogenic, superconducting magnets and nanotechnology. That is when we were able to put it all together. The amount of electrical power we need is enormous. We also had to build the world's largest capacitor bank. We charge it using the high voltage electrical grid up on the surface. That is what caused the electrical disturbances in Canneto. We are creating a magnetic field of 200 teslas with a pulse duration of 100 milliseconds.

"That's impossible," Perry said. "No one is even close to achieving that kind of flux density. How do you even know about all this?"

"Perry, please just let me finish. We were able to solve two problems at once. We used the magnets as giant electrical filters to dampen the feedback loop created by the neutrinos. It solved our instability problems while increasing our flux density. The particle accelerator is very carefully controlled to prevent the feedback loops in the beam from starting a chain reaction. It took decades to develop the techniques to control the reaction without it going critical. But, just in case, we built it below sea level, as a safety measure. In case things do go wrong, the cavern can be completely flooded with saltwater in less than an hour, simply by switching off the pumps. The explosion would be completely contained."

Perry heard the low hum of massive pumps in the background. He thought it an illusion at first, but the sphere was rotating. A round window at the top of the sphere slowly appeared and descended like a setting moon.

"The BiniSphere is completely self-contained," she said. "We power it and control it electromagnetically. There are no outside connections of any kind. We use internal gyros for aiming the beam."

"What beam?" Perry asked. But he already knew the answer.

Remembering the glitch in the KH-11's power supply and the experiments Howell had been doing at NNSS, Perry finally understood what was going on. They weren't trying to take out the PIT sensor. They didn't even know it existed. These people were trying to take out the entire satellite by destroying the nuclear power plant.

"It is a columnated beam of high-density Majorana neutrinos," said Christina. "We can transmit in any direction. To absorb vibrations and stabilize the beam, the BiniSphere floats in 50 tons of mercury. There are two centimeters of mercury between its walls and the hole it is floating in. It is essentially frictionless and very precisely balanced. A single person can rotate the sphere by pulling and pushing. Do you see the grid of latitude and longitude lines marked on its surface?"

Perry nodded in disbelief.

"They coincide with the latitude and longitude of any point on the earth's surface. But that is not accurate enough. The beam must fall within feet of its target and the earth is too elastic. The earth's crust shifts with the tides, 30 centimeters, a foot, twice a day. That, combined with the lack of exact coordinates, well, we are essentially shooting in the dark."

Christina pointed at the round window in the sphere. "That is the exit aperture. With your camera we could shoot a beam of Majorana neutrinos so powerful and so precise that nothing would get in its way."

"My camera? We?" Perry asked with a steely edge in his voice. "How are you a part of this? Shooting at what?"

"The warheads, Perry."

Christina turned towards him and saw the dread in his face.

"No, no, you do not understand!"

Perry turned and ran fast, back through the doorway and into the hall.

"Wait!" Christina yelled.

He jumped into the golf cart. As soon as the dashboard lit up, he took the wheel and drove back down the tunnel at full speed. Perry turned a corner in the tunnel, and he slammed on the brakes. He jumped out, grabbed a case of bottled water sitting in the back of the cart and dropped it onto the driver's seat. The dashboard turned back on. He pressed an icon on the control panel shaped like two elevator doors, and the cart took off without him. He knew he couldn't go back to the surface the way they'd come. There were people up there trying to kill him. And he sure as hell wasn't going to stay here and help Christina.

During their ride to the BiniSphere, he'd noticed several emergency exits with oblong, steel doors, like ships use to seal off compartments. He figured they were there in case the particle accelerator failed. He ran for the closest one, rotated the latches and pushed the steel door inwards. Stepping over the high threshold, he saw a sealed capsule. It was large enough for five people. He looked up and saw a long dark shaft going straight up, but there was no ladder. He rotated the heavy latch on the capsule door and looked inside. When he saw the five life jackets hanging from the ceiling, he realized what it was, a lifeboat. They were under the ocean. Perry climbed inside and closed the hatch. Seeing a red lever in the center of the ceiling, he yanked it down without a second thought.

Perry felt as if he'd been shot out of a cannon. A massive column of water crashed down into the shaft, and the capsule slammed sideways. A blast of compressed air from somewhere below propelled him upwards, as if he were in a high-speed elevator. A small glass port in the side of the lifeboat showed nothing but darkness until it shot up and out of the seafloor in a storm of air bubbles. The boat tumbled, rolled and twisted before settling into a slow ascent. When the capsule broke the surface of the sea, the hatch popped opened. The lifeboat immediately filled with water and began to sink. Perry realized it was not designed to float once its passengers were delivered to the relative safety of the surface. He floated out and looked south, seeing that he wasn't more than 500 meters offshore. Once again, he swam toward the beach.

Christina ran into the hallway in time to see Perry heading back the way they'd come. For a moment, she considered letting him go. But she had to explain, he had to help her. She walked over to an intercom panel.

"He is heading back to the elevator, just track the cart's location." she said. "Let him get there before shutting the cart and the elevator down. I do not know who they are, but those people were trying to kill us. I will talk some sense into him while he is staring at those elevator doors wondering what is waiting for him up on top."

Christina found another golf cart down the hallway and drove back toward the elevators. She was 50 meters away from the emergency exit when she heard the explosion. Her ears popped as the pressure inside the corridor changed. Alarm bells sounded and a loud groaning echoed from behind her. A concrete door the size of a house rolled closed. Up ahead, another door closed. She ran toward the escape hatch. Just as she arrived, a column of cold seawater blasted through the opening, knocking her into the far wall. A second later it stopped. Christina, dazed but alive, sat up and looked towards the exit. As designed, if someone neglected to close the hatch, the pressure of the water would close it. She walked over and pushed on the hatch, knowing it was a waste of time. The extreme water pressure would never allow that door to open. A few minutes later, the alarm bells quit, and the doors at each end of the hallway slid back open. Christina jumped into the golf cart and headed for the elevator. She was just pulling up when her phone rang.

"Christina! What is happening?" her uncle asked. "I was just notified an escape pod has been activated."

"We were under attack at the house. Perry said they were American para-military and they were trying to kill us."

"Where are you?"

"I am all right. I had to bring Perry down here to the BiniSphere. We are out of time. We need his help. Our secret is getting out."

"Stay where you are. I will be right there."

"I have to go find the camera. It is somewhere in the house."

"No!" her uncle replied. "I will call Don Tumeo. His people can be there in twenty minutes."

"It cannot wait. The camera will disappear."

"No, Christina. I forbid it!"

"The gunmen must be gone by now, and I am already at the elevator. I need to get the camera before the polizia arrive."

Christina hung up the phone and called Steve, her second in charge.

Atwood and Martinelli pulled with all their strength, but the wine cellar's steel door didn't budge.

289

"Gregory! Get a breaching charge over here!"

Gregory opened his satchel and removed a compact coil of detcord and C4. When they heard the muffled sound of Garret's Barrett Atwood spoke into his mike. "What's your status?"

"Law enforcement has arrived. It's time to bug out," said Garret. "I've got them pinned down at the car, but that won't last long."

"We still have a few more minutes," said Gregory. "Their radios are jammed so they can't call for reinforcements, not until they fall back from their position."

"Get that door open!" commanded Atwood.

"Ready," Gregory said. "Fall back!"

The three men pressed their backs against the stone wall on either side of the door, covered their ears, and turned their heads away. An instant later, the blast forced air from their lungs, and they were showered with debris. They ran through the smoke and hit the door running, colliding with each other. The door held.

"Again! Hit it again," yelled Atwood.

The three of them hit the door simultaneously, and the hinges gave way with a loud screech.

Atwood's men entered the dark interior while he covered their six at the entrance.

"You won't believe this," said Martinelli.

Atwood ducked his head into the cellar.

"It's empty, but look at this," Gregory said, illuminating another door on the back wall. "Compared to this one, the front door was made out of rice paper."

"God damn it!" Atwood said. "We just can't get a break. Use some more charges to… "

"I don't have enough for this door," Gregory replied. "I wasn't expecting to have to break into a bunker."

"Wait! What if…" Martinelli put his hand on the latch and pulled. The door swung open.

Stepping into the room, Alpha Team heard the elevator ascending in the shaft. They readied their weapons.

Nearing shore, Perry noticed someone standing in the sand. The man was watching him while talking on the telephone. It was Steve, the Australian from the beach bar. There was no avoiding him, so he kept swimming. As soon as he got his feet under him, he waded through the waves.

"G'day, mate! Havin' a bit of a day I hear."

"Fuck you!"

Steve held out the phone. "It's for you."

Perry took the phone and brought it up to his ear.

"Perry, please listen," Christina said. "This is very important."

Perry hung up and punched Samuel's number into the phone.

"You have to let her explain, mate, before ya get hurt."

"I've heard enough of her lies. What do you know about all this?"

"I'm a physicist as well."

"You're a... Samuels! I need some help here!" Perry spoke into the phone as he backed away from Steve.

Steve pulled out a second phone and pressed a button that deactivated Perry's phone.

"Samuels? It's Perry. Hello? Hello!"

Perry looked over at Steve.

"Sorry. Can't let ya be doing that."

"Who the hell are you?" Perry asked, drawing his weapon and pointing it at Steve.

"Wow! Calm down ya bugger. I'm just a physicist. I specialize in neutrino research. I had to stop what I was doing and rush up here topside to make sure you were okay. Whether ya like it or not, you're on the inside, you're one of us now."

"The hell I am. You're all a bunch of fucking maniacs. Do you know how many people you're going to kill if you start triggering our nukes? Even if they don't reach critical mass, the radiation will kill millions! Do you think there won't be any retaliation?"

Steve's head tilted sideways. "What are ya talkin' about? We're not killin' anybody. Come back to the bar and let me explain."

Perry's thoughts were racing. He needed information to make sense of what he was hearing and decided the Aussie might have some answers.

They walked back to the tiki bar and Steve began mixing some drinks while Perry sat down on a bar stool.

"Now isn't this a lot nicer than the last time we met? You were in sorry ass shape there, skipper. How's your head feelin'?"

"Never mind my head, tell me what you know about all this."

Steve poured a Mai Tai over a tall glass of ice and slid it over to Perry.

"What do ya know about Majorana neutrinos, Mr. Franklin?"

"Excuse me? Someone's trying to kill me. I've just been shot out of some kind of science fiction underwater fortress, and you want me to sit here sipping a Mai Tai while discussing nuclear physics? Are all of you insane?"

"Look, everybody's safe, and our people are going after those shooters as we speak. The crisis is over. If ya want to understand what we're doing, we need to have this discussion."

Perry shook his head, took a sip of the drink, then spoke.

"Theoretically, Majorana neutrinos are different than normal neutrinos because they have a mass associated with them. Normal neutrinos are essentially massless, which is why they don't interact with other particles."

"Very good, but ya said theoretically. It's more than theoretical," Steve said. "It's a fact. We've been working on this for over seventy years."

"What do you mean 'we'? The whole world's been working on nuclear physics for that long."

"We've been working solely on generating Majorana particles, and we've finally built a device that can do it, in mucho large quantities."

"So, you've been building a doomsday machine this entire time. That's something to be proud of."

"We are very proud. But, it's not a doomsday machine, in fact, I guess ya might call it an anti-doomsday machine."

"By blowing up all our nukes?"

"Of course not. That wouldn't be very productive, would it? And, we couldn't do that even if we wanted to."

"We've done our own experiments. We radiated enriched uranium with a beam of the Majorana neutrinos and it began breaking down, we started a runaway fission reaction."

"How close were you to the source of your neutrinos?" Steve asked.

"From the nuclear reactor? Maybe twenty meters."

"Reactor? Ya can't do that, mate! You'll get yourself killed. You have to use a particle accelerator."

"Our calculations… "

"Your calculations are wrong. We use a particle accelerator and it's completely safe. We can radiate nuclear material all day long and not trigger a chain reaction. We just break it down into its subcomponents."

Perry thought for a second. "So, if the warheads never go critical, then… "

"If you continue to radiate the uranium, or even plutonium, with a Majorana particle beam you end up with…?"

"Well," Perry replied. "If you breakdown uranium, I guess you'd end up with a bunch of krypton and barium."

"Exactly, and with plutonium, you'd end up with some rubidium and a few other radioisotopes. The point being, there's not going to be any big boom in the foreseeable future."

"So, you're telling me you've built a machine that can neutralize a nuclear bomb, anywhere in the world?"

"Not a nuclear bomb, Skippa. Every nuclear bomb."

Perry thought of the repercussions.

"I know what you're thinkin', mate. MAD, mutually assured destruction. How do we take out one country's nukes without causing an imbalance and someone getting an itchy trigger finger, aye?"

Perry nodded.

"Politics ma man, politics."

"What do you mean?"

"If some country, say the good ole US of A, starts seein' the radiation from their nukes decrease do ya think they're going to announce it to the world? Tell everybody 'Hey, we can't wipe ya off the face of the earth anymore.'"

"I imagine not," Perry said. "But it will cause a lot of panic. We might not be perfect, but we're the strongest deterrence in the world, stopping all those crazy fucks like Kim Jong Un."

"Exactly, that's why we save the State's nukes for last. We start with the most radical, unstable countries and work our way up. Our calculations show that we can have the entire world free of nukes within six months."

"Except for one problem," Perry said.

"Yeah, except for one problem. We don't have an accurate way of aiming our beam."

"How do I know you're telling me the truth?"

The Australian leaned forward across the bar and looked hard into Perry's eyes.

"Faith, mate. Faith."

"Faith? In what?"

"Look into your heart mate. What do ya think Dr. Christina is trying to do here?"

"What's her part in all of this?"

"Her part? Didn't she tell ya?"

Perry shook his head.

Perry and Steve heard tires skidding and they looked toward the gravel parking lot. A Toyota Land Cruiser came to a sliding stop.

"Looks like ya have some reinforcements," Steve said.

Chapter 21

Day 10 (Continued)

As soon as the elevator emerged from the elevator shaft, Christina locked eyes with Atwood. She immediately hit buttons to stop its upward progress, but it was too late. The platform rose into the cellar and stopped. Three high-capacity assault rifles were trained on her.

Gregory lifted the gate, grabbed Christina by the back of her shirt collar, and yanked her out.

"Where's Franklin?" Atwood asked.

"Gone," she said.

Gregory yanked her shirt down off her shoulders, ripping the buttons off and pinning her arms behind her.

"Cuff her," Atwood commanded.

He brought his face inches from hers and said, "We don't have time to screw around. I'm only going to ask you once. If you fuck with me, that man is going to throw you down the elevator shaft. Do you have any doubt in your mind that we are capable of this?"

Christina shook her head.

"Where is Franklin?" he said.

"I do not know. He escaped."

"Escaped? I thought you two were fuck buddies."

"Not anymore," she admitted. Christina realized that all these mercenaries needed to do was take the elevator to the bottom of the shaft, and all her secrets would be revealed. Her security team was no match for these professional killers. She decided the best course of action was to stretch this conversation out as much as possible to give Leo's people time to prepare.

"He discovered I was the enemy."

"Bullshit! He's a traitor. He's working with you."

"No, he had no idea what was going on. We were watching him closely, gaining his confidence, but he never revealed what he was here to do. We had our suspicions, but he did not tell us anything."

Atwood eyed Christina, looking for deceit. He didn't see any and decided there would be plenty of time later to interrogate her more thoroughly. By the time he got through with her, she'd be spewing with the intel they needed.

"This must be the entrance to the facility," Gregory said looking at the elevator.

"There's no time to go back for the rest of the C4," said Atwood. "We'll never get the girl out of here in one piece."

"Roger, we'll have to leave it up to Sheehan and his torpedoes."

Leo drove his car hard through the curves. He skidded around the last turn and slammed on the brakes. Ahead was a police car parked crossway in the road.

Leo jumped out just as a bullet punctured his hood.

"Father! Get down! Get Down!" cried one of the carabinieri.

Leo dove to the ground behind the police car where the two officers were crouching.

"A sniper has had us pinned down for the last five minutes. Our radios and cell phones are not working. We can not call out."

"I have taken care of that," Leo said.

"You called the chief? How did you know?"

"Christina and our American house guest were attacked, but they were able to escape."

"Escaped?" asked the officer. "Then why are the gunmen still here?"

Leo thought for a second, and a chill ran up his spine.

"Oh, my lord. They must have captured Christina."

"Do not worry Father, as soon as our backup gets here, we will surround them."

"Sergeant, as soon as my people arrive, you will need to stand down."

"What do you mean?"

"I did not call the chief. You do not have the resources for this. Don Tumeo's men will be here shortly."

"Tumeo's men? What are they... "

A barage of bullets impacted Leo's vehicle, sending shards of glass, metal, and rock spinning through the air. They fell to their bellies behind the squad car and peered underneath at the front of the LaTorre home.

Garret had had about enough. Now that the priest was on the scene, he decided he was getting way too old for this shit. He keyed the com.

"Lead," Garret said. "You guys need to get the hell out of there, reinforcements have arrived."

"Roger!" replied Atwood. "I'm sending Brett to get the camera. Then we'll head back to the OP. Let him know when you're ready to lay down cover fire."

"Roger," said Garret.

Garret watched through his scope as Martinelli ran out the door of the wine cellar and into the house.

A few seconds later, "Overwatch! I'm ready. Give me cover."

"Hold!" Garret yelled. "I need to reacquire the targets."

He saw Martinelli run out the front entrance and straight for the Pelican case sitting on the ground behind Perry's car.

From his vantage point under the police car, Leo watched as Martinelli ran out the front door of his home and straight for Perry's car.

What is this fool doing? he wondered. *He's coming right for us.* Then he spotted Perry's case lying on the ground. *The camera!*

Leo heard the junior officer next to him stand and then BOOM, BOOM, BOOM. Martinelli had been reaching for the bag when puffs of fabric burst from his upper body. He tumbled to the ground.

The sergeant, lying prone on the ground, pointed his service revolver under the car and fired three more rounds into Martinelli's chest.

"Stop! Stop!" Leo yelled. "They have Christina!" He reached over and pulled the younger officer to the ground just as another barrage of 50 BMG rounds impacted the top of the car.

"You might hit Christina," Leo said. "Wait for my people."

Leo knew that the likelihood of hitting her with a stray round while she was inside a stone home was slim to none. He was more worried about the camera. Both of them were willing to give their lives for the BiniSphere, and the camera was the last piece they needed to succeed.

As he and the officers withstood the massive assault from the 50 Cal, they watched as Martinelli slowly rolled over onto his stomach. Leaving the camera behind, Martinelli crawled back to the house, trailing a stream of blood.

"How can he possibly be moving?" Leo asked.

"Body armor," the sergeant replied. "One of the rounds must have struck an arm or leg."

He raised the pistol again, but Leo said, "No, let him go. They cannot get away."

Christina sat motionless in the corner of the damp cellar, the zip-cuffs biting painfully into her wrists secured behind her. The courage she'd initially mustered had quickly eroded. She knew there was no chance she'd be surviving this ordeal. The look in their eyes could not be mistaken.

She twisted slowly toward the elevator, looking for an escape route. They'd closed the sliding gate.

"Doc!" she heard Attwood say. "Grab the girl. We're moving out as soon as Martinelli gets back with the camera."

Doc grabbed her wrists and yanked her savagely to her feet.

She yelped in pain.

They dragged her into the rear courtyard just as Martinelli emerged from the back door of the house. His left arm was drenched in blood.

She wondered where Perry was. Was he part of this? Was he the target, or was she? Why was she being taken captive?

"What happened?" Atwood said to Martinelli. "Never mind."

Doc pushed Christina to the ground and removed a tourniquet from his med-pack.

"I'm just going to slow the bleeding for now. We'll patch you up as soon as we get back to the OP."

Martinelli nodded silently.

Atwood keyed his mike. "What the fuck Overwatch! You're supposed to be covering. Kill those sons-of-bitches!"

All Atwood heard in reply was a double-click of static and the resounding cracks of Garett's rounds striking steel.

The three men led Christina out of the courtyard and into Leo's garden. That is when she saw Nonna, on the ground by the doorway. A single bullet hole in her forehead.

A small stream of blood had run across her cheek and dripped to the ground. Christina fell to her knees next to Nonna's body. She screamed a volley of Italian curses at them until Atwood struck her in the side of the head with the butt of his rifle.

Doc was the biggest and strongest of the three. He lifted Christina and slung her over his shoulder. They slid down into the ravine and followed the dry stream bed uphill until they reached a small goat path to the right. Christina was half-conscious by then. She recognized the overgrown path and knew where it led. She had often played in the ruins of the old frantoio when she was a child. She knew every nook and cranny of the deserted building. She also realized it was a perfect hideout, well-hidden from the road. Almost everyone had long forgotten about it. It was so overgrown with vegetation, it was barely visible from the sky. She thought it almost fitting that this childhood place of exploration and vivid adolescent fantasies was going to be her final resting place. She watched as if in a dream, while the three men, all breathing heavily, climbed the path quietly toward the adjacent hilltop. Then she passed out again.

Christina woke when she was slammed to the ground, Doc landing on top of her. He was crushing her face into the stony earth. He wrapped a large hand around her throat.

"If you make a single sound, I will snap your neck."

Christina heard the cars racing down the mountain road. Through an opening in the trees, she saw a black SUV skid through a tight turn and then a second SUV. Once they had disappeared, Gregory yanked her to her feet and pushed her forward.

Chapter 22

Day 10 (Continued)

"Your husband's quite lucky," the doctor said. "His radial and ulnar artery were both cleanly severed. If it weren't for all the adrenaline running through his body, he wouldn't have even passed out. Once his blood pressure went back to a reasonable level, his arteries contracted enough to stem most of the bleeding. That and the unfinished tourniquet saved his life.

"When will he be out of surgery?" Brenda asked.

"It will not be long. I've removed all the shrapnel and cleaned up the bone fragments from his wrist and stitched up the laceration on his forehead. My resident is closing his arm right now. But, it's only temporary. Once the swelling goes down, we'll go back in to finish the job. We'll need to cut and shape the bone and build a skin flap. When we're finished, he'll be in good shape for a prosthetic."

"When is the next surgery?" she asked.

"It depends on the swelling, might be as soon as tomorrow."

"Oh God. Thank you, so much."

"We'll come get you once he's in the recovery room."

"I'll be right here."

Leo was still lying prone behind the squad car when he heard the roar of powerful engines coming down the mountainside.

"They are here," he said to the sergeant lying next to him.

"Who is here?"

"The people who can put an end to this."

The shooting had stopped for a good five minutes, so Leo looked over the hood. He watched as two Ford Excursions slid around a curve up the mountain behind his house. The rear vehicle stopped at a wide opening in the road commanding a view of the terrain below. Dark figures poured from all the doors. The first vehicle kept coming and soon pulled into Leo's driveway. The black SUV had been upgraded. It had heavy-duty push bars bolted to the front bumper, high-power light strips above the front and rear windshields, and a turret jutting from the roof where an M2 50 Cal machine gun was mounted. It was manned by a gunner wearing a ski mask and body armor. The vehicle continued across his yard, stopping only when its front bumpers struck the rock wall of the house, creating a protective barrier at the front entrance. The front and rear doors on the side facing the entranceway popped open. Five masked men in full battle uniform streamed from the truck and into the house. Leo heard yelling and crashing for several minutes before the men exited.

Leo yelled to them. "There is a sniper up on that knoll directly west of you."

The gunner swung his M2 around and immediately laid down cover fire as the rest of the men ran to the squad car. When they kneeled next to Leo, the two carabinieri holstered their weapons.

"I am sorry, padre," one of the masked men said.

Leo recognized the voice. Andreo, Don Tumeo's head of security.

"She is not there," Andreo said.

"Did you check the wine cellar?" he asked.

"Si`, there has been some damage. They used explosives to breach the door. The elevator car was at the top of the shaft. Your Christina does not appear to have escaped by that route."

Leo stared at a masked man standing next to Andreo. The man's eyes were dark and bloodshot, his lower lip split and swollen.

"Simon?" Leo asked.

"Si` Padre, do not worry. I promise you; we will find her."

Andreo said, "We have closed off the mountain completely. They will not get far. As soon as we know your niece is safe… "

"We will slit their throats from ear to ear," said Simon.

Brenda entered the recovery room and saw Stan sitting up in bed, drinking water through a straw.

"Hi, darlin'," he said. "Are you okay?"

"Never mind me," she replied. "You almost died!"

He looked down at the stump where his left hand used to be.

"I guess sewin' it back on wasn't an option."

"There was nothing left of it," she said matter-of-factly. "Maybe now you'll keep your promise about retiring."

Brenda was a loving and patient woman, but she was very, very pissed.

"How could you leave me in there like that, you were…"

"I'm really sorry. I had no choice. They were comin' after me and…"

"Shut up!" she yelled. "It's over. You have a decision to make. It's either me or the job."

"Yur right. It's over, I'm retiring. Let me get these loose ends tied up, so we don't have to be looking over our shoulders for the rest of our lives."

"Whatever it takes," she said. "You've got a week to get this mess straightened out, and then I'm out the door. With or without you."

She knew this was her only chance to make an impression on her husband. She'd never leave him like this, weak and defenseless, but he didn't have to know how she really felt until they were safe, away from the line of fire.

Stan nodded. "Okay, you win. Please git me a phone, and there's a piece of paper in my pants pocket with a couple phone numbers on it. I need to make some calls."

"Samuels. Keep an eye on the Aussie," Thomas ordered. "I'll talk to Franklin."

"Glad you guys are here," Perry said. "How'd you find me?"

Thomas showed Perry his phone. It displayed a map of their position, a red dot flashing on the beach where they stood.

"When you tried calling, our software stripped the GPS data from the phone you were using."

Thomas' phone rang, and the map swiftly shifted across the Atlantic to the outskirts of DC. Thomas touched the answer icon.

"Thomas!" Stan said. "What's happenin'?"

"We've got Franklin, sir. He's fine. We found him on the beach, drinking a fucking Mai Tai with some Aussie."

"It figures," Stan said. "Let me talk to him."

"Stan," Perry said. "I found the source of the neutrinos. The facility, it's huge!"

Perry spent the next five minutes briefing Stan on what he'd seen.

"Perry, yur tellin' me this BiniSphere can take out every nuke on earth?"

"That's what Christina and this beach bum are saying."

"Do ya believe them?"

"Actually, yes, the physics sounds about right."

"Okay, this is very important," Stan said. "Sheehan's people are buildin' their own BiniSphere, or whatever they call it. They're using one of our Ohio-class guided-missile submarines to power it and steer it. The sub's docked in Groton, at the General Dynamics Electric Boat docks."

"But that's impossible. They can't power the neutrino beam using a nuclear reactor. It has to be done with a particle accelerator."

"Well, that's what they're doin', and they want this technology all to themselves."

"What do they plan to do with it?"

"I'm afraid they want to use it for more than just ridding the world of nukes. If the US was the only nuclear state... it would destroy the entire balance of power around the world."

"No one country should wield that kind of power," Perry said. "Especially with the narcissistic president we're saddled with."

"But can the Sicilians be trusted with it?" Stan asked. "What if they want to do the same thing? What if they want to be the one and only superpower in the world?"

"Stan, that is too big of a question. I'm just an engineer who stumbled into this mess."

"Damn it, Franklin! A decision has to be made, and if we don't make it right now, it will be made for us. I can see what's happenin' here on my end, and it scares the crap outta me. They're goin' to destroy that BiniSphere of yours and eliminate all the loose ends. Hell! I'm sittin' in a hospital bed because of it. If we don't do somethin', Sheehan will git the technology, and it will be outta our hands. But that won't matter, 'cause we'll all be dead."

"I only see two choices," Perry said. "We give the particle accelerator technology to Sheehan and run like hell, or we give my sensor technology to the Sicilians and hope they're telling the truth. And Stan, the Sicilians don't have any nukes. They have never been and never will be a superpower. It's not in their DNA."

"There's a third option," Stan said.

"What's that?"

"We don't tell Sheehan's people they need to use a particle accelerator and we simply destroy the BiniSphere and everything that goes with it. We maintain the status quo."

"Destroy it?" Perry asked. "It's amazing technology."

"Maybe too amazing. Maybe the world's not ready for it."

"Like Ettore... " Perry mumbled to himself.

"What?" Stan asked.

"Ettore Majorana. He knew the world wasn't ready for the nuclear age. He tried to stop it, he committed suicide because of what he knew."

"I don't understand."

Perry was quiet for several long seconds.

"Oh my God!" Perry said.

He remembered the picture hanging on Christina's kitchen wall. The tall, thin man with his arms wrapped around Nonna.

"The BiniSphere... Bini. That was Ettore Majorana's nickname. Christina's grandfather! He changed his name from Ettore Majorana to Bini LaTorre. It's the same person. He faked his suicide."

"Who?" Stan asked.

"Why didn't I see this sooner? Christina is Ettore's granddaughter!"

"What does that have to do... "

"Steve!" Perry yelled back towards the bar.

"Yeah, mate."

"What's Christina got to do with all this?"

"Are ya kidding me? She's the freakin' boss man! She's the genius behind all of this."

A chill ran down Perry's spine.

"Stan!" Perry said. "Sheehan doesn't want me. It's Christina he's after."

"Steve, where is she?" Perry yelled.

"Don't know. We've been trying to contact her. Her phone's not working. Neither is Father LaTorre's."

"Stan, did you hear that?"

"Yeah. That's not good."

"They used jammers at Christina's house," Perry said. "And she knew my camera was still there."

"Let me talk to Thomas," Stan said. "Then I'll call my guy on the kill team."

Perry put the phone on speaker.

"He wants to talk to you," Perry said.

"Thomas here, sir."

"We've got to find this LaTorre woman. Make sure Sheehan's men can't git to her. If they git the intel they need, our whole goddamn world's gonna be lookin' a lot different. Help Franklin and the local folks find her. Protect her at all costs. The kill team sniper is a friend. I'm goin' to call him. I'll text you back, let you know if he's with us or against us."

"Yes sir, we're on it."

As soon as Stan disconnected, Perry said. "We have to find Christina. She's the key to all of this."

"We're on it," Thomas replied.

Stan made his second call.

"Garret! You were right," Stan said. "They came after me. What's yur status?"

"We got orders to hit Franklin and capture the girl. I did my best to lay down cover fire to keep them separated but no joy. They got her. They're at the OP."

"Shit," said Stan.

"I haven't seen Franklin since he ran into the house," Garret said. "I'm assuming he's dead."

"I just talked to him. He's okay."

"Good. Stan, are ya all right? What happened?"

"Never mind me. I took care of most of 'em. I don't think anyone will be comin' back soon."

"I wouldn't count on that," Garret said. "You don't know who you're dealing with."

"The hell I don't. Your boss is DDNI Sheehan. He's the one callin' the shots. Franklin's no traitor, he's one of ours."

"He's using us to take out our own people? I knew we couldn't trust that shit bag!"

"And Atwood knows damn well what's goin on, too. He's been keeping you guys in the dark the whole time. Garret, I need yur help."

"What do you want?"

"You remember Thomas and Samuels?"

"Of course, good guys."

"They're on station. This woman is essential. We can't let Sheehan git hold of the intel she has. I have a terrible feelin' about this. Text me the position of your OP and your radio codes so we can listen to what Atwood is up to. Then sit tight. I'll have my guys git back to you with our plan of action."

"Will do."

"Oh, and Garret. Just between you and me. If the shit hits the fan and we can't git Christina back… under no circumstances do we allow Sheehan's guys to exfiltrate her. Ya know what you'll have to do."

"I hope it doesn't come to that but, yes, I'll take care of it. There's no way she's leaving with those bastards. Knowing what they'd do to her, she'd thank me in the afterlife."

Stan hung up the phone and swung his legs off the bed before Brenda could back into the room to stop him.

Samuels drove the SUV hard up the mountain road while scanning, side-to-side, searching for traps. Thomas, riding shotgun, looked at his smartphone, reading the message Stan had sent. Perry and Steve sat silently in the back.

"Okay, here's the intel," Thomas said. "We're dealing with a four-man kill team. Their mission was to capture the woman, kill Franklin, and destroy the facility. Their OP is in an abandoned building, a half klick up the road from the LaTorre's home. Their sniper, Garret, is on our side. He's in an overwatch position several hundred meters north of the OP. The only thing they've been able to accomplish is to capture the woman."

Hearing that Christina had been captured, a stillness enveloped Perry. He became hyperaware of his surroundings, as if a fog had been lifted, exposing the entire world to him. It was almost an out-of-body experience. All fear was gone. He felt like a machine: recording every sight and sound around him, analyzing every possibility, predicting every action. All doubt left his mind. He was getting Christina back, and no one was going to stop him. He studied the road in front of him, recalling every curve.

"I'm going to kill every one of them," he whispered.

A kilometer later, the speeding SUV slowed to avoid hitting a line of stopped cars. Thomas swerved into the oncoming lane. The road ahead had been blocked by a dump truck that had lost some of its load. A man tried to wave them down, but Samuels accelerated. The man jumped out of the way as the SUV pitched up and over the debris.

As they sped past, Perry saw that the dump truck's bed had been tilted back. He looked behind them, in time to see the truck driver bring a phone to his ear.

Perry yelled, "Stop! There's a trap up ahead."

The Toyota's brakes locked. Perry fell forward onto the center console. The vehicle skidded to a halt, but it was too late. Gunfire erupted. He felt the Toyota shift left, then right, as if settling into the ground. Masked men on the side of the road had shot out the tires.

Chapter 23

Day 10 (Continued)

Christina was hauled through the partially closed barn doors and thrown onto a pile of broken olive crates. She cried in silence as her eyes adjusted to the dim interior. She searched for ways to escape. Off to the left, she saw a small, make-shift table made from more of the crates. It contained different sized, camo-colored boxes, one with an antenna protruding from it and a set of headphones hanging from the side. A video monitor sat on the table. In each quadrant of the screen was an image displaying the four sides of the frantoio. She watched as one of the men sat down next to the comm station and pulled her laptop from his backpack. Blood was dripping from the fingers of his left hand, but the bleeding had slowed considerably.

"DJ," said Atwood. "Keep an eye on her while we load the van. Call Garret on the radio, tell him to get back here pronto."

"I'm on it," he replied.

"Doc, patch DJ up and give him some pain killers. We need him operational."

Doc grabbed his med kit and went to work.

"Overwatch, what's happening? Their security forces responded way too quickly."

"I don't know," Garret said. "I'm looking at them now. They're at the house. They don't look like polizia, and they're armed to the teeth."

"We need to get out of here," Atwood said. "Lay down some more cover fire to hold them still and then get back here, pronto."

Garret swung his rifle back to the south to surveil their escape route. Scanning the road leading into the mountains, he saw a glint of light, and then another. He zoomed in and picked out the dark silhouettes of two more vehicles parked on the side of the road. He spotted two men with high powered rifles prone on the ground, covering the LaTorre home from the high ground.

"Lead!" he said. "The escape route's compromised. There's another team blocking the road."

"Shit!" Atwood said. "Can we blow through them?"

"Not a chance," Garret lied. He could have taken out the second team from his elevated position but no one else knew that.

"You'll have to egress on foot to the north," Garret said. "I'll cover your retreat. We'll meet up at the entrance to the highway tunnel."

Garret knew that the only chance he'd have to separate Christina from the kill team was if they were on foot. Then he'd pick them off, one by one.

Thomas' and Samuel's doors flew open before the SUV had come to a complete stop. They poured out in one smooth motion, their weapons raised and readied. They'd been trained well. Recognizing that not a single round had entered the passenger compartment, they held fire while taking up positions behind the open doors.

Perry saw Leo and the two police officers come running around the bend in the road. He jumped out and yelled. "Lower your weapons! That's Christina's uncle. Lower your guns, now!"

When Thomas and Samuels lowered their weapons, the masked men did the same.

Perry ran to Leo. "Christina's been taken, we know where she is."

Perry was in no mood to waste time. When Leo swung his fist, Perry crouched and shouldered his forward momentum into Leo's midsection. He lifted the padre up and back, before body slamming him to the ground. Perry drove his knee into Leo's chest and grabbed his throat in a vice-like grip.

"I don't have time for your bullshit," he said. "I'm going to get Christina. Don't get in my way."

Monsignor LaTorre lay on the road with the breath knocked out of him. Unable to speak, he looked Perry in the eyes and nodded.

Steve ran up, pulled Perry off Leo, and helped Leo up off the ground.

"Are you alright, padre?" he asked.

"I am fine," he choked, brushing off his clothes.

Thomas asked. "Who's in charge of these men?"

"I am," said Don Tumeo's security chief, Andreo.

"They're in an abandoned building further up the road," said Thomas. "But they won't be there for long."

"It must be the old frantoio," said Leo.

Thomas spoke into his mike and switched his comms to speaker.

"Garret, repeat what you just told me," he said.

"They have the woman and they know you have teams on the road blocking their egress. They plan to go north on foot, down the ravine."

"Roger," replied Thomas.

"The ravine leads straight to the highway tunnel entrance," Leo said.

"How many men do you have?" asked Samuels.

"We have ten," answered Andreo. "Five are on the upper road, blocking that escape route and five down here."

"Time is critical," Thomas said. "We need to storm that place before they can interrogate her."

"No!" Perry and Leo said at the same time.

Leo said, "Christina would rather die than give away her designs. We have some time."

"Father, you need to understand," said Thomas. "These are ruthless men, they will get what they need from her, and quickly."

Perry said. "If you storm the place, the first thing they'll do is kill her."

"We can't take the chance of them escaping," Thomas said. "This is more important than one woman." He looked back at Samuels, "Get your gear! We need to take that building."

Andreo nodded to one of his men. A second later, bullets hit the ground around Samuel's feet. Everyone froze.

"It will do you well to remember where you are and who is in charge," said Leo. "Andreo and the rest of his team are good at what they do."

Perry interrupted. "Leo, we don't have time for a pissing contest, we need their help. Thomas and Samuels are two of the best-trained warriors in the world. There are none better at getting what they want, when they want. We just need to adjust their priorities."

He said to Thomas, "We're going to get Christina back with or without your assistance. It's your choice."

"Whose goddamn side are you on, Franklin?"

Perry drew his weapon and racked a round into the chamber. He raised the gun, centering it on Thomas' forehead, and said, "I'll tell you exactly what side I'm on. I'm on my side and you either get in line or you die. You decide, it's now or never."

Thomas wondered if Franklin had the guts to pull the trigger. *The guy's a freaking geek,* he thought. *He doesn't have the stomach for this. He didn't even want to come to Sicily.* But there was something in Franklin's voice. Something, in all the years of knowing him, he hadn't heard before. He thought back to Saudi, when Franklin took on those bodyguards to save the life of a teenage girl. It had changed him.

"Fine," Thomas said. "As long as they don't leave here with Ms. LaTorre, we're in."

"Good," said Perry. "Andreo, tell your people the kill team's sniper is on our side. Have them hold positions north and south of the frantoio."

Andreo looked toward the monsignor for guidance, and Leo nodded.

Perry, recognizing that Leo was ultimately the one in charge of this group, turned to him and said, "Have the two carabinieri fall back to where they can get phone reception. We need roadblocks east and west on the highway and the surface roads in Canneto. We have to move fast."

Leo nodded and, in Italian, issued commands to the two officers.

"We need a map of this mountain." Perry said.

"I have one in the house," said Leo.

Perry said, "Everybody! Move!" and he ran towards the house. Leo, Andreo, Steve, and Thomas ran after him.

Perry swept debris from the kitchen table, and Leo laid out a contour map of the mountainside, placing his finger on a small black square that indicated the position of the abandoned frantoio.

"They are right here," said Leo.

Perry said, "Where's Garret's position?"

Thomas looked at the coordinates Stan had sent him and pointed at a set of small concentric rings on the map.

"He's right here. On this little knoll, just shy of the hilltop to our northwest. He has a clear sightline to us, to the frantoio, and to Andreo's men on the upper road."

Perry still felt the throb in his hand from Garret's round ripping through the Pelican case and was glad Garret was on his side.

Perry turned to Andreo. "We'll need your men to slowly close on the building, on foot and keep to the road. We don't want them to feel trapped. They'll kill Christina if they think there's no other way out. We just want to limit the exit routes out of there. If they go north on foot, they'll walk right into Garret's kill zone."

Perry's finger followed the set of tight, v-shaped lines indicating the narrow ravine leading down out of the mountains. As Leo had described, it led right to the entrance of the highway tunnel piercing the mountain below them.

"If Garret doesn't succeed and they enter that tunnel," Perry said, pointing to where the ravine intersected the highway, "they'll grab any car they can stop. We'll have absolutely no idea what car they're in when it emerges from the other end. We can't let them reach the tunnel."

Thomas said, "Samuels and I will take the SUV with the 50 Cal and cover the tunnel entrance."

"Hurry," Leo said. "Once they leave the frantoio, they can reach that tunnel entrance on foot faster than you can by car. You will need to drive down the mountain to Canneto. The entrance ramp to the highway is ten kilometers to the west."

Perry said, "Andreo, once your men get to the building, herd the kill team down the mountain. When Garret engages them, you'll need to block any retreat. If they manage to get past Garret, we'll kill those bastards as soon as they step onto the highway."

Everyone nodded in agreement.

Perry said, "Give me the radio."

Thomas handed it to him and he keyed the mike. "Garret, this is Franklin."

"Go ahead."

"We are going to feed them right to you."

"Roger."

"As far as I'm concerned," Perry said. "You're one of the bad guys until proven otherwise. If that woman is harmed in any way, I will hunt you down and kill you."

"Affirmative," Garret replied. "There's one other thing you guys might want to know."

"What's that?" Perry asked.

"Once Sheehan learns that our team was unable to destroy the facility, he'll send one of our fast attack subs to finish the job."

"How do they know where the facility is?" Perry asked.

"The SEALs on the *New Mexico* were able to retrieve the navigation console on the sunken dive boat. It had the exact coordinates. They'll sneak in and torpedo the shit out of that area and get out before the Italian Navy can even respond."

"Got it," Perry replied and handed the radio back to Thomas.

Thomas said, "We need to move out. Franklin, you, the padre, and your Aussie friend need to leave this to the pros."

Perry didn't like it but knew Thomas was right. He nodded.

"Here's a radio so we can stay in contact. Andreo, I have an extra one in the truck for your team. These radios are just like Atwood's; they're impervious to the jammer."

Andreo and Thomas stepped over the debris littering the kitchen floor and left the way they came.

Martinelli slipped off his headset and signaled Atwood over to the comm set.

"You're right," he said. "The microphones are still working. We've been compromised. They know where we are."

"How's that possible?" Atwood asked.

"Garret. He's been feeding them intel."

"That fucking traitor! I knew something was off with him. That's why Franklin and those cops are still alive."

"We don't have much time," Martinelli said, "They're moving their people into position along the road. They want to squeeze us north on foot."

"So Garret can pick us off, one by one," Atwood nodded. "Okay, well, we'll have a better plan."

"Doc, go up the backside of the hill behind Garret. Let me know as soon as you've taken him out, then we'll move out with the girl. Meet us at the highway."

"We need to hurry," Martinelli said. "Two of their men are driving down to the highway to intercept. They'll be there in fifteen minutes."

Christina overheard their plan and felt slightly relieved, knowing that Don Tumeo's men were coming to rescue her, just like they'd promised years ago. But, if her captors reached the highway, they'd have a good chance of escaping. She knew the terrain well; she'd hiked the ravine many times, all the way down to the beach. The overhanging trees created a natural tunnel. If they took her in that direction, they'd be under cover most of the time, no one seeing where they were going. She scanned left and right, trying to remember the details of the dark interior. She had to find a way out.

The frantoio was an old but solid structure built into the Sicilian mountainside. Sunlight filtered down through the tree branches and through the holes in the roof, illuminating the solid concrete floor in a swaying patchwork of light and shadows. The massive wooden beams spanning the interior had sagged to the point where they resembled the shallow ribs of an ancient ship. Spider webs and bird nests filled the crevices.

Memories flooded back. Many years ago, she'd lost her virginity here. It was the night of their high school graduation. She and Mario left their families behind at the house and went for a long walk. They'd been close friends the entire senior year but had only just kissed for the first time a few weeks earlier. She knew they'd soon be going off to different colleges and different lives, but maybe, just this once, they would go further than just kissing.

Christina rolled slowly to her side and sat up. She saw the long trench running down the center of the concrete floor. It was about two feet wide and one foot deep. One end of the trench opened out into a wider circle surrounded by bent, rusted bolts embedded in the concrete. This was where the giant olive press once stood. Back then, the men hand cranked the iron press, slowly extracting the olive juices. At the other end of the trench, just out of sight, was a narrow opening in the floor. She remembered it. It led down to the lower level. In the times before electric pumps and centrifuges, this is where the precious Sicilian nectar streamed for settling, filtering and bottling. Her memories were vivid, even now, twenty-five years later. That was where she and Mario had gone to explore. Outside access to that lower level had been blocked years ago. She'd assumed it was one of Sicily's many earthquakes that had caused the collapse. The stone wall on the far side of the building had caved in causing the upper floor to fold down on itself. It completely blocked the entrance as if it were a giant door to a crypt. There were only two ways to enter or exit. Down the disintegrated staircase on the far side of the building or through that narrow opening in the floor.

Christina had to escape. She knew they'd eventually break her. The question is, how long would it take them, and how much would it hurt? The BiniSphere was only days away from being operational. All she and her team needed was a little more time and a little help from Perry. She was the weak link. The greater the distance she put between her and her captors, the more time they'd have to retrieve Perry's camera and become operational, and the more time they'd have to rescue her.

It was years ago, part of their unparalleled level of security. All of Christina's team had been required to go through rigorous training. They had used the facilities at the Hotel Za' Maria. They were in a beautiful room with large windows overlooking the sea. She remembered it vividly. The training was held in mid-summer. It was a hot sunny day outside. Her team of a dozen had arrived, mostly men, some women. It was 10 a.m. Everyone was wearing shorts, short-sleeved shirts, or dresses. The air conditioning had been a welcome relief from the sweltering heat. It was running full blast and quickly dried their sweat-dampened clothes. But, an hour into the briefing, she was chilled and looking forward to getting back into the heat.

The training was being conducted by three of Don Tumeo's men. They were hulking, muscular, scarred men in their mid-forties. In contrast to her group, the men wore jeans, flannel shirts, and jackets. She assumed, under those jackets, they were armed. They looked and acted like ex-military. She'd seen the leader before; he went by the name Andreo and was the head of the Don's security team. She didn't believe he was an evil man but undoubtedly ruthless, someone to not be on opposite sides with, someone who'd slit your throat without a second thought.

Andreo briefed them on the importance of maintaining situational awareness, on surveillance techniques used against them, on computer security and passwords, internet scams and phishing schemes. Even on how to escape and evade capture if they thought they were being followed. The classroom briefings on what to do if they were captured were stirring enough, but when they went through the mock interrogation exercises, her nerves still recoiled from the memory.

It was 2 p.m., they'd spent four straight hours in the air-conditioned classroom, and everyone wanted to get out into the warmth of the day. Even for just a few minutes, just to melt away the chill they were feeling from the hotel's all too efficient cooling system. She had skipped breakfast, and her stomach growled. She held her tongue, though, not wanting to show any weakness in front of Tumeo's men. But when one of her female scientists finally interrupted Andreo and asked about lunch, she felt more than relieved.

"Lunch?" Andreo said. "Do you think your captors are going to worry about your lunch?"

"Can we just take a break for a few minutes?" the woman asked. "Just to warm up, it is freezing in here."

Andreo looked at his men and said, "It is time we moved onto the practical exercises."

They were led down to the hotel's basement; all of them very familiar with this level of the building as it concealed the main elevator shaft that led to the BiniSphere. It was a perfect front. The hotel housed many visitors. Their team dressed as businessmen and women, or members of the hotel's staff. One of her scientists even enjoyed dressing as a local farmer, just stopping by for a quick breakfast before heading out to the fields.

Andreo ordered Christina and her team to remove their shoes and socks. Then, one by one, their hands were bound behind them with zip-ties.

Andreo said, "This is the most important part of your training. It is critical for your survival."

Awkwardly shuffling in their bare feet and restraints, they were led into a windowless, empty conference room and lined up against the back wall. The room was even colder than upstairs and she felt the breeze from the air conditioning vents. It was running full blast. Goosebumps formed on her bare arms and legs. Her nipples stiffened, and a shiver coursed throughout her body. She saw that several of her people were visibly shaking.

The leader explained that an interrogation was all about the illusion of control, and the loss of that illusion.

He said, "Your captors will play with your emotions. They will let you believe there is a way out and then, in a split second, snatch it away. They will scare you, they will starve you, they will freeze you, and they will hurt you. Then they will offer a respite, an escape from the nightmare. All you will need to do is cooperate."

"I am ready to talk," one of her men blurted out, and everyone laughed.

The conference room was instantly plunged into darkness and spotlights, mounted to the ceiling, were lit, blinding them.

Andreo's booming voice yelled out in the dark, "This is not a game! Do not move!"

That got everyone's attention. They all stood still and waited. Scraping and clanging noises emerged from the darkness behind the blinding lights. She assumed it was part of the plan, to spook them.

One of Tumeo's men stepped into the light. In one hand he carried a large brown glass bottle labeled "Alcohol," in the other hand was a pump-up garden sprayer. He put them both on the floor, opened the top to the sprayer, and slowly poured the contents of the bottle inside. He screwed the top of the sprayer back on and started pumping.

One of her junior engineers said, "Okay, this is bullshit, I'm freezing my ass off, I'm out of here," and he walked towards the door.

Christina said, "Jeremy, get back in line. You knew what you were getting into when you signed up for this."

Jeremy kept walking towards the darkness, his bare feet slapping on the floor, then they all heard a loud shatter of glass and felt shards raining onto their legs and feet. Jeremy stopped instantly. Christina looked back toward the man with the sprayer. The glass bottle that had been sitting on the floor next to him was gone. Everyone was quiet.

From the darkness, Andreo said calmly, "You are all free to walk out of here anytime you choose."

Everyone stood still, the only places on the floor without glass shards were under their feet.

"That is what I thought. We will proceed."

The man with the garden sprayer crunched through the glass and approached the line of scientists. He held up the wand and squeezed the trigger, spraying a fine stream of liquid onto their bare arms, legs, and feet. Christina felt an instant chill, so cold, it felt as if it were burning. She shivered, tried to slide her feet away but was stopped by the wall behind her. Then the scent of the solvent reached her nose.

The leader stepped into the light. He was holding a lighter. He flicked it to life and a tall blue flame rose from the top.

"Is anybody still cold? Need a little warming up?"

Everyone was shivering, even Steve. Andreo singled him out, the biggest and toughest of her team, and brought the lighter close to his legs.

"Hey, man! That's a little too close. Back off!"

Christina thought this was getting way too dangerous. They could all go up in flames. She was about to say something when she realized the scent wasn't quite right. It was close, but it wasn't alcohol. The liquid was very cold but had quickly changed to a burning sensation. She looked down at her bare legs and saw that the solvent had already evaporated away. Leaving behind a slight reddening of her skin. She knew alcohol didn't feel like that, then she recognized the scent. Dichloromethane. One of the most potent solvents known. It was the main ingredient in paint remover and caused severe burns. Except, when sprayed as a mist, in its purest form, it is so highly volatile it evaporates too quickly to cause anything but a mild redness. On the other hand, the fumes displaced oxygen. They could all die from asphyxiation. *Tumeo's men are good, very good,* she thought, realizing that the air-conditioning had been deliberately cranked up to the max. It quickly purged the fumes from the conference room. She relaxed a little and wondered what was next.

Andreo stepped back into the darkness and she heard a loud screeching, followed by the sight of a twin-sized metal bed being slid into the light. There was no mattress on it, just the metal mesh and the support springs.

"Do I have any volunteers for the next demonstration?" he asked.

No one stepped forward, no one said a word.

"What? Do you not trust us?" Andreo seemed to enjoy playing the part, perhaps too much.

Finally, Steve, her lead scientist, spoke up.

"Fine Mate, have at it."

Andreo's men crunched through the glass and approached Steve. They eyed him for a few seconds, then turned toward Jeremy, still standing halfway toward the door.

He put his hands up. "Whoa. Hold on! No, not me."

They walked over and grabbed him under his arms. He struggled as they lifted him up and headed for the bedframe.

Christina yelled. "Okay, that is enough! This exercise is over! We are done!"

The men stopped, with Jeremy suspended between them.

Andreo stepped out of the darkness and said. "As I told you all, this is about the ILLUSION of control and loss of that illusion. Signora, your control over what is transpiring here is an illusion. You have all signed on to this program and agreed to undergo this training. You have no control over this situation."

"You are going too far," Christina said. "Someone is going to get hurt, and I am still in charge here."

Andreo turned to the man suspended between the two mobsters. "Jeremy, please explain."

"Dr. LaTorre, I was asked ahead of time to volunteer for this and I agreed. I was picked because I was the smallest of the men, I looked the most vulnerable. I've also agreed to this next demonstration. They'll proceed until I've had enough. All I have to do is give them a thumbs up, and they'll stop." Jeremy looked back at Andreo. "That is, I hope they'll stop."

Andreo laughed and nodded, "Not to worry, we will take good care of you. Now, will someone shut off that damn air conditioning? I am getting cold."

The whole group, still shivering, nodded in agreement.

One of Andreo's men turned on the heat, and they went on to demonstrate the fine art of waterboarding. It was hard for Christina to watch, even knowing that Jeremy could bail at any time. Her high opinion of him was elevated to a new level as he withstood the onslaughts of the three large men. But finally, he cracked. Coughing, spitting, retching, and convulsing, he finally gave the signal for the men to stop.

After retrieving Jeremy's shoes and sliding them on his feet, they walked him over to a chair to recover. The leader then approached Christina and looked straight into her eyes.

"Our final demonstration is solely for you men," he said, staring at her. "Do I have any volunteers?"

Christina knew what was next. It was obvious. She also knew she wasn't going to have one of her female subordinates go through this. Andreo knew that too. She nodded.

He looked at the group and said, "Let me assure you, this has not been prearranged with your boss. This is real, and this will be painful to watch."

His two men cut the zip tie binding Christina's wrists, picked her up roughly, and threw her onto the bed. They retied her arms to the headrail.

The leader knelt by her side, menacingly wrapped his massive paw of a hand around her delicate neck and, with a sneer, bent in to whisper in her ear.

"The same goes, signora, anytime you want us to stop just give me a thumbs up."

Christina nodded.

"Father Leo would kill me if he knew what I was going to do, but this is important for your team's survival. I will need to put my hand on your privates for a few moments. Is that okay?"

She nodded again, but not as quickly.

"Oh, and forgive me for asking, signora. You are wearing underwear, are you not?"

"Of course," she whispered.

327

He released his gentle grip on her neck and nodded to his men.

Each man, as if rehearsed, stood on either side at the foot of the bed frame. In unison, they grabbed her knees and roughly spread her legs apart.

Christina jumped, resisted for a second and then lay deathly still. She felt her heart beating through her chest.

Steve said, "Okay, we get it. That's enough."

The leader jumped toward Steve viciously, pinning him up against the wall as Andreo's men tied her legs down against the sides of the bed.

"I will tell you what is enough, stronzo figlio di puttana!" he yelled. "When I get what I came for!"

Steve's jaw clenched tightly.

"Go ahead," Andreo whispered. "Make it worse for her."

Steve was silent.

Andreo returned to her bedside, knelt and put his rough hand on Christina's bare thigh, just above the knee. He then went on to describe in vivid detail what he was going to do to her while the captive audience looked on in shades of terror and embarrassment.

Christina, listening to his description, almost laughed at the absurdity. She was calmed by what he whispered in her ear. Her uncle surely would cut off his balls and stuff them down his throat if he harmed her in any way.

The leader grabbed the hem of Christina's dress and yanked it up over her head, exposing her lower body to everyone. He watched her clenched fists closely, waiting for a sign, for the thumbs up, as he slid his hand slowly up her inner thigh.

Christina knew it was coming, but her body still stiffened when he roughly grabbed her genitals.

Steve jumped forward, instantly wincing as glass penetrated the bottom of his feet. Andreo's men stopped him from taking another step. Andreo looked up at Steve and then at the rest of the men. They were visibly shaken by what they were seeing.

Andreo kept staring at them and said, "Dr. LaTorre, are you feeling any pain right now?"

"No," Christina said. "Just a little embarrassment."

"Are you ready to tell me all your secrets?" he asked.

"Not very likely."

"What about you, Steve? What about any of you men? Are you feeling any pain right now? Any of you ready to talk?"

They all adored Christina. Some even worshipped her. Seeing their boss in this position, knowing it wasn't real, but not knowing how far Andreo was willing go, made their blood boil. One by one, they all nodded.

"Just stop it!" Steve yelled.

Christina finally laughed to break the tension. "Okay, okay, I think I have had enough," she said. "You are not very good at this, Andreo. I am actually starting to get turned on."

Everyone chuckled nervously as he quickly removed his hand from her groin.

Andreo pulled Christina's dress back down, and the men untied her.

"You all have buttons that your captors are going to push," he continued. "Especially for you men. These women here are a lot stronger than you can imagine, they are a lot stronger than we are when it comes to this kind of shit. Hell, they are born into it. Into being physically dominated and penetrated by us."

"But only when we choose," Christina said as she sat up on the bed.

"Si`, signora, and I apologize for any embarrassment I might have caused."

"No harm done," she said. "I think you were more embarrassed than me."

"Let me assure all of you," Andreo said, turning back to the group. "Sooner or later, you will break, you will all spill the secrets of this program."

"Then why even try?" one of the women asked. "Why put ourselves through this?"

"Because," he said. "Once they have gotten all they need from you, once they have extracted every bit of information, they will kill you."

He waited for that to sink in.

"I want you to hold onto this one thing and hold on to it very tightly. Keep it tucked away deep down inside the darkest places of your mind. The longer you hold out, the longer you endure, the longer we have to find you. And in your darkest despair, also hold on tightly to this. When we find you, when we find them, they will suffer unthinkable horrors, for days, if not weeks. They will pray for death by the time we get finished with them, and only then will they get their wish. Anger is a strong emotion. BE ANGRY, BE VINDICTIVE, BE VENGEFUL," he bellowed. "It will give you the strength to hold on."

Christina sat on the broken crates in the frantoio, watching the men prepare to leave. Her Nonna had been murdered by these bastards. She was angry as hell. She was vindictive. She was vengeful. She was going to escort these monsters to the gates of hell. Christina jumped up, ran around the corner and dove headfirst into the narrow opening in the floor. She fell through the blackness and landed on her back with a squashing thud. She felt wetness on her bare arms. She smelled a sickening stench and instantly realized what she had done. They were using the opening in the floor as a latrine.

God, she thought as she rolled out of the filth and struggled to her feet. *How long have these men been here?*

She heard clamoring of feet above her and knew it wouldn't take long before they came down the stairs. At the opposite end of the building, furthest from the stairs, she saw a shaft of light. It was coming in from a small broken window high up on the wall, way too small for her to escape, but she ran for it anyway. She reached it just as she heard the wooden stairs buckle. She turned in time to see Martinelli crash through the rotted steps and land in a plume of dust and broken boards. She leaned against the wall directly under the window with her arms still bound tightly behind her and slid to the ground.

It must be here, she thought as she searched in the darkness.

She felt a prick, and then smoothness. A piece of broken glass. She sat frozen, not wanting to make a sound. It was hard to hold on to the glass; her hands slippery from the filth. She felt it cut into her hand as she frantically sawed. Christina watched Martinelli step out of the dim light filtering down from the stairway and into the darkness.

"Yeah, I'm fine," Martinelli yelled. "Toss me a light. It's too dark down here."

She kept sawing as she listened to the footsteps above her and then she heard a thud.

Martinelli stepped back into the light to retrieve the flashlight and then back into the darkness. He was taking no chances. He knew there was only one way out, through him. He methodically scanned the floor in front of him, back and forth.

The beam steadily moved forward as she continued to slice at her bindings. She knew they would capture her again; she was just doing what she was trained to do. Adding a few more seconds, a few more minutes to her life. Martinelli's light finally panned across her legs, then pointed up to her face, blinding her.

"You didn't really think you were getting out of here, did you?"

Christina drew her legs up to her chest and whimpered.

He saw she was shaking. He almost felt sorry for her as he grabbed her blouse and hauled her to her feet. Smelling the stench, he mistakenly thought she had soiled herself, a split second before the piece of jagged glass ripped through his carotid artery.

Christina pushed hard, but it was overkill; he was already stumbling backward, his eyes wide in shock. She landed on top of him. The puddle of light from the window illuminated them.

Martinelli opened his mouth to scream, but his airway had been savagely sliced open. Blood splattered Christina's face as he tried to yell.

She looked down at him, perversely calm, and said, "Welcome to hell."

Christina grabbed his holstered Beretta with her bloodied right hand and picked up his flashlight with her left. There was only one way out, and when the other man realized what happened, he would not underestimate her the way Martinelli did. But all she needed was time, and she just bought herself a bunch of it. Christina worked her way back to the stairway, crouched in the darkness, and waited.

Atwood watched the monitors, checking their perimeter while waiting for Martinelli to return with the girl. One camera was pointed up the road to the south. He saw movement, men on foot working their way down each side of the road. They were coming.

"Martinelli! What's taking so long?" he yelled. "We've gotta move."

There was no reply.

He looked back at the men coming down the road and then switched the monitor to his internal cameras. They'd set them up to cover the ingress and egress points from the building. A new set of images appeared on the screen. One camera was outside, pointing in through the sizeable barn-door entrance. Another camera covered a doorway in the back that led outside and down. The third was an infrared camera. They'd set it up in the basement to cover the wooden stairway, just in the remote case someone was able to gain access from below and tried to sneak up on them.

"God damn it!" he muttered.

On the edge of the image, up against the wall, he saw the bright thermal signature of someone sitting on the ground. The warmth of Christina's hand stood in sharp contrast to the cold steel of the weapon she held.

He yelled again. "Martinelli, get up here, leave her behind if you have to, we gotta go!"

Atwood watched the glowing figure on the monitor shift and raise the weapon, pointing toward the stairway. He realized Martinelli was dead.

Atwood ran through the building, setting the charges they'd placed around the frantoio to the "Ready" mode. He grabbed his weapon and the remote detonator. He hadn't heard from Doc yet, but they were out of time. He had to move. Atwood ran out the back door, down along the side of the building and placed a small C4 charge against the base of the wall. He stepped around the corner and leaned against the wall, knowing Christina was in the exact same location as he was, but on the inside. He switched the remote detonator he was holding to "CHNL 4," flipped up the red switch cover and pushed the "FIRE" button.

Christina was blown sideways as the wall next to her all but disappeared. Chunks of cinder block and the remains of the staircase pelted her. She was blinded, her ears rang, and she choked on the cloud of dust. She cleared her eyes in time to watch a hand reach out of the cloud and grab her by the hair. She clawed in the rubble for the gun, but it was gone.

Atwood dragged Christina outside and down the hill a dozen meters before throwing her onto the ground. He dropped a knee to her chest, knocking the air from her lungs. She coughed and struggled but couldn't move under his weight. Atwood turned the detonator selector switch to "ALL" and flipped the "DETONATE" switch from "MANUAL" to "AUTO." He brought his face to hers, shoved his Glock under her chin, and said, "I'm going to make this very easy for you. Run or die."

Chapter 24

Day 10 (Continued)

Doc hid behind an outcrop at the top of the hill. He pulled up the digital map on his tablet and compared his position to Garret's. They all had encrypted electronic tags to keep track of each other's position. He saw the flashing red dot at Garret's position, as well as the red dots of Atwood's, Martinelli's and his own. The latter three tags were still located in the frantoio, right where they'd placed them after learning of Garret's treachery.

Doc was in a perfect position. The only problem was Garret. The man was one of the best snipers in the world, and you don't get to live very long in that business without being very, very careful. He hoped that since Garret had switched sides, he wouldn't be on guard for someone sneaking up on him. Garret's enemies consisted of only three men, and Garret thought he knew exactly where they were.

Doc left his rifle behind and unholstered his sidearm. He slowly crawled up to the top of the rise and peered down. At first, he didn't see him, just a hillside of rocks, brush and scrub trees. He scanned slowly back and forth, then he spotted him, not more than 10 meters away. Garret was hidden under a broad-leafed tree; the suppressor on the front of his gun and his big feet were the only thing that showed.

A sharp explosion echoed across the hillside. Doc jumped, a branch snapped, and he saw Garret roll quickly while drawing his sidearm. Doc fired but had no clear line-of-sight. A rock next to Doc splintered from the impact of a round, and he felt the sting of either stone or lead hitting his cheekbone. He kept firing into the bushes, round after round until his receiver locked back in the open position. He rolled back from the edge, slapped in a new magazine, and rolled back into firing position. At that moment, Doc came eye-to-eye with Garret's silenced weapon.

"If you'd used your suppressor to preserve your hearing," Garret said, "you'd have heard me coming."

Doc learned Garret's lesson the hard way; it was the last lesson he'd ever learn.

Garret pulled the trigger and a dark hole instantly appeared in Doc's forehead.

Perry, Leo, and Steve waited in the rubble of what was left of the LaTorre's kitchen.

Perry paced back and forth, crunching the wood and glass underfoot.

"We're missing something," he said, concentrating on every detail of what had transpired over the last 10 minutes.

Leo looked as if he'd aged ten years. His brow was furrowed. He was looking down at the floor in deep contemplation. Steve looked out the window toward the frantoio.

Perry keyed the radio. "Thomas, you there?"

"Yeah," came the reply. "We're almost at the entrance ramp to the highway."

"Their mission. You said they were supposed to kill me, capture Christina and destroy the facility."

"Roger."

"How would they destroy the facility?"

"You know that answer, Franklin. Lots of C4."

"Shit!" Franklin keyed the radio again. "Andreo! Pull back, pull back!"

The explosion rumbled in through the broken windows. Perry and Leo ran to the window in time to see a small cloud of dust rise out of the trees.

"It's too late," Steve said. "She's gone."

"No," Perry said. "Something's not right. The explosion should have been bigger."

"What?" Steve asked.

"If their mission was to blow up your facility, they'd have a lot more C4 than that. They're going to blow the entire frantoio to stop Andreo's men. That first explosion was a diversion."

Perry keyed the radio again.

Garret slumped to the ground. His left arm was numb. He looked down at the blood pouring from under his tac vest. The vest had blocked most of Doc's rounds, but as he was rolling away, one shot caught his upper arm. *Bullets can do funny things*, he thought. *Once they enter the human body, there's no telling where they're going to go.* He lifted his arm painfully and clearly saw the exit wound in his arm and a re-entry wound in his armpit. Pinkish foam was oozing out with each breath he took. The bullet had entered his chest cavity. He tasted the metallic tang of blood in his mouth. It was all so surreal. So academic. If he were on that road below him, surrounded by those men down there, he'd have an excellent chance of surviving. But not up here, not on this hillside. Even if he radioed down for help, he'd be dead, drowned in his own blood, before they got to him. He coughed up a mouth full of the pink foam and spat it onto the ground. He reached into his pocket and pulled out a used wrapper from the energy bar he had for lunch. He stuffed it in the hole under his arm to seal the wound and prevent his lung from collapsing. It would give him a few more minutes of life, at least until his right lung filled with blood.

Andreo was leading his men up the road toward the frantoio as his other team worked their way down from the other end. Both teams were within a hundred meters. The explosion had drowned out Perry's command. Andreo signaled his men forward.

"Set a perimeter around the frantoio. Hurry!"

They all ran up the road. Twenty seconds later, the ancient building was surrounded.

Garret slid back down the hill to his rifle and got back into position. He scanned the frantoio. Through the settling dust he spotted the two figures working their way down the ravine. He keyed the comm connected to Thomas' radio.

"Targets are working their way north, down the ravine."

"What happened?" Thomas asked.

"Don't know." Garret coughed up more blood. "It's only Atwood and the woman."

"What happened to the rest of his team?"

"Gregory came after me." Garret took a labored breath. "He's dead."

"What about the other guy?"

"Don't know."

"Okay, well the plan's still working, take out Atwood."

"Not sure if I can, I'm hit," he wheezed.

Garret sighted his Barrett on Atwood and Christina. They disappeared and reappeared behind the trees shrouding the ravine. He squeezed the trigger. The gun bucked painfully and he watched the round strike the dirt between Atwood and Christina. He knew he had just as much chance of killing her as he had at killing Atwood. But, either way, he'd have accomplished his mission, his final mission. He hacked up more blood and fired again. The round struck an outcropping of rock, showering Atwood with a mini-avalanche of fist-sized stones. He saw Atwood fall and then climb back to his feet.

Andreo heard the exchange between Thomas and Garret on the radio and yelled to his men.

"Christina's clear, she's down in the ravine. There's a target in the frantoio. Go, go, go!" Andreo yelled.

He led his first team over the debris and in through the bombed-out basement wall. The first man of Andreo's second team ran through the barn doors on the main floor of the frantoio. A second man entered through the barn doors and then a third. What they neglected to see was Doc's small proximity sensor mounted to the wood frame of the doorway. It was counting: Intruder 1, Intruder 2, Intruder 3. In their rush, they failed to see the 20 kilos of C4 strategically placed around the foundation. Andreo's radio crackled and Perry's voice rang out. "Pull back! Pull back!"

Christina saw Atwood fall under a shower of stones and she bolted. She jumped from rock to rock, trying to create distance as Atwood struggled to regain footing. She'd hiked this path many times and knew it well, but as hard as she ran, he stayed five meters behind her. She pushed harder, but she had a splitting headache that was sapping what little strength she had left. A couple minutes later, she was utterly exhausted. She'd used up her adrenaline and along with it, her will to fight. She slowed and looked back. Atwood had slowed as well. He was matching her pace.

I am helping him, she realized.

"Keep going, or you're dead," Atwood yelled.

Christina shuddered at what she knew was in store for her and wondered if she should just let him kill her. Sooner or later, she'd talk, tell them everything. It would be so easy to just quit and let the work go on without her. But it was her grandfather's dream, her parent's dream, and she'd always felt it was her responsibility to finish it. She had to... for them. One of the greatest achievements of mankind, complete denuclearization. For it to fall into someone else's hands, for it to be used as a weapon... the image of Nonna laying in her garden filled her thoughts and her anger returned. She was not giving up without a fight. This monster had a long way to go before he would be safe from her, or her uncle, or Don Tumeo's men. They were surely on her trail right now.

Christina continued climbing down the mountain, occasionally allowing her foot to slip, or pretending to lose her balance to slow their progress. Ten seconds later, a deafening roar rolled down the mountainside.

The second explosion knocked the remaining glass from the broken kitchen windows and the air from their lungs. Perry, Leo and Steve struggled to remain on their feet as a mushroom cloud of smoke rose into the air. As the debris settled, they saw where the trees had been felled. There was a gaping hole in the forested mountainside and a clear view of the frantoio's jagged foundation.

Leo seemed to shrink visibly. His complexion went white, and pain covered his face like a funeral veil. He turned away from the window and picked up Perry's gun from the table. The padre wanted to kill somebody. He wasn't as certain as Perry and the rest of them that Christina had survived.

Leo turned to Perry and asked, "Where is your camera?"

Without hesitation, Perry said, "It's on the ground behind my car."

"Steve, you are second in charge. Take it down to the BiniSphere, see if it is still working. Do what you need to make it operational."

"But padre," Steve said. "What about Christina?"

340

"We have all prepared for this. We do not know when she will be back." In a lower voice, almost a whisper, he said, "or if she will be back."

"Don't give up," Perry said. "Thomas and Samuels are highly trained in rescuing hostages."

Leo ignored Perry. "Go. Do it. You are of no use to us here."

"What about the attack sub?" asked Steve. "We need to evacuate the facility."

"No, I will take care of that," Leo replied.

Steve nodded and left the kitchen. A few minutes later, he returned with the camera.

"It looks okay," Steve said. "The bullet missed the camera."

Perry was revolted by the sight of it, wishing he'd never built it, wishing he'd never invented the nanotubes, wishing he'd never come to Sicily. He was the cause of all of this, and it made him sick to see the destruction he'd wrought.

"The nanotubes," he said. "They're in the Pelican case. You'll want them to boresight the camera."

"No need," Steve said. "Christina gave me some."

Thomas and Samuels sped eastbound on the highway at over 120 mph. They were getting close. Samuels slid out of the passenger seat and into the turret. The wind made his cheeks flap as he racked a round into the chamber and set the weapon to full auto. The roar of the air was deafening, but not enough to hide the report from the explosion. They saw the massive plumb of smoke rise into the sky south of them and knew immediately what had happened. Atwood had rigged the building with C4.

Up ahead they saw the tunnel and Thomas slowed the SUV. They spotted the body on the side of the highway. A woman. Her head resting in a pool of blood. Thomas slammed on the brakes and the vehicle came to a stop 30 meters away.

He keyed the radio. "Andreo, what's your status?"

Perry's voice came over the speaker. "It's gone. The entire building. It's leveled."

"Roger," Thomas said. "We have to assume Leo's men are out of play."

"Are you at the tunnel?" Perry asked. "Do you see them?"

Thomas didn't reply.

"Hello? Thomas? Are you there?"

"Affirmative. We're at the tunnel."

Samuels heard sirens in the distance. Looking behind him, he saw several cars had stopped. Half the drivers were on their cell phones, but none ventured out of their vehicles. He assumed the 50 Cal machine gun sticking out of the roof had something to do with that. He climbed down from the turret.

"We gotta go. It's too late." Samuels said.

"We need to find Atwood and whoever is left of his team."

"We won't be able to do that from behind bars. We're sitting here, heavily armed, looking down at a dead body."

The sirens were getting louder. Thomas looked in the rearview mirror. The cars were backing up. In the distance, he saw flashing lights approaching. He stomped on the gas and entered the tunnel.

"We might not know where he is, but we know where he's heading," Thomas said.

"Sigonella?" Samuels asked.

"Yup, let's go finish this."

"What about Franklin?"

"The woman is dead; I don't think Franklin is Atwood's priority right now."

Thomas and Samuels exited the other end of the tunnel at full speed and the radio came back to life.

"Thomas, do you hear me?" Perry said.

"Roger. The police are there, we had to go," he said.

"The police? Why?"

"I'm sorry, Franklin. She was lying on the side of the road. She'd been shot in the head."

Chapter 25

Day 10 (Continued)

The radio clattered to the table, and the kitchen fell silent.

This can't be happening, Perry thought. He felt physical pain, his knees were weak. Just like the Saudi girl, he was responsible for another innocent death. He'd rather die than live like this.

Leo turned and stared out the back door, at the courtyard and his garden beyond.

"Go," he said to Steve. "Finish it."

Steve was crying as he walked out the door. When he reached the wine cellar, its door a crumbled mass laying on the ground, he called back. "We're going to find them, Father. The people responsible for this."

Leo did not respond, he just stared.

Perry followed Leo's gaze, through the courtyard, and out the archway to the garden. The colors seemed more vivid, almost garish. It was too bright. He wanted darkness, emptiness, stillness. Then he saw the wrinkled hand, just barely visible, at the threshold of the gate. A moan escaped his mouth. Perry ran. Reaching the archway, he looked down at Nonna. His knees buckled and he dropped to the ground. He looked back at Leo and saw tears streaming down his cheeks.

"I'm sorry," Perry said. "It's my fault, I should have never come here."

Squeezing Perry's Glock tightly in his hand, Leo walked over to him.

Perry didn't care anymore. He shifted his gaze back to Nonna and her bag. The contents of freshly picked vegetables, a small piece of needlework, and a jar of canned fruit had spilled onto the grass.

"Just do it," he said, waiting with anticipation for the end.

After an eternity, he looked up at the priest.

"My son," Leo said. "You have no evil in your heart. You did not come to kill, but death followed you nonetheless."

Perry nodded and waited.

"There is evil in this world," Leo said. "and my family has sworn to fight it with every ounce of our blood. Our work is not finished. We grieve later."

Leo offered a hand to Perry. Perry took it and was pulled to his feet. They stepped back into the courtyard, and Leo removed his suit jacket.

"Please," he said.

Perry took the jacket, returned to Nonna, and draped it over her head and shoulders.

Perry returned, and they walked to the wine cellar where Steve was waiting. Leo looked back toward the garden.

"That is exactly where my mother would have wanted to pass. On the threshold to her garden, the threshold to her family home."

Perry nodded and pulled his Glock from Leo's hand.

"I'll be needing that," he said.

Leo's cell phone rang as they stepped into the dark interior of the cellar.

Leo looked at Perry.

"The jammers are very powerful but only have a short lifetime," said Perry.

Leo nodded and answered. "Si`,"

...

"Si`, there was a bomb. Your men are gone. I am sorry, Don Tumeo. We have lost our Nonna, and Christina as well."

...

Leo turned suddenly and walked out of the cellar.

"No, not in the blast," he said. "Down where you are, at the entrance to the tunnel."

...

"Che cosa!"

Leo ended the call.

"Contact your friends! The woman down at the tunnel. It is not Christina!"

"What!" Perry said, his mind racing.

"They do not know who the woman is. Don Tumeo only knows that it is not Christina."

Perry ran into the house and grabbed the radio. Leo and Steve followed him.

"Thomas, are you there?"

"Go ahead," said Samuels.

"That wasn't Christina. Atwood still has her."

"What! Do you know where they are?"

"No, he must have hijacked the dead woman's car. They're gone."

"Do you know the make and model? Give us anything," Samuels said.

"Negative, no idea. We won't know until the polizia can identify the woman."

There was a long pause before Samuels replied.

"Franklin, there's nothing we can do. We have nothing to go on. The polizia are going to think it was us who killed the woman. They have witnesses."

"You have to do something," Perry said.

"We are. Atwood has the power of the US government behind him. His best bet is to return to Sigonella. They'll have a plane waiting for him."

"It's too long, too far. We need to find them now!" Perry said.

"The polizia are already setting up roadblocks. If there's any way you can convince them to stop looking for us and focus on... I don't even know what to tell them to focus on, but we're going to have a hell of a time reaching Sigonella with all of the carabinieri searching for us."

Atwood grabbed Christina as soon as they stepped out of the drainage ditch. He dragged her the last few feet to the road and immediately threw her into the path of an oncoming car. The driver swerved and slammed on the brakes but not without striking the left guard rail and then swerving back to the right. It was a glancing blow and the vehicle slid to a stop just shy of the eastbound entrance to the tunnel. He ran to the driver's side of the red Volvo as Christina yelled, "Vai! Vai! Non fermarti. Non fermarti!"

Despite Christina's pleading to not stop, the driver, a woman about Christina's age, opened the door. Atwood grabbed her, dragged her out of the car and over to the curb. Without a hint of remorse, he put a bullet between her eyes and dropped her to the ground.

Christina wailed, "Why? She was innocent! You did not need to... "

"Shut up!" Atwood yelled.

The sound of another car echoed out of the westbound tunnel. Christina scrambled to her feet and ran several meters towards the median before stopping.

Atwood smiled; she wasn't going to let him kill another innocent person. The car shot out of the tunnel and continued without a clue to what was happening.

He grabbed Christina and led her back to the car. Pressing the trunk latch, he lifted the lid and threw her in. Before closing it, he pulled a Leatherman from his belt and clipped the cable for the internal emergency truck release.

Christina, surrounded in darkness, banged and kicked at the trunk lid but soon realized she was getting nowhere. She had to use her head. She poked and prodded with her fingers, searching for something, anything she could use to escape. She pulled up the carpet under her and found a large hinged cover. *The spare tire, maybe a tire iron,* she thought. But no matter how she positioned herself, the cover was too large to open with her on top of it.

She turned, faced forward and tried releasing the folding rear seat. *Locked. Maybe the tail lights!* She wondered. *Maybe I can break one.* She searched blindly and found nothing. The lights were not accessible from the inside. Lying there, catching her breath, her eyes adjusted to the darkness. After several minutes, Christina noticed a speck of light coming from the floor. She touched it. It was a round piece of plastic, a couple inches in diameter. She pushed down on it, and the light disappeared. She rolled over and pushed her hand into her back pocket, looking for something to pry with. All she felt was one of the packages of nanotubes she'd gotten from Perry's Pelican case. She tried the other pocket and found what she was looking for, her car keys. She used the key to pry the plastic cap out of the hole, and a flood of light and fresh air entered the trunk.

Now what? she wondered.

She thought about yelling but knew it was useless. Atwood would be the only one to hear her. She wondered if she could trail something behind the car, something to arouse suspicion, but, except for her, the trunk was empty. She peered through the hole, at the outside world, and waited. Ten minutes passed, what seemed an eternity, before the car slowed. She prayed there was a roadblock. She felt a series of broad, sweeping curves, and then the Volvo accelerated again. She knew where they were. He'd taken the exit ramp for Sant'Agata di Militello. He was taking her into the mountains. There would be no roadblocks. There would be plenty of privacy and plenty of time for Atwood to interrogate her, to hurt her, and to kill her. Within minutes she felt the tight curves: left, right, accelerating, slowing down. The air streaming in through the small orifice in the floor of the trunk cooled. She lay still and wondered what Leo and Perry were doing. Did they know she was missing? Had they found Nonna? They must have. It sounded as if the whole mountainside had blown up. They must have heard it. But what if they were there when the frantoio blew. Were they even alive? Christina shook her head. "No," she said out loud. "Do not lose hope." She remembered Andreo's training. 'We will find you... and when we find you, when we find them, they will suffer unthinkable horrors.' Her anger and vengeance returned, and she realized how they could find her... if they were smart enough to figure it out.

Leo pulled out his phone and dialed. "I will call the chief of the Carabinieri, but there is little hope of finding them without a description of the car. There are too many roads, too many cars."

Perry looked at Steve, who hadn't said much since the explosion. Then Steve's words came back to Perry. He'd forgotten them in all the turmoil. He prayed, he hoped.

"You said Christina has some of the nanotubes?"

"Yes," Steve said. "She's been analyzing them, trying to figure out how they work."

"Where are they?" Perry asked.

"She gave me a bag and kept the other one. She treated them as if they were the future of mankind. I don't think she'd have gone far without them."

Perry grabbed the camera from Steve and turned it on.

"If they are here in the house, the camera will completely saturate at such a close range."

Perry scanned the camera back and forth, pointed the lens towards the upstairs, and scanned again. The camera flashed bright red. His heart sank. They ran out of the kitchen and up the stairs. Pointing it at Christina's room, he saw nothing. He scanned again. When the lens was pointing toward his bedroom, it bloomed again.

"That's from my tubes, not hers." He went into his bedroom and stepped out onto the balcony.

"There's a road map on my dresser," he said. "Bring it out here."

Leo handed Perry the map, and he quickly laid it on the floor, positioning it so it was oriented to the north. Looking down at the map, he sighted along the highway heading east and pointed the camera in the same direction.

"She has enough nanotubes that it might just work."

"If she has them with her," Steve reminded them.

Perry ignored him, slowly and carefully scanning the camera back and forth, up and down, in ever-increasing arcs. Nothing.

"It's got to be there, there's enough in that packet if she's not too far away. If I can only get it into the field-of-view."

Perry adjusted the sensitivity higher, sighted along the highway on the map, pointed the camera again to the east, and began a new scan. Going even slower than before, he panned the camera left and right, up and down. Still nothing.

Leo said, "What if they were headed west instead of east?"

"Too dangerous," Perry said. "He'd need to find a place to turn around on the highway and then head back through a murder scene. There might have been witnesses who'd seen him take the car. He wouldn't chance it."

"What about south, into the mountains?"

Perry remembered the mountain road he'd driven on the day he had arrived.

"It would be hard for him to blend in with other traffic, but it's worth a try."

Using the map on the floor, Perry resighted the camera on the azimuth where the SP 289 intersected with the E90 highway and slowly scanned to the right, into and through the mountains.

"A small red square immediately appeared on the display screen.

"Got it!" he yelled. Then he saw another square, and another, and another.

"What the hell?" Steve said.

Perry scanned the camera further to the right, following a trail of red squares leading further south and into the mountains.

"She's leaving a trail of breadcrumbs. That's why the signal is so small."

He followed the squares south until the signal bloomed brighter.

"There she is!" Perry said.

"What is going to happen when she runs out?" Leo asked. But he already knew the answer. "I'll call the Don…"

"There's no time! The farther away they get, the weaker the signal. Get the polizia to set up roadblocks."

"Si`, I will try, but the mountains are filled with back roads. It will be hard to stop them, to even find them without your sensor."

Perry snatched the camera from the tripod, stuffed the map into his pocket, and the Glock into his waistband. He ran out of the room and down the stairs.

"Perry," Leo said. "We do not have a working car."

Perry looped the camera strap over his shoulder and ran from the house. Reaching Leo's garage, he yanked the doors open.

"Please," he prayed. "Please, God, let it start."

He jumped onto the padre's CB750, slid the choke closed, turned the key and pressed the start button. Nothing. He tried again. Not a sound, not a click. *The battery*, he thought. He popped the side cover off and saw that Leo had disconnected it. Perry screwed the terminal back onto the battery post and tightened it with a wrench. He turned the key again, and the Honda roared to life. Perry backed the bike out of the garage, popped it into gear, and rocketed out of the driveway.

The closest entrance ramp to the E90 was 10 minutes away, and that was going west, in the opposite direction.

The surface streets were no better. There was too much traffic, too many intersections, he'd never catch them in time. Then he remembered. On one of the tight curves in the road leading up to Christina's house, there was a small dirt road. It had a chain strung across it, and a sign, Ingresso Vietato, Manutenzione Della Strada Principale. The road seemed to lead straight down the mountain to the highway below.

Perry reached the narrow maintenance road and squeezed the motorcycle between one side of the chained pole and a small tree. He slid more than rode the bike a half kilometer down to a maintenance building sitting right at the edge of the highway. He steered the Honda along a sidewalk that ran between the building and the guardrail, he crossed the westbound lane and the median and accelerated up onto the highway heading east. He looked at the speedometer. It was pushing 200 km/h. He did a quick conversion in his head: 120 miles per hour. The old 750cc, 4-cylinder still had plenty of horsepower. He leaned down between the handlebars, lowering his wind resistance, and the bike gained more speed. Perry hugged the outside edge of the passing lane, not slowing for anything or anybody.

The tunnels were the worst. His headlight wasn't working, and there were wet patches from water dripping from the ceiling. He banked through the dark curves, and the bike bucked and shook on every hidden puddle. He'd have to straighten it for a split-second and then bank even harder as the tunnel wall approached.

As Perry rocketed toward the SP 289 intersection, he knew he had a few things going for him. It just might save Christina's life. On the highway, he was able to travel twice as fast as Atwood, who wouldn't want to attract attention by speeding. On the mountain road, he could take each curve at max speed because of his perfect spatial memory. He'd already encountered those same curves on his first day in Sicily.

Perry banked through another curve on the highway and locked up his brakes. The handlebars shook wildly, and he lost control. He released the brakes as fast as he'd hit them. The bike straightened, and he shot between two stopped lanes of traffic.

A roadblock? That was fast, he thought. But he had no time for this. He twisted the throttle open and prayed that no one opened a door or changed lanes. He clipped one rearview mirror and had to duck under another mirror belonging to a semi-truck, but he made it to the front of the line. He searched for a gap in the roadblock. There was none. His heart sank as he slowed the bike. The polizia were standing outside their vehicles, all looking straight at him. An officer jumped into his car as if ready to give pursuit. Perry looked for an escape. He thought about turning around, but then a gap appeared between the police cars. The officers waved at him frantically. Leo had gotten through to them.

Perry revved the engine to a high pitch and popped the clutch. The front wheel of the 750 raised off the ground several inches before settling back down to the pavement. He shot between the police cars at over 80 miles per hour. He now had a completely empty road in front of him. He looked back for a second and saw one of the officers take up pursuit. Perry stepped through the gears and twisted the throttle wide open. He wasn't waiting. Five minutes later, he saw the exit sign. SP289, Parco dei Nebrodi.

Perry slowed and took the exit. At the bottom of the ramp, he pulled off onto the side of the road. He turned on the camera and searched the mountains south of him. He immediately saw the closest of the nanotubes. Judging by the strength of the signal, they weren't more than a few kilometers away. Perry followed the line of detections up and slightly to the left. He compared that to the road map he'd pulled from his pocket and nodded. He took off just as the police car, lights flashing, siren wailing, shot by at full speed, heading east on the highway above him.

Atwood had spotted the roadblock from over a kilometer away. They were descending the south slopes of the Nebrodi mountains, the thick forest periodically opening its branches to serve up wide vistas. He spotted the flashing lights and the line of vehicles down below, right where the SS289 entered the village of Cesaro. Atwood pulled the car over and punched away on his GPS, instructing it to find alternate routes. He was surprised at the results. The mountain was filled with a maze of tertiary roads: narrow tracks farmer's used to access the patchwork of plots that spread out across the southern slopes of the mountain. He accepted the GPS's deviations and soon turned left off the main road and headed down a steep dirt trail.

Reaching the valley floor, he drove toward and then around the city of Bronte and soon intersected with the SS284, a major road that wound around the western side of Mount Etna. His plan was to work his way south, eventually taking some more of the smaller back roads to Sigonella, less than an hour away. He pulled the sat-phone from his backpack, dialed Sheehan's number, and put it on speakerphone.

"What's happening down there?" Sheehan asked.

"I've got the woman. We're coming in hot. Tell them to get the plane ready."

"Good, what about Franklin?"

"It all went to shit," Atwood said. "Your guy, Garret, he turned on us. He let Perry go. Martinelli's dead, and I've been unable to contact Gregory."

"You're a bunch of fuckups!" Sheehan yelled into the phone. "If you don't get that LaTorre woman back here, you're going to be just as dead as your partners!"

"Just have the damn plane ready."

Atwood disconnected the sat-phone and drove ten more kilometers before spotting the next roadblock. They knew where he was heading. He pulled the car onto a side road and looked up towards the steaming slopes of Mount Etna.

They won't expect this, Atwood thought.

Christina had a good sense of where they were. About 30 minutes had passed since they'd exited the highway. The cold mountain air had warmed again. The car slowed, came to a stop, turned left, and accelerated to a higher speed than before. They were down in the valley, south of Nebrodi Park. She took another small pinch of the gold powder and dropped it through the hole, marking another intersection. She prayed that Perry had figured out what she was doing. She looked at the remaining amount in the small zip lock bag and prayed that he'd figure it out in time.

Perry descended out of Nebrodi in a series of full-throttle accelerations and full panic braking. Several times he'd slid close to the edge and had dropped the bike once in a tight curve after hitting a patch of loose gravel. He came to a stop when he saw an opening in the trees and a panoramic view of the valley below him. The sun was setting as he scanned the landscape with his camera, following the SS289 down to a town at the bottom of the mountain. There, he spotted the roadblock.

"Where are you damn it!" he said.

He wondered if they'd made it through the town before the polizia had setup the roadblock. He raised the camera higher, looking across the valley toward Mount Etna. He swept the camera back and forth and finally got a set of detections that led down the mountain and into the valley.

"There you are."

He saw they'd taken smaller roads to avoid the roadblock, but at the expense of speed. They were now on a normal road, heading south. Perry put the motorcycle back into gear and continued his red-lined pursuit.

The billowing smoke from Mount Etna rose high into the darkening sky, the dull red glow of the lava fields becoming more visible as the light ebbed with the setting sun. Atwood maneuvered the Volvo higher and higher, trading one threat for another. He spotted a man on a motorcycle a few hundred meters behind him. It had slowed and was matching his turns at each intersection. If they had tracked him down, he knew it would be a lot more than just a motorcycle following him. He was sure it was only a coincidence, but he didn't like it, and he wasn't going to take any chances. He saw the slow progression of the lava flows way above him, lazily rolling over the older layers of black volcanic rock as if the mountain were bleeding, the flow thickening, darkening, and crusting over like a scab. Atwood knew the bleeding wasn't going to stop, not yet. He used the map on the Volvo's navigation screen to guide him closer and closer to the lava fields.

The wind blew from the southeast, pushing super-heated air down the mountain and over the two vehicles. Whenever and wherever the lava rolled over puddles left behind by the earlier rains, jets of steam and molten globules of rock exploded hundreds of feet into the air. Perry closed the distance between them while trying to decide the best course of action. He saw only one head in the passenger compartment and assumed Christina was locked in the trunk. He couldn't just start firing, he'd be more likely to shoot her than Atwood. He needed to know what Atwood was planning. His motorcycle was no match for the car. He swerved the bike left and right, avoiding the hot embers lying on the roadway, and then he saw the long arcs of the lava traveling through the sky. They splatted down ahead of him with a spray of sparks. One thing he did know. Atwood was going to get them all killed if he kept maneuvering closer to the lava field.

The wind carried the heat across the mountainside. The chill he'd felt earlier had disappeared. He was getting hot, as if sitting in front of a gaping oven. His exposed face and hands had turned red. That's when he realized what Atwood was up to. He was in an enclosed vehicle. Perry was exposed to the elements. A minute later, the Honda sputtered and jerked. Perry twisted the throttle, but it only slowed more. He downshifted, trying to get more power, but as soon as he pulled in the clutch, the air-cooled 4-cylinder engine seized. Perry stopped the bike, pulled out the Glock, and ran fast as the Volvo disappeared around the next curve.

Atwood swerved to avoid several larger puddles of lava that littered the roadway and looked once more in his rearview mirror. It worked. The motorcycle was gone. He checked the navigation map and saw that a road was coming up on the right. It led down the mountain, away from this inferno. The lava was getting closer. He could smell burning rubber and felt the heat radiating in through the driver's-side glass. The car wasn't going to last much longer. Then all hell broke loose.

Christina heard a splat, and the car shuddered and swerved. She heard glass break. She smelt the sharp, pungent, burnt-match odor of sulfur dioxide. The acrid scent triggered a flood of memories, and a primal fear grew in the pit of her stomach. She felt the side of the wheel well; it was hot. Another louder splat made her ears ring, and the lid of the trunk caved in several inches. She instinctively pushed hard against the lid to hold it back and felt the burning heat. She jerked her hands away as the car slowed to a stop. *Why are we stopping?* she wondered. Panic coursed through her veins as she curled up in the center of the floor, trying not to touch the top or sides of the trunk. She lay there, feeling the cool floor, and wondered why. She twisted and looked through the hole. Directly under her, she saw the answer. The plastic fuel tank was insulating her from the hell going on outside. She put her mouth to the small opening in the floor and screamed.

Perry rounded the bend in time to see the car come to a stop. The roadway was blocked by a flowing red river. Then he heard her scream. He kept running as Atwood made a three-point turn and headed back towards him. The car accelerated, and Perry stopped. Above him, he saw more lava, working its way down the mountain, heading for where he was standing. He knew they'd be trapped if they didn't get out of there soon. He raised his 9mm and waited. This was the only way out, and he had the advantage. It's hard to aim a gun when you're driving a car while he could accurately put round after round into the driver's seat. But the car stopped again, halfway between him and the river of lava. Atwood jumped out and ran back to the trunk. He was too far away for an accurate shot, so he could only watch as Atwood pulled Christina out. Perry's heart went cold. Even from that range, he could see she was white as a ghost, the fight had been drained from her. Her face, arms, and legs were bloodied and covered in grime. Oblivious to the heat, Perry kept the gun raised and walked forward.

Atwood dragged Christina to the downhill side of the car, effectively blocking them from the heat, and watched as Franklin approached. He'd already had low expectations of him but now realized Franklin was a fool. There was only one obvious outcome here. As long as he had Christina, Perry would never shoot. All Atwood needed was to wait until Perry was within range.

Christina yelled, "Perry, stop! Do not come any closer."

Atwood grabbed Christina's hair, pulled her face close to his, and placed the barrel of his pistol against the side of her head.

"If you make a move, I'll blow your fucking head off," he told her.

Christina cowered, slid down the side of the car, and fell to her knees, crying.

"Please do not kill us," she pleaded while holding onto Atwood's leg. "I will do whatever you want."

"You're damn right, you will."

Franklin closed to within 25 meters. That was close enough. Atwood raised his weapon, sighted on Franklin's center of mass, and squeezed the trigger. Atwood felt a sudden movement and then a jolting, electric pain shot up through his groin. His gun fired. He fell backwards. But Christina pulled him closer. Excruciating pain reached all the way up to his stomach. Christina rose to her feet, cocking her wrist as if her car key were a fishhook. Christina ripped the key from his scrotum and ran. Not towards Perry, but in the opposite direction.

Atwood stumbled back to his feet. Knowing that Christina had nowhere to run, he turned toward the more immediate threat, which was closing on him at full speed. Atwood raised his gun and shot again.

Perry heard the first bullet whiz by and felt the second. It impacted just below his right shoulder. It knocked him off balance, enough so that the third bullet only grazed his scalp as he fell to the ground. His world went dim for a few seconds. When he could see again, he looked up, expecting to find the barrel of Atwood's gun a split second before dying. Instead, Atwood was walking away from him, towards Christina. Perry grabbed his gun, jumped to his feet, and ran. Time slowed as he watched Atwood approach her. She was standing at the edge of the lava flow, her back turned towards them. Perry ran harder. He was gaining on him, but not fast enough. Atwood was five steps from Christina when she turned around. Her eyes met Perry's, and she smiled lovingly at him. He thought that odd. Then, in utter shock, he watched her turn and run into the lava field. Perry yelled, raised his weapon, and shot.

The caseless, TacOps 9mm parabellum round uses a 115-grain solid copper, hollow point bullet. It is designed to bloom open like a daisy when it strikes flesh. The first round struck Atwood in the back of the left thigh, creating an entrance wound nine millimeters in diameter. The exit wound was much larger. Atwood stumbled forward, recovered on his good leg, and swung around fast, his weapon already in position. Perry, still running, shot again. The second round struck just below Atwood's armored chest plate. The bullet pinwheeled through his intestines, shredding them like confetti. It didn't stop until it struck Atwood's spine. The bullet had lost too much momentum to sever the spinal cord. If it had, he would have crumpled to the ground like a rag doll. The shock wave did the job. Atwood tried to regain his balance, but his legs didn't obey. His feet slid more than stepped and he shuffled backward as Perry kept coming. Atwood's heels eventually struck the hard crust at the edge of the lava flow. The third bullet struck Attwood squarely in the chest and he fell backwards, landing flat on his back in the river of molten rock.

Perry reached him just as his short-cropped hair ignited. Atwoods scalp was covered in a fantastic glow of colors before quickly turning black. He looked up at Perry in disbelief. He tried to sit up, but his synthetic clothes had melted, bonding him to the viscous lava like eggs to an ungreased frying pan. Perry heard fat sizzling and popping. Atwood's body jerked, and small jets of fire and steam shot out from under his torso and buttocks. Perry knew it would take a while for the pain to kick in. But it eventually would. He lowered his weapon and watched the man struggle as he drifted downstream. The screams started a short time later.

Perry did not want to look up, he didn't want to see what remained of Christina. He looked at his feet, not even noticing the blood dripping down his right hand and over his Glock. He choked and turned away. Perry looked towards the car and saw another river of lava crossing the road. He was trapped. But not necessarily concerned. His vision was fuzzy, and he had trouble keeping his balance. He assumed he'd gotten another concussion. His head hurt, his arm hurt, his heart hurt, but it didn't matter. It was over.

When he heard Christina's voice, he thought he was hallucinating.

"Perry! Perry!"

He ignored it.

"Damn it, Perry! You are going to die if you do not get over here."

He thought that odd for a hallucination. He turned around and saw Christina waving her arms over her head.

"What the hell!" he said.

"You must run, fast!" she yelled. "You only have about five seconds."

He looked at her, not understanding. Then the image of Atwood flooded his consciousness. Atwood's body didn't sink into the viscous lava, it floated on top, as if he were laying on a mattress. Of course, he realized. The density of rock is much higher than a human body.

"Hurry, you are running out of time!" Christina yelled.

He took one last look at the mountain, saw the river of lava moving closer, and ran. He had no choice. The woman he loved was waiting for him.

Chapter 26

Day 11

Sheehan sat alone in the Situation Room, trying for the tenth time to contact Alpha team. No one answered. A day had passed since Butch, the last one standing from his Bravo team, had called with the bad news. And now with Sheppard dead, he had no idea what was happening in Canneto. His only source of information was the live spy satellite feed being displayed on the wall in front of him. It showed a burnt out hulk of a building on the side of a mountain near the LaTorre villa. Dozens of emergency vehicles and almost a hundred men were still combing through the debris, looking for survivors.

President Blake stormed into the room.

"What the hell's going on, Sheehan? My chief of staff just told me we have three dead spooks at the residence of one of our ONI employees. What have you done?"

"I'm sorry sir, it was supposed to look like an accident, the team must have rushed into…"

"I don't want to hear your excuses. As soon as Sheppard's out of surgery, he's going to start talking."

"What? Sheppard's alive? I was told he was…"

"Shut up!" the president ordered. "I should throw you under the bus right now."

Sheehan jumped out of his chair and faced Blake.

"You can't, sir."

"What do you mean, I can't?"

"You're in this as much as I am, Jim. You and I have met several times without the DNI in attendance. How do you think that's going to play when people learn what I've been trying to do for you?"

"It's called plausible deniability, you fool."

"Maybe so, but you do know I'm a very cautious man."

"No. Not considering what you've managed to…"

"What I've managed to do is have Max Howell record our quite detailed phone conversations. He was more than amenable given his reluctance and the extreme nature of the work you have directly ordered him to do. He needed to cover his own ass."

President Blake stared at the DDNI with rage in his eyes.

"Jim, relax, this isn't over yet. If we can pull this off, they'll forget all about these minor transgressions. You'll be the greatest American in modern history and the ruler of the world."

Blake was still steaming, but at least he was listening.

"The *USS New Mexico*, one of our Virginia-class fast-attack subs, is in the Mediterranean right now. I used it last week to search for Franklin. If we don't hear from our Alpha team in the next twentyfour hours, we'll have to assume they failed. The only option left is to use the sub's torpedoes to destroy that facility."

"I thought you were trying to capture their head scientist. What about the stability problems with the phaser? Don't we need the technology to…?"

"We don't have time, sir. These Sicilians know that we're after them. There's no chance of us getting to the technology, now. They're going to be looking directly at us, we're a threat to them. We must strike before they do. Once they're out of the picture, we have some more breathing room to solve the stability issues on our own. Howell is making great progress in New London, preparing the *Rhode Island*. They're working 24/7 and have already powered up the phaser. They've been able to increase the output power to 15 percent of the theoretical limit and still maintain stability. Howell believes they can reach 50 percent, it's enough for them to start breaking down the nukes. We just need to buy ourselves some time."

"So, you're asking me to authorize an act of war before we can even use our phaser."

"Yes, sir. Every ounce of our nanotubes, 100 kilograms, is sitting on the *Rhode Island*. They won't be hard to find, especially with Franklin helping them. Once they do, they'll have no choice but to eliminate the threat."

"I can't believe I let you talk me into this."

"Jim, it's a single covert strike, and it's underwater. The Sicilians might suspect where it came from, but they'll never know for sure."

"Some of them will," Blake said.

"Look, where do you think all these scientists are right now? What do you think they're doing now that they know we're trying to stop them."

Blake turned back to his map of the world. "They're going to attack us. They're going to take out our nukes."

"Exactly. We need to be preemptive. Any people who might suspect we're behind this are going to be in that facility, preparing for war."

"Do you have the coordinates?"

Sheehan reached into his pocket and handed Blake a piece of paper.

"How did you get this?"

"The dive boat sir. The SEALs on the *New Mexico* dove on the wreck, searching for Franklin's body. They retrieved the navigation console from the cockpit. It took a few days, but they were able to extract the memory chip and read it."

"It had the position of the facility? Why would…"

"The dive captain was trying to prevent Franklin from finding the facility. To do that, he'd have to know exactly where the facility was. He'd apparently set up a proximity alarm to warn him if they were getting close. When the CO of the sub couldn't get a hold of Sheppard this morning, he went up the chain of command."

"And that was you?"

"Yes, sir."

Blake hit a button on the telephone. His chief of staff answered on the first ring.

"Yes, sir."

"Get the DNI, the Secretary of Defense and Chairman of the Joint Chiefs of Staff in here immediately."

"Yes, sir."

After ending the call, the president asked, "What about Sheppard?"

"Mr. President. Lt Col Sheppard has directly disobeyed orders. He's killed three American heroes here in DC, and he's conspired with a compatriot to eliminate our Alpha Team in Sicily," Sheehan said. "That's treason, he needs to be dealt with immediately."

"Get it done. No more screwups."

"Yes, Mr. President."

After Blake walked out of the situation room, Sheehan pulled his phone from his jacket pocket and pressed the "Stop" button on his voice recorder.

Brenda returned to the waiting room and sat, not even noticing the small man wearing scrubs. He was sitting in the corner, reading an outdated People magazine. His ID badge had gotten twisted, only the back was showing. Brenda had kissed Stan goodbye a halfhour earlier, as he was being wheeled in for his second surgery. She'd gone down to the cafeteria for a coffee and returned in preparation for the long wait. The operation was expected to take three hours. She'd barely gotten her first sip of coffee when Stan's surgeon came walking towards her. He was trailed by a younger doctor who she assumed was the resident. She thought it odd. *Why wasn't he doing the closing like last time?* she wondered. She stood. When she saw their expressions, she fell back into her seat and covered her face.

"I'm so sorry, Mrs. Sheppard. We really don't know what happened. As soon as our anesthetist applied the propofol, Mr. Sheppard's heart stopped. We were unable to resuscitate him."

Brenda, sobbing, didn't hear a single word he said.

The small man in scrubs got up from his chair, dropped the magazine on the end table, and walked away.

Chapter 27

Day 12

A wide stone archway opened out to the veranda overlooking the sea. The waves were crashing on the rocks below, and a northerly breeze carried the spicy scent of pomelia, a white fleshy flower that bordered the estate. A dozen of Don Tumeo's men bordered the property as well, each one of them carrying a Beretta Mx4 submachine gun.

Perry sat on the veranda, shirtless, his right arm resting in a sling, his shoulder bandaged. Christina, sitting next to him, leaned back and inhaled deeply before asking.

"It hurts like hell. That's how it feels," he answered. "I wish you'd quit asking."

"You do not have to be a child about it," she said. "It is not like the bullet did any real damage."

Christina's ears still rang from the explosion at the frantoio, and she had injuries of her own, all of them superficial, except for the dull ache in the pit of her stomach. She missed Nonna terribly.

"Thanks for the sympathy," he said.

"Perry, you know how I feel about you. But I cannot let that get in the way. We need your help. We cannot do this without you."

"It's too dangerous. They're going to destroy the BiniSphere, and there's nothing you can do to stop it."

"I did as you asked. I have evacuated all our personnel, but you told me yourself, they are building their own. Do you really want that to happen? Do you really trust your government that much? To have that kind of power?"

"Do you trust yours?"

"We are not the government, and we have no nuclear weapons to hold over the rest of the world's head. Italy does not even have a nuclear power plant."

"I don't care. Why not just leave things as they are, maintain the status quo?"

"You know there is no such thing as maintaining the status quo. Sooner or later, someone is going to push a button. A dictator, a terrorist, a religious fanatic, a confused leader of a free democracy. Or just simply by accident. There are over 14,000 warheads spread across the earth. Sooner or later, it will happen, and millions of people will die. You can change that."

"We might be speeding things up if we start dismantling the world's nuclear arsenal."

"Yes, that is a remote possibility, but compared to the alternative, a virtual certainty that we will destroy ourselves... especially from what I hear about your president. He cannot be allowed to have that kind of power."

Perry put his hand on Christina's. "I can't let you go down there. I'm not going to lose you again."

Christina leaned over and kissed him. "You will not have to. You will be right next to me."

"That makes me feel much better."

"You have the technology. You know how the nanotubes work, and you know how to interface the camera. We do not have time to figure it out for ourselves."

Perry shook his head and got up from the lounge chair.

"I need to talk to Stan, see if he's learned anything more about when the modifications to the *Rhode Island* will be completed."

Perry turned towards Don Tumeo's house and saw Thomas and Samuels walking towards him. Their somber expressions didn't seem out of the ordinary; they always looked that way.

"Let me have your phone. I need to call Stan, get a status on Sheehan's sub."

"I'm sorry Franklin. I'm afraid that's not going to happen."

Ever since Perry and Christina's brush with death at the hands of America's elite warriors, he had lost all patience with every one of them.

"Give me your damn phone," he ordered.

"I'm really sorry, Perry," Thomas said. "I know he was your best friend. He's gone. They killed him."

Perry looked at Thomas as if he hadn't heard him, then at Samuels.

"What?" he said.

Samuels nodded. "They caught the guy who did it."

"How?"

"A neurotoxin while he was in surgery. I think they called it tetrodotoxin. It stopped his heart."

Christina stood and put a hand on Perry's shoulder. He pushed it aside and turned towards the ocean. He felt numb, as if his body didn't exist. As if he'd melted into the landscape. He stood and stared for several long minutes. The rocks and crashing surf reminded him of Ocean Point. He wished he was home, with his family.

He thought about the last time they were all together. It was his dad's birthday. Julie, the kids, and he had driven up from Boston to stay at the cottage for the weekend. The three of them sat on the porch, watching the kids play in the front yard. They were drinking a summer cocktail that Marta had whipped up. It had mint leaves and rum. The sky was deep blue with bright white billowy clouds. They were always billowy up there. *Why couldn't things just stay the same?* he wondered. *Why did Dad have to die alone, in the woods, on that trail? They said it was a massive heart attack, that he was dead before he hit the ground, but why did he have to be alone?*

"You are not alone, Perry."

He jumped, not realizing he'd spoken out loud.

Christina put her arm around him again and laid her head on his shoulder.

"I just want to go back home. I miss my family."

"We can never go back," she said. "Nothing ever stays the same."

Christina started crying. Perry wiped a tear from her cheek and put his arm around her. They stood for several minutes, the four of them, in silence. Only the sound of the waves and the breeze in the trees recorded the passage of time.

Perry broke the silence. "Call your people. Get them back to work."

Christina looked up at him.

"Right now!" he said.

Leo stood at the window of Don Tumeo's study, looking out over the expansive back yard where his niece stood with the three American spies. He picked up the phone and dialed a number he knew by heart.

"Buongiorno. Secretariat of State's office. How may I be of service?"

"This is Monsignor LaTorre. Is Cardinal Girolamo available?"

"Si`, Father! I will find him immediately."

Cardinal Petri Girolamo presided over the Holy See Secretariat of State, the oldest and most important department of the Roman Curia, the central body through which the affairs of the Catholic Church were conducted. The cardinal, sometimes described as the prime minister, performed all the political and diplomatic functions of the Holy See and the Vatican.

The Sicilian Mafia and the Vatican had been supporting the development of the BiniSphere since the spring of 1938.

Throughout the decades, it was a problematic relationship, but not unknown in the history of Sicily.

In the late 1800s, when Sicily became a province of unified Italy, chaos and crime had spread across the island as the Italian government tried to establish itself. Roman officials had met with the Cosa Nostra clans, asking them to rein in the dangerous, independent criminal bands. In exchange, officials looked the other way as the Mafia continued its protection shakedowns of landowners. The Vatican coordinated these efforts while relying on the mafiosi to monitor its massive property holdings in Sicily and keep tenant farmers in line.

After World War II, major construction of Majorana's underground research facility began in earnest, using Mafia-controlled construction companies that had dominated the post-World War II building boom. The inherent secrecy of both the Vatican and the Mafia allowed the BiniSphere's development to accelerate and expand without a single breach in security. Every scientist, engineer and technician was carefully vetted, each one of them knowing the deadly consequences if they betrayed the famiglia.

Both Leo and Christina detested the mafiosos but knew they were a necessary evil. They never would have come this far without their support or their secrecy. Leo's father, Ettore, may have been the brains behind the BiniSphere, but the Cosa Nostra were the muscle.

"Leo!" said Cardinal Girolamo. "I just heard about your problems. How are you?"

"We are all safe. We are with Don Tumeo at his estate."

"I am so very saddened to hear about your Nonna. She was an angel. I am praying for her."

"Thank you, Petri, I appreciate your prayers, but she is in good hands. It is the rest of us that I am more concerned about."

"Your Christina. Was she harmed?"

"She is recovering. It was mostly superficial. But she is despondent… and very angry."

"I understand. And the BiniSphere?"

"We have an immediate threat, Your Eminence. If you could speak to the minister of defense. There is a US fast attack submarine in our territorial waters. They have orders to destroy us. It must be stopped."

"Of course! I will speak to him immediately."

"Thank you, Cardinal, I am in your debt."

"No, Leo, we are in yours. You have sacrificed much for the good of all of us."

"Thank you, I must go now. We have much to do."

"Very well, attend to your matters, and please, tell Don Tumeo I am sorry over the loss of his men."

"I will. They will most certainly need our prayers. Even then, their salvation may be in question."

Chapter 28

Day 13

The *USS New Mexico* had spent the last 12 hours slowly threading its way underneath a staggering number of Italian surface vessels. The Block V Virginia-class attack submarine had recently undergone modifications that included a new propulsion system, quieting technologies for the engine room, and the application of advanced coating materials on the hull to absorb sound. The *New Mexico* was one of the stealthiest submarines in the Navy and that was the only reason it had gotten this far. But there were limitations when the entire Italian Navy appeared to be looking for them.

Captain Dawson told his executive officer, or XO, "We're within range to the target. Bring her to a full stop and set her down on the bottom. Comms, send a message to Washington. Tell them we're ready to launch. Awaiting orders."

"Aye, sir."

Two minutes later, they felt the soft landing of the sub, eight nautical miles north of the BiniSphere.

"Judging by the number of contacts on the surface, it seems like someone knew we were coming," said the XO.

"I agree, we're lucky we got this far. But no matter, they're not going to know where we are until we launch the torpedoes. Then we'll get out fast."

Several of Christina's team were inside the BiniSphere, making the modifications needed to mount and align Perry's camera to the exit beam. It was not an easy task. The highly sensitive camera was being bolted to a device capable of producing megawatts of neutrino energy. Most of that energy, 99 percent of it, was directed out into the world as a tight, columnated beam. But the remaining energy, only one percent, leaked into the surrounding environment, enough to affect the performance of the highly sensitive camera.

Perry had been working feverishly for the past 24 hours, running calculations on the computer, feeding his results into the remote wireless connection he'd set up between his laptop and the camera.

"It should work now," he said. "Try again."

Christina's crew climbed out of the sphere and sealed the hatch. Steve went to the control console and pressed a series of switches. The gyroscopic motors spun up, and the entire sphere slowly rotated.

"Point it at Christina's house," Perry said. "The nanotubes are still there."

"Doing it," Steve said.

Perry watched as the exit port for the beam rose and panned to the left. He turned back to the computer screen displaying the output image from the camera. It was totally black until the line-of-sight of the BiniSphere approached the house. The screen saturated red.

"We got it!" he said. "The optics are working."

Perry's handheld camera was small by comparison to the immense optics used by the BiniSphere. His camera was designed to detect small amounts of neutrinos at relatively short ranges, tens of kilometers at the most. The BiniSphere was designed to radiate energy onto a target located on the opposite side of the planet. They had mounted the camera to a small optical port used for measuring and controlling the output power of the BiniSphere. In that position, the camera was looking straight down the axis of the neutrino beam. The problematic part was synchronizing the camera to the output beam. If the camera were powered on at the same time the beam was transmitting, it would be destroyed immediately. The trick was to turn the camera on a split second after the neutrino beam had been turned off. Within that tiny window of time, the camera would catch the avalanche of Majorana neutrinos cascading off a target, more specifically, a nuclear warhead.

"Great, but now for the real test," Christina said. "Steve, enter the coordinates for the Tricastin power plant in France and set the power to 5 percent."

"Yes, ma'am."

"A nuclear power plant," Perry said. "That'll set off a bunch of alarms."

"No," said Christina. "The chain reaction in a power plant is much slower than a nuclear bomb. It would take us a lot longer to radiate it with enough energy to neutralize it. At low power, we can radiate the fuel rods for several hours, if not days, before anyone noticed a degradation in performance."

"We're ready," Steve said.

Perry adjusted a few settings on the camera and activated the synchronization software.

"Okay, I'm good. Fire it up."

The BiniSphere hummed, and red pricks of light flashed on the computer screen, but there were no detections.

"Nothing," Perry said. "That's just background radiation. I've adjusted the timing of the camera so it will ignore natural radiation from closer sources, but some of it is still leaking through."

"We are not on the target yet," Christina said. "Steve, activate the search and track algorithm."

Steve clicked on the computer screen at his counsel, and the BiniSphere started vibrating. There was no perceptible movement from the giant globe. Scanning a small patch of earth, only a few hundred meters wide, from over a thousand miles away, didn't require a whole lot of movement. The BiniSphere was rotating only a tiny fraction of a degree. Then the vibrating stopped.

"It's tracking." Steve and Perry said in unison.

Christina, along with the dozen other scientists working for her, watched the displays. A set of red squares danced across the video feed from Perry's camera. A stream of heavy neutrinos was pouring from the fuel rods, ever so slowly depleting the power plant's nuclear material.

The 70-year dream of the LaTorre family, of the Majorana family, had finally been realized. But they could only savor the moment for a few seconds.

"Okay," Perry said. "We can't stand here congratulating ourselves. There's an attack sub out there that wants to blow us out of the water. Steve, break lock and pan the beam up; we need to start scanning the ocean floor. Point it directly above us and start sweeping north. The range of their torpedoes is fifty kilometers, but they'll need to be within ten to have any chance of hitting us. There's no target in the water for the sonar to lock onto. The torpedoes will have to use their inertial navigation system for guidance, and the INS loses accuracy the longer the torpedo is in the water. If we can find them before they get within range, we can shut down their reactor. They'll be helpless, stranded on the bottom. We'll send their position to your warships, and they can finish them off."

"Perry, what is wrong with you?" Christina said. "We are not going to kill all those sailors, that is not what we are here... "

"They're coming to kill us. They're committing an act of war with no provocation."

"It does not matter," she said. "If they are stranded on the bottom, we will rescue them."

"But they'll still be a threat. They'd still be able to launch their torpedoes."

"We do not even know for sure if they can damage us. We are a hundred meters underground."

"If one of their warheads is triggered close to one of your escape tubes, the pressure wave could travel all the way down to your facility, blow out your escape hatches and flood your tunnels. You're willing to take that chance?"

"Of course I am. We all are."

"That's crazy," Perry said, his mind running in overdrive. "I have another idea. How fast can you modulate the output power of the beam?"

"What?"

"Damn it! Will you just once do what I ask? I need the maximum frequency response of the output power. How fast can you turn it on and off?"

"It is about 10 kilohertz," Christina said. "But it falls off fast with increased power. What are you...?"

"That will work. Who's your top software guy?"

"Our top programmer is a woman, Anna."

"I need her. Someone get me a microphone. Hurry!"

The BiniSphere was making large sweeping scans, rotating back and forth, then notching down and scanning back and forth again. Three minutes later, the scanning stopped.

"I've got it," Steve said.

"Are you sure?" Perry asked. "Could it be one of your own ships, one of your subs?

"Perry, I told you, Italy does not have any nuclear power plants, even on ships. Nothing!" Christina said.

"Okay, okay, I get it," he said.

"Steve," Christina said. "Contact the fleet, give them the coordinates."

Steve grabbed the phone and dialed the direct line to the fleet commander. At the same moment, a young Italian woman walked into the control room.

"This is Anna," Christina said to Perry. "She is the best software programmer in Sicily. What do you need her to do?"

"Anna, come here," he said.

Perry sat her down at a control console and said, "I don't need the best, I need the fastest modifications you can make," and he explained what he needed her to do.

The *New Mexico's* sonar operator keyed his mike. "Captain, three ships have altered course, they are on a direct bearing to our location.

"Shit," said the captain. "Comms, any word from Washington?"

"It's coming in now, sir."

The text slowly emerged on the Comms console.

"Captain, launch is approved. I repeat, launch is approved."

"Prepare to fire, flood torpedo tube 1," ordered the captain.

"Aye, sir. Flooding torpedo tube 1... torpedo tube 1 is flooded."

"Flood torpedo tube 2," ordered the captain.

"Aye, sir. Flooding torpedo tube 2... torpedo tube 2 is flooded."

"Fire torpedo 1, fire torpedo 2," ordered the captain.

A slight vibration ran through the *USS New Mexico* as a blast of high pressure air blew the two high-speed MK-48 torpedoes from their tubes.

As part of the BiniSphere's elaborate security system, an array of acoustic sensors had been installed on the ocean floor. The array surrounded the underground facility in a 3 kilometer arc to the north and was used to track the many surface vessels that populated the local waters. A klaxon sounded, and red lights flashed. Then the sonar operator's voice rang out over the loudspeakers.

"Two torpedoes have just been launched, eight kilometers directly north of us. On a heading of 175 degrees true. They are coming straight for us."

"What's the speed?" Perry yelled across the room.

"145 kilometers per hour,"

"We have two minutes to stop it," Perry said.

Perry pushed the software programmer from her seat and sat down at the computer console.

The *New Mexico's* sonar operator put his hand over his headphones and stared intently at the computer screen displaying the acoustic signals from the two torpedoes. He adjusted the output power and threshold settings and shook his head. He keyed his mike.

"Captain! You need to hear this," he said.

Captain Dawson ran over and put on the extra headset. He heard the roar of the torpedoes' super-cavitating rocket motors and then the unmistakable sound of a voice.

"*USS New Mexico, USS New Mexico*, this is your target speaking. We have a lock on your position. With a simple push of a button, we can destroy your ship instantly. You must immediately abort your attack…"

"Where's it coming from? Quick! What's the range and bearing?"

"That's the problem, sir. There is no range and bearing. It's coming from inside the sub."

"What?"

The XO ran into the control room.

"Captain Dawson, there's something strange happening in the engine room. Our power plant readings are fluctuating wildly, and the radiation monitors on our Tomahawks are sounding."

The captain ran down the central gangway of the sub and into the weapons bay.

"Sir, the readings indicate the Tomahawk's nuclear cores are unstable," said the weapons officer. "The radiation is oscillating wildly. I've never seen this before."

He handed his captain the tablet displaying real-time plots of the sensor outputs.

Dawson watched the energy plots jump up and down on the screen and said, "Give me the headphones."

Captain Dawson slipped the headphones over his ears and contacted sonar.

"Sonar! Patch the audio through to me."

"Yes, sir."

"… you have 40 seconds left before we detonate your entire magazine of thermonuclear warheads. *USS New Mexico, USS New Mexico*, this is your target speaking. You are committing an act of war by firing on us. In 30 seconds, we will destroy…"

The captain watched the fluctuating radiation plots on the display screen as he listened. They were synchronized with the audio coming from his headphones. The nuclear warheads were literally speaking to him.

"… you have entered sovereign territory. You have exactly 20 seconds before we destroy you."

The captain ran to the control bay.

"Sir," said the XO. "Propulsion just called. Our reactor power is fluctuating wildly. They need to shut it down."

"Initiate self-destruct on torpedo 1 and torpedo 2, immediately!" the captain yelled.

The blast wave from the two torpedoes rocked the entire facility and alarms sounded. Thirty seconds later, Christina started receiving status messages on her control screen. The damage was minor.

"Perry! It worked," Steve said. "They fell for your bluff."

Perry, Christina, and Steve watched the monitor as the sub's tracking vector swung to the west.

"It's moving away," Steve said. "They got the message."

"How did you do that?" Christina asked.

"It was simple," Perry said. "I had your programmer, Anna, send the input signal from a microphone to your output power control module on the BiniSphere. The neutrino beam puts a lot of internal stress on the nuclear material. By modulating the output power of the beam... "

"... you can make the subs nuclear warheads and reactor vibrate, at audio frequencies," Christina said.

"Not much, not much at all," Perry said. "It was a very, very soft whisper."

"So soft that no one was able to hear your voice unless they were using a sophisticated listening device," Steve said.

"Exactly. Like the type of acoustic sensors that might be used on a nuclear submarine," Perry replied. "The sonar operator got the message loud and clear."

Christina smiled for the first time in days. "Can you imagine the look in their eyes when their radiation sensors went wild, and their warheads started talking to them?"

Steve patted Perry on the back. "Outstanding mate! Now what?"

"Now we go after bigger fish," Perry said. "Let me at your console."

Perry sat down at Steve's workstation and used the mouse to pan the Google Earth image west. He zoomed in, panned, and zoomed in again.

"Here it is. Set up another search pattern centered on this location with five-kilometer legs. It'll be there somewhere. You can't miss it."

Steve went to work, setting up the BiniSphere for the next phase of their plan.

Perry pulled Christina aside and said, "You've got this covered. I have to go."

"Go? What do you mean? We are just getting started."

"You don't need me here. I'd just be a distraction, and I have work to do back in the US."

"Perry! You are not a distraction. I want …"

With his good arm, Perry pulled Christina close. "You're letting your emotions control you."

"That is ridiculous," she said.

"Christina, you just let me commandeer your entire facility for the last few hours," he whispered. "You gave me full access to your computer systems. I was your enemy a few days ago. You would never have let someone like me do that."

"I trust you. You knew what you were doing."

"Well, you shouldn't," he said. "I'm not like you."

"What does that mean?"

"Up until yesterday, I was ready to walk away and let your BiniSphere be completely destroyed. You knew that, and yet you still gave me full access. You shouldn't have trusted me."

"Oh Perry, have you not learned yet? That is what we do. We have faith in people doing the right thing."

"Well, I don't believe in faith. The 'right thing' to do isn't always that simple."

"I do not understand."

"After your programmer finished making the software changes, I stepped in and made a few of my own. That countdown was real. If that sub hadn't backed off, I would have wiped them off the face of the earth, killing every sailor on board and leaving a patch of nuclear waste the size of a small city."

"You cannot set off a nuclear warhead with the BiniSphere," she said.

"Christina, all of your research and development is based on using a particle accelerator to energize the phaser. That's because your country has such an aversion to working with nuclear energy. When I first developed the nanotubes, they were going to be used in a device to detect nuclear material that was being proliferated around the world. That project failed because of instability issues between the neutrinos and the nuclear material we were trying to detect. At close ranges, they feed off each other. I ran the numbers. I could have triggered a low-level explosion of that sub's S9G nuclear reactor. The software timer I set up was real. If they hadn't aborted, the neutrino beam would have gone to 100 percent. Every sailor would have died within seconds."

"What is wrong with you! Why would you do that?"

"I told you, I'm not like you. I would have done it just to save a single life. Yours. You wouldn't have done it to save your entire team, your entire project."

Christina stared at him in disbelief.

"You are right," she said. "You are not at all like us. You need to leave."

Chapter 29

Day 14

Sheehan hung up the phone and said, "*The Rhode Island's* preparing to get underway."

"It's about time," said the president. "What's the status of the phaser?"

"It's operational, but they've been unable to exceed 40 percent of power. That's as good as they can get."

"Will it work?"

"Yes sir, Howell assures me it will. It will just take longer than expected to eliminate the warheads. The facility in Sicily is another story. We have no idea what effect, if any, it will have on the BiniSphere."

"BiniSphere?"

"That's what they're calling it, sir."

Sheehan and the president had been inseparable ever since they'd received the secure message from Captain Dawson. The strange attack on the *New Mexico* meant they were out of time. The BiniSphere was operational. When Captain Dawson played the recorded message of the event, Sheehan recognized the voice. It was Franklin's.

The chief of staff knocked and walked in.

"Mr. President," Davis said. "I have an urgent message from DNI Gonzales. It appears she's been in contact with a…" Davis checked his notes. "a Mr. Perry Franklin, who wants to speak directly to you and DDNI Sheehan."

"Franklin? Have the director come over immediately," the president said.

"I'm sorry, sir, not the director, it's Mr. Franklin who needs to speak with you. There's also a Mr. Thomas accompanying him."

"Franklin's here in Washington?"

"Yes, Mr. President. He said it has something to do with the location and purpose of a ..." he checked his notes again, "phaser. The DNI also voiced her displeasure at not being in the loop on this but seems to think it's imperative that you meet with Franklin immediately. For some reason, she declined my invitation to attend the meeting."

Blake turned to Sheehan. "Have you heard back from your team yet?"

Sheehan shook his head. "Something's gone wrong. We better hear what he has to say."

"Davis. What's on my schedule today?"

"They're downstairs at security, sir."

"Oh, uh, okay! Send them right up."

"Should I tell the DNI to attend?" Davis asked.

"No, that's not necessary. Mike and I will talk to Franklin alone."

A few minutes later, Perry and Thomas walked into the Oval Office.

"Deputy Director Sheehan, Mr. President," Perry said. "Thanks for seeing us on such short notice."

As soon as the chief of staff closed the inner door, Perry removed an inhaler from his pocket.

"Sorry," he said. "My asthma always acts up whenever I'm in DC. Must be something about the swamp this place was built on."

Perry brought the inhaler to his mouth and pressed the button.

"Mr. Franklin," Blake said. "What's the urgency that can't wait?"

"As you know we've been investigating the shutdown of one of our KH-11 satellite's PIT sensors."

For the next fifteen minutes, Perry provided a very detailed account of his activities in Sicily, minus the interactions with Sheehan's kill team or his visits to the BiniSphere.

"Franklin," Sheehan said. "Why are you wasting our time with this? Sheppard had been keeping us appraised of the situation. We know full well what you've been doing."

"You mean up until you had him eliminated," Thomas said.

"That's ridiculous," the president scoffed.

"Oh, you didn't know about that, Mr. President?" asked Franklin.

Sheehan said, "I understand that you and Sheppard were close, but we had nothing to do with his death. From what I understand, he died on the operating table. I'm sorry for your…"

Thomas stepped closer to Sheehan, saying, "You know damn well what happened to Stan and you will pay for that."

Perry put his hand on Thomas' arm. "We're not here to discuss Stan. We're here because of the BiniSphere."

"BiniSphere? What are you talking about?" the president said.

"It's a particle accelerator, it's in Sicily. I just wanted to come over here to keep you guys up to date."

"I told you. We know what's happening in Sicily," Sheehan said.

"Oh, that's right. The fast attack sub you ordered to destroy it. I guess you had a good idea where to find us."

"What do you want, Franklin?" asked the president.

Perry scanned the room for almost ten seconds before addressing the president.

"Okay, where was I. Oh yeah. Did you know that the surface area of an adult male's lungs is about 75 square meters? That's about the same size as a tennis court."

The two politicians looked at him, confused.

"Our lungs act like giant wet filters. We suck in about 10 liters of air per minute. So, we've each filtered about 200 liters since I've been here. I've calculated the diffusion rate of 200 grams of the thorium-fluoride nanotubes, the average respiration rate of a male adult - although I suspect yours is a bit higher right now - and the approximate size of this beautiful office you have here. Taking that all into account, I think we're ready."

Perry pulled out his cell phone and pushed the speakerphone function.

"You're not allowed to have a phone in here," Sheehan said.

"You know, I hear if you talk to the right people you can get away with just about anything."

Perry spoke into the phone. "Samuels, can you hear me?"

"Loud and clear, Franklin."

Perry looked at Sheehan. "Samuels, and Thomas here, are my guys. All your guys are dead."

"I don't know what the hell you are talking… "

"Shut up, Mike," said Blake. "I'll ask you one more time Franklin, and then I'm locking the two of you up. What do you want?"

Perry ignored the president and spoke into the phone. "Are you tracking us?"

"I have all four of you," Samuels replied.

"Tracking?" Sheehan asked. "You think I give a shit that you're tracking us with your magic powder?"

"Oh, don't you understand? It can be used for more than just tracking our enemies. Light us up," Perry ordered.

A column of light instantly appeared in the far corner of the Oval Office. It shimmered and glowed a dull red, cutting an angle from floor to ceiling.

"The neutrino beam is set to low power," Perry said. "But still, I wouldn't get in its way. The particles are quite hot."

Sheehan retreated to the far side of the president's desk.

"Okay, Samuels," Franklin continued. "Turn up the fireworks."

The column of light immediately flashed bright white, blinding everyone's eyes like a flashbulb and disappeared with a loud snap.

Blake and Sheehan stared at the empty space where the beam had been.

"Here's the deal," Perry said, waving the inhaler in front of them. "I filled the room with nanotubes as soon as I walked in the door. What you just saw is a demonstration of what happens when you illuminate those tubes with an intense beam of Majorana neutrinos. That beam came directly from Sicily. You don't want to see, no, excuse me, you don't want to feel what happens if you are illuminated by that beam. That flash you saw was the thorium-fluoride instantly vaporizing. Since it's much more diluted when spread through the room, it's not that hazardous. But, given the amount of tubes you've absorbed into your lungs, it would not be a pretty picture if they were vaporized. The moist, mucous membrane catches the particles with every inhalation. If you were to be hit with that beam, the intense heat would sear your lungs, and the thorium-fluoride gas would disperse through your bloodstream. It would be an agonizing death. And, in case you're wondering, it will take years for those tubes to work their way out of your system. During that time, we will be watching you. Are you catching on?"

"We understand," said the president. "What do you want?"

"That's the simplest part. There are only three things you need to do. One, you stop all activity concerning the nanotubes, which means you immediately dismantle the phaser you're installing on the *Rhode Island*. Once it's dismantled, we'll take possession of the nanotubes. Two, Mr. Sheehan retires, effective immediately. Your life in the public eye is over."

"What!" Sheehan said. "Mr. President, you can't let him do that."

"Oh, he will," said Perry. "Because he gets to keep his job."

"And three?" asked Blake.

"You, Mr. President, will sit back and do nothing when your phone starts ringing off the hook about our nukes degrading. You can tell STRATCOM to investigate, calculate, negotiate, whatever the fuck you want, but you will take no direct action to stop us."

"You're crazy. You'll leave us completely open to a nuclear attack!" said the president.

"Don't worry, the US will be the last to lose their nukes. Believe it or not, there are crazier people out there than you. We'll take them out first. Understand?"

"We understand," said the president.

"Good, and remember, there's a big brother, well, actually a big sister, out there, and she's watching you."

After Franklin and Thomas left, the president said, "You're finished, Sheehan! I can't believe you got me into this shit."

"Jim, this isn't over yet. We know where they are. We can hit them hard with our phaser, shut them down."

"It hasn't even been tested yet. If it fails and they know we tried, we're dead."

"How will they know we tried?" he said. "They don't even know that we're ready to launch."

"You better be right, Mike. Call Max and give the order. As soon as this BiniSphere is destroyed, get to work taking out the nukes, and start with North Korea. They've been a constant pain in my ass. And get the STRATCOM commander in here, we need to put our guys on high alert."

"Yes, sir."

For the last 48 hours, Christina and her team had been watching the *USS Rhode Island* as it sat at the pier in New London. They were using Perry's camera to keep track of it.

Because of the large quantity of nanotubes inside the sub, they didn't even need to illuminate the ship with the phaser.

"Christina!" Steve called out as he watched his monitor. "They're moving downriver."

"It is too soon," she replied. "Perry said they needed a week to dismantle the phaser. Maybe they are going out for a routine exercise."

"No," Samuels said. "Not with the nanotubes installed. Something's not right."

"Okay," Christina said. "Power up the BiniSphere and set it for low power. If we can track the position of their reactor and compare it to the position of the nanotubes, we can calculate a pointing vector for the sub."

"Why don't we just shut them down right now?" Samuels asked. "All we need to do is radiate the nanotubes, break them down."

"If what Perry tells us is true, the tubes are too close to the sub's nuclear core," Christina said. "If we irradiate the nanotubes, we might create a feedback loop with the reactor. It could go supercritical, create a meltdown."

"I sure hope they get far enough out to sea before they try anything," said Samuels. "They'll pollute the entire northeastern seaboard if they're not careful."

Captain Wainwright's crew steamed the sub down the Thames River, through New London Harbor and out into Long Island Sound. He needed room to maneuver. At 560 feet, the Rhode Island was one-tenth of a mile long. Compared to the average 250-foot depth of the continental shelf, she'd be sailing in relatively shallow waters until they reached the edge, seventy nautical miles south, where the ocean bottom dropped away to depths of over 3000 feet. But they were under strict orders; they didn't have time for the three-hour trip.

Only the captain and Howell's team knew the real purpose of their mission. The rest of the crew were kept in the dark, only being told that a calibration of the new acoustic modifications had to be performed.

Howell required extreme precision, more than what the ship was capable of while underway. Currents, tidal drift, thermal inclines made it virtually impossible to achieve and maintain the precise heading and dive angle required. The sub needed to be secured, immovable, anchored to achieve the extreme depression angle Howell had given the captain.

"Okay, Howell. Are you ready?" said Wainwright.

Howell sat in the command and control center, in front of two monitors. All the signals from the phaser and the PIT camera had been routed to his terminal, as well as to the helmsman's screen.

Howell switched on the PIT camera, checked the status of the phaser one more time and said, "I'm ready."

"Helmsman, set a course of 165.3 degrees true."

"Setting course of 165.3 degrees true. Aye, sir," the helmsman replied.

Five minutes later, the helmsman said, "Sir, I have Race Rock Light off our port side."

"Roger. Diving Officer. You have the conn."

"I have the conn, aye, sir," the officer echoed back as he took control of the vessel.

Race Rock Light, to their northeast, and Valiant Rock Light, one mile to the southwest, marked the demarcation line between Long Island Sound and Block Island Sound, a heavily trafficked area commonly known as "The Race." This relatively narrow channel was a major shipping route to and from southern Connecticut and the northern coast of Long Island. Depending on the time of day and the phases of the moon, the tidal currents flowed in and out of Long Island Sound at speeds of up to 3 knots. Over the centuries, these currents had carved deep underwater gorges into the ocean bottom. In less than 500 horizontal feet, the ocean floor plunged from a depth of 30 feet to over 300 feet. This was where Howell and the Captain had agreed to conduct their first operational test of the phaser.

The diving officer barked commands, and the crew responded. Several minutes later the 18,000-ton submarine hovered at the bottom of one of the gorges.

"What's our depth?" the captain asked.

"In 325 feet of water, sir."

The captain pressed the intercom. "All hands, all hands, this is the captain. Secure all stations. Secure all stations."

"Okay, let's slowly flood the forward trim tank and drop her nose onto the bottom."

"Aye, sir."

Thirty seconds passed before the nose of the *Rhode Island* slowly dipped forward.

"Ten degrees," the helmsmen called out.

"Twenty degrees."

Howell heard equipment shift and small overlooked items slide off tables to the floor.

"Thirty degrees."

Howell leaned forward, his seat belt tightening against his waist.

"Thirty-five degrees."

The captain said, "Hold ballast."

"Holding ballast, aye sir."

"Forty degrees."

The downward pitch came to a slow stop as the nose of the submarine settled into the sand.

"What's our angle?"

"We're at forty-two degrees, sir."

"Howell?" the captain asked. "Will that work?"

"Yes, I believe so."

"Proceed."

The helmsman activated a switch that extended the secondary propulsion motor. It had recently been installed in the aft section of the sub. Called the "outboard" by the crew, the motor's prop could be pointed a full 360 degrees in azimuth and +/- 45 degrees in elevation. Using a joystick and throttle lever installed on his console, the helmsman could precisely adjust the pitch and yaw of the submarine.

He used forward propulsion from the main screw to keep the sub's nose anchored securely into the bottom while delicately maneuvering the ship's stern up, down, left, and right with the outboard. Five minutes later the camera displayed a small red dot on its screen.

"Gottcha!" Howell said. "Hold it right there!"

He immediately reached over and turned on the phaser.

"Christina! That is no test," Steve said. "They're moving the ship into position. We have to do something!"

"We cannot," she replied. "It is too much risk. We will kill thousands of people."

"If they shut us down, they'll have complete control over the world's nuclear arsenal," said Samuels. "We can't let that happen."

"The end does not justify the means," she said. "We are better than this."

"Christina!" said Steve. "They're preparing to attack us. We have a right to defend ourselves."

"We are not in real danger. You know that."

"They killed your grandmother. Doesn't that mean anything to you?"

Christina nodded and clenched her teeth.

"It means everything to me, but Nonna would not want us killing a ship full of innocent sailors or risk radiating the northeastern seaboard of the United States. If she were here, she would be cutting the head off this snake, and that is precisely what we are going to do. Swing the BiniSphere back towards DC. Samuels, find out where the president and Sheehan are. Let's remove the head of this snake.

Steve was entering the last known coordinates of the president into the BiniSphere's computer when a warning flashed on his display screen.

"The nanotubes are heating up!" he yelled. "They're attacking us!"

"Increase the coolant flow," she ordered.

Christina watched the PIT camera display intently as it saturated red and then the signal disappeared.

"They did it, they destroyed our camera," Steve said.

"I have the target," Howell yelled to the commander. "Keep it steady. Keep it steady!"

He brought the phaser power up to 40 percent and watched as the red dot floated across the screen. "You have to keep it on target," he told the helmsman. "We need fifty seconds."

The helmsman leaned over his console, carefully maneuvering the outboard, trying desperately to keep the *Rhode Island* steady.

"This is the best we can do in these currents," the captain told Howell.

"We're drifting back and forth; we need more time on target."

"Can't you increase the power?" the captain asked.

"Not without destroying the phaser."

"It's going to be destroyed one way or another if we don't shut down that facility in Sicily. This sub and every other nuclear weapon we have is going to be useless."

Howell nodded and slowly increased the phaser power to 45 percent.

"It's stable," Howell said. "But I still need more time."

"I'm trying," said the helmsman as he jockeyed the joystick back and forth.

Howell monitored the status of the phaser and was relieved that the power levels were remaining stable. He wondered if the surrounding seawater was providing a stabilizing effect as he slowly adjusted the output power to 48 percent. He felt a slight vibration running through the ship and started to turn the dial back.

If the *Rhode Island* had been in deeper waters, the effects of the explosion would have been minimal. But that wasn't the case. If the blast had been caused by an interaction between Howell's phaser and the sub's nuclear power plant, the effects of the explosion also would have been minimal. But that wasn't the case either.

Unknown to Howell and his team of experts, or to Christina and her team, were the interactions that occur when placing a source of dense Majorana neutrinos close to a thermonuclear warhead. The research by both teams had been focused on radiating thorium-fluoride nanotubes with neutrinos from either a well-controlled nuclear reactor or a particle accelerator. The resulting beam of more massive Majorana neutrinos could then be used to degrade a nuclear warhead from thousands of miles away. Little had been investigated on exposing thorium-fluoride nanotubes to a dense beam of radioactive particles from a nuclear warhead. There was no need. Nuclear warheads were very stable and did not produce dense beams of radiation. The problem that was overlooked involved the physical construction of a nuclear warhead. To initiate a nuclear reaction, the radioactive core of a warhead is molded in a spherical shape which is then compressed using conventional explosives to create a critical mass. It's called an explosive lens. To the detriment of the *Rhode Island's* crew, this lens could focus not only an explosive charge, it could focus a stream of Majorana neutrinos into the center of the plutonium core. And the opposite. It could focus the resulting release of radioactive particles inside the warhead back onto the nanotubes.

When Howell activated his device, the phaser's beam of heavy neutrinos left the auxiliary machine room, traveled down the centerline of the sub and entered the missile compartment. In a perfect world, the stream of neutrinos would have been precisely columnated in a tight laser-like beam that traveled along the central gangway, exiting through the nose of the sub. 98.7 percent of the phaser's energy did just that. But a small percent of the neutrinos traveled off-axis from the central beam. These stray neutrinos illuminated the warheads of the twenty-four

Trident II ballistic missiles as they rested quietly in their vertical launch tubes. The sub's weapon systems officer, sitting at another control station, was monitoring his arsenal when he noticed an increase in radiation. He assumed it was the new neutrino drive causing the anomaly, not his warheads, but like all good missileers, he knew it was better to be safe than sorry, especially when it came to nuclear warheads. He had just clicked his mike to apprise his commander of the anomaly when Max Howell increased the power of the phaser from 45 to 48 percent. The feedback loop reached its own critical mass, and the reaction was unstoppable. The explosion vaporized the *USS Rhode Island* within microseconds, sending a half-mile wide radioactive bubble of superheated steam up through the water column.

Christina and the rest of her team stared silently at the blank screen, thinking the camera was dead. Then they saw the tiny flashes of red.

"Turn up the sensitivity and restart the scan," Christina ordered.

The BiniSphere scanned the area around the sub's last known position, and the computers slowly painted a picture of wide devastation. Almost a full minute passed before one of her scientists asked, "Isn't there anything we can do?"

Tears streamed down Christina's face. She felt helpless, as if it were her fault. All she and her family wanted to do was stop the madness, to neutralize the threat, to save lives.

"There is!" she yelled, "Steve, bring the BiniSphere to full power. Quickly! Continue the sweeping pattern. Somebody find out what the tides and currents are doing. Now people! If we can neutralize the radioactive plume before it reaches the coast, we can save a lot of lives."

The United Nations' Comprehensive Test Ban Treaty Organization maintains a string of highly sensitive underwater hydroacoustic sensors designed to detect the unique signature of an underwater nuclear explosion. These sensors are placed at strategic locations around the globe and can triangulate the position of an underwater detonation with a relatively high degree of accuracy. When the *Rhode Island* vaporized into a massive cloud of radioactive steam, this sensor network immediately transmitted the location of the detonation to all members of the CTBTO. Minutes later, the commander of the US Force's Northern Command raised the nation's Force Protection Condition from FPCON Bravo to FPCON Delta, the highest threat condition of the military's counter-terrorism threat network.

President Blake was sitting at his desk when Joe Davis ran into the oval office followed by the president's secret service detail.

"Sir, we're under attack!"

"What?"

Two agents ran around the side of the president's desk and grabbed his arms. "We need to get you into the air immediately."

"Oh, my God. Where?"

"Off the eastern coast of Long Island. We need to go!"

The agents lifted the president to his feet.

"Wait!" the president replied.

"Sir, we have strict procedures. Marine One is inbound,"

"I'm well aware of our procedures, what is the threat?"

"It's a nuclear event, sir. It happened south of New London, Connecticut."

Blake knew immediately it was not a nuclear attack.

"Stand down," he ordered. "Get the Joint Chiefs into the Situation Room immediately. Call Deputy Director Sheehan, get him in here as well."

"But sir."

"Now!" he yelled, slamming his fist on the desktop. "We just lost the *USS Rhode Island*."

Chapter 30

Day 21

A week after the loss of the *Rhode Island*, scientists across the world were still dumbfounded by the surprisingly limited release of radiation that had resulted from what was essentially the most massive dirty bomb ever released upon the surface of the earth. The calculations showed that the radiation should have exceeded the meltdown of the Chernobyl power plant by an order of magnitude. Many of the experts attributed the relatively small release of radiation to the depth of the water, the prevailing tidal currents, and the inherent safety of the warhead design that prevented the nuclear cores from achieving critical mass under any but the most precise circumstances. Many other scientists, looking at the strange isotopes created from the explosion, just had no explanation whatsoever. All their data, all their models, simulations, and projections showed that thousands upon thousands of lives should have been lost because of the superheated cloud of radioactive steam that had been released in such close proximity to the most densely populated area of the US.

Sheehan poured a tall glass of Johnny Walker, walked over to his leather couch and sat back. He put his feet up on the coffee table, took a long sip of the scotch and turned on FOX News. When he heard the talking heads below the breaking news banner, he knew his career was officially over. An unknown source close to the administration had leaked that Sheehan had been the one that ordered testing of the *Rhode Island's* new stealth propulsion system in a densely populated area. President Blake had no choice but to fire him. It could be a lot worse. He had solid evidence to prove that Blake had full knowledge of the activity and had authorized the testing himself. Sheehan could take the president down with him, but the leverage he held over the most powerful man in the world was a lot more valuable than his ego. Except for Franklin, Christina's team and the president, no one else knew the truth. Except, of course, the people at the other end of the insurance policy he'd setup earlier that afternoon. Sheehan was not finished dealing with Franklin, Christina, or the BiniSphere.

It was dark when Perry parked his BMW a block from Sheehan's home. The brownstone Victorian row house was located near the corner of Q and 13th street, just north of Logan Circle. The 19th century architecture combined with the light drizzle and fog gave the impression of an old street in the heart of London. The glow from haloed streetlights glistened off the wet pavement as Franklin walked the remaining hundred yards. He spotted a total of six Secret Service agents wearing knit hats and dark raincoats. Two approached him on the sidewalk while two others stood at the entrance to Sheehan's home. In the distance, he saw two more covering the approach from the other direction. Three black SUVs were parked out front. He assumed there were more covering the rear of the house.

Two hours earlier, Franklin had been standing in the rain next to Stan's wife, Brenda, looking down at a casket descending into the ground. He was stirred from his reverie when his phone started vibrating. He'd turned it off before the funeral. When he looked at the screen and saw it was

DNI Gonzales, he knew the phone had been remotely switched on.

When the *Rhode Island* had been destroyed, Franklin knew that Sheehan and Blake would not keep their bargain. He immediately briefed Gonzales on every detail of his mission in Sicily as well as the activities of her own deputy director. After verifying Perry's claims with Thomas and Samuels, she unofficially placed Sheehan at the top of their terrorist threat list. She and Stan had been close friends and she was appalled that the president was allowing Sheehan to walk around free. She immediately ordered the NSA to keep close tabs on every second of Sheehan's actions. Audio and visual surveillance was set up in his house and car, spyware was installed on his phone, and a live feed was transmitted to the NSA and Samuels, who had remained at the BiniSphere. Samuels was to act as a liaison between the US Intelligence Community and the Sicilians as the world's nuclear age slowly melted into oblivion.

Perry approached the two agents blocking his path and pulled out his ID. One of the agents inspected his credentials and said, "The president is already inside." He escorted Perry to the front door, where the two other agents let him pass into Sheehan's home.

"What's this about?" Blake asked when Franklin entered the front room.

"Mr. President. Thanks for meeting me here. We need to make a slight adjustment to our arrangement."

"An adjustment?" said Sheehan. "Bullshit Franklin, we've met all your demands to…"

"No, actually you haven't," Franklin said. "You see, Mr. President, I briefed DNI Gonzales on all your activities, and she's been keeping a very close eye on Mr. Sheehan here. For some reason, they feel he's a national security threat."

"That's ridiculous," said the president. "He might have been overzealous in his protection of our country, but…"

"Over the last few days," Franklin said. "Mike has been having some covert conversations with the Russians."

"That's a lie!" Sheehan said.

"During those conversations, which the NSA has recorded, he proposed a plan to provide information regarding the nanotube technology and the location of the BiniSphere. In exchange, he'd be given a high-level position within the Russian government. I'm sure you can understand, we felt the need to intervene."

The president looked at Sheehan but was silent.

"Jim, please," said Sheehan. "How can you let this nobody walk all over you?"

"How?" asked the president. "I was a fool to listen to you. Mr. Franklin and I might be at odds, and I'd squash him like a bug if I had the opportunity, but I never questioned his loyalty to this country."

"Loyalty! He's single-handedly responsible for dismantling our entire nuclear arsenal. He's a traitor! If he hadn't put his technology into the hands of the Sicilians, we wouldn't be…"

"What he did was rid the world of the most dangerous, most powerful weapons known to man. Along the way, he and his Sicilian friends managed to save tens, if not hundreds of thousands of Americans who would have died because of your bumbling. I might not agree with his approach to disarmament, but for the first time in seventy years, we will not have nuclear Armageddon hanging over our heads."

"But, we're no longer a superpower! We're just like the rest of them," Sheehan said.

Blake shook his head. "I have no doubt that we'll figure out better ways to annihilate each other, and I'll make sure the US is the best at it. In the meantime, the death of our sailors and scientist on the *Rhode Island* might go down in history as an accident, but there's no denying the fact that you directly ordered the murders of Lt Col Sheppard and Ms. LaTorre's grandmother."

President Blake turned for the door. "Consider yourself under house arrest."

"You can't do that, Jim," Sheehan yelled. "I know too much. I will not go down without taking you with me."

Blake ignored him.

Perry's heart pounded, and his face flushed with anger. He'd thought that Nonna had been collateral damage, killed in the fog of battle, and he'd dished out his retribution, watching Atwood fry on a river of lava. But now he knew. Nonna's death was premeditated murder, ordered by Sheehan.

Blake saw the look in Franklin's eyes and pulled him by the arm.

"Not now," he said. He led Perry outside and down the granite steps to the sidewalk.

"The Russians. How much did he divulge?" the president asked.

"Not enough, according to Gonzales. Sheehan was leading them along until he had firm guarantees. What are you going to do with him?" Franklin asked.

"Me?" Blake replied. "You made it pretty clear the other day in the Oval Office what the Sicilians would do if we broke our deal."

"I did," Franklin said. "But I can't ask Christina to kill someone in cold blood. She's had enough trauma for a lifetime."

"Fine, I'll have Gonzales take care of him."

Perry nodded.

"And Franklin, I don't ever want to see you again. Leave DC and never return."

"That's perfectly fine with me, but I'm not leaving until Sheehan has been dealt with."

Perry stood on the sidewalk and watched as the president turned and walked towards his waiting limousine. He wanted to do it himself, to kill Sheehan with his bare hands. It would be simple. He'd just wait until all the president's men were gone.

Blake was halfway to the car when they heard the loud screams coming from Sheehan's house. Blake turned back and they both ran up the steps. The two agents waiting at the car caught up to them and pushed Franklin aside. They drew their weapons and pressed the president into a corner of the entranceway, shielding his body with theirs. Four more agents ran up the steps and burst through the front door.

"Clear!" came a command a few seconds later.

Perry followed as they rushed the president inside and closed the door.

Sheehan was lying on the floor of the living room. Blood poured from his mouth and nose. The president and Franklin watched in disbelief as he writhed in a fetal position. A full minute passed before he was still. One of the agents called 911, another started CPR.

"You're wasting your time," Perry told them. "He won't be recovering from this."

"What happened?" asked the president.

"I think Christina overheard our conversation about Nonna. I asked Gonzales to send live audio and video feeds to Samuels at the BiniSphere. You know, just in case any action needed to be taken."

"What were you saying about your traumatized scientist?"

Perry thought back to the time he'd spent with Nonna and the perpetual smile she always carried for those she cared for. She'd seen something in him that he had yet to see in himself. His voice cracked.

"You need to understand, Mr. President. Nonna was a very special signora."

"I guess so. And that's an extraordinary girlfriend you've got there, as well."

"Yeah," Franklin said. "She's pretty intense."

Chapter 31

A month later…

Perry threw the asphalt shingles up onto the roof one at a time. He grabbed a hammer and a handful of roofing nails from the shed and climbed the old wooden ladder. The steep pitch of the roof forced him to step slowly and carefully as he worked his way up to the crumbling brick chimney. It was an annual ritual. The extreme temperature swings, the powerful ocean winds, the thick winter snow, and his sagging cottage always led to leaks. The water worked its way around the chimney seams and eventually puddled onto the hearth. Every spring, he'd tar the cracks and crevices, and every fall, before the first snow, he'd replace any shingles that had broken loose. With every swing of the hammer, a shock of pain ran through his injured shoulder, but at least it was a dull pain. The bullet wound had healed, and he'd replaced his doctor's prescription for physical therapy with long days of chores and maintenance on the cottage. Except for the daily dose of ibuprofen, or Vitamin I, as the athletes liked to call it, he refused to take pain medication. He told himself he needed to keep his mind sharp while the world settled into its new, nuclear-free reality. But, at some subconscious level, the pain was a sort of penance, a distraction veiling the deeper loss he was feeling. He'd finally realized the world didn't really need him. It was doing just fine without him. The sacrifices he'd made in the name of patriotism. Losing Julie, his kids, any close relationships, they were all just excuses to keep others at arm's length. He liked the emptiness, being here, alone, making his own decisions. No need for give and take, no wasted time negotiating and compromising.

When Perry finished the repairs, he sat on the eave of the roof and looked out over the water.

"It's better this way," he said as the wind whistled through the trees.

He inhaled the scent of the pine floating in with the cold, crisp air. Grey, billowy clouds drifted in from the northwest. Snow was coming. He reminded himself to call Rick. He'd promised Perry he'd deliver a couple loads of firewood before the first snow. If he didn't get here today, Perry would be digging the wood out of a snowbank to stack it under the shelter he'd built. That was enough motivation for him to climb down from the roof and go inside. He tried calling Rick's phone, but it went immediately to voice mail; typical occurrence in this area of spotty cellular coverage. He assumed Rick was out on another delivery.

Perry made a cup of coffee and walked down to the shore. As he had a thousand times before, he sat down on his favorite granite rock and watched the waves as they marched across the inlet and crashed at his feet.

Twenty minutes later, he heard Rick's truck. He looked back just in time to see it pull behind the house. Perry thought about going to watch him dump the first load, but he was enjoying the solitude too much. He decided he'd catch up with Rick when he returned with the second load.

"Thanks for the ride," she said. "I had no idea there were no rental cars available in Boothbay."

"There are in the summah," Rick said. "We pretty much shut everything down late Septembah, aftah the leaves fall. They're only a few hundred people crazy enough to stick around these parts for the wintah.

"I am lucky I found you."

"Ha! It wouldah been hard not to. You'll probably meet the whole wintah population within the first week. Lucky you got here before the first snow. I usually don't bothah plowin the airfield. You wouldah had ta land at Bath or

Augusta, but then why go through all that trouble when you couldah just driven up from Boston."

She pulled her backpack down from the cab of the truck and thanked Rick one more time before venturing through the back of the cottage.

"Perry?" she called out.

The room was filled with the smell of freshly brewed coffee mixed with the smoky scent of oak logs burning in the fireplace. Her fears melted away. The warmth enveloped her like a well-worn wool robe, and she felt more comfortable than she had in a long time. She walked through the cottage, looking at the small details that made a house a home. Old mismatched dishes rested in a strainer by the black iron sink. A grocery list was stuck to the refrigerator. The floorboards creaked as she worked her way through the house to the living room.

"Perry?" she called out again.

In the middle of the room, facing the fireplace was a well-worn leather recliner. She sat on the edge of the chair and studied the framed pictures sitting on the mantel. She saw the picture of two young girls holding a small, buff-colored dog and smiled. Seeing the front door cracked open, she rose and stepped onto the porch. Her heart quickened when she saw the solitary figure sitting down on the rocks.

Perry watched a seagull dive for a fish, and a childhood memory returned. He'd been about twelve years old. He was fishing on this same shore. He was reeling in a Spanish mackerel when a seagull swooped down and snatched it up. In one swift gulp, the seagull swallowed the fish. It shocked the younger Perry; he wasn't sure what to do. They were in a tug of war, and he knew he couldn't let the seagull win. The fishing lure inside the fish would kill the seagull. They battled for several minutes; the seagull desperately trying to fly away, Perry desperately trying to reel him in. Perry loosened the drag on the reel to avoid breaking the line, and the bird soared into the sky like a kite, fishing line streaming out behind him. Eventually, the bird tired and gave up. It

411

spit out the fish. Perry still remembered the smile that spread across his face over thirty years ago. The excitement from a little unexpected adventure, a challenge in a long series of challenges that, for better or worse, had defined his life. He wondered why he hadn't felt that exhilaration from his latest adventure, the biggest adventure of his life.

Perry felt the warmth of her body moments before her arms gently wrapped around him. For a second, he was afraid to move, afraid that he'd break the fantasy. When her warm breath brushed past his ear, and she kissed the side of his neck, he smiled.

"How'd you find me?" he asked.

"Franklin, you are such a fool."

Epilog I

Within days of the loss of the Rhode Island, North Korea made a completely uncharacteristic offer to dismantle their entire nuclear program in exchange for lifting of sanctions and the implementation of favorable terms for international trade. For almost a year, the loss of the world's nuclear weapons was the best kept secret ever known, aside, of course, from the BiniSphere. When it was noticed that all the major superpowers were transitioning billions upon billions of dollars into the advancement of conventional weapons... the truth came out. For better or worse, mutually assured destruction was no longer an option. Wars were going to be a lot messier, a lot longer and a lot safer. Mankind might still be at risk of extinction, but at least the rest of the planet had a chance to survive.

Conspiracy theories continued to abound concerning stealth technologies and advanced propulsion systems. In a strange twist of fate the theories spurred research into neutrino drives that had amazing thrust potential, as long as they were nowhere near a nuclear power plant.

Epilog II: A Little Bit of History

In 1939, a group of Hungarian scientists that included émigré physicist Leó Szilárd attempted to alert Washington to ongoing Nazi atomic bomb research. The group's warnings were discounted. Einstein and Szilárd, along with other refugees such as Edward Teller and Eugene Wigner, "regarded it as their responsibility to alert Americans to the possibility that German scientists might win the race to build an atomic bomb, and to warn that Hitler would be more than willing to resort to such a weapon." To make certain the US was aware of the danger, in July 1939, a few months before the beginning of World War II in Europe, Szilárd and Wigner visited Einstein to explain the possibility of atomic bombs, which Einstein, a pacifist, said he had never considered. He was asked to lend his support by writing a letter, with Szilárd, to President Roosevelt, recommending the US pay attention and engage in its own nuclear weapons research.

The letter is believed to be "arguably the key stimulus for the U.S. adoption of serious investigations into nuclear weapons on the eve of the U.S. entry into World War II". Some say that as a result of Einstein's letter and his meetings with Roosevelt, the US entered the "race" to develop the bomb, drawing on its "immense material, financial, and scientific resources" to initiate the Manhattan Project.

For Einstein, "war was a disease ... [and] he called for resistance to war." By signing the letter to Roosevelt, some argue he went against his pacifist principles. In 1954, a year before his death, Einstein said to his old friend, Linus Pauling, "I made one great mistake in my life—when I signed the letter to President Roosevelt recommending that atom bombs be made; but there was some justification—the danger that the Germans would make them ..."

Wikipedia

"It was then that Fermi, trying to make me understand the significance of this loss, expressed himself in quite a peculiar way; he who was so objectively harsh when judging people. And so, at this point, I would like to repeat his words, just as I can still hear them ringing in my memory: `Because, you see, in the world there are various categories of scientists: people of a secondary or tertiary standing, who do their best but do not go very far. There are

414

also those of high standing, who come to discoveries of great importance, fundamental for the development of science' (and here I had the impression that he (Fermi) placed himself in that category). `But then there are geniuses like Galileo and Newton. Well, Ettore was one of them. Majorana had what no one else in the world had [...]'"

Erasmo Recami
Professor of Physics, University of Bergamo